WOLF BRIDE

ELIZABETH MOSS

sourcebooks
casablanca

Published by Sourcebooks Casablanca, an imprint of Sourcebooks, Inc.
P.O. Box 4410, Naperville, Illinois 60567-4410
(630) 961-3900
Fax: (630) 961-2168
www.sourcebooks.com

Originally published in 2013 in Great Britain by Hodder & Stoughton, an imprint of Hachette UK.

Library of Congress Cataloging-in-Publication Data
Moss, Elizabeth (Novelist)
  Wolf bride / Elizabeth Moss.
      pages cm. — (Lust in the Tudor court ; book one)
  (trade paper : alk. paper) 1. Great Britain—History—Henry VIII, 1509-1547—Fiction. 2. England—Court and courtiers—History—16th century—Fiction. 3. Historical fiction. 4. Erotic fiction. I. Title.
  PR6112.A497W65 2015
  823'.92–dc23

                              2014050017

        Printed and bound in the United States of America.
            VP 10 9 8 7 6 5 4 3 2 1

And graven with diamonds in letters plain
There is written her fair neck round about:
"*Noli me tangere*, for Caesar's I am,
And wild for to hold, though I seem tame."

Sir Thomas Wyatt, "Whoso List to Hunt"

One

January 1536, Greenwich Palace, near London

THE SOFT GIGGLING FROM within the queen's chambers could be heard all the way along the corridor to the gardens. If they were caught, Eloise thought, the penalty would be death. Lady Margaret might be standing guard at the door to the west wing, against the king's approach, but there could be no secrets at court. Already the courtiers were whispering of the queen's infidelities, though discreetly, not in so many words, fearing the king's anger if the news should come to his ears.

Eloise had been sent to the queen's privy chamber with a pure white ermine mantle to guard Her Majesty against the cold. Now she did not know whether to knock and risk the queen's anger at being disturbed, or go back to the bedchamber with her mission undischarged.

With the queen's fur mantle draped over her arm, Eloise flattened herself against the wall and peered through a crack in the ancient oaken door. She had hoped the rumors were not true, or that the gossipmongers had exaggerated. Yet what she saw was enough to condemn the queen twice over.

Radiant in a billowing gown of yellow silk, Queen Anne was sitting on a man's knee beneath the casement window. The man was Sir Henry Norris, one of the king's own Gentlemen of the Chamber. His arm was tight about her waist. She was protesting, but with a smile on her face.

"Your lap is too hard for a lady's comfort, Sir Henry. Let me down before you do me some mischief!"

"I have never heard you complain before that a man was too hard, Anne."

The queen laughed, leaning back against him. Her slim white throat was adorned with pearls, a strand of wayward hair peeping out from under her black velvet hood.

"I do not know why I allow you to speak to me in such an insolent fashion, Sir Henry."

"Do you not?" he murmured in her ear, and Eloise saw the hand at the queen's waist slip upward, cupping her breast in an openly possessive gesture.

Queen Anne gasped, and slapped his hand away. "One of these days…" she began warningly.

"One of these days you will go too far, Norris, and find yourself out of all favor," a deep male voice finished for her, and the queen looked up, smiling gratefully.

There was another man in the chamber, Eloise realized. She watched this man kneel before the queen and jolted with horror, recognizing him from his profile.

Sir Thomas Wyatt, a gentleman of courtly disposition, and a poet of great wit and intelligence. Surely he too was not involved in the queen's dangerous inner circle?

Sir Thomas had always seemed so well mannered and quietly spoken. Eloise refused to believe he was one of those ambitious courtiers who surrounded Anne like hungry dogs whenever the king was absent.

Wyatt was murmuring, "Forget Norris's insolence, and permit me to amuse you instead, my sweet lady." His hand brushed Anne's cheek, an intimate touch which suggested they were more than mere friends. Certainly if the king had been present, that touch alone would have earned them both a pass to the grim Tower of London. "Do you have some small token I could borrow? A jewel, perhaps?"

Anne looked deep into Wyatt's eyes. Then she smiled, slipping a large emerald ring off her finger. It glittered greenly in the sunlight. "The king gave me this as a gift at New Year," she confided. "Will it do?"

"It is perfect." Wyatt's voice seemed to waver, becoming husky. "Like its wearer."

"Will it be returned to me soon? I do not begrudge it to you, Sir Thomas, but the king may notice its absence."

"You may have it back if you can find it, Your Majesty." Sir Thomas Wyatt hid the ring behind his back. "If you cannot find it," he murmured, "I will be forced to claim a forfeit from you."

Watching through the crack in the door, Eloise saw him shift the ring from one hand to the other. Then he presented both closed fists to the queen.

"A challenge?"

Queen Anne gurgled with teasing laughter, still seated with indecent intimacy on Norris's lap. She leaned forward to choose, her bosom on show, then hesitated a moment, biting her lip as though in doubt. Her wavering hand hovered first above one fist, then the other.

With a sudden lightning stab, she chose the left hand. "That one!"

Sir Thomas turned his hand over. His palm was empty. Queen Anne gave a little cry of disappointment.

"You were unlucky this time, Your Majesty," the poet murmured. "For if you had chosen the right hand…"

Slowly, he opened his other hand; the emerald ring was nestled there, gleaming. Before she could snatch it back, Wyatt clenched his fist again.

"A kiss," he reminded her softly.

The queen's eyes widened, and a tiny ripple of fear seemed to move through her countenance. She did not refuse him though. Sir Henry Norris made some small noise of protest but Anne ignored him, leaning forward with her gaze on Wyatt's face. At that moment she looked like a woman dazed, unable to resist the temptation before her.

Eloise stared too, unable to believe her eyes. Surely the poet would not dare kiss the queen on the lips?

The sound of running feet in the corridor made Eloise turn, springing back guiltily from the door.

She had only meant to peep through for a moment, but had found herself caught by the scene before her. Now it seemed to her that the rumors of infidelity might be true after all. If the queen was flirting with courtiers like this behind King Henry's back, it might have gone beyond kissing with one or two of them.

Eloise shuddered. The horror of what might happen to Queen Anne when the king discovered the truth did not bear thinking about.

It was Lady Margaret, a few years her senior and already one of the queen's most trusted ladies-in-waiting, who had interrupted her. Margaret was agitated, holding up her gown to run, her cheeks flushed, her unbound hair flying about her face.

"Out of my way, girl!" she gasped, pushing Eloise aside. "The king is coming! The king is coming!"

But she had been heard from within. A second later, the door to the queen's privy chamber was flung open. Flushed and with her eyes sparkling, Queen Anne stood on the threshold. She pulled in her jeweled skirts to let Norris and Wyatt pass, ushering them out of her private quarters.

"Hurry!" she whispered, watching as the courtiers slipped down a shadowy side corridor that led out to the queen's privy garden.

"Where are my ladies?" she demanded, turning to Margaret.

"In the rose chamber, Your Majesty."

"Quickly, then," Queen Anne insisted, hurrying along the corridor into the rose chamber. With deliberate dignity, she seated herself near the fireplace. Her color was high, yet she did not seem too discomposed by the king's sudden arrival. The sound of men's voices could be heard in the corridor now. "Fetch me that embroidery."

While Anne set a few lopsided stitches into her embroidery frame, Lady Margaret bent over her mistress, whispering urgently in her ear.

"Henry will suspect nothing if we can only keep our heads," the queen replied sharply.

"Yes, Your Majesty."

The flustered lady-in-waiting tidied Anne's black velvet hood, pulling back her hair so her slender neck—so admired by King Henry in the early days of their courtship—could be more clearly seen. Anne sat straight in the chair, gazing down upon her embroidery with apparent absorption, her sallow cheeks lit with a blush which was already fading.

Her chief women, who had been lounging at their ease on velvet cushions strewn across the floor, rose in a whisper of silk at the king's approach and arranged themselves about the queen's chair.

Eloise hurried into line with the other maids of honor, shaking out the crumpled folds of her court gown. Hers was made of yellow taffeta, for they had all been instructed to wear yellow that month, in celebration of the death of old Queen Katherine, who had been the king's wife before Anne.

Eloise had only come to court a few years before, a northern girl with little taste for court life. To her father's relief, the new queen had seemed willing to accept her as a maid of honor, where the old queen, Katherine of Spain, had not been interested. Even so, Eloise was not blinded by gratitude. She did not think it wise of the queen to risk her husband's displeasure in this dangerous way, flirting with his courtiers behind his back.

She could almost understand Anne's flirtation with Sir Thomas Wyatt, who was a poet and stirringly handsome. But not Norris, an older courtier whose appearance and manners were far less appealing. Besides, her position was already dangerous. It was rumored that the king was growing bored of his new wife, even though he had disrupted all of England—and even split with the Holy Roman Church—to divorce Katherine and marry Anne instead. There were whispers that he was looking elsewhere for a wife, and all because Anne had failed to bear him a son and heir.

Perhaps the queen had fallen in love with Wyatt, Eloise reasoned. That would explain her flirtatious behavior. A woman in love must follow her heart.

But could Her Majesty be in love with two men at once?

The door to the queen's apartments was flung open, and King Henry entered the room, accompanied by Sir Thomas Cromwell, one of the most feared and hated men in the country.

All the ladies sank to the floor as the king entered, their heads bowed, and Eloise followed suit.

Rising on his command, Eloise glanced at the king with sudden apprehension. Would he speak to her again today?

Although her family was too obscure to make her an eligible match, the king's eye had lighted on her more than once in the three years since she had come to court. But then King Henry seemed to study all the queen's younger ladies with interest, admiring their figures and their hair, their dancing and their features, as though weighing up each one as a potential companion for his bed.

Indeed, King Henry had taken more than one lady-in-waiting as his mistress since his marriage, much to Anne's fury.

Yet what could the queen do but accept her humiliation? Henry was the king, and the king's word was law.

Anne had risen too, and was curtsying to her royal husband. He raised her, kissing her hand in a leisurely fashion. It made Eloise wonder how he had wronged the queen this time, for he was rarely courteous toward his wife these days.

"How is your head today, Anne? Still aching?" His sharp eyes slipped to her belly, a little rounded under the stiff yellow-gold gown. "And how is my son?"

Anne muttered some polite reply, but the king did not seem to be listening. His hungry gaze was already roving the room. Soon it found Eloise.

His Majesty came forward, smiling indulgently at Eloise. One hand stroked his neatly trimmed beard, the other rested on his hip, where the heavy folds of his richly embroidered suit hid his liking for sweetmeats.

"You keep so many maids of honor, Anne, I cannot number them all. What is this pretty thing's name?" Cromwell came forward to murmur discreetly in his ear. The king nodded. "Ah, Eloise. I remember now. A sweet young maid from the North Riding."

She curtsied very low, though his lascivious attentions made her skin crawl. "Your Majesty honors his poor servant too much."

"Where such an honor is deserved, it can never be too much." The king seized her hand as she rose, kissing her fingertips, his touch lingering on her skin. She did not know where to look, so stared at his vast doublet, the contrast of red velvet beneath the slashed yellow sleeves, and the ornate gold chain that hung about his neck. "Your father has come back to court at last. Have you spoken with him yet?"

Eloise was startled. "My father is here?"

Sir Thomas Cromwell came to the king's elbow again, his sallow face expressionless. "Your Majesty? I believe the queen wishes to speak with you about the arrangements for your forthcoming tournament."

Gently and with due reverence, Cromwell steered the king back toward his wife, then turned to look on Eloise thoughtfully.

"Your father, Sir John, has returned to court in the company of his neighbor, Baron Wolf," Sir Thomas told her coolly.

It was clear to Eloise that the king's chief minister did not wish Henry to become too interested in her. For this intervention, Eloise was most grateful. She herself took no pleasure in the king's flattery, but knew that it would be just as dangerous to spurn it as accept it. They said he had hunted Anne Boleyn in the same persistent way before she gave in and became his mistress, refusing to believe any woman would not please her king by lying with him, virgin or not.

"I believe your father intends to make a match between you and Lord Wolf, and has come to beg the king's blessing on your impending marriage," Cromwell continued. "For myself, I trust it will be a happy and fruitful union."

She blanched. "My…my marriage?"

But Sir Thomas Cromwell had already moved on, having not heard—or tacitly ignored—her question. For King Henry was not speaking with his wife according to his intention, having spotted Jane Seymour instead amongst the queen's ladies. He was now eyeing Jane in such a lewd fashion it brought color to that lady's cheeks, though she did not seem reluctant to receive his attentions. Cromwell did not interfere, but watched them carefully. It was no secret that he disliked Anne. Perhaps he hoped the king would push her away in favor of Jane Seymour if this new pregnancy ended in yet another miscarriage.

Eloise did not hear another word that was said until King Henry had left the queen's apartments, for she could not quite believe what Sir Thomas Cromwell had told her.

She remembered Lord Wolf from her childhood; a grim, disagreeable old man, he had been forever in a bad temper because his son was either away serving the king on campaign or else plaguing his heart out with his dissolute ways.

Surely her father could not expect her to marry such a

man? Lord Wolf must be nigh on sixty years of age, and thrice widowed already.

"I must speak with Simon at once," she muttered, taking her friend Bess aside while the other maids gathered excitedly about the queen to discuss the king's visit. "If Her Majesty asks where I am, will you tell her I am unwell and have retired to bed?"

"Of course." Bess looked concerned though, following her to the door. She was a sweet-natured girl, but biddable, and did not approve of Eloise's secret meetings with Simon. "But do nothing rash, Eloise. If your father has arranged a marriage for you, it is pointless to pursue Simon. He is a younger son and has no hope of providing for you."

"Wealth is not everything," Eloise said hotly. "We love each other, and that is all that matters."

—✺—

Simon was her most perfect man. Dark-eyed, fair-haired, he might not be a knight, or set to inherit a vast fortune, but he was handsome and clever, and always knew how to make her smile again when she was unhappy. Only a year apart in age, they had been more like brother and sister when she first came to court, but in the past year, things had grown more serious between them, until Eloise found she was quite in love with him. His quiet humility was what she admired most about Simon. Although his father was a baron, he did not strut about like the other young men at court. The youngest of five sons, he was largely ignored by his father, so came and went as he pleased, and had wooed her with a gentle patience which she found deeply pleasing.

After sending him a note, Eloise hurried to their favorite meeting place, a small privy garden on the north wing of the palace. It was a beautiful spot in any season, though she preferred it in spring, with the flowers just opening their buds. Today, the January weather was chill and sunny, no wind but a slight bloom of frost on the flagstones as she swept through the cloisters, her yellow gown raised slightly to avoid soiling the hem.

To her relief, Simon soon appeared, ducking his head as he passed through the arched doorway to the cloisters.

"Eloise!" Simon clasped her hands, kissing them as the king had done earlier, though now she thrilled at the warm lips against her skin. "You look flushed. Are you in trouble with the queen again? I have warned you not to be so free with your speech. She will not tolerate impertinence, even less now that she and the king are so estranged."

"My father has come to court," she told him urgently, "and intends to offer me as a bride to Lord Wolf."

Simon nodded. "Yes, I have seen Sir John."

"You have seen my father?" She stared. "Have you spoken with him?"

"Not spoken, no. But I saw him with Lord Wolf only this morning." Simon shrugged. "They say King Henry has given his blessing on the match. The queen may not wish to release you from her service, for she dislikes it when her maids are wed. But she will bow to the king's will in the end."

Simon turned her palm upward and kissed it lingeringly, teasing her skin with his lips. She thought he would at once suggest that they marry in secret, but instead he looked up at her with a sorrowful smile.

"I know this marriage is not what you had hoped for. But perhaps you will find a comfortable life with Lord Wolf, even if there is no love between you. I hear his family have become very wealthy since the fall of the church. Not that such gifts of land are undeserved, for his lordship has served the king well these past ten years. He is a brilliant soldier, by all accounts."

"A brilliant soldier?" she repeated, shocked by this careless acceptance of her fate. "Is that all you can think of, when I am to be enslaved forever to this stranger?"

A thought hit her and she frowned. "Wait, Simon, you must be mistaken. Lord Wolf is an old man, all but bedridden. How could he have served the king in battle so recently?"

Simon laughed, shaking his head. "That was Wolf's father, my love. The old lord died at Yuletide. His son is the new baron."

"His son?"

A vague memory came to her of a sullen, grim-faced youth watching her play as a young child, sitting astride a wall in their old apple orchard. Had that boy been her prospective bridegroom? She had seen him again maybe once or twice when growing up on her father's estate. But he had been away so often, fighting for the king, she had barely known him.

Not quite such a terrifying prospect as an elderly noble, it was true. But he was not her beloved Simon. And if he had spent the past ten years on a battlefield, she doubted they would have much in common.

She knew it was rare for a girl to choose her own husband. But Simon was at least of noble birth, and she had hoped her father would look kindly on their match.

"I hardly remember him."

"I told you, he's been off soldiering for years."

"He's a stranger, I know nothing about him. Though I do re-member there was some scandal… He was betrothed when I was still a child. But the girl ran off with someone else before they could be wed." She looked at Simon wonderingly. "Maybe that's why he never married, for he must be almost thirty years of age."

"No doubt he will be eager for an heir, then," Simon mused, tracing a finger across her lips.

Simon did not seem to care that she was being married off to this stranger, that she would soon be sharing another man's bed. She did not understand. Did Simon not love her? How could he remain so calm in the face of this disaster?

"I cannot even remember his name," she pointed out, trying not to be angered by his calm demeanor, "and now I must marry him? It is unjust."

"True," Simon agreed somberly, "but it is your father's will."

She raised her face to his, looking for some sign of grief or torment. "But do you not love me, Simon? I thought we were to be wed."

"Oh, my sweet fool," he muttered, suddenly his old self again, his eyes dark with passion. He gripped her by the waist and pulled her close. "Of course I love you. How can you doubt me?"

Simon kissed her fiercely. She felt her fears dissolve under that searching mouth, her lips parting daringly to admit his tongue. His kiss deepened and she clung onto his shoulders, her head spinning pleasantly.

"You are so very beautiful, Eloise," he whispered against her cheek. "I am only surprised no other man has tried to claim you before now."

His lips slid down her neck to the low-cut bodice of her gown, kissing the soft skin there just above her breasts. He groaned her name under his breath, clasping her more tightly. Then his hand moved slowly round to cup her breast, squeezing it, but gently, as though afraid she might repulse him.

For once Eloise did not push him away, telling him they must wait until they were married. Instead, she allowed him to caress her, sighing with pleasure as his fingers sought her nipple through the stiff fabric and played it skillfully.

"Simon," she breathed, and raised her head, kissing him back.

Perhaps he was right: this was no time for doubts and arguments. He was her beloved, and she was his. Their lives would be intertwined forever. But whatever Simon was planning that would allow them to be together, she wished he would share it with her.

Simon had pushed her against the wall in his passion, kissing her more forcefully, and she had not protested. But now the stones felt cold against her back, and she shivered, opening her eyes to the gray sky above them. His knee pushed against her gown, nudging her legs apart.

"No, Simon, we must not," she groaned.

"Why not?"

He kissed her palm then placed it firmly against his own body, showing her how aroused he had become.

"It is cold, I grant you that, but we will be quite safe here if we are quick. There is no one about to see us. They will all be in the presence chamber at this time, attending the king."

"But…we are not yet married."

"Who cares for that?" He kissed her again, his tongue pushing into her mouth. Then, as if sensing her reluctance, he sighed and raised his head. "What's the matter now? Come, speak your heart to me. Are you afraid Lord Wolf will discover you are not a maid on your wedding night?"

She stared, speechless with astonishment that he could consider making love to her and still allow her to be married off to a stranger afterward.

Speak her heart to him? It was hard enough not to let the hurt and anger show on her face. Had Simon no intention of marrying her himself? She had foolishly assumed by his kisses that he intended to suggest an elopement and a secret wedding before her father could intervene, but apparently such a thought had never been in his mind. He had used her. And he had not finished the task, it seemed.

"Do not distress yourself, my dearest Eloise," he whispered in her ear, his hand once again caressing her breast, only this time in a more lewd manner, pinching her nipple. "I can teach you a trick that will make your husband think you are still a virgin. The queen herself must know it, for she was surely no maid on her wedding night. Yet the king found nothing amiss."

"How dare you say such a thing of Her Majesty?" she exclaimed, pushing away his hand. "You must know how it disgusts me."

"My love, all I mean is that we need not let this arranged marriage stand in the way of our pleasure. True, it is a long way to York. But you will return to court soon enough. Lord Wolf is too ambitious a man to remain in the cold north forever." His smile teased her. "And then we can lie together at court while he is busy with the king or campaigning abroad."

"You expect me to cheat on my husband?" she asked, feeling sick.

"Why not?" Simon patted the bulge in his crotch with every indication of pride. "I am an excellent lover, or so I have been told. I will give you no reason to complain."

"Simon, please tell me you are jesting," she demanded, and promptly hated herself for clinging to the fast-fading hope that he loved her. "We could run away together, and marry under assumed names."

"What, and risk the king's displeasure? I think not. And how would we live, my sweet, when I have no hope of income? You must know that being a younger son, I cannot marry you, however much I love you. I can only marry a woman with a large fortune, or else look forward to a life of chastity and cold knees in the church." Simon winked. "And we both know that would not suit me. Besides, if I get you with child as a married woman, who is to say it is not your husband's?"

Anger boiled inside her at this insult. "What?"

"Oh, these arrangements are quite common at court. They say the king fathered many of the young pages you see about the palace these days, some with the husband's eager consent."

He smiled down into her face, oblivious to her growing fury, no doubt thinking her merely nervous at the idea of surrendering her maidenhead. "My dearest Eloise, do not be afraid to raise your skirts to me. There will be pain, a little at first, but you will enjoy it after that, trust me. And when you are Lady Wolf, we need not be apart when you are at court, but can love with even greater freedom than now, for a wife is watched less carefully than a maid."

The sound of footsteps in the cloisters saved her from slapping his face in rage, which she had been about to do. Eloise pulled hurriedly away from him, and even Simon had the grace to look embarrassed as a group of young girls passed through the cloister, accompanied by their governess, a stern-faced woman who eyed them both with disapproval.

"That was close!" he exclaimed once they were alone again, and made as though to pull her back into his arms.

"No, leave me alone, Simon," she told him fiercely. "I think you had better go, for I see now how mistaken I was to…to trust you."

He hesitated, then shrugged, seeing the contempt on her face. His hands dropped and he took a step backward. She was relieved that he did not appear interested in pressing his suit.

"Very well, if you must go to your marriage bed a foolish and inexperienced virgin, that is your own affair. By all accounts, Lord Wolf is as hard a man as he is a soldier. He has an ugly limp, you know, and rough soldierly manners." Simon looked pointedly at her. "He will not take you gently, maiden or not. You may regret submitting to him unspoiled."

"Go!" she insisted, a sudden heat flaring in her cheeks at this description of her wedding night.

Simon bowed reluctantly, and turned on his heel, but could not resist saying over his shoulder, "If you change your mind, Eloise, send me a note. And don't forget my offer. When you come to court as Lady Wolf, I will not refuse you if you are looking for a lover behind your husband's back."

Eloise stood in angry silence when he had gone, cursing her own blind folly. How could she have been so deceived in Simon? She had thought he loved her, but in truth he had only ever loved himself and thought to enjoy her body without commitment. And to think she had almost permitted him to take her virginity.

"What a touching scene," a voice drawled behind her, and a man ducked his head under one of the archways, stepping out from the shadowy cloisters into the garden.

She spun, cold with dread that anyone might have witnessed the intimacies that had passed between her and Simon.

The man walked with a pronounced limp, though his body looked fit and strong enough despite it. He was not fashionably dressed like most of the other courtiers; his clothes seemed to be designed more for riding and comfort than dancing with ladies, for he carried a crop in one hand, and his boots were dirty from the stables. Yet she could tell from the fine cut and costly material of his rich claret-colored doublet that he was a nobleman, and a wealthy one at that. His red-and-black hose were tightly fitted, and she found herself staring at his powerful thighs and the prominent bulge of his codpiece.

Then she raised her eyes to the man's face and felt sick. For although he was much changed, his black hair cut short, his angular body grown tall and strong, his face harder and older, she knew him at once from her childhood.

It was the old baron's son, Lord Wolf. The very man her father intended her to marry.

"Forbidden love in a privy garden," Lord Wolf continued, his tone light, though his blue eyes were cold as he looked her up and down. "Listening to you two reminded me of one of Chaucer's tales. The old fool, his beautiful young wife, and the cunning lover. I am only sorry to have missed its torrid consummation. But no doubt that will be arranged as soon as my back is turned."

Eloise curtsied, managing a cold, "My Lord Wolf," for what else could she do but try to remain as collected as the queen had done, nearly caught flirting behind the king's back?

Yet she knew in how much danger she stood. If Lord Wolf reported her meeting with Simon to the king, along with what he had witnessed of their lovemaking, she would be utterly disgraced. She had heard whispered tales of unchaste maids of honor whipped from the court, their wicked names never to be spoken again in the queen's presence.

Did that fate await her now?

Two

"ELOISE TYRELL." LORD WOLF bowed in response to her curtsy. His blue eyes seemed to mock her as he straightened. "My chamber overlooks this charming garden, and has a most stubborn casement that lets in the cold—and the sound of voices below. For which I shall be forever grateful. At least now I will have no illusions about my new bride's willingness."

God's blood, why had she kissed Simon so openly? This wealthy baron would not wish to marry her now. Not after hearing Simon's suggestion that they should meet and couple shamelessly behind his back once she was Lady Wolf.

Then she realized belatedly what he had said…

"New bride? You surely do not still intend to marry me?" she demanded, staring.

"Why not?" Lord Wolf shrugged. "From what I overheard just now, your maidenhead is still intact, even if your honor remains in question." His smile was unpleasant. "Unless you were lying to that boy?"

"No," she told him defiantly.

"Well then, there can be no opposition to the match. I need an heir, and your father will welcome my help with his debts." He examined her through narrowed eyes. "You are a little thin for my tastes. But if you can learn to obey me, you will do. All I require is a girl to produce a few sons and not make too much of a nuisance of herself about the place. Do we understand each other?"

Eloise did not know what to say. She wished it was possible

to refuse this marriage, but she did not wish to be beaten for her disobedience, nor put away in some quiet place of contemplation for the rest of her life. Her childhood friend Sylvia had refused her father's choice of bridegroom, and had been beaten so badly that she lost her sight in one eye. Now Sylvia kept to her rooms through shame, and spent the days in prayer. For what else was left to her, scarred and disfigured as she was?

Eloise did not believe her father would beat her as Sylvia had been beaten if she refused Lord Wolf's proposal. But he would certainly punish her for dishonoring him.

I will not suffer like Sylvia, she told herself fiercely. It was clear that Lord Wolf would not trouble her except in pursuit of an heir, and she would at least have a large manor house to run once they were married. There was no shame in wanting to make her life comfortable.

Besides, Lord Wolf was not unsightly, and was certainly more honest than Simon. Her father could have found her a worse husband, she considered.

"Yes, my lord," she replied, lowering her gaze before his in a mimicry of obedience.

She would never sleep with Simon—nor any other man— behind her husband's back. It was not in her nature to hold a man's honor so cheaply. But it might be possible to keep the baron at a distance after she was safely with child.

After all, once the question of his heir was taken care of, what else would Lord Wolf want her for?

He approached her, limping, his face thoughtful. "So docile, so quickly?" he murmured. "Is that possible?"

Eloise had wanted to appear submissive before Lord Wolf; she knew he would expect his bride-to-be to acquiesce to his every demand. Yet to her dismay, she found she could not keep up the pretense. Not when questioned with such directness. There was something in his voice that dug at the truth and would have it out.

Eloise tilted her chin to look him boldly in the eyes. He was taller than she had realized. "My lord, I am grateful you do not intend to shame me before the court by refusing my father's offer. But I cannot pretend to look on our marriage with anything other than dislike." She paused, then added flatly, "You are not my choice of husband, as you know."

"Yes, I was a little startled to see my promised bride in the arms of another man. But if you can overlook my ugly limp and my rough soldierly manners," he said, an ironic gleam in his eyes as he repeated Simon's unflattering description, "then I can over-look a single mistake on your part. Assuming it is never repeated, of course."

He raised his hand, and she flinched. But it seemed he did not intend to strike her. The rough split ends of his hazel riding crop touched her on the forehead, so lightly it was almost a tickle, then slid down to her mouth.

Slowly, the crop traced the outline of her lips with a sensual threat, and Eloise shivered, unable to help herself.

Lord Wolf watched her response, narrow-eyed, then lowered the hazel crop again. This time he traced it down her neck to the gentle swell of her breasts, his face unsmiling.

"Eloise?"

She tried to reply but could not. His blue eyes seemed to have penetrated Eloise to her core, leaving her utterly entranced, as though caught in some kind of spell. Did Lord Wolf possess some magical power? Why else would she feel so utterly drawn in by his gaze?

"Do you remember me?" he asked, drawling again. "From when we were children?"

She struggled to remember him, that sullen-faced youth watching her from a distance. He was too close to her now, his gaze too demanding. Her heart raced at his proximity. The memory of him as a boy came back to her slowly. No, the two images could not be pieced together. The edges were too jagged. He was a man now, and she would soon belong to him.

"A little," she conceded.

He stroked along her breasts with the crop. "You were such a skinny little thing. I am glad to see you have filled out." His smile was appreciative. "I would have come for you sooner, but I had not yet made my mind up. I was betrothed once before, you see, and my memories of that time are not happy."

She nodded silently.

"But of course, you spoke of it to your suitor. It seems my youthful indiscretions are a topic of gossip for every court slut."

She was startled by the sudden harshness of his tone, and jerked away in angry surprise.

"My lord?" she questioned him, and heard the haughtiness in her voice too late. But Eloise refused to cower before him, even if he had caught her in an embarrassing situation with Simon. She had blood in her veins, not milk. It was better he should know it before they married, rather than after.

He dropped the riding crop and grabbed at her wrists, dragging her toward him with hidden strength.

"God's blood," he told her thickly, "I swear to you that our marriage will never be food for gossip. I will not stand to be cuckolded, I promise you that. Once we are married, you will belong to me and admit no other man to your bed. Is that understood?"

"Yes," she replied, staring at him, his face so close she could feel the warmth of his breath, see the strangely long lashes that hid his blue eyes.

"Swear it," he insisted. "On your life."

"I swear it, my lord." This man, she thought, would not be as malleable a bridegroom as she had hoped. "I swear it on my life."

"Good."

That had been the right response, she thought, still staring at him. The squall seemed to have dropped as quickly as it blew up, though his smile was still fierce.

Lord Wolf slipped an arm about her waist and drew her easily against him, tucking her into his body. He was tall and hard-bodied, easily more than six feet of pure muscle under his soldier's plain doublet, and she felt breathless, knowing she would not be able to fight him off as she had attempted to do with Simon, not if he deliberately chose to dishonor her.

"Let's have a kiss to seal your oath," he said shortly, and bent his head to hers.

She had thought Lord Wolf would give her a token kiss, like that given by a bridegroom after the marriage vows had been exchanged. Some cold and bloodless meeting of lips to remind her that she belonged to him now. But his mouth took hers with a kiss of such ardent fervor she could barely stand beneath it, her hands clinging to his shoulders. She was dazed, her body under assault, not expecting the wave of violent passion that swept through her in the wake of his embrace.

His kiss was bold and darkly possessive. Lord Wolf was sure of her acquiescence, she realized with a shock. Nor was he wrong. Eloise found her lips parting beneath his, her tiny gasp an opportunity for his tongue to slip inside.

Seeming to sense her surrender, he lifted her slightly, pressing her against the cold stone wall, just as Simon had done, and lowered his head again to claim her lips.

He tasted of heat and long summer nights, his scent as well as his hands enticing her closer, reminding her of spice and oranges. She had meant to resist, but it was impossible. His tongue traced slowly along her lower lip, then dipped back inside, stroking and flickering, promising the kind of sensual pleasures she had only dreamt of before in the privacy of her bed.

In a few ecstatic seconds, she had forgotten Simon's boyish, enthusiastic kisses. This was beyond mere physical desire. His body weighted strongly against hers, he no longer needed to hold her still. His mouth teased and played her, one hand cupping her face, the other stroking her long hair.

Eloise moaned under his kiss, her eyes closing with pleasure. She felt new worlds opening up as he touched her, parts of herself suddenly springing to life under his hands. Her breasts tingled in a way she barely recognized, her nipples taut, pushing against the neckline of her gown. Between her thighs a strangely sweet ache had begun to throb, her flesh there slick with unaccustomed longing.

"Yes," he muttered, as though she had spoken, and kissed all the way down her neck to her breasts, following the line his riding crop had taken.

Her skin felt scorched by his mouth, a new desire flaming inside her, stronger than any passion she had hitherto experienced. She was shocked but excited, recognizing that impulse for what it was: a desire to lie with this man in complete abandon, to be possessed by him, and to let him see her own needs, naked and urgent.

He raised his head and kissed her mouth again. This time they clung together with equal passion, her hands gripping at his broad shoulders, her tongue sliding against his, instinctively bold, inviting an even deeper intimacy.

He laughed huskily, drawing back a little. "I thought so," he murmured.

She could not quite believe that she had been kissing him back, her lips tingling and swollen. Was that what he meant? That he had guessed at her passionate nature beforehand, perhaps when watching her with Simon?

Eloise drew back, turning her head away so he could not kiss her again. "Please," she whispered.

His gaze followed her, heavy-lidded with desire. "Please yes, or please no?"

"I am not ready to…"

"You think I mean to take you here, in this garden, where any man may stumble across us?" He laughed, but did not release her. "I'm not your young suitor, who would have pinned you against this wall and taken you like a serving maid in the buttery. Where is the pleasure in such a rushed coupling?"

Lord Wolf kissed her again, but more gently this time, slipping his tongue into her mouth, seducing her with the hard warmth of his body.

"No," he murmured against her mouth, "when I make love to you for the first time, Eloise, it will be in a comfortable bed where I can look upon you naked and enjoy your body for as long as I please."

She was still hazily trying to shake off that sensual image of married delight when there was a sound of brisk footsteps in the cloister behind them.

"Ah, there you are, my lord!" With a shock, Eloise recognized her father's voice and dragged herself free from Lord Wolf's arms. "And my daughter… But I see you two are getting on well."

She curtsied to her father, her cheeks deeply flushed. "Father, I beg your forgiveness, but I must attend the queen before she misses me."

"Of course," her father said, his tone almost jovial, and kissed her on the forehead.

She examined him worriedly, for her younger sister Susannah had written that winter to say their father was unwell. But he seemed to have recovered. Once a man of imposing stature, her father was now stooped, his hair graying, his face lined. Nonetheless Sir John was still an active man, enjoying a ride or hunt most days, and seemed to have taken no harm from the lengthy and arduous journey south from their estate above York. No doubt he was delighted to find them together, she thought. With the wealthy Baron Wolf as a son-in-law, he would soon be able to rebuild much of their tumbledown estate.

"It is most seemly that your duty to the queen should come first," her father continued, smiling. "Besides, there will be plenty of time for us to talk on the journey back to Yorkshire. Do not stare, my dear. You had best start packing your things and bidding your friends farewell, for we shall depart as soon as the queen gives permission for you to be released from her service. I shall send word ahead of our plans, and hope to see you both married in early spring."

"So soon?"

Lord Wolf looked across at her sharply, his brows arching at her exclamation. "The sooner the better," her prospective bridegroom remarked, already cool and controlled again, all traces of passion gone. "The court is a dangerous place for an unmarried woman. You will be much safer at your father's house while we await the reading of the banns."

"Dangerous?" her father queried, looking from one to the other in surprise.

"Forgive me, father, my lord," Eloise repeated, curtsying with her head bowed. "The queen is most strict and I do not wish to be late."

Turning before either of them could stop her, Eloise slipped away through the cloisters and hurried back to the queen's apartments.

The love she had long felt for Simon had been revealed to her today as false, a shadow of love that had not survived the dawning of Lord Wolf's appearance. How could she have believed Simon would be true to her? What a fool she had been. No wonder his lordship had laughed at her for encouraging such a youth in his attentions.

Yet she was not easy in her mind about this arranged marriage either. There seemed no way out that would not lead to disgrace and punishment. Yet if she could find an escape, she would take it. For although married life with Lord Wolf would never be dull, he was too experienced a lover to have felt the same way Eloise had done when he was kissing her, her blood on fire for him, her lips suddenly tingling with passion.

His desire would soon fade once they were married. Lust was a thing of the moment, easily forgotten by a man.

Then she would be left in the cold, abandoned while he moved on to a new woman—just as the king seemed likely to do if Queen Anne could not bear him a son.

—⁓—

The presence chamber was crowded, a chill February sunshine falling through high windows to warm the vast room. Standing in groups in doorways, or leaning wearily against the tapestried walls, gentlemen waited to present their petitions to the king. Courtiers and ladies of the court paraded themselves in brilliant silks and velvets like birds of paradise. The restless hum of conversation in the privy chamber rose and fell as each petition was presented, some pleas more interesting or contentious than others.

At last the name "Sir John Tyrell!" was called out by the chamberlain, who struck his staff of office with a dull thud thrice on the floor.

Head held high, Eloise followed her father through the massed courtiers toward the high dais. There, above them, King Henry and Queen Anne sat enthroned, side by side, a lavish cloth of gold draped behind their heads.

This audience with the king had been delayed by several weeks, a period of waiting which had severely tested her nerves. Yet it could not be helped. Soon after her father's arrival at court, King Henry had been thrown from his horse in a jousting accident and knocked senseless. He had swiftly recovered, thank the Lord, but it was whispered that his leg had been crushed and he might never dance again.

Outwardly, the king seemed his usual ebullient self. Those who attended him in his privy chambers, however, told of sudden, restless bouts of violence and temper such as they had never seen before.

Though that was small wonder, for Queen Anne, no doubt ter-rified that His Majesty might die, had miscarried her unborn child mere hours after his accident. Now the queen sat beside her husband like a wax effigy, white-faced and still, the king's physicians having only recently pronounced Anne fit to leave her bed.

It was said the child miscarried had been a boy: the male heir to the throne so longed-for by the king.

Eloise knelt behind her father on the cold stone flags. That morning she had dressed demurely in a plain gown, covering her hair with a simple hood. She hoped that by appearing unattractive to Lord Wolf, he might choose some other girl to marry. But she suspected he would see straight through that strategy.

The other maids of honor giggled, winking at her. Lady Margaret hushed them with a frown, one eye on her grieving mistress.

A quick movement caught her attention, and Eloise glanced sideways through the crowd. It was Simon, splendid in pale yellow velvet, pushing through the other courtiers to stand against the wall near the dais. She had to bite her lip, looking hurriedly away before her color rose.

So even Simon had come to watch her humiliation. How had she been so deceived in him?

Eloise had watched such marriage negotiations many times as one of the queen's maids of honor, standing behind the dais or seated at the queen's feet. Now it was her turn to be brought forward and her prospects discussed, a mere chattel in the hands of her father. Being in the queen's service, it was up to the king and queen to decide her fate.

"Lord Wolf!" the chamberlain announced, bowing.

She did not look up, but heard footsteps on the stone floor and felt his gaze on her face.

Wolf paused beside her. "Eloise," he said quietly.

It would cause unwelcome comment if she did not respond.

Proudly, she lifted her chin, forcing herself to meet his gaze. "Lord Wolf."

Lord Wolf took her hand and raised Eloise to her feet. "I do not like to see my future wife kneeling like a servant."

She was surprised by this gesture, then caught a warning glitter in his eyes as he glanced past her at Simon, still leaning against the wall tapestry.

Wolf was not concerned for her welfare, she realized with a flicker of anger. He was telling every man there that she was his possession.

The king had watched this exchange with interest, an avid look on his face.

"I trust you slept well, Wolf? Though as I recall, you're a man who can sleep anywhere, even among the dead on a battlefield. Look at this brave fellow, Anne. A better swordsman would be hard to find in all of England." King Henry held out his hand, and Wolf knelt dutifully to kiss it. "So you've finally chosen a bride to warm your bed. Well, it's about time you secured your line, and she's pleasurable enough to look on. You have my blessing on the match, as I told you yesterday. But did you have to find her among Anne's own maids? The queen does not wish to part with her, for she needs all her ladies about her at this time."

"Forgive me, sire. I am most loath to distress Her Majesty with my request, but it is a good match and I should be less of a man if I did not pursue it wholeheartedly." Lord Wolf stood back from the dais, bowing to the queen. "My eye first fell on the lady when she was a girl. Now the wars are over and Eloise is grown to womanhood, I crave Your Majesty's permission to claim her."

Queen Anne studied Eloise in silence, then turned her gaze to Lord Wolf. "I have no desire for Eloise to leave my service," she declared, unsmiling. "The king has spoken to me on your behalf, and, believe me, I do understand the pressing nature of your claim.

But you must look elsewhere for a bride. If I allowed my maids of honor to leave court and be wed whenever they wished, my lord, I would have no women left to attend me."

Her father fell on his knees before the queen, his head bowed in deference. "Forgive my impertinence in taking away one of your ladies, Your Majesty. But as Lord Wolf has said, my eldest daughter is over-ripe for marriage. Indeed, if she waits much longer, she may never be wed at all. I would be very glad to see her wed to Lord Wolf, if Your Majesty could graciously consent to release Eloise from service. For once she is wed, I can find a suitable bridegroom for my youngest daughter Susannah, who is now of age and much admired amongst the landowners in the north."

Queen Anne drew breath as though to deny him, but the king laid his jeweled hand heavily over hers.

"Come, my love," King Henry told her, his voice unmistakably cold. "Lord Wolf has fought stoutly for England and our throne. I have rewarded him for his service with land and goods. You can readily spare him one of your maids of honor for a wife."

The court held its breath, waiting for the queen's response to this veiled reprimand.

Queen Anne looked at her husband a long moment, and a flush crept into her cheeks. Stiffly, she turned her head toward Lord Wolf.

"Take her then, my lord, and I wish you joy of her." Her voice was almost shrill. "But I trust Eloise will be speedily returned to me whenever I send for her in the future. Indeed, if she is not with child by the summer, she may take her place here at court amongst my married ladies-in-waiting."

Lord Wolf bowed courteously. "You have my humble thanks, Your Majesty, and my promise as a soldier on that."

It was over. The next petition was already being announced by the chamberlain. Eloise felt a despairing rage within her as her father was dismissed. She wanted to cry out to the king and queen, "What about me? Are my feelings not to be consulted? I do not even wish to be married to this man!"

But the decision had been made for her. She had no choice but to curtsy and follow her father and Lord Wolf from the chamber. She had been handed over to the enemy.

———

Her last days at court passed swiftly. Soon the morning arrived for their long journey to the north. The cold weather had eased a little and sunshine thawed the frost in the courtyard as Eloise was led outside to the covered litter in which she would travel home. She had packed her meager belongings, and dressed as warmly as she could in a traveling gown, two pairs of thick woolen stockings beneath her skirts to keep out the cold, and a shawl about her shoulders.

She had also been honored with the lavish parting gift of a gold and pearl brooch from the queen.

Eloise suspected this was as a reward for her silence though, rather than given out of love. She had, after all, witnessed the queen entertaining Wyatt and Norris in her chamber without the king's consent.

That would not end well, she thought, fearing for the queen now that another pregnancy had ended in bitter disappointment for the king. But she could understand such infidelity rather better now, facing her own arranged marriage with a stranger. Anne had been coerced into a royal union with a man past his best, who had since lost interest in her beyond his need for an heir. Perhaps she was even in love with one of those courtiers, Eloise thought compassionately. But it would be dangerous for her to flirt too openly. Since his jousting accident, King Henry's temper had grown more notorious by the day; God only knew what he would do if he suspected his wife of adultery.

In the courtyard, the day was gray and chilly. She helped her young maidservant Mary climb into the covered litter, for the queen had insisted she take a girl with her on the journey. Then she looked about for a groom to help her too.

"Eloise! Wait!"

She turned, hearing the shout, and her lips tightened when she saw who it was.

Simon came hurrying down the steps into the courtyard where her covered litter stood waiting, a rolled-up paper in his hand. Much to her relief, Lord Wolf had not yet emerged from the palace, and her father seemed too busy speaking to the driver to have noticed her former suitor.

"My love," Simon said, embracing her. His lips touched hers, though he did not seem aware of how still she held herself beneath his touch. "I'm so glad I caught you, Eloise. I could not stand the thought of you leaving court without so much as a farewell."

"It would be best if we did not speak to each other again," she told him frankly. "I am to be married soon, remember."

"I told you, we need not let your marriage to Lord Wolf stand in the way of our desire." Simon smiled, holding out the rolled-up paper. "Take it, and let my words warm you on your journey north. Only do not show it to your betrothed."

"I cannot take it, Simon."

He seized her hand, stroking her palm intimately with his thumb, and pressed the letter into it. "Don't break my heart with this coldness. At least read what I have written to you, my love."

"You must not call me that. You know that you do not love me." Frowning, she shook her head at his hurried protest. "You only love yourself."

"So cruel?"

"So honest," she said drily.

"My dearest love," Simon replied, his look pitying, "you will find honesty a worthless enough commodity in a marriage. No wife and husband were ever true to each other, whatever promises they may have made at the altar. And you do not love Lord Wolf," he added pointedly. "You are only marrying him because your father wills it. Why be faithful to a man who will be your jailor for the rest of your days?"

She looked into his eyes. How deeply she had thought herself in love with Simon once. He still seemed so handsome and charming, it was hard to remember the careless nature of his deceit. Now she knew him for a young man who would think nothing of lying in order to dishonor a maid, or even of stealing a woman from her husband's bed, so long as their night together brought him satisfaction.

"Because it is my duty," she told him, and felt a chill of despair creep through her heart at those awful words.

"What's this?" a voice asked coldly behind Simon, interrupting them. "Fond farewells from your lover?"

Lord Wolf!

Horrified, Eloise realized she was still holding Simon's letter. She could only imagine what it contained, intimate words of love that could earn her a whipping for wanton behavior if her father or his lordship discovered it about her person. She thrust the rolled-up letter down into her bodice, and drew her shawl about her shoulders to hide it.

Simon had flushed. He bowed to them both, stammered something about archery practice, and disappeared back up the steps into the palace.

"How gallant of him to stay and defend your honor," Lord Wolf drawled. "Come, the morning is already half gone. It is time for us to depart. I have arranged for some of my men to accompany us back to Yorkshire for your protection. Some of the roads in the north can be dangerous for unwary travelers." He saw her worried glance at the litter, which would barely house more than two persons, and smiled. "Your father and I will ride alongside, so you will be undisturbed."

He handed her up into the covered litter where young Mary was huddled in the corner, looking very nervous at the prospect of her first long journey. Eloise settled back against the cushions, her face averted.

To her dismay, Lord Wolf leaned forward. "Just one more thing," he murmured, and pressed a kiss on her lips.

She sat still beneath his kiss, her heart beating violently. She could not help remembering how he had touched her in the garden, and the powerful surge of desire she had felt. Even now it was difficult not to respond, to keep her lips closed beneath his and not lean into his masculine scent.

Then his hand slipped to her bodice, and he withdrew the letter she had hidden there.

"Now what could this be, I wonder?" he commented, straightening.

He unrolled the letter, reading though it with a hard face. Then he tore the letter into a dozen pieces and scattered them across her lap.

"Whatever Simon was to you once," he told her coldly, "I advise you to forget him. You are mine now; do you understand?"

Lord Wolf did not wait for an answer, but jumped down from the covered litter and strode to his waiting horse.

Eloise dropped the curtain down so she could no longer see him, and sat in silence, her maid staring at her in horror. She wondered what had been in that letter. Had Simon repeated his suggestion that they should meet behind her husband's back and make love?

If only she had thrown that damned letter in Simon's face!

The horse pulling the litter began to move. The whole litter jerked, curtains swaying. Mary gave a little cry and clung onto her seat.

Outside, Eloise heard the jingle of harness and reins, Wolf shouting orders to his men in a curt voice, then the clatter of hooves beside the litter as the cavalcade made its slow, lurching way out of the courtyard and through the palace gates.

She brushed the torn pieces of letter from her lap and sat in an angry silence for the first few miles of their journey, eyes closed as though trying to sleep, but frowning. She could not help touching her lips from time to time, still tingling from his mouth. How could he arouse such pleasure in her body with just one kiss?

Whichever way she looked at it, there was no avoiding the truth of her situation. Wolf was to be her lord and master, and it seemed there was little she could do to escape him.

Three

THEIR FIRST DAY OF journeying was exhausting; the litter jolted from side to side as the roads worsened north of London. By the time they reached the wayside inn where her father had arranged for them to spend the night, Eloise was too weary even to contemplate dinner. She slept in the cramped chamber she was sharing with her maid, then she and Mary rose at dawn the next morning to breakfast and continue their journey.

The next day was just as cold. A bitter wind snatched at the litter curtains, lifting them with every gust. Eloise wrapped herself in furs, glancing out at the occasional flash of green countryside. More accustomed now to the lurching progress of the wagon, she tried to sew her sampler at first. Needlework reminded her of long days of incarceration in her childhood, forced to sit and be docile with the other girls when what she wanted was to ride free across the fields. Yet she knew such domestic skills would be expected of her as Lady Wolf, so she persevered for a while, aware of Mary's curious gaze on her face.

Her good intentions did not last long, however. Watching the intricate movements of the needle made her feel sick. Soon she laid her sampler aside, staring restlessly at the men riding alongside the litter. How much less tedious it would be if she too could ride home, she considered. But such a long ride would be unthinkable for a gently reared lady of the court.

"Have you ever traveled before, Mary?"

Her maid shook her head, wide-eyed. "Never, Mistress. I was

born in Greenwich and never left there before, nor ever wanted to. They do say it's terrible cold up north."

"I'm afraid it can be in the winter," Eloise agreed.

"And there are ruffians on the road, or so I heard. Robbers and murderers!"

"Further north it can be dangerous to travel unaccompanied. We should be safe enough though, with all these stout-hearted soldiers about us. Robbers rarely attack wagons where there are so many armed men to overcome."

Mary seemed unconvinced. But she gladly accepted a drink of ale when Eloise suggested they open the basket of provisions her father had procured from the inn.

The ale seemed to loosen the girl's tongue. Her face was soon flushed, her conversation less shy. "Are you looking forward to your wedding, Mistress? It will be exciting to dress you for the marriage feast. My last mistress died of childbed fever, but she looked lovely before the altar. Only sixteen years of age, she was, but pretty as a magpie with black hair and white skin." Her maid looked at her appraisingly. "With your golden hair, you would suit scarlet or deep blue for a wedding gown. With poppies or cornflowers in your hair."

"I have hardly thought of what to wear," Eloise murmured. "Not that it matters yet. My wedding is still far off."

Mary looked at her coyly. "Is that so, Mistress? I thought you would be wed as soon as we arrived in Yorkshire, from what they were saying at court."

Eloise looked at her sharply. She disliked the idea that she had become a source of court gossip, though she supposed it was inevitable with a bridegroom of Lord Wolf's stature and reputation. He was handsome and influential enough to have drawn the eye of many restless wives and maids at court, and could have had his pick of the younger women for a bride. Though she had heard no gossip against him in that way. It seemed her prospective husband had been careful to avoid entangling himself with any one mistress in particular, whatever discreet pleasures he might have taken on his returns from the battlefield.

He was a clever man, she had to grant him that.

"And what were they saying?"

"Only that his lordship was most impatient to be wed," Mary whispered, watching her with a sly smile on her face. "That he would barely wait for the banns to be decently read in church before dragging you off to his bed."

"Mary!"

"Forgive me, Mistress." Her maid bit her lip, looking down at her hands. "Though there's no shame in a man's impatience. At least his lordship will not be an indifferent husband."

Eloise did not know how to answer that, so she bade the girl hold her tongue and pass her a box of sweet comfits. But she felt uneasy at the thought of Wolf's impatience.

In a hastily arranged marriage such as this, where the unfortunate bride was all but whipped to the altar, indifference on the husband's part would be a blessing. The thought of Lord Wolf's desire was alarming, though she knew it was merely desire for an heir. She should do her duty swiftly and produce one. Then his lordship might leave her alone.

She tried to sidestep the prickling awareness that she might not find accepting Lord Wolf in her bed such a hardship.

"I still say cornflowers for your hair," Mary muttered, then fell silent under Eloise's stare.

It had been important to bring a maidservant with her as a chaperone, even with her own father as one of the party, but she would have preferred to bring someone less talkative. Since none of the other maids could be spared, Mary had been assigned to her. The girl was several years older than her, and did not seem much in awe of her now they had left court.

Still, it was a long journey to the cold reaches of the North Riding, and there would be few at home who knew so much of courtly life. Mary would at least be able to make her gowns and dress her hair in the latest fashions; as Lady Wolf she would be expected to look more elegant than she had ever looked at home, and a maid who had served the queen's ladies would make her the envy of her neighbors.

"Let's try to get some sleep, shall we?"

Mary nodded her assent and settled back, closing her eyes, though the likelihood of getting much sleep was remote with the litter swaying so violently.

The wagon bearing them took a sharp bend and Eloise lurched, clutching at the seat rail. The curtain blew back momentarily in the gusting wind, and she caught a glimpse of Lord Wolf riding alongside the litter.

The day was cold and gray. Cloaked against the wind, Wolf sat upright in the saddle, gloved hands resting lightly on the reins, his head turned away. At that moment, as though sensing her gaze, he looked round and their eyes met.

Then the curtain dropped again.

She lay back, trying in vain to sleep, the image of her bridegroom burned into the darkness behind her closed lids.

———

It was dark before they reached the wayside inn where they would break their journey that night. It was a small, remote tavern at the foot of a steep hill, not so welcoming as the bustling place they had stopped the night before. A man came out with a lantern to light the way while another carried their baggage inside; both leered at her and Mary in the drafty inn courtyard, only looking away when Lord Wolf swung down from his horse and began issuing abrupt orders.

Eloise stretched her aching legs, glancing up at the wintry night sky where the first stars were coming out. She was glad their journey had ended for the day, sore and tired after so many hours spent in a swaying litter. She was beginning to think even riding would be preferable. But of course her father would never allow such a thing, for the roads were too dangerous this far north and unsuitable for a woman on horseback.

"Hurry up inside," Lord Wolf said curtly, taking her by the elbow and almost pushing her through the narrow passageway into the inn.

He spoke a moment with the surly-faced innkeeper, checking their provision of chambers, then gestured Eloise and Mary toward the cramped and winding stairs to the first floor.

Thrust into a bedchamber with little attempt at civility, her maid following after with a candle, Eloise turned to glare at him. "My lord!"

"You'll want to rest a short while before supper," Wolf commented, ignoring her fury at this treatment. His gaze rested a moment on her creased cloak and gown. "And perhaps change your attire."

"I should prefer to eat in my chamber," she told him coldly.

"You kept to your chamber all yesterday evening," he pointed out. "Tonight I wish you to dine downstairs with us, where you can meet some of our companions on this journey. But have a care what you wear. This is a small place and unused to unmarried female travelers. No doubt you saw the way those ruffians eyed you in the yard." His smile disturbed her. "I would not wish to have to defend your honor."

She stared at him, speechless.

"Half an hour," Wolf told her brusquely, turning away. "Your father and I will wait for you below."

The inn chamber was bare and low-ceilinged, with a threadbare tester bed for herself and a straw mattress on the floor for Mary. She prodded the mattress with her toe, and a mouse ran out from underneath. Mary gave a little shriek, but said nothing, merely looked at her new mistress with trepidation.

"You can share the bed with me," Eloise promised her. "First though, you had better help me look respectable for this meal."

Mary dressed her by the light of their single candle, its flame flickering with every icy draft that blew in around the loose window shutters or under the door. Much to Eloise's relief, Mary had thought to bring a small hand glass in which she was able to study herself.

She held it up while Mary combed out and arranged her hair. A narrow-chinned face frowned back at her, pale and not particularly pretty, with unfashionably fair looks. She was no dark court beauty. Yet somehow she had managed to procure a wealthy lord for a husband. And she had even thought Simon in love with her once, though his intentions had not been honorable. Perhaps Queen Anne had been right to say her charms, like the queen's own, lay below the neck.

Eloise pinched her cheeks to bring some color into them after the long, dreary journey. Would Lord Wolf be as disagreeable a husband as he was a suitor?

"A clean ruff," Mary murmured, and Eloise straightened to receive it, holding still while her maid fastened the fresh ruff in place.

She tried to guess at the intimacies of her wedding night, with nothing but young maids' gossip to fuel her imaginings. Brought up in the country, she knew how animals coupled, but had always hoped that love between a man and a woman would be a more dignified affair. Soon she would know the truth. She felt like a virgin sacrifice in one of those ancient Greek tales mentioned by the poets, left chained to a rock to appease some ogre. Part of her dreaded the appeasing of the ogre, while part of her was curious to become a woman at last.

At least she could be in no doubt that Lord Wolf desired her, that he was unlikely to mistreat her. She told herself it could have been worse: an infirm old man for a husband, or a drunken brute. But in truth she would have preferred a man she loved. Not this sharp-eyed, cold-tongued stranger.

Downstairs, she found a long room with a fire burning in the stone hearth and a trestle table set for supper, an array of serving men bustling to and fro with platters, trenchers, and cups for the wine. Her father was already seated at the head of the table, stately in his furred robe and embroidered cap, drinking wine. The other gentlemen were standing, conversing together by the fireside. Among them she saw the tall figure of Lord Wolf and looked hurriedly away before he saw her looking, determined to appear more modestly behaved than she had done at court.

"There you are at last, Eloise!" her father exclaimed impatiently, and gestured her to the seat on his left. "Come and sit beside me, my daughter. Supper is ready to be served, we have been waiting only for you."

But Lord Wolf intervened before she could sit.

"Sir," he said coolly, "if I might first introduce my bride-to-be to this company? Some of these gentlemen are to remain in my service once we are married. Your daughter should perhaps know their names as well as their faces."

"By all means, my lord," her father agreed hastily.

Eloise nodded as each man was introduced to her, then gave them all a deep curtsy, her eyes demurely lowered. "Sirs," she replied.

She knew none of the men except one, Hugh Beaufort, a young man she had seen a few times about the court, though they had never been introduced.

Hugh was not a rugged, weathered soldier like the other fellows, but a courtier who worked for the king in some clerical post. A handsome, fair-haired gentleman with long, powerful legs clad in black hose, broad shoulders, and a pair of wondrous green eyes, Hugh's appearance took her breath away. He was also the only one to kiss her hand as they were introduced, his bow and flattering compliments very much in the French manner.

If only Hugh Beaufort were her prospective bridegroom, she thought drily.

Introductions over, Lord Wolf drew out her chair and she sat down, thanking him in a murmur. From the cold gleam in his eye, she suspected that he knew precisely what she was trying to do. But this charade was for her father's sake, not his. She was not married yet, after all. Her father had often complained that she was too fiery and willful. Perhaps if she seemed submissive in the face of this marriage, he might change his mind and listen when she pleaded to be allowed to remain unmarried.

"You must forgive my lack of manners earlier," Wolf commented, leaning forward as he pushed in her chair. "I was concerned for you in that cold wind, exposed to the stares of the inn servants."

She said nothing, taken aback by his sudden civility. Then she saw his gaze light on Hugh Beaufort, and wondered if he had read her thoughts about that gentleman.

Wolf straightened and took his place facing her father at the other end of the table. The others in their company waited until his lordship was seated before they too took their seats. She found herself opposite Hugh Beaufort, and smiled back at him when the courtier gallantly passed her a dish of partridges.

It might do Lord Wolf good to think he had a rival for her interest. Though in truth she had no desire to marry anyone, not even a courtier as handsome and flattering as Hugh Beaufort. Now that she knew how deceived she had been in Simon's courtship, she suspected no man could be trusted where his sexual instincts were concerned.

"Thank you," Eloise said with deliberate friendliness, helping herself to the succulent meat.

The partridge had been simply cooked—no rich or piquant sauce as she was accustomed to enjoying at court—but her hunger was sauce enough. The long cold journey had left her starving.

"What brings you so far north, Master Beaufort?" she asked. "I thought you served the king, not Lord Wolf."

His green eyes lit with amusement, Hugh Beaufort glanced from her to Lord Wolf. "Yes, I serve the king. But the road north from London is notoriously treacherous for single travelers, so I travel on the king's business in Lord Wolf's company."

"And what will you do in the north, sir?"

Hugh hesitated, again glancing down the table at Wolf, who showed no response. He dragged a partridge out of the dish himself and began to wrench at its breast meat with his knife.

"It is no secret," he told her, shrugging. "I go to oversee the dismantling of some of the larger monasteries and priories in that region, to ensure all is done fairly and in accordance with the king's wishes. It is no small task, and could take several months to complete. Lord Wolf has very generously offered to accommodate me at his home during my time in the north. But I do not anticipate being much at leisure there. My work for the king is too demanding."

She had listened with interest to his description of his work, and could not help being pleased at the thought that he would not be returning to court immediately. Hugh Beaufort seemed an intelligent man with excellent manners, and it would be good to have a courtier on hand to remind her of how things had been at court. Time often dragged in the vast wild stretches of Yorkshire, with little music and dancing or poetry to be had, and she had grown used to a more entertaining life at court.

"Forgive me, sir, but have I not heard you play the lute and recite at court before the queen?"

Hugh Beaufort laughed somewhat uncomfortably. "What a memory you must have. I admit, once or twice I have been fortunate enough to be granted that honor. Though I am by no means skilled at the lute, nor is my poetry to be admired." He paused, his voice becoming husky. "I am no Thomas Wyatt."

There was a flicker in his green eyes which spoke of wariness, perhaps even an awareness of danger. A sliver of ice entered her heart. She wondered what this courtier knew of the queen's secret dalliance with Thomas Wyatt, and what it might mean for Queen Anne if suspicions about her character were beginning to be whispered about the court.

Her reply was careful. "Thomas Wyatt is a most wonderful poet, is he not?"

"He is indeed." Hugh drank from his wine cup, not meeting her eyes. "Wyatt has a gift for versifying almost to rival the classical poets of Rome."

His response had been guarded too. Eloise turned her head, and was taken aback to see Wolf watching them both intently. He was not eating, his brows drawn sharply together as though in a frown.

Was he angry that she was conversing so freely with Hugh Beaufort? Or was it the subject of their discussion which met with such narrow-eyed disapproval?

She hesitated for a moment, wondering whether to look away and discreetly cut off the discussion. Then the heat of rebellion burned in her heart. They were not yet married. She was still free to converse with whom she liked, and she liked Hugh Beaufort. Not in the same way as Simon, but she guessed he could be a good friend to her. And she would be in need of friends in the months to come.

"Do you write poetry?" Hugh asked her after a moment, refilling both their wine cups from the flagon.

"It has been known."

Hugh grinned at her, then seemed to catch Lord Wolf's eye. His smile faded and he took a large mouthful of partridge, effectively bringing the conversation to an end.

Her father grunted, scattering a pinch of salt over his meat. "Well, my friends, we have made good progress and should be back in the North Riding the day after tomorrow, by my reckoning." He looked down the table at Lord Wolf. "Once home, we must discuss a date for this wedding with the priest. The sooner the better is what I say."

"Indeed," Wolf said darkly.

"Once Eloise is safely wed, I shall set about arranging a date for my younger daughter to marry. There is a gentleman in the north who has asked me repeatedly for her hand, the old goat." Her father took a leisurely swallow of wine, then wiped his wet mouth on his sleeve, returning to his northern manners now they had left the court. "He is nearly as old as me, and no doubt she will not be happy with the match. But Susannah needs a firm hand and a husband's guidance, just like her sister here. Their mother was the same, God rest her soul." He crossed himself, then set to his meal, finishing his thought with his mouth crammed with meat. "So take heed, Lord Wolf, not to spare the rod once Eloise is under your protection. An obedient wife will serve you better than a wayward one."

Eloise bent her head to her trencher, and finished the meal in silence, her heart beating fast, surprised by her own anger. She felt some antagonism toward her father for his blustering talk of beatings and obedience. But she had heard his thoughts on women and marriage before; they were nothing new, and indeed Susannah had only rarely been beaten for disobedience when they were growing up, for she was their father's favorite. Mostly her temper had sparked at this stern bridegroom who wished to show her off to his company of gentlemen, but would prevent her from speaking in too friendly a manner with any other man.

There would be little hope of pursuing the courtly life once married to Lord Wolf. For if she spoke or sang or read poetry in the company of gentlemen as she had been wont to do at court, her new husband would soon make her—or the gentleman in question—suffer for it. She would be less his wife than his possession, and kept under close scrutiny.

As the last course was served, her anger faded away and an intense tiredness took its place. The wine was stronger than she was used to, a coarse, dark red that made her head spin, and Master Beaufort kept refilling her cup as soon as she drained it.

Whenever she glanced up at Wolf, his face seemed to be in shadow. Or were her eyes slowly closing while she was still sitting at table?

Carefully she washed her fingers in the water bowl set before her, then dabbed at her mouth with the napkin. She felt overwhelmed by fatigue. All she could think of was the bed in her chamber upstairs, where no doubt Mary would already be asleep, having taken a dish of supper with the servants before bedtime.

"Shall I light you upstairs to your chamber?"

Turning her head wearily, she found Wolf at her elbow, a lit candle in his hand.

"I thank you, yes," she said huskily, not bothering to conceal her fatigue.

Wolf drew back her chair and she rose unsteadily, bidding her father and the company good night. Hugh and the others rose from their seats with polite bows, but Eloise kept her eyes lowered. As she glanced at her father, she had caught a frown on his face and knew her conversation with Hugh had indeed met with his disapproval. If she did not wish to find herself confined to her chambers on their return home, she would have to be more careful how she behaved in public.

Now that she was promised to Lord Wolf, it was no longer acceptable for her to speak so freely with other men, however innocent her intentions. It was a sobering thought.

"This way," Wolf murmured.

The corridor was unlit and deserted. Wolf gestured for her to go ahead of him, then climbed the narrow stairs in silence, limping slightly.

Near the top, Eloise stumbled, catching her foot in her gown. Lord Wolf caught her at once, steadying her.

"Thank you," she managed, very aware of how close he was standing.

His eyes gleamed with amusement in the candlelight. Did he know how nervous he made her?

"My pleasure." Outside her chamber door, he paused, still gripping her by the arm, the candle held high to examine her face. "I hope you enjoyed your supper tonight. And the company."

She nodded without speaking, wishing he would simply allow her to retire.

"You seemed to take a keen interest in Hugh Beaufort," he remarked, watching her.

"He is an interesting young man."

"I would advise you not to find him as interesting as you found Simon," he warned her coldly. "You are promised to me now, body and soul, and no longer free to smile at whomever you wish. In a very short time you will be Lady Wolf. Whatever liberties you may have enjoyed at court, we will soon be back in Yorkshire, and I shall not permit any scandal to be attached to my family name." His eyes dwelt on her face. "Is that clear?"

"Yes," she said gratingly, and shook her arm free from his grasp. "Perfectly clear, my lord. Though I dislike being punished for another woman's fault."

He stared, frowning.

"I seem to recall this is not your first betrothal," she remarked, and saw a grim look enter his eyes. Slightly startled, she backed away. "Have I your permission to go to bed now?"

He gave a bow, his smile icy. "Of course," he agreed, his lips tight. "Granted you intend to sleep alone."

She fumbled behind her back for the door handle, not quite trusting him enough to turn her back on him until she was safe inside her chamber. But how insulting he was!

"Does my maid count?" she demanded hotly, throwing open the door.

The last embers of a small fire remained in the grate, their reddish glow illuminating the rough plaster walls. The threadbare curtains around the bed had not been fully drawn, and through the gap she noted that the maid was taking up most of the bed, her fair face flushed, her nightcap askew.

Eloise sighed, realizing she would have to undress herself for bed. Well, she could hardly complain at finding Mary asleep. She had told the girl not to wait up for her.

She turned to close the door and found Wolf still leaning on the threshold, looking into the bedchamber with a dry smile.

"What a touching scene."

"Good night, my lord," she said, rather more sharply than she had intended, closing the door on him.

He stuck his booted foot in the way. His blue eyes narrowed on her face. "Have a care, Eloise. I would not wish us to become enemies. This might not be a love match, but you agreed before the court to marry me. Or had you forgotten?"

No, she had not forgotten. But did Wolf have to make her feel so uncomfortable? Surely it was enough that she had accepted her fate, knowing how useless it would be to fight this arranged marriage. Must he now rub her acquiescence in her face by acting the jealous husband before they were even wed?

"No, my lord."

"Excellent." The smile returned to his eyes as he beckoned her closer. "Come then, and kiss your betrothed good night."

She stared, hardly able to believe he was serious.

Wolf laid a finger on his lips. "Here," he told her softly, and waited, his blue gaze locked on hers. "On my mouth."

Hesitant, Eloise remembered how he had kissed her in the cloistered garden at court, so powerfully it had left her shaking afterward, dazed and unsure of herself. But she would not allow this man to think her a coward.

Leaning forward, she placed her lips against his. The contact burned, their breath mingling with the scent of wine. She felt again the lure of some passion she had yet to discover, and closed her eyes instinctively. His arm curled about her waist, pulling her close, and to her own surprise she did not resist.

His tongue slipped between her lips, gently exploring, and her whole body jerked in heated shock at such an intimate contact. Here in the dark, on the very threshold of her bedchamber, his embrace seemed even more of a sensual promise than when he had kissed her in the palace garden.

Still kissing her, he cupped her breast, kneading it gently through the thin fabric of her gown, then stroking his fingers back and forth until her nipple began to tingle and swell. It felt nothing like the way Simon had touched her there, and Eloise held her breath, shocked at the sudden hunger burning inside her.

When he tugged the lacy bodice lower, exposing her breasts, the hunger became molten, coursing through her veins and setting her entire body alight. She had not thought it possible to feel more excited by a man's touch. Then his head bent and he seized one nipple between his lips, dragging it fiercely into his mouth. Her nipple stiffened to a peak under his merciless tongue, so taut it was almost painful, yet still she did not push him away.

Unable to help herself, Eloise made a small noise under her breath which sounded suspiciously like a moan of pleasure.

Lord Wolf pulled back, his expression oddly tense as she opened her eyes and stared up at him.

If his lordship had thought her unwilling before, she had just given herself away. Her lips tightened under that searching gaze. She was irritated with herself for allowing herself to be seduced, then angry with him for taking advantage of her father not being present.

Yet to her surprise he did not kiss her again. It was almost as though he had been testing a theory rather than making a serious attempt to seduce her.

"We make another early start tomorrow." Carefully, Wolf dragged up her bodice to cover her breasts, and left her with a curt bow. "Sleep well, Eloise, and sweet dreams."

Four

"I MUST CONGRATULATE YOU in your choice of bride, my lord," Hugh Beaufort remarked, riding ahead of the litter with Lord Wolf. "She is quite ravishing."

Wolf smiled, hearing the hesitancy in his companion's voice. "But…?"

"Very well, my lord. Though pray do not bite my head off for an honest opinion which you have solicited. Not wishing to cause you or your betrothed any offense, I admit Eloise Tyrell would not be my own first choice for a wife."

"How so?"

The chilly February weather had improved overnight, the day dawning still cold but bright. Now that the sun was higher overhead, Wolf was glad to feel the warmth of it on his back and shoulders. Yet as always, the promise of spring held a darker note for him. For it was in springtime that he had lost his mother, and knelt as a child beside her fresh-dug grave while the larks soared and sang dizzyingly high overhead.

Wolf's gloved hands tightened on the reins as he remembered that day. The irony of the lark's joyful song had never been lost on him since.

Hugh pondered for a moment before replying.

"Eloise Tyrell is a lively and intelligent lady, to be sure, and goodly enough to look upon. That cannot be denied. But when I eventually marry, I hope to find a bride with a less mettlesome nature. Like our Queen Anne, your intended is of an argumentative bent. While I admired her fiery responses at supper last night, I agreed with her father that a woman like that needs to be disciplined. I would not wish to share my bed with such an opinionated lady." He sounded rueful. "I fear your wife will not take kindly to bridle and bit."

"I must take care not to restrain her too harshly then."

Surprised by that response, Hugh glanced at him. "You intend to indulge her behavior? Is that not dangerous in a wife?"

"To continue your amusing conceit of the wife as mount, I would rather have to rein in a restive wife than be forced to plod along at too sedate a pace."

"And when she bears a child? Will you not demand her obedience then?"

"If my wife is to raise sons worthy of the name Wolf, she must possess some spark of pride and know her own worth as a wife and mother." He thought of his own upbringing at the hands of a proud and fiery woman, who had died while still young. "I must bring Eloise to acknowledge me as her lord and master, you are right there. But I shall not do so at the expense of her spirit. A broken wife is no wife at all, but a poor drudge."

"And yet you gave no sign of indulging her whims last night. Quite the contrary, in fact."

Wolf grinned. "I would not wish my mettlesome bride to have it all her own way, my friend. She must not think me weak."

"You knew Eloise as a youth, did you not?"

"Barely."

Wolf recalled their few encounters, remembering how the young daughter of Tyrell's estate, all long limbs and untidy yellow hair, had impressed him with her wild demeanor. She had been too young then, a child still, climbing trees and riding about the fields without a chaperone. One time he had seen her from afar, a thin dab of a girl flying over hedges and ditches on a restless black stallion most women would have feared to mount. It had occurred to him then that she would make an interesting bride. But he had not been in any hurry to enter into a marriage contract, for he knew she might change once old enough to wed.

Then he had met Margerie at court, a girl fast passing into womanhood, a red-haired creature with pale skin and high, well-rounded breasts.

Margerie had blown him a kiss at supper, and he had sought out her quarters later, eager to lose his virginity. She had been shy but not unwilling. His lovemaking that first time had been awkward and clumsy, and he had known it. Margerie had lain beneath him in silence, her eyes wary and unsure. But he was soon deeply in love with her strange green eyes and elfin beauty.

Straightaway, he had made an offer of marriage and it had been accepted by Margerie's father, a country squire with too many daughters to his name. His future had seemed settled when the king sent him on his first military campaign soon after that, trusting a party of men to his command.

With a soldiering career and a soft-skinned wife for his bed, what else would he need?

Yet when he returned from that campaign, flushed with the triumph of his first battle and eager to wed the girl with whom he was now desperately in love, he found Margerie had fled the court—on the arm of another lover, a penniless young noble from the south.

The news of Margerie's flight was soon all round the court. His pride had been wounded, his already sore heart broken. And he had sworn never to love again, for love was just a mask that hid a man's baser needs.

"But Eloise was always at the top of my list," he admitted, seeing Hugh's glance.

"You had a list?"

Wolf raised his eyebrows. "There is no need to sound so

surprised. You may reach that point one day soon. And it does not hurt to be prepared."

His companion laughed. "I have no wish to marry young, so I have not yet made my list."

The cavalcade slowed as the narrow track turned east, passing through a grove bordered by a shallow, reed-thick lake. Wolf examined the close-growing trees with an experienced eye, watching for signs of ambush, for these roads became more dangerous the further north they traveled.

"No maid has caught your eye at court?"

Hugh looked sheepish, bending to pat his horse's neck. "I find one or two of the queen's ladies pleasing to the eye, I cannot deny it. But none have struck me as perfect."

"Perfect?"

"When I meet my future wife, I hope to recognize her as such at first sight. The French poets liken it to a lightning strike."

"The French are a fanciful people," Wolf commented drily, "particularly when they turn their hands to writing verse. I would advise you to avoid poetry and take a more hard-headed approach when it comes to choosing a wife."

Hugh looked at him. "You do not believe in love?"

"I believe in making the best of things, my friend. Look at me: my bride is fair enough to look upon, and hopefully there will be an heir to follow soon. If Eloise be not too unruly, nor too cold in bed, what should I need of love? Trust me when I tell you it is an empty word, used more by fools and liars than any sensible man."

Wolf reined in his horse, signaling the other riders to stop.

As the cavalcade halted, he pointed across at the lake with his riding crop and raised his voice. "This place has water for the horses and good shade. We shall rest an hour or two here for luncheon, and allow the ladies to stretch their legs."

Wolf dismounted, leading his horse across to the shady grove and lakeside. While the weary animal drank its fill from the greenish water, he glanced back at the litter, where his future bride was already descending.

Hugh's remarks had rankled slightly, reminding him of the first time he had seen Eloise, tousle-headed and soft-cheeked, still a girl, not yet of marriageable age.

He had been little more than a youth himself, his heart still smarting with grief from his mother's death. But he had not been a child anymore. No, that unquestioning innocence had been long gone by the time he saw Eloise and thought her memorable. In those days he had been hungry to be out in the world, fighting the king's enemies rather than sitting at home, mourning his lost childhood.

Had his first glimpse of Eloise Tyrell been a lightning strike?

Nothing so dramatic, he thought wryly. But perhaps there had been an element of compulsiveness about his interest in Eloise. He had asked around discreetly a few months back and discovered that she was still a virgin. It was rumored the king had considered her for his next mistress, though she was no beauty. Her features were a little too irregular, and there was no stately composure in her look.

So why had he chosen her? He had no answer to that.

Grasping the hem of her gown, Eloise came slowly down the wooded slope toward the lake. She raised her head and looked eagerly about herself at the trees and the sunlit water beyond, taking deep breaths.

He watched with interest. No doubt she was glad to be free of the stuffy confines of that curtained litter, even if only for a short time.

Her maid, following more carefully with armfuls of cushions from the litter, stooped to arrange these at the water's edge for them to sit upon.

Suddenly Eloise looked round, seeing him amongst the trees.

Surprise flashed into her face, and a resentment which was quickly hidden as their eyes met.

"My lord," she murmured, dropping a low curtsy. "This...this is a pleasant spot."

He smiled, then his gaze narrowed on his bride-to-be. At that angle, he could see right down her low-cut gown. His gaze dwelt thoughtfully on that shadowy cleft between her swelling breasts, and for a moment he imagined how she would look naked, riding atop of him in bed, long golden hair tickling his chest, breasts thrust toward his face.

Behind the solid leather constraint of his codpiece, Wolf felt his cock twitch and stiffen. He looked forward to their wedding night with a desire so urgent it took even him by surprise.

He had enjoyed many women since that first clumsy night with Margerie, as courtier and soldier, and knew the undeniable pleasure of a willing mouth and a knowing body. But Eloise was a virgin, he reminded himself, and would need to be broken in gently.

One of the men hurried down the slope with a cloth-covered basket of provisions supplied by the tavern that morning for their journey, then returned to where the others were sitting under the trees, passing round a bottle of beer and heartily tucking into their own victuals.

With great eagerness, the maid Mary began to lay out their wrapped parcels of food, then invited her mistress to sit. "There is fish and fowl to be had, Mistress Eloise, and sweetbreads, and a few slices of manchet. Best eat before it spoils."

Seeming to hesitate, Eloise turned to him with a careful smile. "Will you join us, my lord? There is more than enough here for three."

He stared, a little taken aback by this unexpected invitation. But perhaps she was warming to his courtship. Wolf had his own supplies in his saddlebags, but decided he should not waste this opportunity to know his bride better.

"Gladly," he agreed, and threw himself down on the damp grass in a careless fashion, stretching out his legs beside her. "Is there beer?"

"Wine," she murmured, and poured him a cup.

He took the wine with a muttered "Thanks," and tossed it back, entertained by how Eloise's gaze widened at his lack of knightly etiquette.

Well, his manners were more suited to the battlefield than the court, and it was best she understood that straightaway.

"Venison pie, my lord?"

He nodded, and took the thick slab of pie with relish, biting into it so hard the jelly oozed about the sides and ran down his chin. With a harsh laugh, he shook his head when she offered him a napkin, and wiped his chin on his sleeve instead.

Eloise averted her gaze, so missed him grinning like a boy at her expression of distaste. But the maid did not, and stared from one to the other in surprise.

His uncouth manners were partly for show, for Wolf knew well how to behave in the company of ladies. But he would be damned if he had to treat his new bride as daintily as Venetian glassware. She was from the hardy north like him, not a soft-natured southern maid, and must already know the ways of Yorkshiremen to be rough and ready.

Why pretend otherwise just because he had learned to kiss hands and bow in the dance like a courtier?

"Not bad, this pie. At least the tavern's luncheon fare is better than its beds. I might as well have slept on the bare boards last night, for all the comfort I enjoyed in my bed." He paused, glancing at Eloise. "How about you? Were you comfortable in your bed last night?"

To his amusement, she blushed. "Thank you, my lord," she stammered. "Yes."

"I am glad to hear it."

He held out his cup to be refilled, and their eyes met fleetingly as she poured the wine. Greenish-dark eyes, slanted, her lashes long and thick.

Yes, the girl had the makings of a beauty. Not conventionally, for she lacked feminine grace, her curtsy was too awkward, and her lips rather too full and sensual for courtly approval. These days, to be considered truly beautiful, a woman had to have the thin lips and sharp chin of Anne Boleyn. But Eloise would do him very well as a wife.

He noted that her hand shook while pouring, as though the wine flask was too heavy. Not as bold as she had seemed at court, then.

He saw some flicker of emotion in those green-flecked eyes. Fear?

"You will be made most comfortable at my estate, of course," he assured her abruptly. It gave him little comfort to see that look of apprehension in her face. "When we are married, you need not fear losing that privacy and level of service you have enjoyed at your father's home. Mary here will not be your only maid. You may have women to tend your hair, your dress, whatever you wish."

Wolf paused. Her gaze had lifted to his face, suddenly intent. Had Eloise assumed she would be his prisoner once they were man and wife?

The thought was a chastening one, for he had not meant to make his future bride so afraid of him.

"Indeed," he continued, "you may have your pick of my servants for your own personal entourage. You will lack for nothing once you are Lady Wolf."

"You are too kind, my lord."

He was not fooled by her submissive murmur. But he did not press the point. Once they were married, he would have many more opportunities to tame her.

This time he did not finish his wine at once but sipped at it thoughtfully, then set it aside.

Mary held out a small unwrapped cloth, her eyes wide with curiosity. No doubt she too thought him a cruel husband, taking his new bride so far away from the comforts of court.

"Manchet bread, my lord?"

Neither of these women could realize how restrictive Wolf found the English court, how much he loathed his every move being watched and reported back to the king, for his master feared betrayal even from his most loyal servants. If he wished to be free, to walk unobserved by spies and speak his mind, returning to his native northlands was his only option. Though he knew the king would recall him to military service soon enough, and he would have no choice but to obey.

He accepted a piece of bread, dipped it in his wine to moisten it, then finished his meal in silence, for his thoughts had turned sour. For King Henry there was always one more traitor to be crushed, one more rebellion to be put down before it threatened the Tudor dynasty.

Lying back on the grass, Wolf stared up into the overhanging canopy of trees. The green buds of leaves rustled in the breeze. He ran back through his thoughts, surprised by his sudden yearning to be free of the court. Free, above all, to woo his bride without interference from the too-lascivious king.

Eloise would be his wife whether she willed it or no. Yet she held no special significance for him except as a sweet memory from his youth. So why was he suddenly so concerned to put his bride at her ease before their wedding night?

Shouts broke his reverie. Men calling urgently from the road. He was on his feet in a second, his hand on the dagger hilt at his belt.

"What is it?" Eloise looked startled, and her maid gasped as one of the men came running down the slope, a drawn sword in his hand.

"My lord!" It was Hugh. He was out of breath. "Riders coming across the fields from the southwest. They will be upon us within minutes."

"How many?"

"Maybe a dozen, maybe less."

"King's men?"

"I cannot tell, my lord. They've kicked up a dust cloud, and the sun is at their backs. But their mounts look to be rough beasts."

"Stay here, I will send men to guard you," Wolf told Eloise, then returned to his horse and mounted the surprised beast while it was still drinking from the lake.

Eloise ran after him. "Who are they?"

"Ruffians," he threw back over his shoulder, his voice curt. He straightened in the saddle, gathering the reins. There was no time for a discussion, not if he wished to keep her safe. "Get back to the litter and take Mary with you. Hugh will guard you."

He spurred the horse up toward the road; the younger man ran alongside. "You did right to raise the alarm, Hugh. This is dangerous country. We cannot trust they will respect the law."

Hugh looked back at the two women following them hurriedly up the slope. "And the ladies?"

"Escort them to the litter, and have it drawn between the trees for safety. Guard them with your life. The rest of us must be ready to defend this slope. You must pray to God none of those men break through to you."

"Aye, my lord."

Reaching the track where he had left his men, Wolf gave orders for them to find vantage points among the trees and hold their positions in twos and threes. Then he shielded his eyes against the sun and looked southwest to where the swirling dust cloud proclaimed riders approaching.

He narrowed his eyes. Hugh was right. Ten or twelve men, their mounts low northern ponies rather than well-bred horseflesh, and growing nearer every moment.

He glanced up and down the track, which stood sunlit and empty in both directions. They were not far from the northern moors here. These could be some of the moorland bandits who made a name for themselves by attacking travelers and murdering them for their possessions. If so, the ruffians would soon discover they had picked a difficult target.

"Where do you want me, my lord?" It was Sir John Tyrell, his sword out and gleaming in the sun. His face was flushed. "I know I'm no seasoned campaigner like yourself, but I can still fight."

"Your daughter is below in the litter, sir, guarded by Hugh Beaufort. I'm sure she would welcome your stout defense."

"No, no," Tyrell objected. "I'll stand with you here."

"Sir, your daughter needs you more. If any of these ruffians should break through our ranks…"

Tyrell looked grimly at the approaching dust cloud. "Very well, I'll be with Hugh below. They will not reach Eloise alive."

When Sir John had gone, Wolf called out a few last commands to his unseen men, then drew back into the shadows himself.

He waited just within the line of the trees, dagger in one hand, sword in the other. There was no time to dwell on what might have happened if these ruffians had fallen on them unseen. Thanks to Hugh's sharp eyes, they had the advantage of forewarning. When the riders reached the north road, they would find the track deserted, but men with swords and crossbows hidden amongst the trees, ready to defend themselves.

Less than a moment later, the first rider lurched out of the fields, cleared a gap in the hedgerow, and turned toward their hiding place. He was a big man, clad in a leather jerkin and coarse shirt, an ancient battered helmet pulled low across his forehead. His pony was squat and broad-flanked, and it gave a high whinny as he dragged its head about, his sharp gaze searching the road and woods for his victims.

Nearly a dozen men poured after their leader through the gap in the hedgerow, swords already drawn, some with pikes and axes, helmeted and with leather instead of armor.

A poor defense against a crossbow, Wolf thought, but waited another moment until all the men were on the road before lifting his hand.

"Fire!"

As soon as he gave the order, a series of hisses were followed by the thwack of arrows finding their mark, sending five of the unarmored riders into the dust.

"Again!"

Their attackers were in confusion, horses wheeling about, foam on their mouths from the hard ride, some rearing up and striking at the air with their hooves, while the leader yelled hoarse instructions to his men.

"Attack, you cowards, attack! Follow me, they're in the woods!"

The leader and four of the remaining horsemen spurred their mounts past Wolf's position. They left the road, crashing through the trees to the left of his men, just wide enough to avoid their defensive line.

Wolf turned his horse in pursuit, cursing under his breath.

"To me!" he called to Ralf and Hal, and plunged downhill after the attackers.

Under the shady canopy of trees, out of the sun-glare, he could see the men more clearly. They were an ill-disciplined bunch, their faces coarse, clothing patched and ragged in places. Some rode and handled their weapons well though, suggesting training in the past. Renegades, perhaps, or mercenaries fallen on hard times. Not that poverty was any excuse to rob and murder travelers, he thought grimly.

The leader had seen the litter and had turned slightly, making for it across the loose slope. Hugh had not driven it far enough down the slope, and although Eloise's elderly father had his sword drawn, and Hugh was on horseback beside the litter, the two of them could hardly hold off this pack of dogs.

One of the first men was careering toward the litter now, whirling a murderous ax about his head. Hugh pushed forward to meet him, sword raised to meet the punishing blow, and soon forced the man back.

Untrained he might be, but Hugh had natural strength and prowess. Whenever the king held a joust at court, Hugh invariably won through to the final bouts, and always showed his skill with a sword in close combat. Nonetheless, Wolf knew he could not last long against such desperate men.

"I'll have their heads for this," Wolf snarled, and urged his horse on harder.

No doubt the looters believed that a covered wagon, hidden amongst the trees, must hold some precious cargo. Gold coins, perhaps, or jewels. Though even a young woman could be valuable, particularly one for whom a hefty ransom could be demanded if they were bold enough.

Wolf caught up with the leader, pressing his mount hard into the man's horse. The man roared, turning to attack. But the horse was hampering his sword-hand, and he could not seem to wrest it free.

Seizing his advantage, Wolf sunk his dagger into the leader's side, thrusting the blade in deep. Then he shoved the man off his horse, watching as the animal dragged him several hundred feet into the woods; his feet were caught in the reins, his side a bloodied mess.

Wolf wheeled his stallion about and urged him back toward the litter.

"Ralf!"

The young man, riding just behind him, hurried to help Sir John against his assailant. The other three horsemen had surrounded

Hugh, hammering at him with their weapons, taunting the young man like the cowards they were. Hugh looked spent, his horse whinnying and rolling its eyes at every blow, almost unseating him in its fear.

Wolf pushed between the men, parrying the next blow, then thrusting hard under that man's arm to disarm him. The man cried out in agony and fell back, dropping his weapon, his arm hanging useless.

The other two turned on Wolf at once, their lips drawn back in rage, seemingly unaware that their leader was fallen and their attack had failed. The clash of metal on metal rang from tree to tree, echoing about the dense woodland.

Birds flew skyward, chattering in alarm.

Then Hal was there too, his sword slicing one man across the throat, and at last the survivor realized he was alone.

"Damn you all to hell!" the man cursed them, falling back a few steps in angry exhaustion, then set spurs to his horse and made a clumsy attempt to reach the road above.

Breathless, Ralf glanced at Wolf. "Should I pursue the man, my lord?"

"Yes," he agreed, waving him on. "Though don't kill him if you catch up with him, carrion though he is. Bring him back to me. We need the name of their leader."

He turned, concerned at once for the old gentleman. "Sir John, are you hurt?"

But to his surprise, Tyrell seemed unharmed and in good spirits. "Not a scratch on me," he exclaimed, cleaning his sword on the bracken. He gestured to Hugh instead, who had dismounted—or perhaps fallen from his horse—and sunk to one knee on the rough ground. "Our young friend here was more grievously pressed. I'd say he cannot ride, not without assistance."

"I'll survive," Hugh said faintly, but the gash on his shoulder looked ugly and in need of binding. "By Our Lady, it was a good fight though. Who were they, do you think?"

"Local men in search of easy pickings?"

"Dead men now," Sir John remarked sagely.

The curtains to the litter were still drawn tightly shut. Wolf rode forward, bent and lifted one edge of the curtain with his sword. He met the furious gaze of his bride-to-be, and the working end of a dagger pointed toward his face.

"You took no hurt in this skirmish, madam?"

Eloise raised her brows coldly. "No thanks to you, my lord. I thought you would have stayed to protect me yourself."

"I left you in capable hands. My men needed me to command our defense." He felt a stab of irritation at her ingratitude. "Master Beaufort is hurt and cannot ride. He will need to travel in the litter with you."

"There is no room," she exclaimed, then glanced out and saw Hugh, blood streaming down his arm, struggling valiantly toward his horse. Her mouth tightened. "But we shall make room, of necessity. Mary, come sit with me. Master Beaufort may take your seat and I shall tend his wound."

Hugh was helped up into the litter, gritting his teeth against the pain. Having satisfied himself that the man was as comfortable as he could be, Wolf left Eloise busily preparing strips of material to staunch and bind his injury. She was not too dainty to tend a man's wounds, he thought, noting her calm demeanor with interest. Perhaps she would make a good soldier's wife after all.

But there was other work to do. Hastily, Wolf supervised the laying out of the dead men, out of sight of the road; he would have to stop at the next town and order the authorities to give the men a decent burial, ruffians or not. Then he rode into the woods in search of the man dragged away by his horse.

Wolf found the horse grazing quietly a few hundred yards into the trees. His rider was lying twisted on the ground nearby, coarse tunic soaked with blood, his back clearly broken. But when he dismounted, meaning to capture the horse and throw the dead body over it, Wolf saw that the man was still alive.

Kneeling beside the man, he offered him ale from his flask, but the man was too far gone to drink. His throat gargled with blood and his gaze flitted wildly about, before finally coming to rest on Wolf's dagger.

His message was clear.

With a muttered prayer for the man's soul, Wolf thrust the blade into the man's neck. The big vein there pumped out his life in a matter of moments; he died with his head turned away, staring blindly into the trees.

Even if the ruffian could have survived these terrible injuries, Wolf thought, it would only have been to face the hangman. This swift death was more merciful.

Once the work of clearing up had been accomplished, he ordered the cavalcade to move on, and rode ahead of the litter, watchful for any further sign of attack.

But the road remained quiet on their way north, and soon his thoughts returned uneasily to the woman he had decided to marry.

Had he made the right choice, allowing Eloise to spend so many hours closeted with a handsome courtier like Beaufort? Women always felt more sympathy for a man when he was wounded. Perhaps he should have taken some minor scratch in the skirmish himself, just to see her eyes warm with pity at his hurts.

His smile was a savage mockery of his own weakness. Fool! What kind of thought is that?

Was this jealousy? Or mere possessiveness?

There could be no jealousy where there was no love, he told himself drily. He would feel the same for a prize hawk coveted by another man.

"Keep your soft hands off my bride, Hugh Beaufort," he muttered under his breath, glancing back at the swaying litter. "Or I shall not be answerable for the consequences."

Five

ELOISE THREW OPEN THE shutter and leaned far out, reveling in the fresh country air of Yorkshire. How sweet after the stench of court to be home and breathe deep again, even if it was sheep and the musty scent of the farmyard she could smell. From this narrow bedchamber, hers since childhood, she could see the northern gable and the stableyard, and beyond them the rolling hills. Lord Wolf's land lay in that direction, for his was a vast estate grown larger since his father's death, thanks to King Henry's generosity. It was odd to think she would soon be mistress of that great estate, and odder yet to imagine herself a wife. It was barely ten days since her father had come to court, and she had found herself betrothed to a stranger against her will.

A nagging voice within her said, "Not against your will, not that."

Eloise could not deny that she had given her consent to the match. But she had not wished to disobey her father, and indeed Lord Wolf was not the old man she had feared. Though perhaps an older husband would have been preferable, for Wolf was a virile man: she had no doubt what lay ahead. He would demand his rights, and even if she did not mean to grant them, he would soon seduce her.

"Why can I not be stronger and find him loathsome?" she moaned, leaving the window.

She threw herself facedown onto her tester bed, its bedding plump and newly restuffed for her return. The sharp feather quills in the mattress prickled her, so she rolled onto her back, staring up at the faded tester above her head. Lord Wolf knew how to tease and persuade a woman with his lips, that was for sure. Eloise hid her face in her hands and tried not to remember how she had shamed herself by kissing him back. The truth was, she longed to have Lord Wolf kiss her again—if not against her will, then certainly against her better judgment.

And he knew it, he knew it!

Hateful man!

She had seen the laughter in his face, his dry smile whenever she turned coldly away. What other reason could there be for such mockery except that he knew her secret desire?

At least she had taken some comfort from Hugh Beaufort's presence on that last day of their journey north. His wound had kept him subdued, but they had read and discussed poetry together as the litter lurched over the mud ruts, and if Mary had looked upon their conversation with a disapproving eye, Eloise had ignored her maid.

What business was it of Mary's, anyway? She was not yet Lord Wolf's bride and was still free to laugh and talk with other men. Though she had no doubt that such freedoms would soon be severely curtailed.

She heard footsteps on the stairs and jumped up at once, straightening her gown and tidying her unruly hair. It would not be him, of course. His lordship had ridden on to his own estate once he had seen her and Sir John safely installed in their manor. But Eloise did not wish any of her father's servants to catch her lying on her bed like a scared child. She was one of the queen's maids now, soon to be a lady, and she must behave with proper decorum.

The door opened.

It was her old nurse, Morag, flushed with exertion after climbing the stairs but beaming with pleasure.

"Eloise!" she exclaimed, and held open her arms.

They embraced warmly, and then Morag looked her over at

arm's length. She drew a sharp breath, shaking her head. "Well, well. I thought being at court would make you happy, my lamb, with so many gentlemen to notice your spirit and beauty. Yet you have come home with such a sad look about you."

"The court is a hard place."

Morag nodded. "Did I not warn you it would be? But you were so young, you would not listen."

"I know it now."

"And soon you are to be married to Lord Wolf! Whoever would have guessed it, for he rarely came to visit when you were a girl, and everyone thought he would marry some great lady of the court." Her old nurse studied her face closely, as though unsure what to make of that news. "It's all the gossip among the servants, of course. An excellent match, and no doubt your father will not rest until he has told every man, woman, and child in Yorkshire. But now you have met the man himself, and traveled with him, what do you think of your bridegroom?"

"His lordship is…very…"

When she could not finish, Morag raised her eyebrows. "Handsome?" she suggested.

"I suppose he is, yes." Eloise resisted the urge to stick out her tongue at her old nurse. Morag had always known when she had found a man attractive, and had teased her mercilessly about it. "Though I was going to say forthright."

"Of course. He is a northerner."

"And a good soldier."

"Indeed he is. Though rather older than you."

"That signifies nothing these days. Queen Anne is ten years younger than King Henry."

"And Mary tells us in the servants' quarters that King Henry has already tired of his pretty young wife and is looking elsewhere for his amusement."

Eloise stared. "Hush, for pity's sake!"

Laughing comfortably, Morag went to the window and pulled the shutter across. "Have you forgotten this is Yorkshire, my lamb? We are hundreds of miles from court, and there are no spies here to carry our wicked gossip back to fine King Harry. Now come, let me dress your hair properly." The darkened chamber seemed so cozy, just like when she was a child, and Eloise did not object when Morag sat her down on the stool and began to comb out her hair. "Your father has ordered a grand banquet in honor of your wedding, and half the county is to be invited. But for the next month at least, you will live quiet here and prepare for your nuptials. Your father has asked Lord Wolf to come and ride and hunt with him, and you are to entertain him too."

"Me?"

"Do not look so shocked, child. When you are his wife, his lordship will expect you to entertain him every night."

Eloise felt her cheeks burn at the thought. "Oh, Morag! I do not think I can go through with it."

"Nonsense, every bride fears that."

She turned, looking up at her nurse in surprise. "Every bride? You were married once, were you not? Did you... That is, were you unsure of..."

Morag smiled, and bent to kiss her cheek. "Of course I was. The wedding night can rattle most girls' nerves. But I soon learned to love my husband. It was God's will that John was taken from me barely a year later, and after that I sought service in your father's household." Her old nurse gave a little giggle under her breath. "We had to share a house with his parents. I still remember how John would touch and kiss me in the darkness, and how we tried so hard not to make a sound those first few months..."

Eloise could not help laughing too. "Morag!"

"Do you love Lord Wolf?"

She sobered at once, her smile fading. "I do not know him well enough to love him."

Morag hesitated. "Well, give it time. If he wants an heir, he will not hurt or mistreat you."

"I always thought I would marry for love."

"A girl's dream. You are too old to believe that now. Lord Wolf will be as good a husband as any other man, and better for being richer. At least you will never know hardship as his wife. Many women do not even have that assurance when they exchange their father's authority for their husband's. And one day love may come, through habit if nothing else." Morag smoothed her hair. "There, that's better."

She grabbed Morag's hand and kissed her palm. "Thank you," she whispered. "You always know what to do for the best. Will you come with me when I marry?"

Morag frowned. "To Lord Wolf's estate? That will be for your father to decide. I am his servant."

"He will let you come with me," Eloise said confidently.

"Well, we shall see when the day comes. Now you must go downstairs and speak with your father. He wishes to see you before supper."

"What about?"

Morag pinched her cheek, her smile teasing. "My pretty lamb, you are soon to be married. There will be a hundred things to decide."

"I...I am not ready for any of that."

"None of us ever are." Her nurse gestured her to stand, then turned her in the direction of the door. "Now off with you. I have your bridal clothes to arrange."

Eloise paused at the door, looking back. "Morag, where is my sister? I thought she would be here to welcome me back."

"Susannah is visiting your Aunt Eileen at Thirsk. I sent a note up there with a servant this morning. No doubt she will return as soon as your aunt can spare her."

Smiling, Eloise hurried downstairs to her father. She wondered what Susannah would look like now, and found herself quite impatient to see her younger sister again.

When Eloise had left for court, Susannah had been an unruly girl in muddied petticoats, clutching a horn book and still learning her letters. By now her sister must be of marriageable age. And no doubt as pert as ever!

———

As Eloise had feared, her father was adamant when asked if the wedding could be delayed. "No, my dear. You are to be wed to Lord Wolf with all speed—though not without proper decorum. The banns will be read in church, to satisfy the priests, and your marriage will take place before summer comes."

"But why must we hurry to wed?"

"Because Lord Wolf demands it." Her father hesitated, clearly uncomfortable with this discussion. He looked away, coughing delicately. "I did not argue with his lordship. He is a nobleman of some consequence, after all, and knows his own mind. I simply assumed there must be some good reason for his haste."

She stared, not quite understanding. Then it hit her. Her father thought she and Lord Wolf had anticipated the wedding night.

Anger buzzed in her head like a wasp; she took a deep breath to dispel it, not wishing to lose her temper with her father, however much he had slighted her honor.

"If you mean what I think you mean, then no. I have not been intimate with his lordship."

Her father smiled affectionately upon her, as though glad he had been mistaken. "Why then, it must be your beauty alone that inspires his haste. And what harm is there in that? Come," he told her, rising from his seat, "let us walk together. I have sadly neglected you as a daughter these past few years, and now we may not have many days left for walking and talking together. For once you are Lady Wolf, your first duty must be to your husband."

Eloise said nothing, but lowered her gaze to the floor. My first duty as Lady Wolf should be to myself, she thought grimly. But her father had never understood her rebellious nature, so she kept that thought secret. To him a woman was a mere possession without opinion or feeling, to be passed like a chattel from father to husband, so that a woman could only speak her mind and run her own life once she had become a respectable widow.

If Lord Wolf also held such views, she thought fiercely, he would find himself at war with his wife from the first day of their marriage.

She spent the day with her father, even dining cozily with him in her private chambers, for he was still tired after their long journey. For a while it felt like the years before she left for court, when she had been close to her father, and sat with him in the long evenings, reading aloud to him or sewing her sampler while he dozed. Sitting there in the firelight, she could almost believe her betrothal to Lord Wolf, and her days at court, had been a dream. It was a comfortable thought, for the court was a more menacing place than she had realized as a girl, too eager to be out in the world and ignorant of its traps and dangers.

The very next day though, that dream of innocence fled, leaving her with nothing but cold reality.

Morag woke her early with an urgent cry, exclaiming, "Wake up, my pet! He is come to see you, he is waiting for you below."

She stared from her bed in drowsy confusion while Morag bustled about the room, throwing back the shutters to let in the cool February light and shouting orders to the other servants to bring a bowl of water and scented soaps for washing.

"Who is come?"

"Your betrothed, who else?" Morag shook her head, pulling back the bed covers. "Hurry, girl, shake off your sleep. You are to dress and ride out with him."

"Ride out with Lord Wolf?"

"Did I not just say that?" Morag shook out a riding gown, then turned as the door opened. "Ah, Mary! Put the bowl next to the bed and aid Mistress Eloise. Quick, quick. Oh, I should not have left you sleeping so late if I had known he would visit so soon. But what man could ever be patient when his mind is on love?"

Sighing, Eloise slipped out of bed and helped Mary remove her thin nightrail. There seemed little point in trying to wriggle out of seeing Lord Wolf. Soon she would have to see him every day, whether she wished it or not. She washed carefully, then held out her arms and allowed them to dress her for riding, staring out at the blue sky and the soft outline of the distant hills.

Was Lord Wolf's mind on love?

She rather fancied he had come to ensure she had no chance to change her mind. Wolf struck her as possessing a jealous nature, so that her time spent in the litter with Hugh Beaufort might have angered him. Yet he had placed the wounded man there himself. If he was now suspicious of her fidelity, it was a trap of his own making.

Leaning over the stairs, she caught a glimpse of Lord Wolf with her father in the hall below. His black hair framed a hard-boned face, his plain cap set at a slant, his fine riding gloves gripped in one restless hand. Once again she had an impression of power, an indomitable will that would not easily be swayed by a woman's argument.

It was hard to believe she would soon be in this man's bed, and under his control. It was not a comfortable thought. Yet how could she persuade her father to change his mind?

Wolf was telling her father, "I have offered a substantial reward for information, but these gangs are often very tight. We may never catch the men involved."

"Villains!"

Wolf turned and saw Eloise descending. His sharp blue gaze traveled over her riding gown, then he bowed. "Mistress Eloise, it is good to see you again."

She curtsied low to both men, forcing herself to be polite. "Good morning, Father. Lord Wolf."

Wolf himself wasted no further time on pleasantries, she noticed drily.

"I trust you are rested after your long journey," he said, "and can face a morning's ride? I have brought a mare for you, as a gift, and would like to show you some of my land."

"That is very generous of you, my lord." She looked from him to her father. "But ride out unaccompanied?"

Wolf shrugged. "I thought your sister, perhaps…?"

Her father interrupted, his expression concerned. "Sadly, my lord, my younger daughter is not at home. Susannah has gone to visit her aunt, who is forever ailing. A letter has been dispatched to summon her home again. If you wait until tomorrow, my lord, I'm sure she will have returned by then."

"I do not wish to wait," Wolf told him, with little attempt at civility.

"Of course not, my lord," her father agreed hurriedly. "In that case, one of my servants can ride out with you. It will not take long to organize."

"Sir John, your daughter and I are betrothed to be married. The wedding will take place within a month, or so you have assured me." Wolf pulled on his riding gloves, his body tense with impatience. "Surely we need no chaperone for a few hours' ride across the fields? I shall bring your daughter home unmolested, I swear it."

Her father said nothing, but glanced at her as though in need of her agreement.

"Lord Wolf is quite right. We have no need of a chaperone while riding out together," she agreed, and kissed her father on the cheek.

She added significantly, "If his lordship swears to return me safely to you, then I trust his word."

Leading her out to the stableyard where their horses stood saddled and waiting, Wolf gave her a dry smile. "So you trust my word as a gentleman, do you?"

"To my father, yes."

The smile widened to a grin. "But not my word to you as a husband."

"You are not yet my husband," she reminded him lightly, and nodded for him to lift her onto the sturdy chestnut mare.

"More's the pity."

"I did not wish you and my father to fall into an argument, that is all."

His hands settled tightly about her waist, bringing her close to his body as he lifted her. "I see."

Their eyes met, and she caught a tang of his masculine scent of leather and horses. Then she was perched on the sidesaddle, looking down at him in the sunlight. She felt warmth in her cheeks and hurriedly dropped his gaze, unwilling to let him see how much his closeness affected her.

Wolf handed her the reins, then mounted his own stallion with ease. He glanced at her assessingly. "I remember seeing you riding alone when you were a girl. Clearly your father allowed you more freedom in those days. Did you often ride out with the queen's ladies at court?"

"Hardly ever," she admitted.

"But you have not forgotten how to ride?"

She raised her chin, turning to glare at him. Was he mocking her? "I'm a country girl, my lord, I grew up around horses. Of course I have not forgotten." As though to prove her point, she hooked her foot about the saddle harness for added security, gathering the reins in her gloved hands. Then she gave the mare a smart kick. "And up!"

The mare broke into a trot, clattering out of the stableyard.

Jolted about across the cobbles in an undignified fashion, Eloise was glad when the horse reached the dusty grass of the long walled track which led back to the road.

She heard the stallion's hooves behind them, then suddenly Lord Wolf was alongside her.

Grinning wickedly at her expression, he rode past and urged his horse through a narrow gap in the wall.

"Come on, this way! Is that the best you can do?" he taunted her over his shoulder. "I've seen a nun on a donkey ride faster."

"Swine!" she muttered, trying to persuade the mare to turn round and follow the stallion through the gap in the wall.

Lord Wolf had turned his horse and was making for the open fields to the north at an infuriatingly easy canter by the time she had galvanized her reluctant horse into a trot again.

He slowed his mount to a walk, waiting for her to catch up with him, then laughed at her flushed and breathless state.

"I thought you said you could ride?"

Was he trying to make her lose her temper? Well, she would not give him the satisfaction. She counted to ten, then said sweetly, "I'm sorry, my lord. I didn't realize you wanted a race."

"Oh, that was just a gentle start. We haven't even galloped yet. Perhaps I should have carried you before me, not given you your own horse." He stroked the pommel of his leather saddle, his smile teasing. "There's plenty of room for two, you know."

Much to her chagrin, she felt a sudden rush of heat between her thighs at this suggestion. In her mind's eye, she saw herself seated on the saddle before him, but facing him, her skirts raised, the two of them kissing and coupling urgently.

Eloise looked away at once, gulping in the cool morning air. Had she no shame?

His eyes narrowed on her face. "What is it? What's the matter now?"

"Nothing."

Those sharp blue eyes of his saw far too much! To distract him, she glanced back the way they had come, shielding her eyes against the sun.

"I can hardly see the manor house from here," she murmured, gazing back at the thatched roof of the dairy, half-shrouded by trees, and beyond that a milky trail of smoke from her father's kitchens. The main house was invisible, hidden by a dip in the land. "I don't know this area at all. But then Susannah and I were never permitted to ride beyond the North Field boundary as children."

"In case the wicked wolf and his son caught you and gobbled you up?"

"Something like that," she replied drily, and risked a glance in his direction. Her pulse was still racing but her tone was deliberately cool, unbothered. He already thought her keen to bed him; he must never be allowed to guess what she had just been thinking, or she would die of shame. "Is that where you're taking me today? To the wolf's lair?"

"Not quite. Though it is on my estate. It's just a place I like to visit when I'm home."

"Is it far?"

"Less than an hour's ride." Their two horses were walking slowly side by side, his thigh pressed close to where she sat side-saddle. Her nerves were stretched thin as she tried to look unconcerned by such proximity, though in truth she had never before felt so light-headed in the presence of a man. He came to a halt and pointed to a striking cluster of trees on a hilltop in the distance, the fields around its base grazed by little white dots of sheep. "The other side of that hill."

"Then we had best get on," she muttered, and urged her mare into a trot, eager to get away from him.

He passed her easily, breaking into a canter. Rather than be sprayed with sods of turf, she let her mare's head go, so that both horses were soon cantering side by side.

Wolf glanced at her, his eyes still narrowed in scrutiny, and she looked away. She guessed that he was trying to work out what had made her so uncomfortable back there.

It would only be a matter of time, she realized in dismay, before he guessed at her rising desire for him.

And then what?

Why had none of the love poems she had read ever mentioned the strength of a virgin's desire?

Because they were all written by men, a voice jeered in her head.

They reached the far side of the tree-topped hill just after noon and stopped in a rough hollow, with boulders and sparse trees, and nobody else in sight. The sun was high overhead, surprisingly warm for February, and after the long ride Eloise was thirsty and in need of somewhere private to relieve herself. Wolf discreetly led the horses to a nearby spring while she clambered over rocks and through trees to find a suitably unseen spot. Afterward, she made her way back to where he was waiting with the horses.

He stripped off his riding gloves, tucking them into his belt, then looked at her flushed face. "Thirsty?" When she nodded, he held out a flask. "I filled it with cold water from the spring. Try some, it's clean."

Dubiously, she put the flask to her lips. At court, drinking river water could kill you, it was so often mired with filth from the palaces. But she was so thirsty…

She drank, then lowered the flask to stare at him. "It's delicious."

"I told you it was good."

He removed his plain velvet cap, dragging his sleeve across his damp forehead. His smile prickled at her nerves. Suddenly she realized how closely Wolf had been watching as she drank, his blue eyes narrowed on her mouth. They seemed more piercing than ever in the sunlight, and all the more dazzling for the blackness of his hair, short and disheveled where he had combed it back with his fingers.

She licked her lips, and his smile became oddly intent.

"Thank you," she managed huskily, holding out the flask.

He reached for it, his gaze still on her face, and their hands touched briefly. A spark of the most intense desire raced through her, setting her veins alight. For a few seconds her chest hurt and she could not breathe; her gaze locked on his. She tried to speak but could not form words. It was as though her mind had shut everything out but the roaring clamor of her senses.

Then he took the flask and turned on his heel, looking about himself. His voice was uneven. "I used to come here as a boy to get away from my lessons. Sometimes to escape the rod. There's a cave down there in the hollow, near the spring. When the weather was fine I would bring a fleece or a cloak and sleep there, away from the hubbub of my father's house. It is a good place to be alone."

Still reeling from that fleeting contact, Eloise found she could make no reply. She gazed about the place instead, surprised and a little enchanted that Wolf would have brought her here, though they were still very much strangers. So this was a private place of his from childhood, a hideout where he could feel safe. She had her own little spots too, secret hiding places on her father's estate, but she could not imagine ever sharing them with him.

"Would you like to see inside the cave?" he asked softly, and Eloise found herself nodding instinctively. Wolf took her by the arm and drew her down into the shadowy hollow, his breath warm on her cheek. "Mind your head as we go in…"

Six

AT FIRST THERE WAS merely a glimmering rock face with shadows ahead, and she went willingly. But then they reached a second passageway, and their bodies blocked the light from the mouth of the cave. The air grew cold and Eloise shivered. It was much darker inside the second cave, as dark as the inside of a glove, and as they ducked their heads to enter the cavern, a strange rustling came from above.

It seemed to Eloise, who was not usually given to dreams and fancies, that something brushed her hair in passing.

A cobweb—or some kind of evil spirit?

She jerked back and clutched Wolf's shoulder, unable to disguise the apprehension in her voice. "What...what was that?"

He laughed softly in her ear. "Bats."

She shuddered, crouching even lower as they entered in case the tiny flying creatures were tempted to come back.

"You used to sleep here? Alone?"

"Alas, I was never able to persuade any of the local maidens to join me for the night," he replied, and she heard rather than saw the smile on his face. "Though if you had been a little older..."

"No thank you!"

Wolf slipped an arm about her waist as she tried to turn round and escape. "A little further in," he murmured persuasively, "there'll be daylight, I promise. A cleft through the rocks up above. Besides, if we keep going, your eyes will adjust to the light."

Once again she caught his masculine scent and closed her eyes, glad he could not see her expression clearly. What did it matter to walk blind in this darkness?

He helped her negotiate the narrow passageway, his gloved hand on her arm. She had to go first, stumbling across the uneven ground, but felt him close behind. Her breathing began to sound ragged to her ears in the enclosed space, and she wondered he could not hear her heart, it beat so loud.

"Look," he whispered, and she stopped, opening her eyes at last. "Over there."

Wolf was right, she thought, feeling oddly off-balance now that her eyes were open again. There was daylight here, filtering down through the weight of rock and earth above them, illuminating the damp rock walls.

Turning her head slightly, Eloise followed the line of his pointing arm, and came face to face with a horse. Not the animal itself, but, even more remarkable, the painting of a horse on the rock walls. To find a painting in this dark space was so unexpected that she blinked and caught her breath, suddenly speechless, staring at what he had shown her.

A horse indeed, but not any horse she had seen. This was a horse from some other world, not her own. Thin curved lines described its back and legs in motion, its proud raised head, a single black dot for its eye.

"What do you think?" he asked at length.

"It's like nothing I've ever seen before. Who drew it?" She looked at him uncertainly. "You?"

Wolf gave an odd laugh. "Not I, no. It was here when I found this place as a boy, and long before that too. I used to lie on this damp rocky earth and stare up at that drawing for hours, wishing I could decipher its secrets."

"You did not show it to anyone else?"

"This may sound strange, but I did not wish to tell anyone

else what I had found, in case they came down here and destroyed the peace of the place." He studied the drawing himself, almost as though he had never seen it before. "Later, I asked one of my father's oldest friends if he knew anything about such things. He was a man of great learning, a true scholar and a visionary. I knew he would not insist I tell others about the place. He came to look at the horse, then told me it had been drawn on this wall in ancient times, before men lived in houses. He said a great northern tribe lived near York once, and perhaps visited this cave as a sacred place, for they worshipped the horse as a god."

Afraid she might destroy the ancient art by touching it, she traced the horse with one delicate finger. "This is a sacred drawing?"

"I believe so, yes."

"A pagan horse god." She looked about the walls, and her eye fell on another drawing. It was a small angular depiction of an animal with sharp ears and teeth, lunging forward as though leaping toward the sacred horse. "And what is that?"

"No sacred animal this time, but my own poor effort at the art of the ancients." He smiled when she glanced at him in surprise. "I wanted to leave something of myself down here, if only in recognition of all those hours spent staring at another man's creation."

She studied his drawing more carefully, seeing how he had tried to copy the thin curved lines of the original, and the sense of motion. "It's a wolf."

"What else?"

He had spoken lightly, but she was not fooled. "It's very good," she said decidedly, then turned rather too quickly when he moved, as though afraid he was going to leave her down there in the chilly, echoing cavern.

Wolf had moved closer, not further away, she realized too late, finding herself maybe an inch or two away from the reassuring warmth of his body. They stared at each other in silence, two softly breathing people in that glimmering space meant only for animals and gods, until she caught a sudden darkness in his eyes. He brushed her cheek with his fingers, bare flesh to flesh.

"Eloise," he whispered.

She had meant to draw back after his kiss, to refuse any further intimacy. They were not yet married, after all. Such things were forbidden between a man and a maid, even when betrothed, and she did not wish to shame her family.

But the moment his tongue stroked her lower lip, gently stealing inside her mouth, she was lost to reason. The weight of the earth above their heads, the running of the sacred horse and the wolf dancing after it, the rock walls gleaming with water and pressing in on them: all these made her lose her senses, no longer aware of time and space, of rules and decorum, of what was right and wrong. Only of his body against hers, and the desire burning in her veins.

She gripped his shoulders, clinging on. Her head fell back under his kiss, inviting his mouth on her throat and the tender skin above her breasts.

He cupped her breast, and she muttered, "Yes," kissing him back as though it were the most natural thing in the world for them to be in a cave, making love in the half-light.

There was a rightness about it when he lowered her to the earth, throwing down his jacket first to protect her from the dirt. She was his prey and he was the wolf, biting her throat so softly she found herself crying out in pleasure, not pain. His hands were so clever they taught her how to sigh and beg, and she stared up in wonder at the running horse on the wall when he dragged down her bodice and freed her breasts, kissing each one in turn. She felt like she was running too, wild and free across the grassy plains, her heart almost bursting out of her chest with the force of her own desire.

"Here," he said, and guided her hand down to his groin. He had unlaced himself, and she felt his cock, stiff as the rock itself, the hot thrust of it pressing against her hand.

She snatched her hand away, but he merely laughed.

"I want you," he told her, his mouth finding her breast again. Her nipple hardened under his lips. "We were made for each other, Eloise."

"Wolf," she whispered, shaking her head, though she was half-tempted to let him take her. How many other men and women had coupled in this cave, watched by the ancient sinewy horse galloping across the rock? How many children had been conceived in this strange, shadowy space?

"There is already speculation that we have slept together before the wedding night, it hardly seems to matter if we do," he muttered, kissing her throat again. "Though I know we should not... I gave your father my word... Not even here, in a place meant for love."

Was this love?

She did not think so, for surely love was a sweet and gentle emotion which stirred the heart. She had felt love for Simon, and thought he loved her in return, until she discovered that he had deceived her.

No, this was not love, but lust. Her blood beat violently, flushing her skin with heat, her skin tingling wherever his hands touched. It felt like a divine madness, this compulsion to touch and be touched, to draw him closer and wrap her limbs around his until their bodies were joined as one.

He took her mouth again, their tongues thrusting wildly together in a dance of desire.

"Eloise," he groaned against her lips, and she felt him raise her skirts, his hands seeking her out, stroking with bold intimacy between her thighs. Her flesh there was already slick, aching with a sweet need for him, and he slid one finger easily inside.

When she arched her back, urging him on, he gasped as though he felt the same impulsive, burning desire that had suddenly burst into flame inside her.

She wanted him too, yes. Her body was shaking with it, her blood on fire.

He kissed her throat again, setting off tiny flames that fed off her skin wherever his lips touched. And while he kissed her, his finger stroked intimately in and out of her moist cleft, filling her with wild excitement.

"Too much," she moaned. "It is too much."

He shifted, withdrawing his fingers from her sex, though she felt his growing impatience. Instead he dragged his thumb back and forth across her nipple, leaving it tingling and erect. His head bent and he sucked it deep into his mouth, massaging it first against his tongue, then nipping at the quivering bud with his teeth, not painfully but with an exquisite torment.

She gasped, clutching onto his shoulders as a spinning sensation threatened to overwhelm her. Suddenly her moist channel was aching for the touch of his fingers, and she wished feverishly that he would stroke her there again, push back inside…

"That pleases you?" he whispered hotly in her ear. "You want more?"

When she did not respond, lost in the bittersweet haze of pleasure he had conjured between them in this sacred place, he took her hand and pressed it once more against his groin.

"Touch me," he insisted.

This time she did not pull away. Her hand moved of its own desire, stroking the hard length of his cock. She heard him suck in his breath, and guessed that her touch pleased him.

Daringly, she closed her fingers about the broad root of his cock, and squeezed. Wolf groaned as though in pain, but did nothing to stop her, so she squeezed him again. His flesh was wondrously smooth, she thought. Experimentally she ran her fingers back up his shaft until she reached the swollen head, which twitched under her touch, swelling even further.

She sighed into the darkness between them, her cheeks on fire, wondering what it would feel like to take such a large organ inside her.

"Squeeze me again," he said thickly, and she complied, eager to please him. He leaned forward, his tongue dipping between her lips, tasting her hotly, dancing back and forth against her tongue, lighting the sweetest of fires in her belly and between her thighs.

"Eloise," he muttered against her mouth. "Do you have any idea what you are doing to me?"

She did not need to answer that, for his shaft had hardened to perfection in her hand, like a miraculous sword sheathed in velvet, and suddenly his fingers were between her legs too, feeling once again for that moist cleft which ached to take him in.

He was going to take her.

She could not breathe. She could not think. Her hips arched against his, eager for it to be over, to know…

"My lord," she gasped, shaking with lust. "Please…!"

"Yes, yes… You are right…" Abruptly he rolled away, panting. "We must not anticipate the wedding night."

"My lord?"

Clearly fighting for control, Wolf lay still another moment in silence, then raised his head, examining her flushed face. "Don't look at me like that, Eloise. There is no shame in being unschooled in love. Trust me, the pain is only fleeting and I shall soon teach you to please me. But this is neither the time nor the place for my betrothed to lose her innocence."

There was chagrin in his face as Wolf got to his feet, brushing himself down, then bent to help her. She could sense his burning frustration, and could have screamed herself, desperate for a consummation she did not fully understand. He crouched before her and pulled her bodice back up, then tidied her gown so that it covered her ankles again, hiding her nakedness beneath.

She sat up, confused, not sure what had happened. Slowly it occurred to her that Lord Wolf had misinterpreted her cry as one of denial, not desire for more.

"It was a mistake to bring you here unaccompanied," he added curtly, not looking at her as he adjusted his own clothing. "I lost my head, it was never my intention to… There will be time enough for us to learn the ways of each other's bodies once we are wed."

Her slick inner channel was still throbbing with unsatisfied need as Eloise stared up at him, slowly registering his words and what they meant. Unschooled in love? Soon teach her to please him?

"What…what are you saying, my lord?" she asked, stammering as her sense of hurt grew. "That I do not please you? That what we have been doing here does not please you?"

He frowned. "That is not what I said. But as a virgin, there is much you do not know about a man's body. I can teach you, if you will let me, and then our time together as man and wife will be more pleasurable."

She pushed him away when he would have helped her to rise. The more he spoke, the deeper the wound grew in her heart.

"So this is not pleasurable now?" Her voice caught on an angry gasp. "Forgive me, I am only a foolish maiden, after all. I cannot be expected to know how to please a man."

"Of course you please me," he muttered, but did not try to stop her getting to her feet on her own this time. He grabbed up his jacket and followed as she felt her way out of the cave, his voice impatient. "Slow down, Eloise. Wait for me. The way is uneven; you could hurt yourself in this darkness."

"I will be more hurt if I stay," she retorted.

Outside, the sun was still bright, the February day still and quiet. The horses, grazing nearby, lifted their heads to stare at them in surprise as they emerged from the cave. Eloise turned to face him, her head held high, and saw his frown deepen into anger as he realized she no longer intended to make love with him.

"I do not understand why you are so distressed," he bit out, watching her.

"Do you not? You told me I do not please you, my lord," she said pointedly. "That you prefer to bed more experienced women."

"Eloise, do not force an argument where there is none. We are betrothed. Of course you please me."

"How?" she persisted.

He gave a hoarse bark of laughter, looking her up and down. "What, must I list your desirable attributes in order to get you back into bed with me? Very well. You are not beautiful in a classical sense, but you have a sensual body and a way of looking at a man that excites the passions. Your breasts are small, but they are high and pert, and will swell once you are with child. To speak frankly, I do prefer the bold lasciviousness of a married woman or a widow to a shy virgin. But it will be no hardship to find you in my bed the morning after the wedding feast." His eyes were hard as granite by the time he finished. "Is that enough?"

Smarting with hurt and shame, Eloise managed a thick, "Quite enough, my lord," and turned toward her horse.

On the long ride back to the manor house, she sat stiff and upright on her sidesaddle, staring at the countryside through teary eyes. He said nothing most of the way, though rode with more consideration than before, keeping pace with her until they reached the track home. There they parted, for Eloise did not wish him to accompany her back to the door, and Wolf was clearly keen to get away as quickly as possible.

He wheeled his stallion about on the deep-rutted track, watching her through narrowed blue eyes. "I shall visit you again in a sennight, Eloise, and trust to find you in better humor."

"Do not waste your time, my lord, for I shall not receive you."

"Enough of this nonsense!" he bit out, his jaw clenched. "Have you forgotten that we are soon to be married?"

"How could I forget," she flung back at him, "when you so nearly broke your word to my father today?"

His stare was fierce. "Very well, I accept that my actions at the cave today were not honorable. In fact, they were thoroughly dishonorable. But you were not so unwilling to fall into my arms as you would like to pretend."

"Good day, my lord."

He swore coarsely under his breath, then rode after her as she turned her horse toward the manor house. "Admit it, this is nothing but hurt pride. You wished me to make love to you with words, to flatter your vanity with false comparisons, and instead I was honest."

This was too near the truth to be comfortable. But Eloise merely repeated, "Good day, my lord," and rode on alone to the house. This time he did not follow her, and a moment later she heard the stallion's hooves thundering back down the track toward the north and his estate.

She needed time to be alone, to mull over what he had said, and decide how to deal with him the next time they met. She could not avoid the marriage any more than she could avoid seeing him again. Their fate was to be together. But she could guard her heart against him, and school her traitorous body not to respond so wantonly to his kisses.

If she did not, he would leave her a broken woman when he finally returned to court. Wolf would take his beautiful and skilled mistresses to bed, and not care one jot how it hurt his wife back at home.

She must learn to be cold, to separate her heart from the clamoring desires of her body. Just as Wolf did.

———

When she entered the hall, saddle-sore and weary, she found a slender young woman with slanted blue eyes and hair the color of ripe corn waiting for her. Eloise looked at her, confused, then suddenly realized it was her younger sister.

"Susannah!" she cried, and embraced the girl with undisguised joy. "I cannot believe how you have grown! Why, you are almost as tall as me."

"I'm not a little girl anymore," Susannah agreed, laughing. "I am eighteen now, and bored of this place where nothing exciting ever happens. I have missed you so much, Eloise. Will you take me with you to court when you return?"

"But have you not heard?" Eloise was surprised. "I am to be married to Lord Wolf within the month."

"Oh, I know all about that. His lordship came to see Father at Yuletide." Her sister laughed at Eloise's expression. "It was all arranged long before they went to court to fetch you. Did Father not write to warn you?"

"I knew nothing of the match until they arrived at court."

"That's so like Father! He loves to keep secrets." Susannah looked at her, suddenly concerned. "But how pale you are. Are you unwell?"

Eloise shook her head, finding it hard to hide her distress from her sister. "No, I must hurry upstairs and change, that is all. I went for a ride with Lord Wolf and…."

"Your gown is dirty," Susannah said, staring at it. "Did you take a fall from your horse? What is it? Has something happened to upset you?"

"Let us not talk here," Eloise muttered, and took her sister by the hand.

Upstairs, she found Mary folding linen in her chamber. She sent the inquisitive girl on an errand while Susannah helped her into a fresh gown. She did not wish to tell her sister everything that had passed between herself and Lord Wolf. But it was impossible to hide that she was upset, and though her sister knew even less about men than Eloise, it would be good to confide in another female. Morag, of course, would offer advice if asked. But she would prefer her old nurse not to know the extent of her troubles.

"So tell me," her sister said quietly, lacing up her gown at the back. "What is wrong?"

"Were you introduced to Lord Wolf when he came to visit Father?"

"Only briefly," she admitted. "I was helping Morag tidy out the linen store when he arrived, so saw him enter the hall and was asked to make my curtsy. But that was all. Father sent me to change out of my work apron, and by the time I descended they had already gone into the study together."

"Did you think him handsome?"

Susannah smiled, reaching for a pale green ribbon to tie up Eloise's hair. "He is a little rough, and his manner with me was abrupt, but then he has been a soldier. I would not call him unhandsome."

"I find him…" Eloise colored delicately, the words hard to say, even to her sister. "Desirable."

Susannah looked round at her at once, sharp-eyed. "But that is excellent. When I saw how ill at ease you were downstairs, I thought you would say the opposite." She finished tying up Eloise's hair. "To find your betrothed desirable is a good thing, surely? Better than to be promised to an ogre."

"You are right, of course. Only…"

Her sister sat down beside her on the bed and squeezed her hand. "Say it before you burst!"

"Only it seems Lord Wolf prefers a mistress to a wife," she blurted out, then dragged her hand away from her sister's and jumped up, pacing the room angrily.

"I do not understand."

"Nor did I, until he made it clear to me that having to instruct a maid in the art of love is tiresome to him and a nuisance. He would rather some married wanton in his bed, who knows already what it takes to please a man!"

"No!" Susannah gasped, staring at her, wide-eyed. "I cannot believe any man would say such things to the girl he is about to marry."

Eloise leaned out of the unshuttered window, cooling her hot face. She took several deep breaths before returning to sit beside her sister, her hands in her lap. "I am to be his brood mare, it seems, my purpose being to breed him an heir, and so my looks are unimportant. When I had the temerity to question what he meant, he told me flatly that my breasts are too small and I am not beautiful, but that I am somewhat wanton in my looks, which makes up for my shortcomings."

"What a beast!"

There was a long silence, then Eloise said in a small voice, "What am I to do, Susannah? I need someone to advise me. Within only a few weeks, I must marry this man and give myself to him. It is all arranged, and to withdraw now would bring disgrace on myself and on our family. Yet how can I go willingly to his bed, knowing what he thinks of me?"

Her sister looked at her sideways. "Well, I know it will be humiliating… But you did say that… Well, you suggested before that you find Lord Wolf desirable. And he is a wealthy nobleman, and one of the king's most trusted soldiers. So perhaps it will not be such a hardship to wed him, despite his insufferable and unforgiveable rudeness." She bit her lip. "Not as much as if you found him smelly and toadlike, for instance."

Eloise burst out laughing. "Trust you to think with your head, Susannah."

"And trust you to think only with your heart," her sister replied, kissing her affectionately on the cheek. "When I marry, I hope to find a man who is both biddable and desirable. For I could never be content to be ruled by a man. But as you say, Eloise, it is all arranged now. Somehow you must listen to your head and not your heart, or this marriage will never be a happy one."

"If only it were that simple," she murmured, and tried to forget the overriding excitement she had felt in the glimmering darkness of the cave.

She desired the man who was to be her husband, despite the knowledge that he looked on her innocence with contempt. That made her both a fool and a wanton for desiring where she was despised, just as she had done with the deceitful Simon. When would she learn to guard her heart more carefully?

"Well, at least Lord Wolf does not know how you feel about his insults," Susannah said blithely, and stretched out on the bed, yawning. "Men become so unreasonable when they have been caught in the wrong, have you noticed?"

Seven

WOLF HAD NOT EXPECTED to suffer an attack of nerves on his wedding day. Yet nervous was precisely how he felt, standing in his best suit before the altar as his bride came floating toward him down the aisle, her broad-skirted gown bedecked with colorful ribbons and silks. Her hair threaded with white flowers, she stopped before him, surrounded by her bridesmaids, all smiling behind their fans and flowers.

He bowed to her as tradition demanded, and his bride curtsied in return, then accepted his outstretched hand.

With her flowers so sweetly fragrant, Eloise seemed more like the pagan deity of spring than a human bride. Yet her hand trembled a little as he took it, and he glanced at her in surprise.

Could she be nervous too?

They had practiced their vows the day before, and he found himself speaking clearly, praying with the congregation, and swiftly following the priest's prompt when told to produce the ring. Then suddenly they were man and wife, and he was leading her proudly back to the church door, accepting Sir John's congratulations along the way. They emerged into cool sunshine to the cheers of the villagers, crowding outside the church to see their new lady.

Limping, he turned to hand his wife up into the covered wagon, its sides decorated with hanging silks and flowers. "Lady Wolf," he murmured, his arm about her waist, and saw her stare back at him, wide-eyed, her face pale.

The children pressed close to the wagon to see the newly wed bride, throwing tiny handfuls of white blossom about her head and calling "God bless you!" in their high voices. At his signal, small cloth bags of coins began to be handed out, a traditional gift from the lord to the villagers on such important occasions.

In a white rain of blossoms, he climbed up beside his new wife, and nodded brusquely to the driver.

"Take us home."

The short journey from the village church to his ancestral home never took long, for it was only a matter of minutes from the kissing-gate to the hall's vast entrance door. Today though, with the wagon moving so slowly through the crowd of villagers, it felt interminable.

Wolf looked at his silent bride. She was more beautiful than he had realized, he thought, and felt guilty at how he had spoken to her that day at the cave. She had made him angry and defensive, unsure why she had rejected him. He had tried to be honest about his view of marriage. But her expression had made it clear she found him offensive and distasteful, and somehow he had never managed to see her alone again since then, to apologize. He wanted to reassure her now, but Eloise kept herself turned away from him, staring out at the villagers along the way, sometimes raising her hand in a wave.

At the hall, the side door stood wide open, a steady stream of servants and local tradesmen passing in and out in the chilly spring sunshine, carrying provisions and rolling barrels for the feast. Up at the main entrance, servants were still cleaning the impressive new windows and sweeping down the front steps. But the door was hurriedly cleared as the wagon came slowly up the track, and a bell rang urgently somewhere inside the house.

By the time they reached the door, his servants had lined up outside, caps in hand, to greet their mistress as she entered her new home.

Wolf himself jumped down to hand his lady out of the bridal wagon, waving the driver aside.

"Welcome to your new home, my love," he said clearly, and heard a ripple of approval from the watching servants.

He might as well not have spoken, for all the attention Eloise gave him. Her face was raised toward the great house, her eyes still wide and staring, as though not quite able to take in that she was now mistress of this place. Then she made her way to the steward and his wife, who acted as housekeeper at Wolf Hall.

"You must be Master Spears," she said calmly, then turned to his wife, "and Mistress Spears."

"Welcome, my lady," the steward said, bowing very low, and stood aside to let her enter the house.

Their daughter, little Joanna, barely seven years old, came tripping out of the doorway with a pretty bouquet of flowers tied with a yellow ribbon.

"Welcome to Wolf Hall, my lady," she piped nervously, and held up the bouquet with shaking hands.

"Flowers! But how lovely," Eloise exclaimed, crouching to take them. "Thank you so much."

She patted the girl's head, straightening with the flowers in her arms, and at last her gaze came to rest on Wolf's face. He saw a sudden hard brightness in her eyes, and limped forward to take her arm. Was she going to weep?

"Shall we go inside?" he murmured in her ear. "It is cold, and our guests will be arriving soon for the feast."

Eloise nodded, and allowed him to lead her inside. Frustrated by her cool demeanor, Wolf wanted to touch her bare hand, to remind her that they were married. But she had drawn on her soft kid gloves on the journey from church, and her touch was that of a stranger.

Hugh Beaufort was already there, looking out of breath as though he had just ridden back from church. He bowed as they approached, then bent over Eloise's hand with courtly deference. "My lady," he murmured. "You are a lucky man, Wolf, to have such a beautiful bride."

Eloise seemed to stiffen at this, but smiled politely enough at the young man. She glanced at his shoulder, now no longer bandaged. "I am glad to see you looking so well. Is your wound quite healed, Master Beaufort?"

"Just the odd twinge now and then," he admitted cheerfully. "Sadly, although I have enjoyed Wolf's hospitality here these past few weeks, now that I am mended there is nothing to prevent me returning to court. Not once my business in the north is concluded."

"But surely that cannot be soon?"

"I'm afraid it may be concluded as early as next month. Now that my wound is healed, I have managed to survey a number of religious houses in the region, and have almost finished my report." He grinned. "Though I could perhaps be persuaded to stay a little longer."

"Then let me persuade you, sir," Eloise said at once, a little color returning to her cheeks at last. "There are few here in the north who know what court life is. Pray do not desert us so soon."

Watching the two of them together, conversing so naturally and without any awkwardness, Wolf had to bite back his jealousy. She was his wife now, and Beaufort knew it. Even a smooth-tongued courtier would not be fool enough to snatch a newly wedded wife from under her groom's nose.

No, what stung more than that was how easy Eloise was with him. Wolf himself had barely managed to get a word out of her since the afternoon of their ride. Now here she was, talking to Beaufort as warmly as though she was half in love with him.

He should never have taken her to the cave, to his private place. What a mistake that had been. He had tried, in a moment of sudden overwhelming desire, to make love to her for the first time in that sacred space. It had seemed a portent of good fortune when she had shown such interest in the ancient drawing of the horse, a sign that they were meant to be together. Instead, he had only succeeded in offending her.

He saw Mary hurrying across the hallway ahead in great concentration, a basket in her arms, and raised his hand to summon her.

"Perhaps Mary should show you the way to our bedchamber," he said abruptly, interrupting their conversation. His teeth were on edge, his tone barely civil despite his good intentions. "It occurs to me you may want to refresh yourself before the feast."

She looked at him blankly; then gave a slight nod. "Of course," she remarked, then walked away.

Beaufort seemed uncomfortable, standing in silence as they both watched his new wife ascend the stairs with her maid. "Forgive me, I didn't intend to…" Beaufort began awkwardly.

Wolf shook his head, at once contrite for having embarrassed his friend with that ridiculous show of jealousy. God's blood, was this how life would be as a married man, always watching his wife for signs of infidelity?

"It's forgotten," he insisted, forcing a smile. "Come, this place will soon be overrun by wedding guests. Shall we go and find a drink?"

—⁂—

Among the first guests to arrive for the wedding feast were Sir John and his younger daughter Susannah, accompanied by a pack of giggling younger cousins who had been Eloise's bridesmaids. Wolf greeted his new father-in-law, then found himself smiling instinctively at his daughter, for Susannah was a lively young thing, and was taken aback by her narrow-eyed stare in return.

Had Eloise told her sister what had passed between them at the cave? The thought made him uncomfortable. He turned, quickly introducing her to Hugh Beaufort to cover the awkward moment.

Hugh was smiling too. He seemed much struck by Eloise's younger sister, perhaps because they were nearer in age. He took Susannah's hand and lingered in kissing it.

"I had no idea Eloise had such a beautiful sister," he murmured gallantly.

Susannah's eyes widened at this courtly compliment; she was no doubt accustomed to the rougher manners of the north. She looked back at Hugh with undisguised interest. "What do you do here in Yorkshire, Master Beaufort?"

"I am here on the king's business."

"Indeed, sir? I seem to remember my sister mentioning you." Her smooth brow wrinkled in a charming frown.

Watching Susannah flirt with the king's clerk, Wolf thought he had rarely seen such beauty in one so young. Fair and slender-hipped, with small but pleasingly pert breasts, there was a perfect symmetry to her face, and her eyes were the deepest shade of blue. She would be a prize for the noblest of men, he thought assessingly. Which was no doubt why her father had so far declined to present her at court, for that would bring her youth and beauty to the attention of King Henry.

And yet he still preferred her sister's less conventional looks. Eloise ran deep as a river, not like this bright and airy stream of smiles and witty asides. He also suspected that Susannah could make more trouble for a man than Eloise, for all her light manners. There was something beneath the surface of that perfect face—the gently upturned nose, the too-swift curving lips and delicate brows—which hinted at buried fire. But perhaps Susannah was more like her sister than he realized, Wolf thought drily.

"You are surveying the religious houses for the king, is that right?" she continued. "Seeing how much each one is worth to the royal coffers."

Hugh seemed embarrassed by this forthright description of his task. He cleared his throat, glancing about as the other guests began to gather in the hall. "It's a little more complicated than that. But yes, in essence."

"The king must place great trust in you, sir."

Hugh smiled uneasily, and Wolf was forced to hide his own amusement, seeing how the young man was gratified by this compliment but unsure if it was wise or even politic to accept it.

"Well, yes… I like to think His Majesty does."

"Will you sit with me awhile before the feast begins, sir, and tell me everything there is to know about court life?" Susannah demanded, her blue eyes bright with curiosity, and indicated an empty seat near the window. "My father will not consent to send me to court, my sister barely opens her mouth these days, and I am so heartily bored of Yorkshire!"

Grinning at Hugh's expression, Wolf watched as he followed a little stiffly in her wake. If he was not careful there, the young man would soon find himself attached to the younger Tyrell girl, and that would be a troublesome knot to untie.

Then he moved away and caught sight of his bride descending the stairs. The other guests turned to stare too; the hall suddenly hushed.

Eloise had re-dressed her hair in a new style, twisting the long fair hair on top of her head with ribbons of white lace and fresh spring blossoms, and her cheeks were flushed, lending her face much beauty. Nonetheless, she kept her gaze demurely lowered as she descended, her maid behind carrying the heavy train of her gown. About her narrow waist a rope was twined, decorated with flowers, and the lacy shawl which had covered her low-cut bodice in church had been removed, leaving her skin bare. Wolf looked at the creamy expanse of flesh above her breasts, and his cock grew rigid in his red leather codpiece.

Convinced that everyone could see his erection, he made no

attempt to disguise it. He felt like a satyr, consumed with passion for some unearthly beauty despite his own physical defects. He wished it was already night and they were alone together in the bridal chamber, so he could tear off that suggestive gown and slake his lust in her body.

"My lady," he managed hoarsely. He reached for her hand, now ungloved. "Your guests are waiting to greet you."

Her fingers touched his and a shock ran through his body, as though he had stood too close to summer lightning. Eloise felt it too, her wide eyes lifting at once to his face.

His voice sounded thick with desire, and there was a rushing in his ears as he led her forward to the feast. "You look magnificent."

"Thank you," she whispered.

It was a struggle to sit through the lengthy feast, pretending to delight in the inventiveness of his cook's many dishes, but in fact picking at the lavishly prepared food with little interest. He had no appetite for anything but love, his gaze constantly drawn to the woman on his left, her profile framed by her headdress of flowers, her hand shaking as they shared the bride cup.

Now and then, Eloise would steal a covert look at him, then glance hurriedly away when she found his gaze on her.

With fierce and growing satisfaction, Wolf realized he was not the only one thinking ahead to their night together. But was Eloise afraid to surrender her virginity at last, or secretly looking forward to his possession of her body?

There was dancing after the feast. The musicians played in the little gallery above the hall, and the benches and boards from the feast were pushed back to make way for the dance. A single tabor marked out the beat, then the haut-boys and hurdy-gurdy steadily took up the tune, music swelling until the rafters resounded. A hush fell amongst the company, the servants hurried to the walls of the room, and the wedding guests looked expectantly toward the high dais.

There was no escaping the traditional bridal dance. Wolf rose to lead his bride out onto the floor, silently cursing his bad leg and wishing he could be whole again.

Eloise paid no heed to his limping gait, turning daintily about him in the complicated steps, her years at court showing as she performed their dance with the graceful bearing of a queen. She made sure not to brush too close to him, however, and when their hands met, her skin was cool, her face aloof.

Wolf bowed over her hand as the dance ended, amidst the applause of his watching guests. "Thank you, my lady," he muttered, then abruptly drew her close before she could escape and pressed his lips against hers, his arm tight about her waist.

The company gasped and laughed at this deliberate breach of etiquette, some clapping their hands with glee, others carefully looking the other way. But his groomsmen roared their approval of these rough-and-ready manners, banging their wine cups on the tables.

Shocked by this public embrace, Eloise stood motionless in his arms as he kissed her. Then stared when he released her, a small spot of red burning in each cheek.

"Now you look like a bride on her wedding night," he told her breathlessly.

Suddenly her father was at his elbow. "Forgive me. May I dance with my daughter one last time, my lord?"

"Of course, Sir John," he said politely, and allowed the man to lead Eloise away. But he had seen the disapproval on the elderly knight's face, and knew his forthright kiss had shocked not only his bride.

Behind him, some of the other wedding guests had risen to dance. Threading his way carefully between them with nods and smiles, he made his way back toward the high dais.

Beneath the high windows, he found Hugh and Susannah dancing together, smiling intimately as they turned to touch palms, then stepped away in the dance. The girl seemed over-young to be dancing with a courtier she had only just met, he thought carefully, pausing a moment to watch them. But she was not a child, so he said nothing and walked on.

It was not for him to spoil the pleasures of others. He had trouble enough not spoiling his own.

At last the hour had come for them to retire. Barely able to look at Eloise, his body gripped with an intense hunger, Wolf called the bridesmen to assemble. Then he seized his new wife by the hand and dragged her through the throng of guests to the stairs, his bridesmen howling like wolves and shouting, "To bed, my lord! To bed! To bed!"

They stumbled up the broad stairs together, escorted to their bedchamber by a riotous pack of bridesmen and women, their faces lit up by flaming torches. At the door to the bedchamber, Wolf thrust the shivering Eloise inside, then turned to defend his territory, mock-fighting the nearest bridesmen. They struggled on the torchlit threshold a moment, then Wolf drew his dagger and they fell back, grinning.

"Let no man or woman cross this threshold until dawn," he cried, then slammed the door shut in their faces and dragged the wooden beam across with a crash.

The chamber had been dressed for their wedding night, flowers everywhere, and crimson silk hangings on the bed to keep out the night's cold. A fire had been lit in the hearth and was burning steadily, its reddish glow flickering across the walls and deep shadows of the room. The black-and-crimson bedcovers had been turned back, the sheets pure white beneath, as befitted a bridal chamber.

Eloise was standing by the bed, her face defiant. "My lord," she began, but got no further.

Throwing aside his dagger, Wolf seized her by the shoulders. His mouth met hers with a violent passion he had been holding back all evening, and he groaned as her lips opened, allowing him sweet access.

"Eloise," he muttered against her mouth, then tasted her deeply. His hands explored her slender back, reveling in the heat of her body through the flimsy gown. "Yes."

She was not fighting him, he realized in surprise, having half-expected Eloise to refuse this intimacy. Yet why should she refuse? They were man and wife now. This was part of the bargain she had made.

"You are so very desirable," he told her softly, and began to remove her gown, trying not to frighten her. But the laces at her back were wound too tightly, and even after he had worked them loose, some hidden catch still refused to release her body. He swore under his breath, ripping at the fragile material in his frustration. The bodice came free at last, leaving her gasping and naked to the waist, her breasts spilling warm into his hands.

"Forgive me," he managed, then bent unsteadily and took her breast into his mouth, sucking on her nipple. She cried out his name, suddenly clutching at his shoulders, as if she shared his urgency.

His groin swelled with excitement and he shifted, pushing her backward onto the bed, unable to wait any longer.

But Eloise gave a little cry of fright as his hands fumbled with her skirts. Her body shook and her hands fought with him, as though she had abruptly woken from a dream to find some attacker atop her.

"No!" she moaned, and stared up into his face.

Taking a deep shuddering breath, Wolf forced himself to remember that Eloise was a virgin and unused to men. Her natural sensuality, the way she had touched and kissed him in the cave, his growing desire to possess her body: all this had blinded him to her innocence. No doubt she had come to their bridal chamber terrified of what many women considered a painful ordeal, the loss of maidenhead. Perhaps her women had been filling her head tonight with tales of fear and agony, of insatiable men and bloodied sheets, intending to prepare her for her wifely duties but merely terrifying the girl out of her mind.

He rolled away and lay on his back awhile, staring up at the curtained bedposts and willing his erection to go down inside the leather confines of his codpiece. The physical reminder of his desire would only scare her further, he suspected.

Once he was sure he had conquered his lust, he risked a look at his new bride and found Eloise staring back at him in trepidation.

"There's no need to be afraid of me," he told her, aware of a prickling annoyance at her fear. "You are safe enough. I may be your husband, but I am no rapist."

"I'm sorry," she whispered.

"No," he reassured her. "There is no need to be sorry. I was too hasty in my greed. I forgot that you are untried."

Carefully, he stroked the hair back from her damp forehead, its golden flowered length tumbled from the pins which had held it so neatly in place during the wedding feast. After a moment, she began to breathe more easily, and he lifted her hand to his mouth, softly kissing her palm.

"Now, what is it you are afraid of?" he asked. "The pain, I am told, lasts but a moment and soon gives way to passion."

But she shook her head, not meeting his eyes. "It is not the pain."

He frowned. "Then what?"

"I…I cannot say."

Wolf considered her in silence. A dark suspicion began to nag at him. "Did you lie to me, is that it? You are not a virgin, and fear my anger when I discover it?"

Shocked, she stared at him. "No, no…" A sudden flush tinged her cheeks as she stammered, "I have never been with a man, my lord, I swear it on my life."

"I am glad to hear it, my lady," he replied, pointedly reminding her that she was now his wife.

"I do not understand why I was afraid. I am truly sorry," she whispered, her hands covering her naked breasts as his gaze moved instinctively to admire them. Her flush deepened. "I came prepared to do my duty. But then…"

"Then you could not go through with it," he finished drily.

"Forgive me, my lord. It was stupid of me to fight against you." She sat up against the pillows, her hands dropping deliberately away to reveal her rosy-tipped breasts. Her bare skin glowed in the firelight, deliciously tempting. "You are my husband and this is our wedding night. I will not try to stop you again. I know it is your right."

He could barely suppress a smile at this bravery. "My virgin sacrifice?"

Her startled gaze shot to his face, then she half-smiled herself. "Something like that," she admitted.

"Well, there is no need to chain yourself to my bed just yet. I'm not in the mood for devouring terrified virgins tonight." He sat up too, but only to reach for her furred night robe. He handed it to her with a brief nod, and saw the worried surprise on her face. "Go on, cover yourself up. I'm not a monster and I'm not angry with you, but I won't be held responsible for losing my resolve if you parade yourself naked in front of me."

"Thank you, my lord," she managed huskily, shrugging into the night robe. "Though I do know my duty. You want an heir, that's why you married me. I will not fight you if you want to…to try again later."

"I'll bear that in mind," he said, his expression serious. "After all, there may be talk in the morning if the sheets are not bloodied. I can keep the groomsmen out, but there'll be no stopping the gossips once the laundry women have been in to strip the bed."

Her eyes widened. "I hadn't thought of that."

"Just another hazard of the wedding night."

He was still consumed with lust, wishing to push himself inside and vent his frustrations on her body. But they had a long time ahead for such pleasures. Now was a time for care and consideration of her innocence, not violence in pursuance of his marital rights.

Wolf swung out of bed and retrieved his dagger from the floor. Seeing her stare in sudden apprehension, he grinned, then began to strip off his shirt.

What, did his fiery bride think him so dangerous? No wonder she had shrunk from him in bed.

Bare-chested, he cut a small nick across his belly, where it was less likely to be seen and remarked upon than if he had cut his arm. It stung, and the blood welled up at once, beading scarlet on his skin. This he smeared across the sheets where he had lain, then stood back to admire the effect.

"Now even the most determined gossip would swear a virgin lost her honor here tonight," he murmured.

He turned, thinking to see relief in her eyes, now that she had been freed from her obligation to surrender herself tonight. Instead she was staring at his bare chest, a fixed expression on her face, worrying at her lower lip with perfect white teeth, her cheeks slightly flushed.

Eloise looked away at once when she caught his gaze on her, her face shuttered.

But he was no fool. That had been desire on her face. And she had responded with heat to his kisses in the darkness of the cave. His bride was not averse to the crippled lord bedding her. Quite the opposite, in fact.

When Eloise had pushed him away with that cry, he had assumed she would need to be wooed over many nights before she came to want him in return. It had been a disappointment after the heat of her previous kisses, but women were often contrary in nature, and his unsightly limp might have put distaste in her heart.

Now Wolf saw it was no such matter. Something other than lack of desire had held her back tonight.

But what?

Eight

THE MORNING WAS COOL, the spring still reluctant to emerge this far north. But at least the sun had come out briefly, Eloise thought, admiring the purple-headed heather and yellow tips of gorse growing sparely on the slopes above Wolf Hall. Her mare shifted beneath her, sighing. No doubt the animal was eager for a brisk ride across the fields. But she, like Eloise herself, would have to wait until the master was ready.

Then at last it came, the signal they had been waiting for. At the sound of Wolf's long, unwavering whistle, Eloise looked up, shielding her eyes.

The small dark speck in the sky blackened and grew larger, hurtling toward them as though for the kill.

On horseback, Wolf raised his tasseled leather glove for the bird to land on. He called, "Here, boy!" then whistled again, waiting patiently.

The hawk spread its wings, stretching out with cruel taloned feet. Its eyes were wild; its demeanor, savage. Eloise tried not to imagine how it would feel to be some small creature, mewling piteously as it was seized by those claws. With a soft thud the hawk landed on the gloved fist, swaying and gripping hard for balance, and then folded back its barred wings.

"Well done," Wolf murmured, and tossed up a gobbet of raw meat as a reward. The young hawk snatched it from the air, then held the meat between its talons to tear it apart. "This young fellow lacks manners and a little training, that is all. He will make an excellent hunting bird in time."

He glanced sideways at Eloise as he spoke, a dry smile on his face. She sat more stiffly in the saddle, looking away. What did he mean by that glance, that wry comment? Did he think she lacked training as a wife?

It had been almost a sennight since their wedding day, and yet he had never since attempted to make love to her. She saw him watching her sometimes, but could not gauge his mood, nor his thoughts. It was almost as though he lost interest in her since that first night when she had refused him. She regretted her instinctive cry of fear, the way she had pushed him away, for her rejection had struck coldness into their marriage bed.

Yet what had Lord Wolf expected? He had deliberately chosen a virgin bride, and could hardly now demand the skills of a courtesan from her.

Eloise gathered up her reins, hoping she would be allowed to retire to the quiet of the women's chamber on their return. It was difficult to face Wolf's looks and silences, painfully aware that their marriage was still unconsummated. She was not experienced in the ways of love, as her husband clearly was, and the intensity of his passion that first night had unnerved her. Yet she had told him that she was prepared to do her duty.

Irritation flashed through her as she nudged her horse away from the straggly bush it was trying to eat. Why did Wolf delay so long if not to draw out the ritual of taking her damned virginity? She grew more on edge each night, wondering when he would finally claim his conjugal rights. And the longer he delayed, the more her imagination worked, driving the heated thorn of desire deeper into her flesh, her body tingling with barely suppressed excitement whenever he so much as glanced at her.

Wolf summoned his master falconer, handing the bird into his care. "Restrict meat," he ordered the man, "until he learns his trade better."

The falconer bowed and withdrew, standing respectfully to one side as Susannah and Hugh Beaufort, their companions on this ride, rode forward. Susannah seemed to be enjoying her visit to Wolf Hall, and small wonder, for their father's head was full of plans for her own marriage to an old friend of his, Sir William Hanney, a respectable knight and landowner of some consequence in the north. It was clear from the way Susannah had so eagerly accepted an invitation to stay that she was finding it hard to dissuade her father against this match, and felt the need to escape the house, if only for a few short weeks.

But Eloise was not too concerned for her sister. Susannah had always been their father's favorite; she would doubtless win in the end, and marry a man of her own choosing.

"Back to the hall, my lord?" Hugh asked, clearly having trouble controlling his excitable mount.

"Not yet," Wolf told him coolly, and took up his reins. "I thought it might be good to stretch the horses' legs today with a longer ride. The old hunting lodge has been closed since the winter snows set in. But spring is here, and it's time the place was opened again to receive hunting parties. We can ride out there, see what kind of repair the lodge is in." He smiled at his friend. "You must be skilled by now at estimating the need for repairs, given all the priories and church buildings whose worth you have assessed for the king."

Hugh grinned. "If it has been as richly maintained as some of the northern monasteries I have visited, you should have no trouble with the place."

"Alas, my friend," Wolf replied, raising his brows, "I cannot boast vast coffers of gold coins to maintain my buildings, not like these Roman priests and nuns."

"Yet rumor has it the king has lavishly rewarded you for your military campaigns these past ten years."

"The king has not been ungenerous, it is true. But I am not

yet able to pave my lodge with gold," Wolf remarked, laughing at Hugh's expression. "The locals would have it that our northern bishops grew so rich before King Henry split with Rome they paved their palaces with gold."

"I've heard that legend too, but seen no evidence of it. Though plenty of the Catholic priests have lived well enough on what they earned from their rents."

"Aye, they have not lived as frugally as men of God should," Wolf agreed, his tone sharp. It struck Eloise that her new husband had little love for the Roman church and its priests. "Nor been as generous to our northern poor as their oaths of poverty would warrant."

As Eloise sat listening to this exchange, her sister came sidling past on her chestnut horse.

She gave Eloise a wicked smile, leaning close, and whispered in her ear, "Do me a favor, dear sister. If you get a chance to ride alone with your lord, pray take it and let me spend a few moments alone with Master Beaufort."

Eloise was not surprised; her younger sister had not bothered to hide her growing interest in the king's clerk. But she was a little concerned that Susannah thought she would encourage Master Beaufort to pursue her sister.

Since they had danced together at her wedding feast, she had seen Hugh glance at Susannah once or twice in a way she recognized as dangerous. He was a red-blooded male and he found her sister desirable, that much was obvious. And his intentions might be honorable.

But what if Hugh Beaufort took advantage of Susannah's innocence and ruined her, then returned to court without wedding her? Her father would never forgive Eloise if she allowed her younger sister too free a rein during her visit. She could imagine his rage if Susannah thwarted his plans for a marriage with Sir William by spoiling herself with this young courtier.

Impatiently, Wolf wheeled his stallion about. "Shall we ride for the hunting lodge, then? It lies about three miles southeast, along the course of the river."

"I say yes," Hugh agreed heartily, and turned to Susannah, his look uncertain. "Would you permit me to ride beside you, Mistress Tyrell? The ground is firm enough here, but it may be soft beside the river. I would not wish you to take a tumble."

Susannah gave him a little smile that was altogether too encouraging to Eloise's mind. "Indeed, sir, I am sure you would not. Thank you, I would be glad of your company."

As the two younger ones rode down the slope together, their horses shoulder to shoulder, Susannah was already chattering away while Hugh listened politely.

Eloise watched them, frowning. Perhaps she was wrong to suspect Hugh of wishing to seduce her sister; he might simply be allowing Wolf time alone with his new bride.

The irony of that gesture nearly made her laugh. She and Wolf had lain together every night since the wedding, but in unnatural stillness and silence, except for those few occasions when he had risen to put a fresh log on the dying fire or stare out of the window at the moon. Sometimes when they were sleeping together, his body would brush against her in the dark, warm and vital, and she found it hard to breathe. Yet despite her trepidation, he had never once touched her more intimately.

Wolf had ridden a short way toward the river, but now turned back, urging his powerful horse back up the hill toward her. He seemed so restless today, she thought, his body charged with energy as though he were eager to be off and doing things. As he came level with her, she caught a glimpse of that impatient look again, swiftly hidden behind his lashes.

"Shall we canter?" he asked, barely waiting for a response before heading off again at speed.

She kicked her mare on, but the animal was already following his stallion with little need for persuasion. Soon she was cantering alongside him, unable to stop herself looking at his strong thighs controlling the horse, his gloved hands keeping tight guard on the reins, the sun-browned expanse of his throat and face.

Yes, Wolf was a rough soldier, not much given to etiquette or courtly ways, just as she had thought when they first met at court. Yet he was not unhandsome for it. Indeed, the more time she spent with her new husband, the more intriguing she found him, the more compulsively she stared at his hard body, and the more she wondered how it would feel to lie beneath him in pleasure.

That did not mean she loved Wolf though. How could she love a nobleman who had chosen her like a mare for the breeding?

She had loved Simon once, before he betrayed her trust, and had thought him both handsome and a gentleman. Yet she could not imagine ever feeling like this for Simon, consumed by a restless desire that prickled at her skin whenever they were together and made each night a torment.

Susannah and Hugh rode just ahead of them, seeming to take pleasure in each other's company. The spring sunshine grew stronger as the clouds rolled away overhead, and by the time they reached the hunting lodge, the day was quite warm.

Susannah, whose fair complexion freckled easily, was clearly worried to be riding out in such fine weather. When Eloise and Wolf arrived at the lodge, an ancient building with a thatched roof and many tall chimneys, she asked at once if they could return to the hall before the sun climbed much higher.

"For I do not wish my skin to burn in this hot sun," Susannah fretted, and stared imploringly at Wolf. "Forgive me, my lord. I know you wished to look around the lodge before we returned."

Wolf seemed less than impressed. But he sighed, and glanced at Eloise. "I will have to show you the lodge another time then. We had better ride back if your sister does not wish to stay."

Clearing his throat, Hugh intervened. "My lord, if you permit it, I would be happy to ride back to the hall with Mistress Susannah. You may then show the lodge to your lady, and return in your own time."

"But I wish you to see it too, Beaufort, before you journey back to London. Your advice on any repairs would be welcome."

"In that case, we could ride out here again tomorrow," Hugh suggested carefully. "Early, before the ladies have risen."

Wolf considered him in silence a moment, then turned his head to Eloise. "My lady?"

"I am not sure..." Eloise began slowly, not wishing to allow anything improper, but her sister interrupted.

"Please, Eloise," Susannah begged, shielding her face with her hand. "The sun is grown so scorching, I must return at once to the hall. But I do not wish you to spoil your pleasure. I know his lordship brought you here so specially."

"Very well," Eloise agreed, but watched in some consternation as her sister turned her skittish chestnut mare back the way they had come and set off home without even a farewell, Hugh Beaufort riding close behind her. Susannah was planning something, she felt sure of it. But it was clear she would not easily be gainsaid, not if her heart was set on the king's clerk.

"They will not come to any harm," Wolf murmured, swinging effortlessly out of the saddle.

"I hope not."

"Your sister may be young and inexperienced, but she is the daughter of a gentleman and not without friends. Do not distress yourself," Wolf reassured her, beginning to lead his horse toward the stables. "Hugh Beaufort has a sound head on his shoulders. He will do nothing to jeopardize his good reputation at court."

When both horses had been safely stabled and watered, Wolf wandered back to where she was waiting and suggested they take a tour of the old hunting lodge.

"There's usually a servant or two living here during the winter months, to look after the place and manage the grounds. Perhaps we could take some wine and refreshments before heading back to the hall," he murmured, glancing sideways at her. She felt the heat in that gaze and shivered, suddenly aware of him again as her husband. "The ride was longer than I remembered. And it is a hot day."

"Whatever you wish, my lord."

But after some minutes of banging the brass knocker to no reply, Wolf frowned and stepped back.

"Strange," he remarked, staring up at the silent building.

"But perhaps they are out in the grounds in this warm weather. Let's walk round and see if we can find someone to let us in."

"And if no one is here?"

"Then someone deserves a whipping for deserting their post. But we can still go inside." He smiled at her expression. "I happen to know where the key to the kitchen quarters is kept."

She sensed that this deserted place was important to him for some reason, so did not argue but followed him through the soft swish of knee-length grasses to the rear of the building. The once-bright paint of its front facade had peeled away, its wooden frame sagged, and some of the main beams were cracked across. Even the roof thatch had become thin in places. Swallows had built their nests under the gable end, swooping gracefully back and forth in the air as they passed beneath.

Eloise wondered if the interior was in the same disrepair. Peering up against the sun, she noted that the high, narrow casements of the upper floors had been shuttered against the elements, their metal struts rusting in streaks. So there was a good chance that the lodge was sound and dry inside, despite its unhappy looks.

The backyard was dusty and still in the sunshine, not even a solitary hound guarding the place.

Eloise looked up and down, but the shady, tree-lined walk to the fields was quiet, and even the small herb garden with its gnarled hedges of yew and bay was empty. There did not appear to be anyone about.

Having thumped his gloved fist on the kitchen door several times and gained no reply, Wolf slipped away to fetch the key from its hiding place in an old dairy. He returned more slowly, his blue gaze on her face.

"Not a pretty sight, is it? I've let the place go somewhat," he admitted, frowning up at the sagging beams and tufted thatch. "But I've been away from home so much these past ten years it hardly seemed worth the cost of repairs. Now that I am married, it would be good to see the old lodge returned to its former glory. My father and grandfather used to hold great hunting parties here. Yes, the place was magnificent in its day. They say old King Henry, our king's father, even came here once or twice with the court. Now look at it." He kicked aside a broken spar fallen from some decayed casement. "I did not care to honor my father while he was alive. We were not close enough for that. Perhaps now he is dead, I can at least restore one of his favorite places."

She said nothing, but laid a hand on his arm. They were still strangers, despite their marriage, despite sharing the same bed every night. But that did not mean she could not understand his pain—and let him know that she did.

Wolf glanced down at her hand, then managed a lopsided smile. "Shall we look inside?"

—⁓—

The kitchen quarters were vast and ancient, full of battered pots and pans hanging from the walls on gigantic hooks and dried herbs dangling in bunches from pulleys. The whole place was dusty and unkempt, but the floor had recently been swept near the back door, and although the bread oven stood open and cold, the hearth contained the fresh remains of a log fire.

Wolf stooped and rubbed some of the ash between finger and thumb. "Less than a week old, I'd say." He straightened, looking about the kitchen. "Fresh water in the bucket there, and not much dust on that candle stump. So there has been a servant keeping house here. But for some reason, they left the place unattended some days ago."

"When we were married, perhaps?"

He turned to her at once, his face lightening. "Of course. All the servants would have been needed at the hall last week."

"So no one needs to be whipped for this."

He grinned. "My lady, if it is your pleasure they should not be whipped for desertion, then they shall escape punishment."

"Thank you, my lord."

He put a finger under her chin, raising it. "So soft-hearted. You would not last two minutes on a battlefield."

"And I am grateful not to be tested in that way," she replied, rather more sharply than she had intended. Seeing his raised brows, she stumbled over her words, trying to explain herself. "A…a woman's strengths are fortitude and patience. Not brute force. I was born to bear children, and that pain will be enough for me when it comes."

His gaze steadied on her face, oddly intent. "Born to bear children?"

"Aye, my lord."

"But on our wedding night…" He hesitated, then took a step forward. Their bodies were suddenly very close, almost touching. "I thought you did not welcome my attentions."

"I did not say that, my lord." Eloise could hardly breathe. She found herself whispering, her voice too loud in the vast empty kitchens. "I was scared, that first night. I did not mean to push you away. You took me off guard."

His gaze lowered to her mouth, searing her with its heat. "I did not 'take you' at all," he muttered hoarsely.

"My lord…"

Wolf grabbed her by the shoulders and bent his head, kissing her so fiercely she felt her head spin. Then she realized why. He had lifted her in his arms and was carrying her out of the kitchen quarters.

"Where are we going?"

He did not reply, but she saw his eyes glitter in the darkness and was afraid.

The lodge was quiet and unlit, all the windows shuttered. He made his way unerringly through the darkened hall, then up a narrow staircase and along the upper landing. The air smelled cold and musty upstairs. It was like being inside a tomb, she thought, and was glad of his arms about her.

All the doors stood shut in the darkness. Wolf kicked one open, breathing heavily, and entered the room.

Eloise blinked. Sunlight was streaming through a gap in the broken shutters. There was an old curtained bed with ornate posts, pushed against the wall, the mattress long since stripped of its covers. He put her carefully on her feet, then turned to a wooden chest in the corner. After throwing open the lid, he withdrew a rich red-and-green silken coverlet from the chest and lay it across the bed to cover the bare mattress.

"There," he muttered, "now it is a bed fit for my bride. And no one for miles around to hear our pleasure."

She stared, her face suddenly hot as she realized what Wolf intended to do. Thoughts and questions raced through her head, leaving her in confusion.

Had he known the lodge would be empty? Is that why he had

allowed Hugh to ride back to the hall with Susannah unaccompanied? Because he had intended this seduction all along?

What a fool she had been. And yet she had wanted this too. He
was her husband, after all. The marriage had to be consummated, or
she could not bear him an heir. It was her duty, and she had accepted
it when she accepted his offer of marriage. But not like this: to lie
together for the first time in a strange place, no one within earshot,
only the two of them alone in this dusty hunting lodge. It was not
what she had envisaged for her first experience of love.

"Did you plan this?" she asked, her voice shaking.

"Does it matter?"

The blood was beating so loudly in her head she could not hear
herself think.

"I don't know."

Wolf stripped off his gloves, then held out his hand to her. She
hesitated, then forced herself to take it. The moment could not be
put off forever. And he was right; at least here they could be private.

He raised her palm to his mouth and kissed the warm skin. "My
lady," he muttered. "I promise I shall not hurt you."

"Of course you will. I am a maid."

"Then I shall make amends for your hurt." He pushed back her
sleeve, kissing the pale skin on her wrist where a pulse beat wildly. "I
will teach you the exquisite pleasure of love, a pleasure you cannot
possibly guess at now, being still a virgin. But only on one condition."

She stared, unsure what to expect. "Condition?"

"Yes, on one simple condition," he repeated, his voice almost as
unsteady as her own. He bent his head again, kissing her forearm. "I
want you to beg me to make love to you."

"You want me to beg?"

"For love, yes."

She gasped as his mouth found the tender spot in the crook of
her arm, kissing it gently.

"I…I cannot."

"Why not? Are you too proud to beg?" He gazed at her, a challenging look in his eyes, then bent his head again. This time his tongue traced a confident line down her throat toward her cleavage. "There can be no pride between us now we are man and wife. This is the natural state of things. You panting for my cock; me pumping my seed into you."

His words shocked and thrilled her with their crudity. His hands tugged determinedly on her bodice, dragging it lower until her breasts were free, her nipples already engorged with excitement.

He did not touch her breasts, but stared down at them through narrowed eyes. "Do what comes naturally, Eloise. Beg me to make love to you."

To make love to her? Did her husband even know the meaning of the word love?

He meant lust, she told herself dizzily, struggling to hold on to what was real here. What he meant was carnal longing, the kind of violent physical desire that had brought King Henry to the edge of madness when he met Anne Boleyn and could not bed her until she was his queen. And yet, the line between love and desire was already blurring in her mind as Wolf's lewd words aroused her, deafening her to reason. His hands played skillfully with her body, reminding her how much she needed this, how deeply she was in his power.

She shook her head rebelliously, though her cheeks grew hot at the sound of him whispering her name. Wolf had called her not "my lady," nor "my bride," but "Eloise." She thought of running away, but knew she would not get far. Besides, if he did not make love to her soon, she would die of frustration. Her body knew that, even if her mind would not admit it.

She wanted him. She needed him. But it would mean nothing if he did not love her. If all this was to him was a means to an end.

"You don't mean love," she finally managed.

He gave a harsh laugh. "Maybe I don't. But I thought you would prefer the word."

"I prefer the truth."

"Very well then, my fearless lady, you shall have it. There will be no more sweet lies between us, no more courtly pretense. Only the naked, unadulterated truth…"

Wolf gathered her in his arms and kissed her face, then her bare throat, then the fragile skin above her breasts. His kisses were light and hot, driving her out of her mind. He teased her, stroking a finger slowly round the curve of her breast, making her wait for his attention.

"No," she moaned, and her nipples stiffened in the cool air, aching for the touch of his lips.

"Yes," he countered, and slipped a firm hand round the nape of her neck, not to caress his bride but to hold her still so she could not escape.

"Please, Wolf, not like this."

"Eloise, you want this consummation as much as I do," he said thickly, lowering his head to her breast. "And this day I intend to make you admit it. Now beg me to fuck you."

Nine

ELOISE STOOD VERY STILL and tried not to breathe too deeply, for his powerful body, pressed close to her own, and its leathery, masculine scent were driving her senses wild. Yet there was no escape from the sensual desire that had her locked in its grip, and Wolf knew it.

His mouth closed about her breast, sucking on her nipple. A sharp, hot surge of lust crashed from her breasts to her loins, charging her with a deep, shuddering excitement. She clutched at his shoulders, and had to repress a sudden violent desire to arch her back and mew like a cat in season.

His throaty laughter cut her to the core. "That's better," he murmured, raising his head to survey her face. "Now you look more like a woman eager to lose her virginity."

No doubt she looked half-demented, she thought, willing her flushed cheeks to cool down and her breathing to settle.

Wolf had her just where he wanted her. Why did he not simply take her and have done with it? She did not understand why he had to draw this out for his own cruel amusement, forcing her to beg for his…

She forced herself to think the word *cock*, though it made her tremble and everything inside her begin to melt. And then she could not stop thinking it, over and over, reveling in the delicious lewdness of such a word.

His cock.

Suddenly she felt it press against her, almost as though he had overheard her wicked and forbidden thought. His cock, stiff in its leather codpiece, nudged her belly, thrusting forward as though in search of her…cunt.

Eloise gasped as his hands lifted her gown, trying to release her skirt from her bodice. He spun her, his fingers busy with her laces, then suddenly he was dragging her skirts down, past her hips, and she was standing almost nude in a puddle of material.

Facing away from him, she stood dazed into silence by his forcefulness, staring at the sunlight slatting thinly through the shutter. Then his hands dropped to her bare hips, demonstrating his possession.

She was his bride, and he would do whatever he wished with her.

With a growl, Wolf jerked her back against his body. Her buttocks seemed to mold to his groin. Then he rocked her slightly forward, stroking over her smooth, naked curves, first exploring her rear and then, slipping lower, the warm secret place between her thighs.

"Eloise," he groaned, and the sound was pure torment. "I've waited patiently for you to show some interest, to demonstrate your willingness. But I can't wait any longer. Your body is so beautiful, and your innocence so alluring. I would have to be a saint to keep my hands off you any longer, and heaven help me, I've always been more sinner than saint."

His hands slipped round to cup her breasts, then he kissed her spine, his breath warm on her bare flesh. "If you won't beg me of your own accord, I'll just have to be a little more persuasive…"

She did not know at first what he meant. Then he scooped her up in his arms and laid her gently on the bed. The silk coverlet felt cool against her nakedness and she caught her breath, wriggling backward as her husband began to disrobe.

He threw aside his black riding jacket, then tore off his loose white undershirt to reveal his chest, just as magnificent as she remembered.

He was like a wild animal, she thought, her gaze hooked on his body, a body honed by years of hard campaigning and riding, no spare flesh on him anywhere. Even the old pale scars on his hip from where his leg had been ruined seemed somehow right to her, an intrinsic part of this man she had married, his limping gait making him more attractive to her.

Finally he dragged at his hose, and she gave a little whimper of desire to see his cock spring out, fully erect, veins straining. She had little experience to go on, but his penis seemed so thick and long she was suddenly afraid that she could never accommodate such a monster inside her.

Wolf smiled, kicking aside the last of his clothes, and climbed onto the bed. The mattress dipped slightly under his weight, the ropes beneath creaking. He crawled across to her body with the slow stealthy movements of a predator.

"Frightened again, my reluctant bride?" he whispered, his blue eyes fixed intently on her face. "Or do you like what you see?"

Her mouth was dry. She could not seem to stop staring at her husband. It was as though she had never seen him before. Though certainly this was the first time she had seen certain parts, she thought wildly. Her gaze flickered over his broad shoulders, the muscular expanse of his chest, then down his flat belly to the triangle of coarse dark hair below, his penis stiff and swollen, so erect that it seemed to brush the underside of his belly.

"I like what I see," he commented, stroking a finger across her lips.

She waited, holding her breath.

His finger trailed down her chin, then her throat, stroking her skin gently until it reached her chest. "You can forget what I said about your breasts. You are perfect, my lovely virgin bride. Now all our marriage needs is for you to see what would make this more perfect..."

Wolf dipped his head and licked at her nipple, the touch of his tongue so delicate it felt like a wet paintbrush across her skin. Her flesh stiffened, tingling under his clever tongue. He stroked and squeezed each breast into a firm peak, pushing them softly together, then lapping from one nipple to the other, his eyes closed, his face utterly absorbed.

She moaned and clutched at the silk coverlet, hands bunching into fists at the tiny hot darts of pleasure shooting through her. He circled one nipple with his tongue, then drew it forcefully into his mouth, sucking hard as though he would draw milk. Her back arched and she cried out wordlessly, rubbing herself against him with sudden wanton abandon.

She closed her eyes too. Her head was in a daze. She could barely remember where they were, or how they had got there. She did not know what time of day it was. All that mattered was the way he was touching her, kissing her, the delicious slide of his tongue across her nipple.

"Oh," she moaned, and could not help herself.

Instinctively, she stretched out to his body, and found herself touching him, her hands drawn first to the broad, raw sweep of his shoulders, then to his pitch-black head, her fingers bunching and clenching in his thick hair, dragging him closer.

Wolf did not flinch from her touch but made a reassuring sound in his throat, his mouth still working at her breast. So she dared to stroke him in silence, exploring his body, trailing her fingertips down the silken steel of his spine. The feel of bare skin was almost too much, knowing that where her fingers stopped at the base of his spine, too hesitant to move on, his body continued, curving smoothly into strong buttocks and thighs.

He raised his head when she paused, his eyes sharp glittering blue. "Now don't stop there," he murmured teasingly, his voice a little breathless. "I was enjoying your hands on my body. Go lower."

The air rushed into her chest, and for a moment she stared into his mocking gaze and could not speak.

Then, haltingly, she managed, "I do not know how…"

"You were not so shy in the cave," he reminded her softly.

Her cheeks burned at the memory of her wild and wanton behavior that day. She had been like a creature possessed in that cave, driven half-mad by his forceful lovemaking and the dark narrow space into which he had taken her. Now though, he was looking straight into her face, and there was no escape from those mocking eyes.

"I have forgotten."

"Then let me remind you." He rolled to one side, took one of her hands, then placed it, firmly and deliberately, on his swollen erection. "There, you see? Nothing to be afraid of."

A spark of pride lit her soul at this remark. Her hand still on his cock, she raised her chin, looking directly back at him. "I am not afraid!"

"That's excellent," he told her, still smiling, and leaned back slightly, looking down at her hand. "Then you will not mind if I show you this little trick."

He moved her fingers apart until she was gripping his girth like a quarterstaff, then taught her how to slide her hand up and down. "Easy," he murmured, watching her closely as she tried a few first tentative strokes. "Don't grip so hard. Yes, that's good. Very good."

It was like being in a dream. She kept her gaze on his cock, not his face, and let her fingers squeeze and relax as they moved up and down his shaft. The head of his cock seemed to grow as she worked, its color a dusky red, fat as a field mushroom. It glistened with fluid, just a few drops beading at the top, and she found herself quite naturally wiping it away with her thumb, then using the moisture to keep each stroke smooth and slick.

"Sweet Jesu," he gasped after a few moments of this slow and steady work. His hand caught hers, unpinning her fingers from his swollen shaft. "Enough, enough. I shall spend my pleasure before I am even inside you."

Inside her?

Her face flushed with heat at the thought of all that thick, hard strength inside her, and by his smile she guessed he knew what she was thinking.

"Not yet," Wolf told her softly. "You still have to beg for it, my lady. Or had you forgotten my terms?"

Her blush became one of humiliation. She had thought— or rather, hoped—that her husband was not serious when he claimed she would have to beg for his attentions. But it seemed Lord Wolf was still intent on taking his revenge. Or training his new bride to welcome him into her body, as he no doubt saw this little game.

Well, she would not beg him to take her. He could go whistle for his pleasure.

But it seemed he had other ideas than whistling. Lewdly, his hands lifted her knees up and apart, spreading her bare thighs open. Then, before she even had time to guess at his purpose, he came to his knees before her and lowered his head between her legs.

She stared down at him numbly; a shocked amazement swept through her that any nobleman should wish to kiss a woman in such an intimate place. Then his tongue began to work firmly at that little nub of flesh between her legs, playing it with such great skill and daring her whole body hummed with a fierce, throbbing excitement she could not contain.

Compulsively, her hand came down, pulling his head closer. "Wolf," she moaned, then felt an old familiar tugging in her belly, a tingling between her legs, and knew that the secret pleasure she had never admitted to anyone would soon possess her body.

Her body on fire, she turned her head away, hoping to muffle her cries in the coverlet.

Kneeling up between her legs, Wolf strummed her moist flesh with long fingers, watching as her body twisted helplessly to avoid the pleasure. "Don't struggle against it," he urged her huskily, stroking his thumb back and forth across her quivering flesh. "Let the sweetness take you where it will. There is no shame in this, Eloise. A woman may experience joy in love as much as any man. And the taste is good. Better than any sweetmeat."

Eloise peered at him from behind shaking fingers, and saw how swollen he had grown, how his chest was darkly flushed. It could not be long now until…

His mouth found her again, lapping fiercely at her flesh. Could he truly take pleasure in such an act? Just the thought of it shocked her.

Suddenly her legs jerked and she gave a wild, high-pitched cry, pleasure bursting uncontrollably between her thighs. Moisture came flooding out, unexpectedly, and she moaned, unable to meet his gaze. There is no shame in this, he had said. Yet she did feel ashamed, and fearful too that he knew her weakness, that she had shown Wolf just how vulnerable she could be to him.

Her husband shifted between her thighs, staring down at her. His penis was so thickly swollen with desire she feared it would hurt to be impaled on such a shaft.

"Beg me to take you," he commanded her, his words slurred with passion. His gaze was hungry, like that of a starving man, and she could see the veins in his neck standing out, astrain with fire. "It will only hurt for a moment. Beg for my cock."

Eloise wanted more than anything else in the world to beg for it, to feel him push his organ deep between her thighs, to let him take her maidenhead and teach her about love. Yet the words of surrender would not seem to come out.

She stared up at him, her lower lip trembling, the pleas stifled just beyond her tongue, caught in her throat.

"Eloise, for the love of God," he groaned, his eyes a misty, tormented blue. "You can't make me wait. Not after this, not now. I have to take you. Don't you see, I have no choice? Don't make me take you by force. I am your husband."

"Wolf…"

"Yes?"

His eyes were urging her to say it. Her body wanted her to say it. But her pride clung on, refusing to let him win. Why should a virgin bride need to beg for her husband's love? It was unjust. It was cruel and unnecessary. He wanted to humiliate her, to show her how low a wife was in his esteem. She licked dry lips, meaning to reject him again, and saw his gaze fix on the tiny movement, his throat swallowing convulsively.

He was afraid too, she suddenly realized. Afraid that she would reject him. And that if she refused his offer, after he had tried so hard to make this work between them, he would never feel able to put himself in this position again. That this was it. The final time of asking.

"Take me, my lord," she whispered. "Make love to me."

Something flickered in his eyes at her barely audible words. Not triumph, as she had half-expected. But relief, perhaps, that she had not forced him to annul their marriage, admitting to everyone they knew that it had been unconsummated.

"Again," he replied hoarsely.

She glared. "You need me to repeat it?"

"Again," he insisted, his voice stronger now. His blue gaze warred with hers, suddenly confident. "I want to hear you say it, Eloise. Beg me."

"I…" She still could not bring herself to obey him.

He smiled, leaning over her, and placed the head of his organ against her damp cleft. And she was on fire again, her hips rising instinctively to accommodate him, her body trembling with an age-old female need to be filled.

"Fuck me, Wolf," she whispered, and meant it. "Shove your cock inside me. Make me yours."

With a groan of excitement, he pushed forward, and there it was. Inside her at last. Just the swollen head, it seemed, but broad enough to make her gasp. The skin there began to stretch as it slipped another half an inch deeper, but she was surprised to find it was not painful.

Wolf nudged her thighs wider apart, settling himself between her legs, taking his weight on his elbows. He stared down at her, a sudden intense need on his face that was echoed deep in her belly.

"Yes," he managed, and she saw perspiration on his forehead.

He was controlling himself, she realized, trying not to frighten her with the strength of his desire. Then his hips jerked, and she cried out, suddenly uncomfortable.

He closed his eyes, whispering, "Only a moment's pain, remember."

Eloise bit her lip as he thrust fully inside, not wanting to show him how much it hurt. But her hands had stilled on his shoulders, her body lying stiff beneath him, and she knew from the angry flash in his eyes that he was not fooled.

He withdrew, and she saw a tiny red stain on the green threads in the coverlet.

Her blood.

She stared at it, feeling a little faint and unreal. She was no longer a maid.

He put his mouth down there again. She cried out then in earnest, her whole body taken beyond what it could bear. But his lips did not stop caressing her, his tongue slotting smoothly in and out of the narrow opening where his other, thicker organ had just entered, and soon she felt her belly clench.

"Oh God!"

"Yes," he told her, his voice muffled against her flesh. "Come for me, Eloise."

She did not need his permission, she thought fiercely; she was already on the edge.

Seconds later, her body exploded in a fit of passion; the small dusty chamber turned black, the walls seeming to shake around them. She cried out strangled words. She did not know what they were, but they made Wolf laugh.

Her rough soldierly husband crawled over her, his body fitting perfectly against hers as though they had been made for each other, their naked limbs tangling together quite naturally. He entered her again, this time thrusting deep and with determination, no longer holding back.

This time there was no pain at his entry, but a wonderful fullness. Her tender flesh ached and contracted about his shaft, squeezing him as her pleasure continued to throb inside. His thrusts pleased and tormented her in equal fashion, filling and emptying her, his dark head thrown back, his own body driving hard toward satisfaction.

Suddenly his face contorted, and he thrust deep, groaning out her name. "Eloise!"

Afterward, she felt the warm, slow seep of his seed escaping but could not seem to move to prevent it. They lay together in a quiet and heavy-limbed contentment, their naked bodies cooling on top of the silk coverlet, both disinclined to speak. Then Eloise heard his breathing slow and deepen, and guessed that Wolf had fallen asleep.

So now it is done. I am his wife indeed, she thought, and eventually allowed herself to fall asleep in his arms.

———

The sound of footsteps brought Wolf instantly awake. He glanced at Eloise, lying naked and asleep beside him on the bed, and knew he must forestall whoever had come searching for them.

Three strides took him across to the door; he grabbed up his shirt and dagger belt along the way. He dragged the shirt over his head, palmed the dagger, then jerked open the door.

"Who's there?" he asked curtly.

A man turned at the sound of his voice, questing further along the dark corridor. His cap came off when he saw who it was, and he came back, bowing. "My lord," he stammered. "Forgive me, my lord. I am Yates, winter steward here, but was called to the big house for your nuptials, my lord."

"So what brought you back in such a hurry?"

"Your lady's sister came back from her ride today with Master Beaufort, saying you were visiting here. Master Spears gave me a pony and sent me back at once, to attend to your lordship's needs." Yates hesitated, glancing uncertainly at Wolf's bare legs and feet. "Forgive me that I was not here to welcome you, my lord. Can I fetch you anything?"

"You came alone?"

"My wife and children follow in the cart, my lord, with a raised veal pie and a brace of pheasants."

Wolf smiled. "For my supper?"

"Aye, my lord."

"Do you keep wine here, Yates?"

The steward nodded.

"Then Lady Wolf and I will be glad to dine here tonight. Set out wine, and the meal, and call us when it is ready. While we are dining, your wife can make this chamber more habitable. We need fresh bed linen for the night, and a fire."

Yates bowed his head, clearly relieved not to be chastised for having abandoned his post. "At once, my lord."

Wolf hesitated, then added lightly, "There is no hurry, Yates. My lady sleeps."

The man smiled then, shyly. "Aye, my lord. May I wish you both very happy."

"Thank you," Wolf replied with an answering grin, then closed the door and trod softly back to the bed.

His bride lay on her side, curled up asleep, the smooth curve of her buttocks like alabaster. He stood a moment, watching her in silence. He had intended to seduce her today, riding out here when he knew the old lodge was likely to be unattended, sending her sister back with Hugh. Yet she had surprised him with her passionate response.

He had anticipated some kind of struggle, perhaps another cold rejection of the kind he had faced on their wedding night. But his instinct that his wife did not find him unattractive had been proved correct. As soon as she was naked in his arms, he had seen the true Eloise, the woman behind the shy bride. She had not been afraid to join him in carnal pleasure, nor to yield up her maidenhead, begging him to make love to her—even against her pride, he had seen that.

And her passionate cries had fired his own pleasure, bringing him too swiftly to his peak.

Wolf had meant to go slowly the first time, to show his bride how such joys could be extended almost indefinitely. But then Eloise had surrendered so fiercely, not lying passively beneath him as he had expected but kissing him back so hard his lip still stung, then tearing at him like a mountain lioness when she climaxed. And yet she had been a virgin, he knew that absolutely.

So he had given in to the heat of the moment and taken his relief. Though what man could have remained unmoved by such a powerful and unexpected response?

He could still feel the liquid pleasure coursing through his body, the tingling aftershocks of his own peak, and felt himself tighten again as he studied her naked sleeping form. He had made love to her, and yet his desire was still as strong as ever. That too was unexpected. He had thought his desire would easily be slaked by the act of possession. Instead, he was growing hard again.

"What have you done to me?" he whispered, then fell silent as she stirred, stretching gently on the bed.

Her eyes opened, focusing on his face. "My lord?"

"My lady?"

Eloise gazed at his white shirt, clearly taken aback to see him out of bed and half-dressed, then her eyes widened at the sight of his dagger. She sat up at once, no longer sleepy. "What is it? Some kind of trouble?" She looked about for her abandoned gown. "I have a knife on my belt."

He loved her natural courage, not shrinking from danger but prepared to join him if she must.

"Leave your dagger where it is, my braveheart," Wolf told her. "There is no danger to us in this place. I heard a creaking just now, out on the landing. But it was only a servant, come to bring us dinner."

Eloise stared. "How did they know to…?"

"Your sister."

"Of course, I should have known." His bride frowned at his shirt again, then glanced down covertly at his bare legs, just as the steward had done. Only it seemed a more disconcerting look from her. "Are you not cold?"

"A little," he admitted, then climbed onto the bed beside her, ignoring the creaking of the mattress supports. "But it will only take a moment to warm me."

She caught his meaning at once, and he was pleased to see she did not draw away. So he had not done very badly before they fell asleep together.

"You slept well?" he asked, stroking the hair back from her forehead.

"Very."

"The sweetest sleep always comes after love."

"Is that what it was?" Her voice was sharp. "Love, my lord?"

His eyes met hers drily. So his beautiful bride still had claws, despite the pleasure he had given her.

"You know a better word for it?"

"You need an heir," she reminded him, not yielding an inch. "You told me so yourself. I am no fool, my lord. I thought we had agreed to be honest with each other."

He remembered their conversation. But only vaguely. That had been before they fucked. He had needed so desperately to be inside her, he would have agreed to anything at that moment. Still, there could be no harm in a marriage where honesty and integrity were the watchwords.

Indeed, an honest union was what he preferred. Only he had some doubts that a woman could ever prefer truth to courtesy.

He took her hand, turning it to kiss her palm. "Of course," he murmured. "And so we shall be. Not love, then. But desire. Naked, honest desire."

"For an heir."

"For you, Eloise." Again, he lifted his gaze to hers. Damn her. Why did she have to question everything? He took a deep breath; told himself to be patient. It was only natural that a new bride should want to understand her husband's motives, to judge her place in his life. "I am a free man, nobody's puppet. I could have married any pretty maid at court, or any woman in the whole of England who would have me. I chose you, Eloise, because I desired you."

"But how is that possible? You had barely seen me before you asked for my father's consent," she pointed out.

Reluctantly, Wolf recalled his earliest glimpse of her as a girl, wild-eyed and unkempt, her clogs muddied, more like a farmer's lad than the daughter of a gentleman. He had known then, in some part of himself, that she would be his in the future. That the girl with the dirty face was part of his destiny.

The stars must have clashed in the heavens that day, linking them inextricably together just as their bodies had entwined on this bed. Perhaps that was why Margerie had left him for another man, because she had not been meant for him. Perhaps that was why he had found his first union with Eloise so very pleasurable, to the point where he could no longer control himself. Because it had felt like a fated moment.

"I had seen enough to know we would suit," he said shortly, not wishing to go into further detail.

Her eyebrows were raised. Her eyes were cold. She did not believe him.

He let the matter drop. There was no way to explain his instinctive response to her all those years ago, not without sounding like a fool. And right now, he had other things on his mind than a stumbling conversation about long-past events.

"You're cold," he commented, looking down at her erect nipples.

She drew the coverlet up to hide herself. "Are we going to stay the night? Without my maid?"

"You won't need a maid tonight."

"But my gown…"

He bent his head and kissed the blue veins on her wrist. Her pulse beat frantically under his lips, her body suddenly tensed as though poised to run away.

"What makes you think you will be wearing that gown again?"

Her eyes sparked mischievously. "You expect me to sit down to supper unclothed, then? In front of your manservant?"

Wolf's eyes narrowed on her face. He had not thought as far as sitting down to supper when planning this little excursion. But then he had expected to have his bride all to himself in this empty, lonesome place. He had certainly not anticipated that a servant would appear, offering them wine and victuals.

"There is a robe in the chest that you could use. And furred slippers. You need not go naked."

"And in the morning?"

"Tomorrow, I shall be your maid and dress you myself."

"You, my lord?"

Her amazed expression and tone of disbelief needled him, and he retaliated without thinking. "Yes, and why not? It will not be the first time I have helped a lady back into her clothes."

That had been the wrong thing to say at such a moment.

Color flared in Eloise's cheeks, and she swung her bare legs to the floor. There was cool disdain in her voice, and he could have kicked himself when he heard it, for his bride had begun to thaw and now he was back where he started.

"I do not doubt it, my lord. If you would be so good as to grant me a few moments' privacy though…" She hesitated, glancing angrily about the chamber. "Where…?"

He rose smoothly and pointed out the discreet wooden screen behind the bed.

"Forgive me, my lady." He stooped, bundling up the rest of his clothing in his arms. With one careless remark, he had ruined the mood for further lovemaking. "I had better see how Yates is progressing with our supper. His wife has accompanied him, I believe. Perhaps I should send her up with a jug of hot water for your hands and face."

"Thank you," she said awkwardly, not looking at him.

Wolf bowed ironically and withdrew, cursing himself all the way downstairs for an idiot.

Ten

ELOISE STOOD BY THE window, her chest tight. It was ridiculous, but she felt trapped in the old hunting lodge, away from her sister and her old nurse. She had thrown back the wooden shutters to breathe in the evening air, lightly scented with spring blossom, but even that freedom could not allay her frantic state of mind. All she could think was that she had betrayed herself with Wolf today.

Looking down into the yard below, she saw the serving man, Yates, fetching in an armful of logs for the hearth. As he puffed past below, muttering under his breath, she wondered what the steward had thought, finding his master and new mistress in bed like that. But no doubt he thought them in love like any other newly married couple, riding out here to be alone, unable to get enough of each other's bodies.

She turned away from the window, suddenly chilled, reaching for the heavy robe that Mistress Yates had laid out on the bed for her. What must Wolf think now? That he could do what he pleased with her, and she would always surrender, bend herself to his will. He must know what she had tried to hide, that she desired him as much—perhaps even more—than he desired her.

Now, of course, his lust would be slaked. He had taken her, the deed was done. Though he would continue to lie with her until she was with child, she had no illusions about that.

She hung the robe about her shoulders and paced the candlelit chamber, wishing there was a mirror or glass she could use to check her reflection. But the lodge had stood empty so long everything but the most basic items had been put away.

Mistress Yates, a cheerful woman with straggling gray hair, had come upstairs to attend her, bearing cloths and a large pan of steaming hot water. Once Eloise had finished bathing herself behind the screen, the steward's wife helped her into her gown, smiling at the small marks on her arms and shoulders where Wolf had gripped her in his passion.

"His lordship be a fine gentleman," Mistress Yates ventured shyly, then found a comb from somewhere and tidied Eloise's hair. "May I wish you both well, my lady."

"I thank you," Eloise murmured. She stood still under the woman's ministrations, thinking. Then she asked. "Have you always served at Wolf Hall?"

"I was born there, my lady. My mother and father were in service to Lord Wolf's father, the old lord, and my grandfather before that." She laughed. "It's in our blood to serve the Wolfs, my mother used to say."

"So you must have known Lord Wolf all his life?"

"Oh yes, indeed. I remember his lordship as a boy. Big strong lad, he was. Take on anyone in a fight, even twice his size. Not very talkative, mind." Mistress Yates clucked her tongue sadly. "And who can blame him for not wanting to prattle on? Not after his mother died so young, poor pet."

Eloise had listened to the older woman talk of Wolf as a boy, and how he had first gone away to war when he was barely more than a child. It was hard to imagine Wolf in his first battle, but she could dimly remember him as a boy. Mistress Yates was right, of course. He had never spoken much, a blunt-mannered soldier in the making. And though Wolf conversed with ease now, she had the impression that he very deliberately never said anything too revealing. But what did he have to conceal?

Standing alone in the chamber now, she heard footsteps on the stairs and shivered.

Wolf.

He knocked lightly at the door, then pushed it open. They stared at each other in silence for a moment, Wolf's eyes intent on her face, Eloise unable to avoid noticing how he had washed and combed back his black hair, and that his boots had been cleaned.

"My lady?" He held out his arm, his voice deep. "May I escort you down to the supper table?"

She was astonished at the physical thrill that ran through her when her hand, ungloved, touched his arm. She felt his body heat through the sleeve of his tight black jacket, and her pulse jumped violently. Her response was a shock, wholly unexpected, for Eloise had always considered herself steadfast and not easily persuaded to love. She had known Simon for months before she found him agreeable to look upon, and almost a year before she had permitted him to kiss her. Now this…

She looked down at the floor, waiting for her pulse to steady. She despised herself for such weakness. One afternoon in bed with him, that was all it had taken to reduce her to this raw mass of emotions.

How had she fallen under his spell so quickly?

"Are you unwell?" he inquired, leading her down the dimly lit stairs. "You look pale."

"A little tired, my lord. That is all."

In truth, her body ached from the unaccustomed intimacies of their afternoon together. She felt oddly weak, and there was a moistness about the apex of her thighs which reminded her at every step of his invasion.

His possession of her had been determined. Violent, even. Yet she had responded like a wild animal with her mate, urging Wolf on as though she had come into season at his touch, eager for seduction.

"Here," he murmured at the foot of the stairs, and gestured her through a narrow doorway.

Supper had been laid out for them in a cozy, candlelit chamber off the main hallway. A good fire was burning in the stone hearth. Wolf pulled out the high-backed chair and she sat down, glancing uncertainly at the steward, Yates, who was pouring the wine into two ornate wine cups, their stems decorated with tiny carvings of flowers and bees. Eloise was still embarrassed that Wolf's servant had discovered them in bed together that afternoon. But the man kept his gaze discreetly lowered while serving her, and gave nothing away in his expression.

Wolf tasted the wine, then nodded to the man to leave. "That will be all for now, Yates."

"Aye, my lord."

When the door had closed behind the steward, Wolf looked at her over the rim of his wine cup. There was a certain hard amusement in his expression.

"You seem on edge. Does the supper displease you? It is not as elaborate a meal as we might have enjoyed at the hall, but I did not think you would mind." His gaze examined her slender figure thoughtfully. "You eat so little when we are at table."

"Not at all, it looks very good," she demurred, glancing about the array of dishes. Indeed, the smell of the food was unusually mouthwatering; it seemed that lovemaking had increased her appetite tenfold. "It merely feels a little odd to be here alone. Susannah will be alone at the hall tonight. She must be concerned by my absence."

"I doubt it," he said coolly, rising to carve a few slices of pheasant breast for her. "Hugh Beaufort is there to keep your sister company, remember."

"They seem very close."

He looked at her sharply. "You disapprove? Master Beaufort may not be noble, nor is he yet a wealthy man. But he has excellent prospects. He is a good friend of mine, besides enjoying the king's special favor. In such troubled times as these, that is worth a knighthood."

"She is still very young."

"But of age."

"And in my care while she is at Wolf Hall," she muttered. He served her with the pheasant breast, then offered her a bowl of spiced beans and vegetables, from which she took only a very little. He frowned down at her frugal helping, then spooned more beans onto her trencher. Before she could refuse it, he also placed a thick slice of veal pie on the side, then returned to his seat again at the end of the table.

"I am master at Wolf Hall," he reminded her, helping himself to the veal pie. "So your sister is in my care while under my roof, not yours. And I have no qualms about allowing her...friendship with Beaufort to continue. She is young, it is true. But Hugh has been about the world. He grew up at court and knows better than to tamper with a gentle-born maid. The connection will be good for her. It is certainly not something you need concern yourself over, my lady."

"You think Master Beaufort intends marriage, then?"

"I have not the slightest idea what he intends with your sister. But I know this. He will not risk his good standing with the king by seducing the daughter of a gentleman, however elderly or obscure. Such misdemeanors are punishable by whipping and exile. Even death, in some instances."

She did not wish to provoke another argument, but she had felt the impact of Hugh's charming smile. He would be quite a lure for her sister, whether he meant to be or not.

Wolf had noticed that she was only pushing her food about with her little dagger, not lifting any of it to her lips.

"Eat," he told her sternly, and for a long moment his gaze clashed violently with hers. She felt weak under that cold, blade-like glare, her pulse drumming in her ears, but she refused to surrender by lowering her gaze. His tone dripped irony as he added, "Or you will hurt Mistress Yates's feelings."

"Well, we can't have that," she managed.

She took a cautious pinch of salt from the shallow well in her trencher, seasoned her food, then rolled back her lace-trimmed sleeves to prevent them being soiled. She cut into the jellied veal pie first, which smelled gorgeous, and took a small bite. It was so delicious, the pastry melting in her mouth, that she cut a larger slice at once. This she devoured hungrily, hoping he would not think her uncouth. It was true that she did not often eat heartily at table, but as soon as she began to taste the food Mistress Yates had prepared for them, her appetite became suddenly insatiable. She even managed to find room for some of the spiced beans and pheasant too.

Wolf ate too, watching her in silence for a while. Then he put down his knife. "Did I hurt you earlier?"

She looked up, surprised by the suppressed violence in his tone, and saw his gaze narrowed on her arm. Glancing down, Eloise found some mild blue bruising where his hand had encircled her wrist earlier, pinning her to the bed.

"It's nothing."

His voice hardened. "It doesn't look like nothing to me. It looks like I manhandled you."

She shrugged, and rather recklessly drained her wine cup. His gaze lifted to her face, then he rose silently and poured more wine for her. Before returning to his seat, he brushed his fingers across her cheek. It was the tiniest of caresses, barely perceptible, and yet her cheek flared with heat afterward as though his fingertips had burned her.

"Forgive me."

She stared at him, not quite sure if he had spoken, the words had been so softly spoken. Barely a breath of sound, in fact.

Had those words been directed at her? Yet who else, if not? Wolf was looking down at the greasy pheasant carcass he had been picking over, but glanced up again cautiously when she said nothing. There was a slight tinge of color to his face too, as though he had been burned by the same fire that had touched her. Then he sat up, tossed one of the pheasant bones into the fire, and watched as the flames licked greedily at its length.

"Wolf?"

His jaw clenched hard and he dragged his stare reluctantly from the flickering fire to her face. "You see, I had been waiting so long to bed you," he began to explain, not quite meeting her gaze, "I couldn't hold back as I intended. It was my intention to take you gently the first time, but... Your response was so powerful... It felt right to..." He stopped, looking down at the table again, his expression shuttered. "I trust I didn't hurt you too badly."

She did not know what to say, but stared dumbly.

"Nor afterward, when I spoke of..." He paused. "It was stupid of me to mention other women at such a time. Forgive me."

It was not what she had thought, she realized, shocked and unable to reply. She had thought him cruel at first, then indifferent, then triumphing in his power over her when he saw how easily she responded to his touch. But it was no such matter. He did not love her, she knew that for certain. There had been no tenderness in his voice when he spoke to her just now, nor in his hands today when he forced her to surrender. But he was neither cruel nor indifferent to her, and if this was triumph, it was an odd kind of victory when the winner could not raise his eyes to hers.

For the first time it struck her that he might have bedded many women, but he had never been married before, and perhaps knew as little as she did about the wedded state. What she had mistaken for cruel dominance might have been merely a clumsy attempt on Wolf's part to make her respect his authority.

Or was she fooling herself, imagining her new husband a saint in disguise when he was in truth—just as he had told her—a sinner?

Yet perhaps Wolf was a sinner with a conscience: a sinner who would take whatever he wanted, in precisely the way he wanted it, then ask her to forgive him afterward? She did not know which version of this man was worse, but felt her desire for him grow as she tried to understand him and failed.

She stammered something incomprehensible, and saw him rise and approach her; he looked down at her with hooded eyes. What was he thinking?

"Come," he said, and held out his hand.

Eloise rose unthinkingly at his command, leaving her meal unfinished, uncertain what was to follow but not scared. There was a high-backed wooden settle by the fire, old and cracked, but broad-seated enough to be comfortable. He sat her there and stood above her, his face expressionless.

"It should have been better," he told her, his gaze dropping to the swell of her breasts in the tight gown. "I will make it better next time."

His fingers played with her wavy golden hair, pulling it free from its pins, seeming to enjoy how it fell loosely about her face. His eyes darkened as he stared down at her. Then he bent and suddenly kissed her on the mouth, taking her by surprise.

She resisted at first, then felt her lips part almost instinctively under that pressure. His tongue darted in, tasting her, exploring her own tongue and mouth, and Eloise gasped. The kiss deepened, grew more demanding, and her body turned wanton under it, her secret place growing moist and warm, longing for him to enter her again as he had done that afternoon.

"Yes," he muttered. "Like this."

His hand clasped the nape of her neck, holding her still, not bothering to be gentle, and something about that dominating gesture inflamed her senses.

She was his chattel, yes. But more than that, she was his wife.

Even if it made her a wanton, she desired her enigmatic husband as much as he desired her.

Wolf fell to his knees before her, a hungry look on his face, and pushed up the skirt of her gown.

She felt cool air on her thighs, and moaned with shame and excitement. "Your servant…"

"Yates will not interrupt us."

Of course not, she thought, staring down at his head. Doubtless he had entertained women here before, as a young man, away from the disapproving eyes of his father, and Yates had served supper in the same way, knowing better than to enter the room again until the young Wolf had taken his pleasure.

He placed her feet on his shoulders. "Open your legs to me," he muttered. "I need to see you uncovered. To feel and taste you. Let me in, Eloise."

She obeyed him without question, her body eager of its own accord to be examined and tasted by him. As her legs fell apart, he slipped his hands up her thighs, slowly, exploratively. She never wore undergarments, for they were considered lewd, and besides it kept a woman's body clean to be open to the air. His fingers found her easily, spreading aside her flesh, finding and stroking her secret core until she gasped. Then his head bent between her thighs, and she felt the warm slick stroke of his tongue across that burning flesh.

Her head fell back against the wooden back of the settle, and she cried out, pushing back at him with her feet. He braced himself against her, pushing his tongue inside, and her legs shook. His tongue ran over the sensitive nub of flesh at her apex, then dipped back inside.

Again she cried out, no longer caring if his servants heard her. Wolf's tongue played her like an instrument, flicking, licking, sucking, and stroking while she moaned and trembled, her rear lifting off the settle as though to urge him on, draw him deeper inside.

"My lord," she managed hoarsely, "my lord."

Wolf pushed one finger inside her slick heat, and at the same time worked feverishly at her nub with his tongue. Although it felt good, it was not enough. He seemed to be learning every inner fold of her flesh, how it worked, why it needed his touch so much, what delicious strokes and pressures it required to make her shake and cry out. But what she really craved was to be entered and possessed again, to be shown in the most intimate, physical way possible that she was his wife.

"My lord, what?" he demanded, his tone almost brutal.

She could not deny him what he wanted. And it was what she wanted too, after all. For this sweet and sticky yearning to be satisfied by the hard length of her husband's cock inside her.

"Take me," she begged him.

He laughed, his fingers stilling on her wet flesh as though his caresses had all been a tease and he had no intention of bringing her to completion. He let her gown drop and stood in front of her, smiling down into her flushed face.

"Come, don't be so eager to bring our pleasure to a close, my bride. You only lost your innocence a few hours ago. There is much else to learn beside the act itself."

Confused, she waited as he dragged his shirt free of his hose, then carefully released himself.

Her hunger grew into an urgent throbbing between her legs when she saw that strong column of flesh spring out into his palm once more. It was just as she had remembered it, an organ made to pleasure and satisfy both of them.

His lips twitched into a smile again at her expression; his fist encircled and tugged on the vein-swollen shaft. His hand moved, and its smooth head glistened as though already moist with longing, growing even fatter. She could not help licking her lips as she watched his movements, imagining him inside her.

"Hungry?"

She stared up at him, dazed with need, then looked back at his cock. It stiffened under her gaze, growing more erect.

Hungry?

Could he be asking what she thought he was asking?

His other hand played with her tousled hair, pushing it away from her face, looping it over one shoulder. Then he ran his thumb across her parted lips, watching her closely.

"You're so very desirable," he breathed, his lids drooping heavily over his eyes as he looked down at her breasts in the tight bodice, her slender figure. She saw him stroke himself slowly, close to her body. His voice almost seemed to shake as he whispered, "If you're hungry, take me in your mouth and suck me."

Half out of her mind with excitement, Eloise ran her tongue across dry lips and saw his gaze fix on that tiny movement with a sudden burning intensity.

"Suck you?" she repeated, also in a whisper, not quite understanding what he wanted but having a good idea.

"Yes, my bride, I want you to suck me. To take my cock into your mouth and pleasure me with your tongue as I have pleasured you," he explained, his language deliberately coarse, as though trying to shock her. His eyes mocked her stillness. "What? Did you think you had no role but to lie on your back and accept me inside you until you were with child? Oh no, my lamb. There is more to be done between a man and his wife than simple, dumb coupling. Much, much more. And I intend to teach you everything I know."

Eloise knew what her husband was demanding, yet found herself momentarily unable to obey, her whole world shifting on its axis as she realized the fundamental error she had made. Her life as Wolf's bride was far removed from that hazy, domesticated picture of marriage she had envisaged at court. Instead of facing the thousand daily boredoms of household management and other duties, it seemed Wolf wished her to be more concubine than wife.

She ought to refuse, to close her mouth. And yet she was excited by his unexpected order.

Her eyes focused on the smooth, shiny head so near to her mouth, the powerful shaft below it. For an instant, she could not breathe, her mind frozen. How could she ever hope to accommodate such a monster in her mouth?

Wolf made an impatient noise under his breath. He put a hand behind her head, pulling her down.

"Suck me, Eloise," he ordered her again, and this time she knew she had not imagined the slight shake in his voice.

Inexorably, she was drawn toward his groin until her parted lips were almost touching him.

She was trembling herself now. But with desire, not fear. At the first understanding of his instruction, she had been frightened, yes, but also filled with a fierce, shameless desire to taste her husband, to "know" him with her mouth, her whole body alive with it. And it was all she could do to hide her eagerness.

What would Wolf think if he knew how much her body yearned for his, a man who until that afternoon had felt like a stranger to her?

Her lips opened, stretching about the swollen head, and for the first time she tasted him. Salty, but clean, and with a faint hint of something else...the scent of love. She had smelled it about herself after he had left her that afternoon, a gorgeous lingering aroma about the bed and her body that had to be his seed.

Now she tasted it in her mouth, and it drove her wild.

His hand tangled in her hair, urging her to take him deeper. "More," he said hoarsely.

She responded, widening her mouth and her eyes too, staring up at her husband as his thick root slipped further inside her. His flat belly was at her eye-level, then his powerful chest, and above that she could see Wolf looking down at her with approval in his face. Approval and growing desire.

Experimentally, she swirled her tongue up and down his shaft, and saw him grimace as though in pain. His shaft jerked and swelled in her mouth, seeming to thicken even more.

He muttered, "Sweet Jesu," under his breath. His fist clenched in her hair, tugging her even closer.

Had she done something wrong? Hurt him, perhaps?

"No, don't stop," he muttered when she fell back a little, her eyes wide, looking up at him in concern. "That was…good. Very good. Keep going."

Encouraged by his praise, Eloise licked more firmly along his shaft, and this time was pleased rather than disconcerted by its nervous jerks. She pulled him out a few inches, and rolled her tongue about the head of his cock instead, and tasted again that sweetish hint of seed. It seemed to be oozing in tiny beads like transparent amber from a hole in the tip.

Daringly, she curled her tongue up tight and dipped it into the hole, tasting him properly.

This time he groaned, stroking her head, and she closed her eyes, her whole being warm and humming with joy. She might not be experienced, but it seemed that just the touch of her tongue could give her husband pleasure.

"Do you trust me?" Wolf asked, withdrawing his length as she moved to lick him once more.

Her eyes flew open and she stared up at him again, slowly returning to reality. His handsome face was hard but inscrutable, his blue eyes darkened, jaw clenched against some tightly controlled emotion. Trust him? What had he meant by that question?

"Because you have to trust me now, Eloise." His voice was suddenly hoarse and his hand seemed to tremble, stroking her hair.

She was startled, for she had never seen Wolf so unsure of himself. "I know it's been difficult for you, forced to leave court, to leave your…friends behind and marry a stranger. And I haven't given you much cause to see me as a friend, let alone a lover. But I need you to leave all those doubts behind now, and trust me. Can you do that?"

Eleven

WOLF KNEW HE WAS making himself vulnerable to this woman, beginning to feel more than lust when he was inside her, something he had hoped to avoid. Yet he could not seem to help himself. He had thought their marriage would be a simple, bloodless transaction: sexual union with a girl he had once ached for as a youth with no experience of the world, grieving for a lost mother. It had seemed to him fitting that he should be allowed, after such hard and lengthy service to the king, to come back here a few months of the year and bury himself in her body, recalling an earlier time before he had lost his ability to love.

That, at least, was how he had expected this marriage to work. In exchange for his protection and the comfort of his wealth, Eloise Tyrell would submit to him, despite her reservations and any feelings she still harbored for her former suitor.

Together they would make a child. Many children, perhaps. His honor would be fulfilled, his name could continue, and Wolf Hall might become a home again, no longer a vast empty shell which mocked him with its silence.

Only he had not expected to feel so much when he possessed her. Indeed, he had not expected to feel at all.

He had thought this burning raw emotion was impossible for him. His heart had been dead since Margerie rejected him as a youth, compounding his fears of women's infidelity. Yet he could not believe in love, he thought, staring down at her.

He did not love Eloise, no more than she loved him. There was no such emotion as love. It was merely the word women gave to their need to be looked after, and which men used to disguise their rutting, beast-like natures.

"I trust you," she whispered in response to his question. "What do you want of me?"

"Tip your head further back." Briefly, Wolf showed her what he needed. His fingers lingered on her neck, her soft skin. "Like this. Open your mouth and throat to me."

His need to come was so urgent he could scarcely control himself. His hands trembled as he positioned her, and he wondered with a flash of dry humor what she must think of him, her lord and master, whose hands were not even steady.

As soon as her head was tilted back, her lips parted wide at his instruction, he fed his cock back inside her mouth. Just the head first, then the shaft, which was more rigid than ever before, almost painful with the need to come. Wolf did not wish to frighten her with his length, but could not help himself. He kept pushing deeper and deeper into her throat, inch by slow inch, until he thought he would come from the incredible pleasure.

He praised her as she struggled, cupping her cheek, softly murmuring her name, keeping her head tilted back when she would have rebelled.

At last he was so deeply embedded that his balls were brushing her chin. He sighed, his fingers brushing her cheek in approval.

"Such a talented mouth," he told her softly. "Who would have thought it of my innocent bride?"

He began to withdraw again, but painstakingly, holding her in position. When his cock was nudging her lips, he told her to taste him, then watched in near insanity while she obeyed, avidly licking her tongue round his swollen head.

Silently, he clamped down on the urge to come. He wanted this to last. When his desire was under control again, he thrust back inside, plumbing the moist depths of her throat.

"Stay very still," he instructed her when she shifted under that thrust, her hands gripping the edge of the settle, her eyes staring up at him wildly.

With firm strokes, Wolf began to fuck her mouth, his breath hissing out with every inward thrust, sucking the air back in as he withdrew. His pace, his pleasure, his choice of depth. All she had to do was trust him not to hurt her.

Her eyes were still open, watching him. He searched her expression but could not read fear there, only desire.

Eloise was enjoying his dominance over her. Her breasts, still encased in that tight bodice, were heaving, her skin flushed with excitement. She wanted him as much as he wanted her, and in much the same way, there was no doubt left in his mind. She did not wish to be taken gently, but possessed by him, owned completely, commanded at every step by her master.

Abruptly, his control snapped. He felt himself swell and thicken in her mouth, and groaned loudly, no longer able to hold back the torrent.

"Yes," he muttered; then drove deep into her mouth. Once, twice, thrice. His cock grew hard as iron and began to pulse, shooting thick spurts of seed into her throat.

Wolf gasped as the intensity of his climax snatched his breath away, his head soaring, his body arched back like a bow being drawn, his vision burned out with flashes of hot red and searing white. Nothing he had ever felt before could equal this, he realized with a shock, and was momentarily stunned by what she had done to him, his brain numb, his entire body taken over by this almost unbearable pleasure.

His fingers twisted urgently in her hair, dragging her close as the last pulse spurted down her throat.

"Taste me, Eloise," he ordered her hoarsely. His need was so great, it was only through an act of pure will that he did not beg, but commanded her. "Drink me."

Eloise gave a tiny murmuring groan against his cock, then swallowed obediently. Her jaw was still stretched wide about him, and he found a wild excitement at the knowledge that she was swallowing his seed.

They remained locked together like that for a few long, lazy moments. His body was trembling, still coming down after the ferocious, high-soaring intensity of his climax. It seemed so natural not to move, his organ coiled heavily in her mouth, still aroused though no longer rigid.

Wolf felt his heartbeat begin to slow and realized that it had been racing as fast during the sexual act as when he was charging into battle, his whole body still recovering from that nerve-jolting explosion.

He looked down at Eloise, studying her flushed face, her tight-closed eyes, the tip of his cock still nestled inside her mouth. It was hard not to wonder if she had enjoyed or hated that moment when he spurted in her mouth and demanded that she swallow it. Certainly she had not recoiled, as he had half-anticipated she would.

Was it possible his bride had taken pleasure in swallowing his seed?

He had never known any woman to enjoy that task, even those trained in the art of love, those plain-spoken whores who followed the king's armies into battle, or the more skilled, soft-skinned courtesans of the court. But perhaps his sudden emission had taken her by surprise, and she had not thought to rebel against his order and spit it out afterward.

He withdrew from her mouth, oddly bereft as his cock slipped from between her lips.

Wolf opened his mouth to speak; then shut it again.

He frowned.

What the hell was wrong with him?

His pulse was still beating hard, his body clenched with nerves. He felt unsure what to say to her, as though afraid he might have distressed her with the violence of his desire. The surprise of that took his speech away, and for a long moment he could only stroke her hair, fumbling for the right words.

"You have left me amazed," he managed eventually, but was left irritated by how unsteady his voice had sounded. He did not want his bride to think him weak.

He linked his arms about her narrow waist and pulled her off the settle, drawing her close enough to kiss her forehead. Then he set her carefully on her feet, ignoring her questioning look.

"Now I shall amaze you," he continued doggedly.

"My lord?"

Looking confused, Eloise stared as he sat exactly where she had been, his glistening cock still exposed. He put his arm about her waist, dragging her toward him. The wooden settle was warm from her body, he realized, and found it amusing that their positions had been reversed.

She stood awkwardly before him, surprise on her face.

He groped hungrily beneath her gown, billowing it out, lifting the heavy folds until her bare flesh was exposed. "What you just did for me was very pleasurable," he told her in a whisper, watching her face. "But it was not enough to satisfy me. Not nearly enough."

Going slow, his fingers began to open her up, two pushing inside, then three, spreading her wide. His thumb played against her fleshy nub until she gasped, suddenly clutching at his shoulders.

He stared, seeing her cheeks flush hard and her eyes haze over with the same desire that was gripping him.

"You want me, Eloise?"

She moaned.

"That's not an answer," he said curtly, and shifted position, driving a fourth finger inside her tight, moist warmth.

"Yes, yes!" Her head tipped back under the onslaught of his fingers, her mouth open and quivering, cheeks hot. She looked like a woman already in the throes of pleasure, he thought, admiring her abandonment. "O sweet Jesu!"

Not as cool as she liked to appear, he thought triumphantly, and felt his own arousal grow with hers. But there was no hurry to end this. He fucked her with his fingers, thoroughly and relentlessly, and she lifted herself for each thrust, hissing as though impatient for what must follow. Soon she was standing on tiptoe to make herself more accessible to his fingers, trembling and unsteady.

Once he could refuse his own needs no longer, Wolf jerked her down onto his lap. "Enough of the lean dishes," he said teasingly, "now for the meat."

Draping her thighs on either side of his, he spread her legs and positioned her with precision, careful as a clock maker as he aligned their bodies. Then he looked into her eyes and slowly, determinedly, fed his cock inside her.

Her groan as her wet lips parted and allowed him entrance was deep and heartfelt. It surprised him, even though he knew she was aroused. But he had no time to consider what that meant, whether it indicated some change of heart from her side. Eloise had been resisting him since their marriage, whether silently with her eyes or by holding back from congress with him. But now she was so wet and ready for him, the large plump head of his cock entered her easily, and soon all he could think about was fucking her.

Her hunger aroused him further, making him want her more keenly himself. "My sweet lady," he murmured, and lifted her up on his lap so he could penetrate her more fully.

She moaned at his girth, the thick shaft stretching her fully. Wolf felt his arousal build too fast, his control slipping again at the snug fit of her cunt.

He hardened inside her, suddenly aware that he would not last much longer, not with her heat and moisture gripping him so tightly. He remembered that until recently she had been a virgin, and the pleasure of that knowledge, that he had been the first to know her carnally, made him even harder yet.

Grasping Eloise by the hips, he began to rock her back and forth, helping her ride him like a horse.

"Like this," he muttered, and sighed when she fell into the required rhythm, aiding his movements. "Yes, that's it."

He gazed directly into her eyes as their bodies slid together and apart, breathing hard, skin to skin.

"You want me?" he repeated

Eloise stared back at him, her eyes wide, the green flecks in those depths darkening with pleasure and need. Her breath was so deep in her throat it sounded like a humming against his chest, a bird trapped there in the hot space between their bodies.

"I…I want you," she admitted huskily at last, and it was all he could do to keep the triumph out of his face.

It was only a single battle he had won though, he reminded himself, and watched his bride through narrowed eyes. Not the war itself. That was still to be fought and won.

His rhythm slowed almost to a halt. He held her tight against him, and his hand slipped down between their bodies, pushing past the bunched material of her skirts to find the place where they were joined. Eloise cried out as he touched her, and he almost smiled at the high-pitched sound, rubbing his thumb back and forth across her taut flesh.

"Then come for me," Wolf urged her.

His lips met hers, his kiss fierce, tongue pushing deeply inside. His thumb continued to stroke her, just gentle enough not to frighten her, trying to bring her to the edge.

He whispered in her ear, "Don't be afraid of this, Eloise. Let go of your fear. Enjoy the pleasure."

But it was only when he pulled back a little to stare into her eyes that Wolf saw how close Eloise had come to the edge. Perspiration dampened her forehead, her hair was deliciously tousled, and she was biting her lip so hard a crimson bead of blood welled up and was wiped away by a quivering tongue as he watched.

That is the face of a woman close to her climax, he thought, and could not remember ever before seeing such a wild, lost look on the face of any woman that he had fucked.

Her eyes blurred with desire and she moaned as his thumb again flicked across the erect nub of flesh between her legs, catching her right at the core.

"Wolf…" She was groaning, her voice barely coherent. Her still-clothed body twisted and jerked against his, working frantically toward her release.

His cock twitched inside her, hardening intolerably at the sound of her voice calling his name.

Abruptly, Eloise stiffened and gave a strangled cry, grinding herself down on his cock as though desperate to get close.

She was coming…

A violent heat suddenly possessed his cock, clamping down over the whole shaft as her throat had done earlier. He gripped her hips and dragged her tight into his body, hearing her cries but momentarily unable to respond. His whole attention was focused on that hot tight spot of ecstasy between her legs where his cock was being squeezed by her cunt muscles.

"God's blood!"

He exploded on that shout, his hips thrusting upward off the settle, his cock shooting seed into her body. The spasms in her cunt were rhythmic, milking him of his seed with long rippling waves of heat. He was being dragged slowly under the waves, no longer able to breathe, his head throbbing with a fierce reddish light, his exultant cries muffled as though they came from beneath the sea.

"Christ, yes!" he managed thickly. "Keep squeezing me. Again, again!"

It was like no pleasure he had ever felt before, and if he died of it, he realized there would be no surprise in making such an end. Only a sense of glorious rightness.

She moaned his name, still clenched tight on him, riding him only with the strength of her own body as the last of her climax began to drain away.

A moment later, he saw the burning intensity leave her face, her body wilting against his as she came to a halt. There was neither fight nor passion left in her, though he sincerely hoped she had been satisfied by what they had done here tonight. Certainly she seemed to have enjoyed what he had shown her, though her limbs were trembling as though with an ague, her hard-torn breaths turning to sobs of relief.

Wolf would have smiled wryly if he could have managed even that tiny gesture. Instead he was too wrung-out for his facial muscles to respond, his face still twisted in a climactic grimace, though his own cries had fallen to silence now. But he understood how she felt. He too had experienced that terrible sexual intensity and been gripped by it, compulsively fucking her, unable to stop or escape until the deed was done.

And now it was over.

Wolf gave a shuddering sigh, managing one last pulsing shot inside her before he too collapsed on her shoulder, exhausted and replete.

She lay against him as she recovered, nestled into his throat like a wild animal, her breathing rapid.

Unable to stop touching her, he stroked his hand down her warm back, playing with the long golden mane that was so disheveled now, its pins long gone.

He was still inside her, enjoying the strange intimacy of their closeness, for he was unused to moments like these. Generally, when he had finished with a woman, she would rise and either clean him before leaving, or simply go without further ado. But that was when he was lying with a whore, or with a married lady of the court whose husband would soon be demanding her whereabouts.

Wolf realized with a start that he had never before had sexual congress with a woman who did not have to leave afterward for one reason or another. He was a little unsure how to end things, what should happen now that it was over.

Assuming it was over. She stirred at last, her lips brushing his throat, and he felt his cock react to the movement, stiffening again inside her.

Her eyes flashed open at the sensation, then widened as he continued to harden. He met her gaze wryly, not sure what to say, not even sure how to react himself.

She stared back at him as though he were a stranger, her voice faltering. "Wolf?"

"It seems my body cannot get enough of you," he admitted, laughing huskily, then felt his brows twitch into a frown, seeing more than just astonishment in those green-flecked eyes.

Was she still afraid of him?

He stroked her cheek softly with his thumb, trying to reassure her. "Forgive me if I hurt or frightened you. It was hard at times to remember your innocence, you gave my kisses back to me so fervently."

Her flush deepened. "You are my husband," she pointed out. "How else was I to respond?"

"Not all wives are so eager for their husband's touch, I can promise you."

He had not imagined the hurt in her voice. Nor the sharp flick of growing anger. "Forgive me if I did aught amiss, my lord. I will lie quiet next time, if mere submission is what you require."

Silently cursing himself for having mocked his bride at her most vulnerable, Wolf withdrew from her body. He removed her firmly, then tidied his clothing, willing his insatiable lust to be still. Just the scent of her body, warm and musky with pleasure, was enough to drive him mad with desire again.

He took two strides to the hearth and crouched to throw another few logs onto the smoldering fire. The wood began to crackle, and flames soon licked about the logs. He stared into its bright heart for a few moments, listening to the sound of her adjusting her gown and returning slowly to the dining table. His nerves jerked as her skirts brushed him, passing close, and it was all he could do not to jump up and make love to her again.

He had come three times already today, and yet was still partially aroused. How was that possible?

There was something about Eloise that seemed to bring out his instinctual, animal side, and while the sex might be raw and compulsive between them, he was not at all comfortable about where that might lead. He had married Eloise, wild and headstrong as she was, with the sober thought that he would soon bring her to heel and tame her. Instead, he was in serious danger of losing control, and he knew from experience that he could never allow that to happen.

Only when he felt in full command of his baser instincts did he straighten and allow his gaze to turn to her again.

The new Lady Wolf had also tried to regain some much-needed control, he realized, studying her with a faint smile on his lips. She had straightened her gown and combed her unruly hair with her fingers, scooping it to one side of her neck in a makeshift plait. Her face was pale, except for a burning spot of color in each cheek, and she kept her eyes discreetly lowered to her trencher when he sat down opposite.

He noted her avoidance of his gaze with interest. Had she too been shaken by their passion, despite her protests?

"Since you ask," he murmured, pouring them both some fresh wine, "I am not in the business of owning slaves, and do not require mere submission from you. Though you submitted very gracefully, I admit. I shall never forget the look on your face when you told me you trusted me, then opened your mouth for my cock." He saw the flash of temper in her face and felt his mouth twitch, trying not to smile. "I feel privileged to have married such a very willing wife."

He thought he could hear her teeth grinding from the other end of the table.

"More wine?" he asked sweetly, pushing one of the cups toward her.

She reached out for the wine cup, her bodice stretching tightly about her chest, and he admired the ripe mound of her breasts from a safe distance. Events had conspired against allowing him free access to his wife's naked body tonight, but he would rectify that as soon as he had an opportunity. And his breath back.

Eloise drank deeply, making no attempt to hide her thirst. Then she wiped her mouth with a napkin and gazed at him. There was a thoughtful look on her face.

"You were betrothed once before, I recall," she commented, then paused, perhaps seeing the effect of her words on his face. "You must have been quite young."

Wolf took a mouthful of wine, but his throat felt as though he were swallowing broken glass. He put down the cup and forced a smile to his lips, but it felt frozen and ugly, a twisted grimace masquerading as indifference.

"A long time ago, yes," he managed, and was surprised to hear how steady his voice was, for inwardly he was burning in the fires of hell. "Twelve years at least. I am amazed people still remember."

"But it is true?" she persisted.

"Unfortunately, yes. When I was a boy, not yet old enough to have ridden to war, I made my addresses to a young lady of the court who seemed eager to receive them, but who later changed her mind."

Coolly, Wolf put the cup to his lips, pretending to drink, but only watched her over the rim instead. He breathed in the fumes of the sweet dark wine, knowing he was already drunk on her body. He could not allow his senses to become more befuddled tonight. Not if he wanted to keep his past secret. This woman was too good at finding his weaknesses and driving a wedge into them broad enough to break down a castle's defenses.

"What was her name?"

He could not breathe for a moment, his chest tight. Then control came back, and with it a cold, hard edge that allowed him to say the word without any hint of emotion.

"Margerie," he said lightly. "Her name was Margerie."

"Was?"

He shrugged. "Is."

She toyed with the remains of her cold meal for a moment, then looked up at him, pity in her face.

"That must have been hard for you, my lord."

Wolf's jaw clenched hard. He did not want her to feel pity for him. Not where Margerie was concerned, at least. Some loves should be remembered for the fool's gold they were, he thought savagely: beautiful and glittering, always just out of reach, the insubstantial dream of a youth in love.

"No harder than for you to come here," he commented, "and be my bride."

"I have accepted my duty," she said simply.

He gazed at her profile as she looked away, finding it strangely beautiful in the firelight. He had thought her features too uneven for beauty when he saw her at court, and her bearing too clumsy. But now he saw she had a grace of sorts, albeit the grace of a wild animal caught in a trap, and a flicker of underlying power that attracted him.

"Am I your duty, Eloise?" he pondered aloud, aware of a cruel prickling under his skin. He saw her turn to stare at him, her cheeks slowly flushing. "What we just did together… Was that your duty, or your pleasure?"

She drew a sharp breath, then suddenly jumped to her feet, turning toward the window. "Hoofbeats," she muttered, and looked across at him.

Wolf frowned, listening to the distant thud of hooves, growing ever louder now. He had been so engrossed in their conversation that he had paid no attention to his military training. She was right though. One horseman, coming fast across the fields, and in darkness too. The message must be very urgent for him to risk his neck.

His hand fell to his belt. It was empty; he had left his dagger upstairs. He threw open the door, ignoring Yates, who was loitering in the dark hallway, and took the stairs two at a time, ignoring the jolting pain in his hip.

"Fetch light, ho!" he shouted over his shoulder at the servant. "Unbolt the front door."

His dagger was in their bedchamber, lying on a chest. Wolf thrust it into his belt, and returned. By the time he reached the bottom of the stairs, Yates had lit a torch and was standing in the open doorway.

The young horseman was unknown to him, though the horse looked to be one of his own. Taken fresh from the stables at Wolf Hall that night, no doubt. The messenger dismounted in one slick movement, then came running across the grass toward the lodge. He glanced assessingly at Yates, then dropped to one knee before Wolf.

"My lord Wolf," he gasped, dragging a scrolled and ribboned letter from his pouch and holding it out. "From His Majesty, King Henry."

Wolf broke the king's seal and unrolled the letter, reading its terse command with a sick feeling in his belly. But it would not do to show any response in front of these men. He nodded coolly to the messenger, spinning him a coin from his pouch, then turned to Yates.

"Fetch our horses, we will be returning to Wolf Hall tonight. You can ride ahead of us in the donkey cart, and light our way." He snapped his fingers at the servant, who was staring at him in amazement. "At once, man. Do you hear me?"

"Yes, my lord. At once."

Once they were alone again, he limped back to Eloise, still standing in the doorway to their dining room. She looked pale, as well she might.

"What is it, my lord?"

He tucked the letter into his belt, not wanting her to see how harshly the summons had been worded, then drained his wine cup. It was a cool night for riding; he needed the heat in his veins.

"You had best prepare yourself for a long journey, my lady," he said directly, since there was no time to waste on a slower explanation. "We are summoned back to court immediately, on pain of death. It is the king who summons us, so I cannot refuse him nor delay even another day."

"To court?"

"You heard me." He did not mean to sound curt, and knew it would undo all the good work he had done this night. Yet Eloise had no inkling of how serious the matter was. Nor was this the right moment to tell her, her frown already suggesting a stormy argument ahead. And she would need all her strength for what lay before her at court.

Concern for her put him on edge; his tone was more brutal than he had intended. "Hurry, fetch your cloak. We must leave."

She stared at him, not moving from the doorway. Her voice was icy. "I shall not take a single step until you tell me why we have been summoned back to court and must leave in the middle of the night like criminals."

Wolf made an impatient noise under his breath, his temper rising swiftly too. "God's blood, Eloise. I am your husband, lest you forget." His return glare was furious. "Can you not simply trust me and do as I bid you?"

"No, my good lord."

"Very well, then. I hoped to tell you in a gentler moment, but you must have it now, so here it is," he said roughly. "Queen Anne has been arrested on suspicion of treasonous adultery, and taken to the Tower of London until her trial."

Eloise blanched at the appalling news, staggering back against the wall as though her legs had suddenly given way. She was afraid, he guessed, and as well she might be. For if found complicit in the queen's adultery, she could lose her head.

He caught her before she fell. Gripping her by the shoulders, he looked down into her ashen face, trying to hide his fear so as not to alarm her further.

"As one of her maids, you have been summoned to appear before Sir Thomas Cromwell to give your testimony."

Wolf wished he could refuse this royal summons and protect her from the horrors ahead. But such a refusal would risk both their lives.

"Now fetch your cloak, and no more arguments. We leave for London at first light."

Twelve

SUSANNAH WAS AGITATED. "BUT why cannot I accompany you back to court, Eloise?" she demanded again, staring anxiously out at the sky. "Please say yes. It will be dawn soon and you will be gone. It is not fair to send me home when you are escaping to court!"

The sky outside was still that cool slate-gray before dawn, though the household had only awoken an hour before, chasing away the darkness with candles and hurriedly kindled fires. Since then, servants had been bustling about, packing chests and provisions for the journey, and from the stables came the repeated clang of iron, the smith having been called to reshoe the best horses in Wolf's stables.

Eloise herself had been busy, sorting out which clothes and shoes to pack, and briefly scribbling down orders for the running of the household during her absence. It irked her that she had not even seen Wolf since the night before. After riding back from the lodge together through the dark fields, her husband had escorted her to her bedchamber, then left her with a curt bow and not returned all night. She did not know why Wolf had gone, nor where he had slept last night—if he had slept at all—but his silence toward her since leaving the lodge had been frightening.

"Forgive me," Eloise told her, "but it is fair."

"How so?" Susannah turned from the window, her loose fair hair swinging. Her fingers plucked at Eloise's gown in a childishly agitated manner, putting the lie to her words. "I am not a child anymore, and Father will not be angry if you take me with you. In faith, he has often said I should go to court and learn my manners. You had your chance to escape. Now this is mine. And Hugh Beaufort is to accompany you back to court as well... Once Hugh is gone, I will be quite alone again in Yorkshire, with nobody to talk to but the cows and sheep. You must let me come with you!"

"Do you not understand?" Eloise exclaimed at last, rounding on her sister. "I am not returning to court to spite your chances with Hugh Beaufort. I have been summoned as a witness. The accusation against the queen is one of adultery, an offense which is considered treason, punishable by death."

Susannah had taken a step back at her outburst. Now she stared at Eloise blankly, her lip trembling. "It is not you who is accused."

"Not yet, no..."

Eloise was thinking out loud, the fear nearly driving her mad, just as it had done in the night, lying alone in her cold bed with nothing to do but remember the queen's secret kisses and forbidden liaisons at court.

"But what if they claim I had secret knowledge of the queen's adultery that I ought to have shared with one of the king's advisors? If she is condemned, and I kept silent when I should have spoken, then I..." She tapped her chest, suddenly finding it hard to finish her thought. "Then I could be held as guilty as Her Majesty, and pay for it with my life."

She fell into silence, unable to go on, staring at nothing.

A voice spoke coldly from the door. "And is it true? Do you have secret knowledge of Queen Anne's adultery?"

Eloise turned, almost dropping the lace-trimmed foreskirt she had been trying to fold into the too-narrow chest.

"Wolf," she breathed, relief flooding through her at the sight of him. His presence always dominated every room he entered, she realized. Even the gray dawn was suddenly brighter and clearer because he was there. Then she realized what he had asked, and belatedly registered the icy chill of his words.

Angry, she thought abruptly. He was angry with her.

"No," she said at once, and straightened her back, forcing herself to sound more certain. If she could not convince her own husband, she would never convince Sir Thomas Cromwell, whose hard eyes saw everything. Besides, it was a half-truth at least. Perhaps even more than that. "That is, I saw the queen talk closely with many courtiers, and laugh with them in sport, as is the fashion at King Henry's court. But I cannot be sure if…"

"If any of them shared her bed?"

Eloise nodded, nervously running the tip of her tongue along dry lips, and saw Wolf's gaze focus on that tiny gesture.

His eyes narrowed, and his gaze lifted slowly, studying her face with a fierce concentration as though he had never seen it before.

She felt a sudden rush of heat between her thighs, recalling their time alone at the hunting lodge, how he had kissed and touched her, giving her such pleasure she had thought she would die of it.

It was a struggle not to show that intimate memory on her face.

For a moment she thought she had succeeded, then saw him shift as though uncomfortable, his face tightening, a slight color coming into his cheeks, and guessed that he had read her thoughts and was growing hard again.

Wolf gave an abrupt nod and crossed his arms. His head lowered, his whole body grew tense, and he watched the packing away of her clothes as though it was suddenly fascinating.

"Very well." His gaze flickered to Susannah, unemotional. "I am sorry you cannot accompany us to court, but I am sure you will understand this is not an auspicious occasion for a first visit. After all, you can hardly be presented to Her Majesty while she is residing in the Tower, can you?"

Her sister said nothing, not quite daring to speak as sharply to

Lord Wolf as she had to Eloise. But there was defiance in her eyes as she curtsied to her new brother-in-law and turned to help Eloise finish packing her clothes.

Hurriedly, Eloise laid out the heavy foreskirt in the chest as best she could, not entirely caring if it would be crushed by the time they arrived, then turned to ask Wolf if she could speak with him in private.

But Wolf had gone as silently as he had appeared.

She stood a moment in silence, biting down hard on her lip. Her mind was uneasy, for she had lied to Wolf.

Had he guessed it?

If they had been alone, she could have spoken more freely. But it was not for Susannah to hear what she knew of the queen's illicit dealings behind the king's back. Safer for her younger sister to know nothing, for ignorance would save her from accusation, just as Eloise hoped that dishonesty would save her own neck.

She only hoped her guilt would not show in her face when she was called to give her testimony before Cromwell. For she had seen Queen Anne both kissed and kissing, on many occasions, and suspected that some of the queen's favorites had been more than just friends. Yet if she held such information locked in her heart, others must hold it there too. The court was not a private place. And there were many among the queen's ladies who had held Anne in contempt, for she had always favored a few and cut others adrift.

Sooner or later, some terrible knowledge would come before the king, and then poor Queen Anne's life would be forfeit…

She glanced impatiently at Susannah, who seemed lost in her own world, standing motionless in the middle of the room.

"If you do not wish to help me, Susannah, then I suggest you get one of the grooms to drive you back to Father's house in the donkey cart. It will be light soon."

Her sister shook her head. There was an odd, martial light in her eyes as she seized a fine lace shawl from Eloise's pile of clothing, folded it three times very poorly, then bundled it into the chest with all the rest. "No, I shall wait and see you off. Father does not know about this summons anyway, so he will not miss me for hours yet. Besides, I wish to bid a proper farewell to Master Beaufort."

Now there was the true heart of her distress, Eloise thought, and felt sorry for her sister. "You are in love with Hugh, aren't you?"

"In love with Hugh Beaufort, the king's clerk?" Susannah stared at her, then laughed rather wildly. "Of course I am not. Whatever would make you say that?"

—◦◦◦—

Eloise went in search of Wolf after her chest had been packed and carried downstairs by two of the servants. She hurried downstairs, expecting to find her husband out at the stables, or perhaps talking with his men by the entrance. But he was not in either place. The cavalcade was already assembled outside, the lead horses being held by grooms, their breath steaming out in clouds in the early chill, harnesses jingling as they shifted impatiently, though no one had yet mounted. It seemed everyone was waiting for Wolf, the sky growing lighter and lighter by the minute.

She found Morag on the stairs, instructing a man who was still struggling down with one of the heavier cases. Eloise embraced her old nurse, who had only recently come to live at the hall, and asked again if Morag would accompany her to court. But once again her nurse begged to be excused, saying she was too old for such a long journey, and indeed Eloise did not think she looked well.

"You are already taking Mary with you," her nurse pointed out, kissing her on the cheek. "She will know how to look after you. You do not need two of us snapping at your heels."

Indeed, Mary was waiting for her in the covered litter, much to the maid's excitement, for the girl had not taken to country living and was quite homesick for court.

"But it is your advice I value most," Eloise told her, tears in her eyes at the thought of what might lie ahead. "What if...?"

"Hush," Morag leaned forward and kissed her on the cheek. "If things get bad, it is your husband to whom you must turn now. Lord Wolf can protect you far better than I."

"Have you seen Wolf?" she asked wearily, rubbing a hand across tired eyes.

Morag looked at her strangely. "No, but you could try the room at the top of the west tower."

The west tower?

Heading reluctantly in that direction, an older part of the house that she had only visited once before, Eloise had to grope her way, finding the corridors and passageways unlit. The flooring was thin and ragged in places, with no pictures or tapestries on the wall to keep out the drafts. The west tower itself was dark, the crumbling stone staircase narrow and winding, with arrow slits at every turn that let in the chill air. The whole place felt unwelcoming and neglected.

With curiosity in her heart, she climbed the stairs, sure that Morag must be mistaken. With everyone waiting below for his order, why on earth would Wolf be up here?

But when she reached the room at the top, Eloise stepped silently through the half-open door and stopped dead, amazed to find Wolf there after all.

He was seated at a desk with his back toward her, quill in hand, writing something, his head bent over a sheet of paper in utter concentration, as though he intended to remain there for hours yet. The tower room was dusty and circular, and stood empty except for his desk and a tall candle beside it, its flame extinguished.

Light streamed in through a series of thin slits in the stone wall, one bright strip of early sunlight falling directly across his bent shoulders and desk.

She had not meant to break the spell. Yet she must have made some inadvertent noise, for Wolf suddenly stiffened and turned his head.

He had not expected to see her. In that unguarded moment before the shutters came down, masking his expression, she met a scorching intensity in his gaze that took her breath away. She was suddenly reminded how dangerous he could be, not just for her heart and soul, but physically. His whole body exuded power and sexual confidence, but his eyes were the key to that power, the gateway to his soul.

Staring back at him with the same intensity, she knew that if Wolf ordered her to strip off her gown right here and kneel before him, to take him in her mouth as she had done last night, she would obey without question. It was only a matter of days since their marriage, and only hours since her husband had possessed her for the first time. Yet it felt as though she had belonged to this man forever, as though they had been made for each other.

Under that dangerous gaze, her body felt new and tingling, her breasts fuller, her hips more inclined to sway, and between her thighs…

His touch had wrought this sudden, miraculous change in her. Eloise could not imagine how it would feel to be with him forever, to be always in his bed, groaning out her pleasure. Perhaps she would die of that bliss, her heart eventually outstripping her body's strength. But what a death that would be!

"Eloise," he growled, standing up abruptly. His chair fell backward with a crash but Wolf paid it no heed. "What are you doing here?"

"Looking for you," she said huskily.

"Clearly," he agreed, his voice terse. "But how did you know where to look for me?"

Dodging that awkward question, she looked past him at the writing desk, where a vellum-bound book still lay open beside his discarded quill. It looked like a small ledger, like one of the books used for the household accounts.

"What are you writing?" she asked, curious to know why he had come all this way up the tower simply to make some notes in that book.

"That's none of your business." Wolf slammed the book shut, then tucked it inside his black jacket where she could not see it.

Turning back toward her, he ran a hand through his thatch-dark hair, leaving it rough and disheveled; his skin was taut over his cheekbones. There was a searing anger in his voice that shook her to the core. "This is my private place. I do not permit anyone else to come up here, not even the servants. Who told you I would be in the tower room?"

Eloise blinked, thinking hard. She did not want to get Morag into trouble over this.

"No one," she whispered, backing away as he came limping violently toward her. "I couldn't find you, that's all. So I kept looking until…"

He grabbed her by the elbow. "Who told you, Eloise?"

Staring into those ice-cold blue eyes, Eloise knew that she was not forgiven. Not forgiven for having been one of the queen's ladies, for forcing him into this arduous journey back to court, for having been summoned before the Star Chamber like a criminal. He had married a plain northern maid, thinking she would live here quietly in the country, bear his children, and calmly await his returns from campaign. Instead, they had barely been wed a sennight when she had been summoned to appear before the highest lords in the land, for having been privy to the queen's dealings with other men. Soon every man and woman at court would know the name of Lady Wolf.

No wonder he was looking at her with such hostility. She had resisted him on their wedding night, then had not known how to please him, and now this terrible scandal was waiting for her at court. He must be wondering how to rid himself of such a turbulent wife before she put him out of favor with the king.

Fear of losing him made her throat close up. She had only just learned how to please him. Now it seemed their marriage would be over before it had properly started. But she would not leave without a fight. His friend King Henry might know a dozen ways to cast off a wife or mistress, but Wolf would find her a difficult woman to dislodge.

She swallowed, refusing to let him see her fear. Nor would she allow him to bully her into revealing it was Morag who told her where to look for him.

"No one, my lord," she repeated, biting out the words so he could see what she thought of his behavior. If Wolf could become this angry over some trifling matter, so could she. "I was passing the stairway below and thought I heard a noise. You must forgive me, I did not know this was your private place."

He looked down at her as though he hated her, still gripping her elbow, his sapphire-blue eyes hard and unyielding. She thought she had never seen him so furious.

"Don't come up here again," he ordered her harshly. "Do you understand me?"

"Yes, my lord."

There was no mistaking the matching ice in her voice now. With a disgusted expression, he released her arm.

"I am glad to hear it," he ground out, and limped past her through the doorway and down the winding stairs. As he descended, a folded sheet of paper fluttered out from under his jacket, as though falling from inside his book. He paused, looking round in the dim light with a frown.

Before he could stoop to pick up the fallen sheet, Eloise acted on instinct and reached for it herself. She turned it over in her hand, just out of reach, her eyes widening. It looked like a letter, its secrets folded away where she could not read them, except for a single word written in bold, black handwriting across the top fold.

Margerie.

Her heart seemed to stop for one terrible instant, squeezing the breath out of her chest. Then it stuttered back into life at a brutal pace.

"May I have that?"

Wolf held out his hand for the letter, his brows clamped together in a lightning frown. Yet the heat had gone out of his voice. The way he spoke to her was calm, almost distant, as though they had become strangers again. His sudden stillness hurt more than his anger, and she wished he was still blazing at her, for she preferred to meet fire with fire, not ice with ice.

Nonetheless, she handed it back, noting with relief that her hand did not shake as it brushed his. She looked into his eyes, meeting his cool stare with one of her own.

There was no point trying to pretend that she had not seen the name of his former lover written so boldly across the letter, but equally there was nothing to say about the matter. After all, what could she ask that Wolf would ever willingly tell her?

How do you still know Margerie, you duplicitous bastard? Why are you writing to her? Do you still love her? Still take her to your bed from time to time?

Does she please you better than I did last night?

The crushing pain inside her chest grew suddenly intolerable. Yet his face remained emotionless. This awkward moment on the stairs with a secret love letter meant nothing to him. That he was writing to a woman he had once been betrothed to should not concern her, his raised eyebrows seemed to say. She was his wife, and not his keeper.

Eloise tightened her lips and tried to pass him on the narrow stair, drawing in her skirts with a rigid hand. "They are waiting for us below. It is past dawn."

She would rather not ask the questions pressing heavy as rocks on her heart than listen to any explanation that was sure to be a lie. The indignity would be too much to bear.

"Eloise!"

His voice was so rough, she could not help herself. She looked up just at the sound of her name, and instantly regretted it.

His eyes were like a blue fire, scorching her. She could feel the heat from him as she lurched onto the same step as him, their bodies brushing, first hips, then shoulders as she turned awkwardly, trying to avoid touching him. It hurt to be so close to Wolf and know he despised her, that the man whose touch she had grown to enjoy no longer wanted her. Then she caught his male scent, deep and musky, reminding her of love in the afternoon, and her heart began to gallop, leaving her faint and in despair.

"Wait!" he insisted, and slammed his arm across the narrow stairway to touch the curving wall opposite, effectively locking her in place beside him on the step. His blue gaze dropped to her mouth, brooding there as though still angry.

"We must leave for court at once, my lord," she reminded him through the clog of salty, unshed tears in her throat, and kept her gaze lowered. "There is no time to delay."

Wolf cursed between his teeth, staring down at her. Then he stood aside, with obvious reluctance, and nodded for her to precede him down the stairs.

He followed more slowly, no doubt pushing the secret letter back inside the book beneath his jacket.

At the front entrance to the hall, he caught up with her again, his hand gripping her shoulder, bending to her ear so the waiting row of servants would not overhear. "I haven't finished with you yet," he muttered, then straightened as one of his men saluted him. "Yes, Fletcher. Is Master Beaufort out there? Are we all prepared?"

"Aye, my lord. We only await your coming."

A slight smile twitched at the corners of Wolf's mouth, and he glanced sideways at Eloise. "Indeed," he drawled laconically, then nodded, drawing on his tasseled leather riding gloves. "Best tell your men to mount up, then. For I have finished my business here and am ready to depart."

He escorted Eloise to her covered litter, one hand pressed lightly into the small of her back, the warmth of that touch burning through her furred robe and traveling gown. Around them the assembled horses jabbed impatiently with their heads, stamping in the cold dawn light, and the cartmen began shouting farewells to those left behind as the first of the luggage carts set off for the south, trundling noisily toward the arched gateway. Wolf handed her up into the fur-lined interior of the litter, where Mary was waiting for her in silent excitement, then he walked away to his horse without another word.

One of the men blew a long staccato note on his horn, and a few seconds later several others took up the call.

"Head south, men!" Fletcher's hoarse shout went up above the din of the blowing horns. He wheeled his liveried mount up and down the ranks, then signaled the six-man horse escort to fall into position beside the litter wagon. "South to Greenwich and the court of King Harry!"

Leaning out of the curtained litter, Eloise watched Wolf swing up into the saddle of his black stallion, his face grimmer than she had ever seen it before. Without even acknowledging her presence, he spurred forward to ride alongside the litter, engaged in some muted conversation with Hugh Beaufort.

Her heart ached at the sight of him, and of Wolf Hall disappearing from view as the litter wagon rumbled through the arched gate and turned south. Eloise looked up at the dark stone archway and was filled with a terrible sense of loneliness and desolation. She sat back inside, leaning against the cushioned velvet seats, and closed her eyes to avoid Mary's curious stare.

Was it possible Wolf too thought her complicit in the queen's guilt?

A cold fear clutched at her heart, for she had indeed been keeping secrets about Anne Boleyn. She had seen Queen Anne too intimate on several occasions with Thomas Wyatt and with Henry Norris, and others too. And now she must either give up her secrets and watch her former mistress condemned to death, or lie and risk her own neck on a charge of treason. She had only just escaped from the dark webs of court, it seemed to her, and now her life might be forfeit.

The litter jerked over the uneven ground, and she felt again the old familiar swaying that would keep her sick for days until they arrived. Rather the sickness of the journey though, she told herself, than whatever trial awaited her at court.

Thirteen

THEY HAD BEEN TWO days at court and no summons had yet come for her from Sir Thomas Cromwell. Eloise looked up for the tenth time from her embroidery and stared at the closed door to their apartments, wishing she could see through its thick studded wood. She knew a guard stood outside that door at all hours, armed with a sword and pike, one of the king's own yeomen. But was he there to protect them, or to prevent her from escaping the coming inquisition?

They had been given lavish apartments near the king's own: high-ceilinged chambers decked out in gold and silver furnishings, soft deerskins on the floor, elaborate Tudor roses painted crimson on the roof crossbeams, a reflection of Wolf's marked favor with His Majesty. But it was whispered that the gentleman whose rooms these had been now languished in prison, awaiting his trial for treason, and she could not help but fret that her turn would come soon.

Their first evening at court, Wolf had absented himself for hours, only returning late at night. His servant helped him undress and bathe before the fire, while she sat up in bed waiting. But he did not come to her, choosing instead to sleep on the daybed in the other chamber.

Jealousy nagged at her heart. Had her husband already taken his pleasures elsewhere that night?

Or perhaps he was afraid that even being alone with her could be dangerous to his reputation. There was still time, after all, for Wolf to disassociate himself from her before she was questioned. He could claim their marriage had not been consummated, or that she had not been a virgin when she came to him, that he no longer acknowledged her as his wife. There were many cunning ways to save his family honor if she went to the block.

The queen's other ladies had been questioned too, of course. Some of her closest intimates had been interviewed at great length, their answers recorded on paper to be studiously compared with other accounts. Because her journey from the north had taken so long, she was one of the last among the queen's maids of honor to be questioned. And it seemed much weight was to be put on her testimony, for some mischievous gossip had suggested an overly close friendship between herself and Sir Thomas Wyatt, one of the unfortunate courtiers accused of sleeping with the queen.

When Wolf had related this unpleasant lie, he had avoided her gaze, his mouth twisting as though disgusted by her behavior. She had denied it at once, of course. But she guessed he must hate her for putting him through this shameful ordeal. Why else would he look like that?

It was late afternoon when voices and booted footsteps sounded in the corridor outside, and she heard the guard come to attention.

Eloise leaped to her feet, knocking over the embroidery stand, her heart racing.

Could this be the summons at last?

If only Wolf was there, to advise her what to do! But he had barely spent a moment in her company since their arrival at court, and had ridden out hunting with the king early that morning. He had not even slept with her again.

It hurt to lie alone at night, staring up at the beautifully ornate ceiling of her bedchamber, wondering where her absent husband was. Yet she could hardly blame Wolf for distancing himself from her. She had seen too many heads turn as she passed, courtiers whispering behind their hands, their expressions either cruelly curious or pitying.

The door was flung open. It was Wolf.

Catching her breath in relief, she sagged back against the high-backed chair. "Wolf," she managed huskily.

He bowed to someone out of sight in the corridor, murmured something in response to an unheard question, then softly closed the door to leave them alone together.

Turning back toward her, dark and straight in his mud-splashed hunting garb, his gaze met hers with a force which shook her. She stared back, instantly on fire for him. His gaze held her so tight she could not move, speaking without words, touching without hands. The blue glare of his eyes consumed her. It was like being struck by lightning, she thought, or staring into the blue dust of a whirlwind only feet away.

Eloise swallowed, shocked by the storm churning within him. What could have happened?

She would have spoken, but Wolf shook his head.

He laid a warning finger on his lips, and she realized he was listening to the men outside in the corridor. After another excruciating moment of stillness, she heard a man's voice speaking softly, then booted footsteps receding along the corridor.

Her husband dragged off his cloak, then limped across to the sunlit window that overlooked the king's gardens. She watched as he leaned out to pull the shutters closed, and found herself staring entranced at the rear view of his body, his buttocks sculpted, his hard thighs and calves outlined in tight black hose.

Eloise put a hand to her mouth, trying to control her passion. But the memory of him taking her on the bed in the hunting lodge reared up large in her head, and her body remembered that pleasure too.

Her palms were suddenly clammy; perspiration broke out on her forehead. She wanted him so badly it was a sweet burning ache between her thighs, a hunger which left her empty and trembling in the early hours, wishing he was inside her again.

By the time Wolf turned, she was standing before him, less than a step away. He looked down at her in the darkened chamber, very still and silent, a muscle jerking in his face.

He was so cold, she thought despairingly. Did he even want her anymore? Was that lust already gone that had inspired him to teach her so many tricks on their first intimate afternoon together?

She touched his cheek, and looked up at him without pretense, letting her own hunger show, too starved to hide what she wanted.

"Eloise," he said harshly. His gaze flashed down to her court gown, the bodice pulled low to reveal the swell of her breasts, as was the fashion, even the rosy tips of her nipples just showing. "God's blood, woman. I could take you right now on the floor, and to hell with whoever is listening."

"Then why don't you?"

She stood on tiptoe so her lips could brush his mouth. His breathing altered, quickening suddenly, yet still he did not move. She laid a hand on his chest, then dragged it slowly and deliberately down to his flat belly. His heat enticed her fingers through the fine shirt and doublet, and she felt his heartbeat begin to race.

Could she seduce this man, inexperienced as she was?

"Wolf?" she prompted him softly, and ran the wet tip of her tongue along his lips, tasting him.

Exhaling sharply, he slanted his mouth over hers, the driving pressure of his kiss leaving her in no doubt of his desire. A second later, his hand tangled in her hair, jerking her toward him. His tongue pushed between her lips, urgent and devouring, stroking along her own tongue, sucking on it until she moaned, then plumbing her depths with silken invasion.

Something inside her caught fire. Flame licked about the edges of her heart, sending her blood thundering through her veins. She tried but could not recall feeling like this with Simon, though his kisses had always pleased her. With Wolf, everything was different. It was like being kissed by a god: an angry god, whose moods were unpredictable and unfathomable, but whose perfect body had been carved out of the warm, living stone of human desire. And she could think of nothing but lying beneath him after the way he had withdrawn from her.

She explored his mouth too, sucking on his tongue, pleased by the strangled groaning noise he made, and did not even care if he thought her wanton. She let him see that he could do whatever he wanted to her, shamelessly rubbing and stroking his body, lost in their long, hot kisses.

Only when her fingers trailed lower, trembling below the waist, did Wolf finally catch her hand and twist it away behind her back. They stood like that a moment longer, both panting, shaking with need, pressing against each other compulsively.

Then Wolf drew a slow, shuddering breath and turned his head to whisper in her ear. "Because the two men who were outside intend to return in less than an hour's time to take you to Thomas Cromwell, to be questioned about the queen."

She drew back to stare at him, all her desire falling away as his words sank in. "Wolf," she managed thinly, then could not think what to say.

His look was grim, but he did not release her. "There is no help for it. You must answer Cromwell's questions and give your testimony. It will be hard. The hardest thing you have ever done. And if you want to come through this unscathed, you will have to trust me."

"Of course."

"I need you to trust me implicitly. To remember what I tell you, and obey without question, to put your life in my hands." His sharp blue gaze pierced her. "Can you do that?"

She sensed an odd, fulminating restraint in him and grew suspicious. "What is it, my lord?" Her eyes widened when he merely looked at her, his face brooding. "What do you know?"

"I fear the queen cannot be saved," he said bluntly, keeping his voice low. "I have never seen the king so brutal, so adamant that he will have his revenge. He believes the world mocks him for a cuckolded husband, and his fury makes him cruel. He calls her a witch and a whore, and his own daughter a bastard. He is angry and intends someone to pay for his disgrace."

"Queen Anne is to die? You are certain?"

He hushed her cautiously, glancing at the door. "Not so loud. You must take care what is said here, there are many spies at court. The queen will not die alone. Do you understand me?"

No, she did not. "But, Wolf, I cannot...I cannot make it worse by telling what I know. It is not in me to condemn her with my testimony."

"She is condemned already by those who judge her. The charge will be high treason, for which a woman's punishment is to be burned alive—if the king commands it. And her lovers will die with her. Even her unfortunate brother Lord Rochford is in the Tower, and may face death along with his royal sister."

She staggered, holding onto him for strength. So the rumors she had heard about George Boleyn's arrest had not been false and malicious, as she had supposed.

"No, no," she whispered. "It is not true. There has been no unnatural love between them. I have seen them together, and it was a brother and sister's love, that is all."

"I believe you," he said shortly, and she saw contempt on his face. "But this is the filth that must be made known to the world before a queen can be executed."

She was horrified. "His Majesty means to have her dead at all costs, then?"

His voice dropped, and once more he glanced over his shoulder at the door. "Thomas Cromwell has persuaded the king that execution is the only path to take if he wishes to marry Jane Seymour."

"Jane Seymour!"

He looked at her, his eyes blue shards of ice. "That is not all. The rumor goes that you were party to some of these adulterous meetings."

"No!"

"So unless you wish to join your mistress in death," he continued coldly, ignoring her outburst, "I suggest you do precisely what I tell you."

She waited, closing her eyes in pain. What kind of world was this where an innocent woman could be condemned to death, and her friends with her, simply so a king could remarry?

"You must tell them you heard and saw nothing. I do not care if you saw the queen naked and at play in her bed with every man at court, you must lie under oath and say you were not privy to Her Majesty's dealings with any man whatsoever."

His gaze searched her face, as though hunting for her weaknesses.

"It will not be easy," he warned her. "They will drive you hard to incriminate the queen. But whatever questions they put to you, however hard they press you, or essay to trip you up with clever words and tricks, you must say nothing. For if you suggest that you had secret knowledge of her adultery, you too may face the ax. Is that clear?"

"Yes," she agreed at once, relieved that he had not asked her to tell the truth. For then she would be forced to admit she had seen the queen kissing and being intimate with other men. "But Wolf, I do believe her innocent. Anne has flirted, yes, and made unwise choices in her friends. But I never saw her take any man to her bed save His Majesty."

"Hush." He laid a stern finger across her lips, then leaned forward to whisper in her ear. "Tell me nothing of the queen, I do not wish to hear it. You will be questioned and that will be an end to it. After today, whatever happens, we will never speak of this again."

She nodded, and he removed his finger, almost reluctantly. They were standing so close her body ached for his touch. A touch she knew she might never feel again, for he seemed to hold her in so much contempt. She wished she could hate him in return. But in truth she did not know what to feel, nor how to look at him without wanting him, for her heart was all topsy-turvy.

Was this how love felt? Could she truly be in love with her husband?

Not that it mattered one jot. Wolf did not love her. No, nor ever would now. This matter of the queen's adultery had tainted her with the same unspeakable disgrace, and by extension, her new name of Wolf. He would never forgive her for that.

"Forgive me, my lord," she whispered.

"For what?"

"For this stain on your family's honor… The name of Wolf…" She could hardly speak, her throat burning with tears. "I have marred all."

His hands stroked up and down her shoulders, his expression grim, but for a moment he did not speak. That moment of silence seemed to stretch between them forever, leaving her desolate and more convinced than ever that he wished she were not his bride. Then his head turned sharply toward the door, as though he had heard a sound in the corridor.

He paused, his eyes narrowed as he listened, his brows knitted together in a dark frown, before looking back at her.

"Eloise, it is best if we do not…" He hesitated, his voice suddenly rough. "I shall not come to your bed tonight. Do not wait for me to return, but sleep and rest yourself."

Her chest was so tight she suddenly could not breathe. "My lord?"

"You are exhausted." His hands dropped to his sides, curling into fists, as though he could no longer bear to touch her. "The long journey south, and now this trial…"

"No," she choked, shaking her head. She seized his hand and pressed it against her breast, wanting him to feel the soft, warm swell above her thudding heart. "There is nothing amiss with me that you cannot heal, my lord."

He stared down at his hand, lying so invitingly on her breast, the tight bodice leaving little to be imagined, her nipple peeping over in courtly fashion. She saw his throat move, swallowing. "I thank you for the compliment, madam," he said huskily, "but fear I cannot oblige you."

Withdrawing his hand, he bowed, apparently oblivious to her silent agony, then walked away into the bedchamber. A moment later she heard him call through the adjoining door to his servant's quarters, who hurried in to help his master change out of his hunting gear.

She was still motionless with disbelief when Wolf came back to the threshold of the bedchamber, the fine white shirt unlaced and hanging open to reveal his muscular chest and flat belly. He paused with his hand on the door, talking to his servant over his shoulder. Then he glanced cursorily in her direction and their eyes met.

She did not think Wolf had ever looked at her so coldly, as though he had already put her aside in his mind, dismissing her as no longer interesting to him.

It was like being skewered by an icicle, Eloise thought, and put a hand to her belly in sudden unbearable pain.

Wolf stiffened, watching her in silence. His handsome face was brutally devoid of emotion, not even a flicker in his eyes to give any hint of what he was thinking. Then he turned away and closed the door, shutting her out.

Wolf stood with his back to the wall in the long shadows of the interrogation chamber, arms folded, his face deliberately impassive as he listened to his wife give her testimony.

It had been difficult to obtain permission to be present during her questioning, but he still had the king's ear, thank God. That influence counted for something, even with this taint on his wife's reputation. Cromwell had raised a crooked brow when he entered the room, guiding Eloise to her allotted place, but had said nothing. Perhaps Cromwell was wary of angering the king, whose temper was so uncertain these days it felt as though the entire court was holding its breath.

Eloise stood before Cromwell in the center of the room, her back very straight, hands clasped together as if praying. Which she might well be doing, he thought, his eyes on her face. For she must understand now that her life depended on this testimony.

"Sir, I swear again that I have never seen Her Majesty Queen Anne closeted in private with any man. To my knowledge, the queen has always been true to His Majesty, and never looked at any other gentleman."

The scribe's quill scratched rapidly over the paper as he took these words down, to be used as evidence at the queen's trial. The man glanced up occasionally at Eloise, his lip curling as though he did not believe a word she said. Wolf felt his hands clench into fists, and had to remind himself to remain calm. But he looked at the scribe with loathing, wishing he could beat that impudent expression off the knave's face.

Cromwell leaned back in his chair, studying Eloise's face. He too was impassive, though his words showed that he shared his scribe's disdain for her evidence.

"Lady Wolf, I can understand why you should wish to protect your mistress the queen. Indeed, your loyalty is commendable. But it is wholly unnecessary. We already have it on good testimony that Her Majesty has been frequently seen in the company of other men since her marriage."

There was a pause: Cromwell waiting, no doubt, for Eloise to speak further, perhaps incriminate herself. Wolf waited too, barely breathing, willing his wife not to give anything away. But Eloise was not so easily intimidated.

When she remained silent, the king's advisor sighed. "Several other of her ladies," he continued quietly, "have admitted to having seen courtiers entertained privily in the queen's apartments, often late at night when the king was absent from court. Indeed, the musician Mark Smeaton has already confessed that he knew the queen intimately, and that she was not unwilling to accept his embraces. Yet you refute his confession, my lady, and expect us to believe you had no knowledge of these secret assignations."

With a sudden show of spirit, Eloise raised her chin. "Because that is the truth, sir."

Wolf almost smiled, and was glad his face was shrouded in darkness. Well said, my bride.

"We have heard that you are intimately acquainted with Sir Thomas Wyatt. Is this true?"

"It is not, sir."

"You have never been…private with him?"

There was color in Eloise's face. Her gaze flickered helplessly to Wolf's face, though he must be but a shadowy figure to her, out of reach.

"No!"

Cromwell too glanced at Wolf, a certain hard amusement in his expression as he willfully impugned his wife's honor.

Bastard.

"It seems strange that we should have such an account of you then…" The king's advisor fingered the paper in front of him ruefully, then set it aside and rustled through the other sheets, in conference with his scribe, as though hunting for one paper in particular. At last, the scribe muttered something, dragging out a loose sheet from a separate roll of documents, and Cromwell accepted it with a nod. "But no matter. We can return to that later, if needs be. For now let us move on, shall we? There is yet much testimony to be covered."

Sir Thomas Cromwell drained his wine cup in an unhurried fashion, then wiped his mouth fastidiously with a white damask napkin. He spread out and consulted the sheet of paper handed to him by the scribe, his gaze slowly scanning through what appeared from a distance to be a list of names.

"Have you ever seen Her Majesty the Queen privy with Mark Smeaton?"

"I have not, sir."

"But you know him? He is a Flemish musician. Considered a great favorite with the queen's ladies, I am told."

"I have never spoken with the gentleman, sir, though I know his face. Master Smeaton is a fair-spoken gentleman, and plays his lute very sweetly. However, I never saw him closeted with the Queen's Grace, nor did I ever hear him petition the queen for any special favor or attention."

"Indeed?"

Her face stiff with outrage, Eloise looked back at the king's advisor. "Her Majesty would never suffer such an act of impertinence from one of her servants."

"Very well." Cromwell's voice was shrewd. "What of Sir Henry Norris, then? He was a frequent visitor to the queen's privy chambers, I have been told. Perhaps you saw him there once or twice yourself."

Eloise's steady look faltered, her heightened color suddenly fading. Wolf drew a sharp breath, watching her intently.

"Sir Henry Norris?" she repeated.

"That is the gentleman, yes. You are acquainted with him?"

"Yes, sir."

"And did you ever see Sir Henry alone with the queen?"

"I…" Eloise looked across at Wolf. He felt sick and his heart began to thud with sudden warning. Was his wife about to betray herself and the queen? Then she licked her lips, shaking her head. Her voice was subdued. "No, sir. I have never seen Sir Henry alone with the queen."

"Nor with any of these gentlemen?" Cromwell sounded ruffled now. No doubt the king's advisor had hoped to bully her into an admission, but Eloise was proving more resilient than he had anticipated. Impatiently, he began to read out the names of those other unfortunate men accused of adultery with the queen. "Sir Francis Weston, Sir William Brereton, Sir Richard Page, Sir Thomas Wyatt, or perhaps Lord Rochford, the queen's brother?"

"I know many of those gentlemen by name and by sight, sir, but I have barely spoken to any of them myself."

Cromwell's gaze sharpened on her face. "Barely?"

"I may have conversed a few times with Sir Thomas at court," she admitted slowly, then drew a deep breath. Wolf wondered if she was recalling his advice not to incriminate herself in any way. "But I have never been alone with him."

"Nor seen him alone with the queen?"

"No, sir."

He looked at her speculatively. "You are acquainted with young Simon Thetford of Norfolk though, is that not true?"

With a start, Wolf remembered the fair youth who had tried so determinedly to seduce Eloise below his window the day they met at court. His name had been Simon. He was sure she had been a virgin at her first bedding. Yet he had often wondered how far that lad had pushed his charms with Eloise; was he now to discover it before Cromwell, that cold-tongued son of a commoner whose rise to prominence at court had astonished and unnerved so many?

Steeling himself for humiliation, Wolf let one hand drop to the dagger he had tucked into his belt before accompanying Eloise here.

He had not been permitted to wear his sword at this interrogation.

No doubt they feared a soldierly man like himself might be tempted to use it in his wife's defense. But it made him feel better to fondle its hilt lovingly, his eyes on Cromwell's face, willing the man to glance his way.

Look at me, you smug bastard, and leave my wife alone. I could have your throat slit before you'd taken two paces to summon the guards.

Eloise too looked shocked at this last name, produced out of nowhere like a jongleur's trick to dazzle the onlookers.

She clasped her hands together more tightly, and her voice shook for the first time as she answered the king's advisor. "S…Simon?"

Cromwell nodded and sat back, shooting a triumphant look in Wolf's direction, as though her guilty reaction was precisely what he had hoped to see at the mention of that name. His brief glance took in Wolf's tense stance, then the hand resting so significantly on the dagger hilt. But he did not back down, turning back to Eloise with a satisfied half-smile.

"You would not wish to see that young gentleman executed, I am convinced. Yet his name has been suggested to us as one of the queen's lovers."

She stared, shaking her head. "No, no. Not Simon. I know him; he would never…"

"You admit to knowing this young man privately?"

Too late she saw the trap he had set for her. Eloise drew back visibly, and Wolf saw her trying to school her expression. Her voice was only a thread of sound. "No, my lord."

"Come, my lady, there is no shame in such an admission. Your husband is an understanding man, and one of the king's fiercest friends. He would not wish you to perjure your immortal soul just to spare his blushes." He paused, his narrowed gaze moving back and forth between the two of them. There was a long silence in the shadowy room as he waited for an answer that did not come. His fingers drummed lightly on the table. "You seem pale, Lady Wolf, and you have not yet answered my question. Are you unwell?"

Cromwell clicked his fingers. A shuffling servant appeared from behind a screen and handed her a cup of wine. Her inquisitor waited a moment while Eloise drank, as though out of deference to her sex, or perhaps the presence of her husband in the same room. Then he began his questioning again, prodding her toward the only answer he wanted to hear.

"This Simon is a comely fellow, and of noble birth too. He would have made a good match, by all accounts. Indeed, until your recent marriage to Lord Wolf here, it is whispered that you and Simon Thetford were often private together. A young man like that would have no qualms spending time alone with any lady of the court, even with Her Majesty, if an invitation was issued."

His wife's cheeks grew hot with rage and embarrassment at this deliberate slur.

Watching her suffer and unable to do anything to prevent it, Wolf ground his teeth, wishing he could throttle the damn man where he sat. But that would merely result in his execution for murder, leaving Eloise widowed and defenseless.

"That is not true, my lord," she replied clearly, and his respect for her grew when he saw how she faced down her interrogator. Her courage remained undaunted, despite the shock she had registered at the sound of her former suitor's name. "I do not know whose was the voice that whispered such wicked falsehoods, but I urge you to lend that testimony no credence. I was a maid when I married his lordship, as I am sure Lord Wolf will testify."

Cromwell glanced at Wolf, as though seriously expecting him to stand forth at this point in proceedings and give him a detailed description of their wedding night.

Resisting the urge to use his dagger on the man instead, Wolf silently nodded his agreement that she had been a maid, and almost snarled when Cromwell shrugged and turned his back, making his disbelief plain.

Doggedly, Eloise continued her own testimony, though her color was still high and she was refusing to look at Wolf.

"Sir," she said, addressing Cromwell directly, her voice steady again, "before my marriage I was never private with any man. And to the best of my knowledge, neither was Her Majesty Queen Anne. I do not know how I can help you further in this matter, beyond what has already been said, and I pray you will excuse me. For I never saw Her Majesty spend time alone with Master Smeaton, nor Sir Thomas Wyatt, nor Sir Henry, nor with any of the other gentlemen whose names you have mentioned here today. And that is the truth, before God Almighty."

Wolf relaxed his hand on his dagger, seeing the defeat in Cromwell's face. That was one hurdle they had cleared, he thought cautiously. But this was King Henry's court, and nothing was ever simple here. There would be other tests to come, and from what he had learned since their arrival, the king himself would be the greatest hurdle of them all.

He only hoped Eloise could forgive him for what was ahead.

Fourteen

ELOISE SAW WOLF MOVE, suddenly pushing away from the wall he had been leaning against throughout her interrogation, and limp to the door before Cromwell had even dismissed her. She watched her husband go in a flutter of panic, not helped by the scribe's knowing smirk as he bade her sign her name below her testimony on the sheet. He had not spoken throughout the long questioning, yet just to see his dark head at the back of the room, and feel his gaze on her face whenever she struggled with a response, had been a kind of reassurance.

Where was Wolf going?

Had those last terrible questions, the ones about Simon's supposed intimacies, been too much for him?

It touched his honor, the malicious accusation that she had not been a maid when they married. After all, if that rumor was believed, any heir she bore him within the first year of their marriage would always be considered suspect.

It was all she could do not to scream with frustration. Who had told Cromwell such a vile lie? Unless she had given the other ladies cause to believe her so much in love with Simon that she would anticipate a wedding ceremony…

Guilt made her blush, remembering how she had failed to hide her interest in Simon. Nonetheless, with Cromwell's sharp gaze on her face, she signed her name with as bold a flourish as she could manage, then curtsied to her tormenter before leaving.

It was dark by the time Eloise was finally escorted back to their apartments by one of Cromwell's aged servants. The chilly palace corridors were lit by flaming torches that flickered in a spring breeze as she hurried past them, almost outstripping the old man who had been instructed to accompany her, too eager to reach the safety of her own chambers to wait for him.

It was late, and most of the courtiers seemed to have finished dining and retired to their own chambers. Nevertheless, as she passed through one of the empty state rooms, Eloise thought she heard whispers and felt hostile eyes watching her through doorways and from behind screens. Yet whenever she whirled in sudden anger, there was nobody there, only a chill breeze flapping at the wall tapestries and the old man smiling contemptuously.

When she reached her rooms, Wolf was not there either. She dismissed her escort and stood in the deserted apartment a moment, terribly lost without him.

"Where are you, Wolf?" she whispered, staring blindly at the one candle left burning against the darkness.

Then she shook herself, shocked by how feeble-minded she had become since her marriage, how incapable she had grown of independent thought and action.

"Come on," she told herself fiercely, pressing her nails into her palms, letting the sharp sting wake her spirit. "You are not weak; you can weather this."

Mary had lit a small fire in the bedchamber and was waiting there, asleep by the hearth, when she stumbled in. She undressed Eloise by candlelight, wide-eyed at all these strange happenings and the frightening atmosphere at court.

"I am glad you are come back, my lady," the maid admitted in an innocently candid manner. She unpinned Eloise's elaborately coiled hair, then reached for the wide-toothed comb. "So you are not to be arrested, then?"

Eloise frowned. "God's blood, Mary, keep a discreet tongue in your head!"

Mary bit her lip, then began to comb out her hair with a long stroke that was not quite steady. "Forgive me, my lady."

Eloise stood thinking for a while, her eyes on the soft gold of a deerskin rug at her feet.

"Mary, who told you I might be arrested?"

The girl shrugged, looking away uneasily. Eloise stared at her. There was something wrong, something Mary was not saying.

"I don't know, my lady," she whispered. "Just something they were saying in the servants' hall."

"But I have done nothing wrong," she exclaimed angrily, "and nor has the queen."

"Of course not, my lady."

Forcing herself to breathe more calmly, Eloise gestured Mary to bring a fresh nightrail and her woolen bed stockings from the chest. As Mary dressed her, she sternly reminded herself how vital it was to remain unflustered in front of her serving maid, whose loyalty to the Wolf household might soon be swayed if she fell from favor at court. Besides, it would only give the gossips more fuel for their vicious insinuations if she lost her temper and said something she ought to have kept to herself. And that would be a betrayal of Wolf's trust.

Assuming she still had his trust, that was.

"Sir Thomas Cromwell wished to ask me questions about Her Majesty," she continued smoothly, more collected now. "I answered them truthfully, and now it is done."

Mary hesitated, turning down the embroidered covers on the bed. "I am glad it is over, my lady."

Eloise managed a wobbling smile at this small gesture of support, and was horrified to find that tears were not far off.

"You may go to bed now, Mary," she told the girl, determined to do the same herself. "Try to get some rest; I am unlikely to need you again tonight. It has been a long day."

It was hard to wait until Mary had curtsied and closed the door

before Eloise could finally give in to her agony. Her eyes were stinging and she had an ache in her chest that was nothing to do with
fatigue, and all to do with Wolf's unexplained absence. What she
needed was to curl up in bed and cry herself to sleep. If sleep would
come after such a day…

And yet how much more the queen must be suffering, she
thought, and buried her face in the pillow as her heart threatened
to burst.

—⁓—

Limping away from the stifling atmosphere of the chamber where
his wife had been interrogated, Wolf had made for the small privy
garden at the base of the north tower. Wherever possible, he had
kept to the side corridors and sought out the shadows, not wishing to
be seen. Occasionally he passed an open doorway and saw courtiers
within, laughing and talking in the candlelight, some reading aloud,
others dancing. The court was frantically keeping itself busy and
amused as though nothing was amiss, as though their queen was not
in the Tower, awaiting her final condemnation.

Beneath their gaiety, however, Wolf sensed a growing terror, of a
kind which would not readily be quietened. Not even by the queen's
trial, for the horror of it all had them in a frenzy, not knowing to
whom Cromwell's finger might point next.

As more gentlemen were drafted in to ask questions and take
evidence of those closest to the queen, the court was becoming a
circus, where those who had previously watched and applauded the
king's cruelty were suddenly the ones whose sufferings were being
applauded. It was no surprise most of the courtiers were frightened
out of their wits.

Reaching the privy garden, he hesitated, staying out of sight by
habit. The breeze blew through the stone cloisters, and he smelled
fragrant flowers ahead in the darkness.

He thought of Eloise, how he had first kissed her in a privy garden like this one, at Greenwich Palace, near the river. She had shown such courage tonight, he thought, and winced inwardly at how desperate she must be feeling, waiting alone in their chambers, not knowing where he was.

But if he was to protect her, that was how it had to be. His jaw tightened. He felt in his leather belt pocket, retrieving the tiny sliver of paper he had found in one of his shoes on their first morning at court. Glancing about to check he was not observed, he read the note again, wishing he recognized the hand.

Written in Latin, the note simply said, *Beware, the king desires your wife.*

Wolf felt again the same quicksilver flash of jealous rage along his veins, then the aftertaste of fear. If true, Henry would stop at nothing to possess her. Not as a wife, for the king would not put soiled goods on his throne, not after the terrible error he had made with Anne Boleyn. Besides, he had Jane Seymour waiting to see which way the wind would blow from Tower Hill.

No, Henry was not looking for that kind of trouble. But he might take Eloise as his mistress, and then demand that Wolf acknowledge the king's children as his own. It had been done before, those cuckolded husbands welcoming the chance for such easy favor and advancement. But the very thought of Eloise in Henry's arms was enough to make his gorge rise…

So how would Henry achieve his seduction if Wolf refused to allow him access to his wife?

The easiest thing would be to discredit and disgrace Eloise, as Sir Thomas Cromwell had attempted to do tonight, thus forcing Wolf to annul their marriage on the grounds that she had not come to him a virgin. Failing that, he might decide to have Wolf killed. Either by stealth, or through some false accusation that would give the king a reason to order his execution.

My name may be next on that list of suspected lovers of the queen, he thought grimly. That would be the quickest and easiest way to empty Eloise's bed.

Someone was coming.

Wolf stiffened, listening to the soft footsteps in the cloisters. The clock had not yet struck ten, but it was time for his meeting. The beautiful and very married Mistress Langley had approached him that morning as he prepared to ride out in the hunt, and whispered in his ear, "You are in danger, my lord. But you still have friends at court. Come to the privy garden below the north tower, ten of the clock tonight, and I will help you."

He read the note again. *Cave, rex uxorem tuam cupiat.*

Was this secret meeting designed to entrap him in some way, leaving the king's path open to his wife's bed?

Wolf shoved the paper back into his pocket, and stepped forward into the moonlight, almost reckless in his desire to meet danger head-on.

He ought to have destroyed the note as soon he found it, he thought wryly. But perhaps he had needed the evidence in his hands a little longer, not quite believing that Henry would allow his overweening lust to rid him of one of his most seasoned soldiers. Not in these dark, unsettled times.

Mistress Langley was cloaked, her hood drawn down. She trod softly through the formal paths of the privy garden, a second figure following behind her.

Wolf waited in silence, his eyes narrowed on that hooded second figure, ready to draw his dagger if necessary. He did not know Master Langley, one of the king's more elevated clerks, but he knew his wife better than most: clever, promiscuous, but always discreet. The perfect mistress, she had borne three children to unknown noblemen, now growing up under the name Langley, yet seemed as seductive as ever.

But who was this mysterious person she had brought to their meeting?

Mistress Langley threw back her hood as she approached, tight red curls framing her face, her white, long-fingered hands adorned with costly rings.

Gifts from some of her grateful lovers, he thought, and lifted his gaze to her face, unable to deny that she was a very handsome woman and reputedly highly skilled in the art of seduction.

She curtsied, a smile glittering in her eyes as she looked up at him. "Lord Wolf."

"Mistress Langley."

"Kate, please," she murmured, and watched with interest as Wolf lifted her hand, pressing it to his lips as he raised her from her curtsy. "How you have changed since you were a youth, my lord Wolf. You look so much…harder. More like your name. It is a shame we are not better acquainted. But I have not seen you much at court these past few years."

"I have been much occupied in serving the king."

"Soldiering, yes." She ran her tongue along her lips, her brazen gaze dropping hotly to his codpiece, and there was little doubt in his mind what she was imagining. "The king speaks so highly of your fighting skills, my lord, I can hardly hear your name spoken without thinking of carnage and bloodshed."

"You wished to speak with me privately?"

Kate seemed annoyed by this deliberate snub, but shrugged. "You are in a hurry to discover my purpose? But of course you are: your wife is accused of conspiring with the queen against the king's honor."

"Those accusations are wholly without substance," he told her sharply, "as Cromwell discovered this very evening, on question-ing her."

She laughed. "You thought your wife guilty?"

He looked at her, waiting.

"No doubt you think the queen guilty too." Kate Langley's voice dropped to the merest whisper, audible only to him and the one in gray who stood behind her, still cloaked and hooded. "You would be alone in that misapprehension, my lord. Such nonsense, only a child would believe those charges. Adultery, witchcraft, devil worship… Even incest with her own brother? Such wild and dizzying accusations. But mud sticks where it will, and if it obscures a name the king wishes to obliterate…"

She did not finish, but Wolf had got her gist. His suspicions had been correct. King Henry wished to drive Eloise out of Wolf's bed and into his own. A creeping horror darkened his heart as he saw what must lie ahead if he failed to change the king's mind.

"Why did you bring me here if there is no way to change the course of events? To mock me?" he demanded, grabbing at her wrist. "Or to offer help?"

"I have never mocked you." She tried to tug her wrist free of his grasp, but could not. "If I can help you, my lord, I will. You are not without friends at court, though many are afraid to speak out against the king and risk their lives. I have been asked to do what I can for you. But you must remember to repay the favor one day."

"I will not be indebted to anyone," he said harshly.

She stared. "Not even for your life?"

"Not even then."

"And your wife's? Do you not care what happens to her?" Her voice was an angry hiss in the moonlight. "Whose bed she may be forced to grace?"

"Damn you!"

Kate wriggled in his grip. "You're hurting me!"

"Speak plainly then, Mistress Langley, and I will not hurt you. Nor your companion." He pushed her aside, turning to face the silent figure in the gray hood, his hand dropping instinctively on his dagger hilt. "Who are you? Speak! Throw back your hood: let me see your face."

It was a woman, he realized with surprise, and felt his nerves jangle as two slender white hands came up to push back the hood. Then she stepped into the patch of moonlight before him, and Wolf sucked in his breath, feeling as though someone had just punched him in the stomach.

"Margerie!"

She was just as he remembered from their betrothal: still ethereal in her beauty, small-waisted, that elfin face unchanged, her green eyes wide and fixed on him in apprehension, as though uncertain of her welcome. Yet there was a new fragility about her, a suggestion that she too had been broken and discarded, and for a moment Wolf felt his whole being tug toward her in sympathy. Then he recalled how she had deserted him for another man, made him a laughingstock before the court, and he stood in silence, his mouth hard, waiting for her to explain herself.

"Wolf." Margerie managed a smile, though a tremulous one. It did not convince him of her goodwill. "Ah, how you have changed since you were a youth. Your eyes are so cold now…"

"As you see."

"Was that my doing?"

His voice was terse. "What do you want, Margerie? You must have heard that I am married now. Or perhaps you came because of that. You should know, I have no need of a mistress."

"So unkind, my lord," she murmured, flinching momentarily, as though accustomed to such insults. Her green eyes studied him in the contemplative way he remembered. "No doubt I gave you good reason to be angry when we last parted. I did not come here to discuss the past though, but to offer you my help."

He would not berate himself for having spoken so harshly to a woman, Wolf thought, nettled by her presence and thrown off-balance by her unexpected offer. Margerie was no lady, and she could never be his friend. And if she was not his friend, she might turn out to be his enemy. Yet her hurt expression rubbed at his conscience.

He thought of the letters he had written to Margerie during those first years after she had run away with another man. Letters he had never sent, but had burned after writing. Letters full of desperate, pleading expressions of his love. Words he could never have said to her face, for fear of opening his heart in public, of breaking down and shaming himself...

And yet now, standing before her in the shadowy palace garden, Wolf felt none of the grand passion of his youth. Only pity for the hurt in her eyes, and guilt for the way he had just insulted her, both aloud and in his heart. Margerie was a woman he had once loved, that was all. Not a demon or a goddess. Just a woman, struggling through life with no male protector, who had come here with Kate Langley to offer him help. And he had just insinuated that she was a whore.

"Forgive me, I should not have spoken to you like that," he said, and bowed. "I will understand if you prefer to leave."

But Margerie was smiling. "No, I will stay, my lord. Whatever you may think of me, I am sorry for what I did, the way I treated you all those years ago. You were still a boy then, and I was too young myself to understand what had happened between us. I thought for a little while that I was in love with you. But it was just a girl's dream of love. I mistook your passion for possessiveness, and could only think of escaping before you trapped me forever."

His eyes met hers, and he nodded curtly. He thought of Eloise, and wondered if she had the same fear. The idea disturbed him.

"Go on."

"I have an idea which may distract the king from pursuing your wife, at least for now, and allow my conscience to be at peace. Given our past *amour*, and the interest of a certain gentleman at court," Margerie smiled, looking at him through her lashes so he could not see the expression in her eyes, "it would be best if I stayed away. But I have asked my dearest friend Kate if she will lend her support to my scheme."

Kate Langley glanced across at him drily. "And I have agreed. Though considering how uncivil you have been tonight, my lord Wolf, I cannot imagine why."

"Because he is so very comely, perhaps?" Margerie teased her.

Kate folded her arms across her chest, accentuating the high thrust of her breasts, then looked him up and down in a suggestive manner. "Perhaps."

Eloise had been asleep for some hours, twisting and moaning in a terrifying dream of ax blades and smoking stakes, when the door opened and closed in the darkened chamber. The sharp draft was what woke her, and the candle flame beside the bed dipped suddenly, then flickered back into life.

She pushed up on her elbow and peered round the heavy bed curtains, groggy with sleep, shaking away the hideous nightmares with an effort.

At that moment, a hand extinguished the candle. She smelled its thick smoke drifting in the darkness. Someone climbed into bed beside her, the whole mattress shifting with a creaking sound. She knew at once that it was Wolf. His masculine scent was so familiar to her now, she responded at once to his presence, her nipples stiffening beneath her thin nightrail.

"Wolf?"

"Hush." His hand found her mouth in the darkness and clamped down on it. "Not a sound."

Wolf pressed his lips to her forehead, her cheek, her throat. With his mouth, he pushed aside the lacy nightrail to find her breasts, suckling on one taut nipple. She could not speak, but her body writhed beneath him, admitting without words that she still wanted him.

He lifted her nightrail and his fingers stroked her flesh. She arched her back, keening silently like a cat in heat. Her cleft was already moist with longing, more than ready for him. He made a rough noise under his breath, and his knee pushed urgently between hers, parting her thighs.

Then Wolf covered her body with his own, pressing her down into the mattress, his hand still over her mouth.

He was completely naked, she realized with a shock. Her hands were still free, so she used them shamelessly, reaching down to rub his shaft as he had taught her.

Already erect, Wolf caught his breath as she played with him. Her hands moved slowly, one fondling the swollen head, the other playing his shaft up and down, excited to find his length hardening even more beneath her fingers, his skin like velvet over steel.

With a sudden groan, as though in exquisite pain, he pulled back from her. His hand sprang free, releasing her mouth.

"No noise," he reminded her sternly, then slipped down to crouch between her thighs.

Helpless to resist, she let her legs fall asunder, and felt him brush the bare skin just above her woolen stockings. Seconds later she had to stifle a cry with her own hand when his mouth settled at the apex of her thighs.

He tongued her greedily, his breathing heavy with desire, then clamped his mouth over her damp flesh, sucking hard until she thought her body would fall apart. A dizzying, spiraling heat threatened to overwhelm her and Eloise grabbed at his black hair, first dragging him away, then jerking him back in to suck her again. It was sheer agony to take his mouth where she was most sensitive, yet the most intolerable privation for him to stop.

Briefly, he lifted his dark head. "Come in my mouth," he ordered her through the darkness, so softly that for a moment she was not sure if she had imagined the words.

Then his mouth descended again, lashing at her tender flesh, tasting her, delving deep…

Her hands bunched first into fists that thumped helplessly into the bolster pillows above her head, then stretched into sharp-nailed claws, dropping to tear at his shoulders. She wanted to know where he had gone tonight, why he had abandoned her so abruptly after Cromwell's questioning had concluded. But the very instant that demand entered her mind it was chased away by the urgency of her desire, a desperation which made everything else seem of little importance.

Each breath was suddenly unbearable. Eloise snatched at the air, shuddering in her attempt not to make sounds, not to weep or cry or flail about, gasping his name.

In the screaming silence of her head she did all that, and more, her voice scratching on the darkness like a diamond, leaving his name behind.

Wolf.

His tongue pushed hard into her cleft, circled the slick walls of her cunt, and was followed by two fingers entering her, pushing slowly inside while he pulled back to suck on her flesh.

That slow penetration was what she had needed to push her over the edge.

Her body arched off the bed and into his face, her mouth wide open in a silent scream of pleasure. Then everything went black.

For one beautiful moment she was floating in mid-air as though falling from a great height, the air miraculously quiet and still about her, the swell and crash of the ocean far below.

Then her body went into spasm, almost shaking him off, and the vast wooden frame of their bed jerked and thudded as she landed again. The sheets beneath her were wet; her cunt was aching and molten beneath his still-working tongue, the pressure of his lips. Yet through all this, she somehow managed not to cry out, the intensity of her climax increased a thousandfold by his command to stay silent.

He pulled away, gasping with her, and leaned above her. His mouth sucked on her breasts, sliding from one to the other, teasing the stiff nipples with his tongue.

"No more," she managed brokenly, knowing he would hear her, despite the threadbare sound of her voice.

Wolf grunted at that, almost as though he were laughing at her, then pushed forward on his elbows, his mouth close to her ear. "Put me inside you then," he breathed.

Eloise angled her legs about his strong, sweating back, drawing him close. The very act of putting him inside her felt daring, as though she were as bold as a man, taking what she wanted instead of waiting to be taken. Yet Wolf seemed to enjoy the way she was handling him, his cock tense with desire as she slotted him with intense care inside her narrow opening.

He slid in deep, entering her with one long thrust. Her body jerked beneath him, his thick root stretching her, filling her beyond what she had thought possible.

Wolf was no longer cold, she thought wildly. Nor was he distant, not anymore. He withdrew almost to the edge, then pushed deep inside, his body hard and forceful, his muscles taut. She moaned and fought not to cry out, though she had been utterly taken over by the way he was fucking her and could barely control herself anymore.

"No." One hand clamped across her mouth, silencing her, and his other hand gripped her wrist, pinning her to the bed.

She ought to have been angry. Yet somehow that masterful restraint only served to excite her more. Eloise dragged her nails down his smooth, broad back, her legs linked about his waist, her whole body on fire for him, and heard him grunt with every thrust.

His heavy cock seemed to swell even further, thickening inside her. His thrusts grew faster, wilder. They were both panting now, their bodies slick with desire, sticking to each other. Then he released her wrist and pushed his hand between her thighs, seeking her cunt.

Cupping her damp sex, he squeezed and rubbed at it, not bothering to be gentle. His roughness drove her nearly mad with excitement.

Her mind closed to everything but the pressure of his hand on her mouth, his fingers playing with her fleshy mound while he was taking her, the hammering thrusts of his cock in and out, stretching her again and again.

She cried out under his hand, her body arching off the bed in the most exquisite pleasure, so intense it was painful. The darkness lit up with white-hot sparks, shooting in all directions at once, and she struggled not to scream. He groaned into her throat and gave another few thrusts, shoving his length so hard and deep inside her she thought she would die.

"Eloise," he cried hoarsely, muffling her name against her skin. Then suddenly he was coming inside her, his thick cock pumping out spurt after spurt of hot seed, flooding her with pleasure.

She lay beneath him for ages in panting silence, unwilling to move and uncouple from him. Her body was heavy and lethargic, and all her cares seemed to have fled, leaving her empty of thought.

Eventually his hand slipped off her mouth, as though he were falling asleep still inside her.

She turned at once, hungry for him again, nuzzling deep into his shoulder, enjoying the slick feel of his skin beneath her cheek.

Wolf had shown her no tenderness tonight.

No doubt he was still angry after the public accusation that she had been intimate with Simon before their marriage, even though it was untrue and he must know it. She had taken kisses from Simon, and a few fevered caresses. But her honor had never been breached, and she had gone to the altar *virgo intacta*.

But at least Wolf had returned to their bed. And he had given her what she needed after that terrifying inquisition by Sir Thomas Cromwell: a brilliant, intense, soaring climax that had wiped her clean.

Had Wolf known how pleasure would soothe her nightmares, she wondered? Or had he come back to stamp himself upon her after those damaging accusations by Cromwell, eager to remind his wife to whom she belonged?

—⁘—

She stirred after the most delicious sleep to find Mary bustling about the sunlit chamber, emptying the covered chamber pot and pulling the bed curtains open. She sat up, stretching and yawning, and slowly rearranged her tangled nightrail. Then it hit her that she was alone.

Eloise stared at the empty space beside her pillow, puzzled not to see Wolf lying there.

"Mary, where is his lordship?"

"Begging your pardon, my lady, I have not seen Lord Wolf this morning. I do not think his lordship came back last night."

The maid paused, and a slight flush entered her cheeks as she realized the potential significance of what she had said.

"That is…I do not know where he is, my lady."

"Oh, his lordship came back." Eloise swung her legs out of bed, still a little sore from the forceful way he had taken her in the night. She tried not to show the despair devouring her soul. "Only it seems he chose not to stay."

Fifteen

WOLF HAD STILL NOT returned by the following evening, and although she was bored, Eloise thought it prudent to remain closeted in their chambers during his absence. She had no idea whether she was still under suspicion after giving her testimony, but it was better not to draw attention to herself by wandering the court unaccompanied by her husband. She did not know where he had gone, but her body still bore the marks of his unexpected visit. Occasionally she pushed back the lace-trimmed sleeve of her gown to see the slight bruise he had left on her wrist, remembering the strength of their desire. The memory left her tingling with pleasure.

When Mary came back from the kitchens with a trencher for her evening meal, she was full of whispers about the queen's impending fate. It seemed that although the courtiers in charge of the investigation could not make the dates fit the queen's movements, this was considered unimportant, for a theory had been put forward that she was a witch and could magically appear at will in any place.

"Are these men out of their wits?" Eloise muttered, stabbing at her food with her belt dagger. Suddenly she had no appetite. The sauce was too salty, and the quail meat tasted like ashes in her mouth. She pushed the trencher away impatiently. "They will have her condemned any way they can. Poor Queen Anne!"

Suddenly, she found herself weeping, and angrily sought a handkerchief amongst the folds of her gown.

The Lord alone knew what terrors the queen must be facing, waiting in her cell at the Tower, while these wicked men conjured up phantom lovers for her on every side. And for what reason? Because she had not yet produced the son and heir King Henry craved, and His Majesty had grown impatient.

"My lady," Mary whispered urgently, hurrying to clear away her barely touched trencher. "I hear footsteps outside. I think someone is coming."

Drying her eyes, Eloise sat up at once and arranged her gown more decorously. Belatedly, she remembered what Wolf had told her on their arrival at court. Whenever anyone visited or the door to their apartments was open, she must always be guarded in her speech and actions. In particular, she must not allow anyone to think she was frightened, in case that was taken for guilt by those who watched.

When the knock came, she called out in a calm voice, "Enter!"

It was Hugh Beaufort. He pulled off his cap and bowed to her politely, but when he straightened, she caught a grim look in his eyes and felt her heartbeat jump.

Had something happened to Wolf?

She drew a steadying breath before addressing him, her hands in her lap. "Master Beaufort, I am glad to see you."

"Forgive me, Lady Wolf, for not visiting you before now. But I have been much occupied with the king and his councilors." Hugh stood awkwardly in the open doorway, looking rather stiff and somber in a black robe, his black velvet cap still in his hand. Behind him she could see a man on guard in the corridor, watching them, his eyes glittering in the torchlight. "The truth is, I...I have been sent to fetch you before the king."

Eloise stared, not quite understanding. "Fetch me before the king?" she repeated slowly.

"Yes, my lady." Hugh stood back, indicating that she should rise and follow him. When she stayed seated, looking back at him in total confusion, he cleared his throat and said more hoarsely, "His Majesty the King bids you attend him in his privy dining chamber at once. Come, I will show you the way."

Glancing uncertainly at Mary, she rose and curtsied. "As you wish, sir."

As Eloise passed the guard, she could have sworn he leered at her. Averting her eyes, she followed Hugh without a word. But inwardly she was going mad with worry. She had thought to be safer at court as Lady Wolf, protected by her husband's powerful name and influence. Instead, she had not seen him all day, and now she was to face the king alone.

Why would King Henry summon her to his privy dining chamber? What had she said or done to merit such an order? She thought back over her testimony and was lost for an explanation. Perhaps he merely wished her to confirm that the queen was innocent, as she had stated. But His Majesty could have read her testimony himself; he did not need her to be present, to admit her misgivings to his face.

Hugh Beaufort strode along the corridors as though she were not there, making it hard for her to keep up. She thought he seemed angry with her, but could not be certain.

The question of Wolf's whereabouts kept nagging at her as she followed his friend. His absence was a thorn driven deep into her heart. Painfully she considered the various explanations for his disappearance. A demanding mistress from before his marriage, perhaps, who had reclaimed his attention. Or a tempting new lover, some pretty woman who had caught his eye in recent days.

"Sir?" When Hugh paused at the foot of a broad, torchlit staircase, she finally managed to catch up with him, hampered by her full skirts. Her voice was breathless. "I pray you, sir, where is my husband?"

His face tightened. "Follow me."

"But—"

"You must follow me, Lady Wolf," he insisted, his voice suddenly harsh.

He fell into step beside her as they began to ascend the stairs. When she looked at him in confusion, not recognizing Wolf's smiling friend in this cold-faced stranger, Hugh placed a warning hand on her arm.

His voice was a wasp in her ear, stinging her into silence. "Ask no questions. Say nothing. You are being watched."

The chamber where the king had been dining privately that evening was not vast and glittering, as she had expected, but rather a small, intimate space where he could be with friends, unobserved by the rest of the court. A few steps behind Hugh Beaufort, she slipped between the two armed guards on the outer doorway, through a darkened antechamber where several men stood whispering together, turning to survey her as she passed, and thence into the dining chamber itself.

Her gaze swept the room uneasily, wondering who would be there to witness her humiliation.

A small table had been set with fine ware, though the platters stood half-empty now, with food spilt on the rushes beneath. The chairs had been pushed back, and the diners now reclined on cushion-covered couches in the soft, flickering firelight of the hearth. In the corner, a woman sat plucking at a harp, her gaze discreetly averted from the royal party.

On the low table between the couches, a chess board had been set, with delicate, carved ivory pieces. King Henry lay at his ease, watching a young woman in a gossamer-thin gown who knelt before him on the floor, apparently pondering her next move. He was speaking to the man reclining next to him, just out of her line of vision, his voice light with slurred amusement as he recounted some disreputable tale. Soft laughter indicated the presence of another woman, perhaps sitting next to the unseen courtier.

Then the king turned his head and caught sight of Hugh, patiently waiting at his elbow.

"Ah, Master Beaufort. Well, have you brought the lady?" he demanded loudly. "Come along then, man. Bring her forward, let us see her."

She could tell from his voice that the king was very drunk. A cold prickle of unease stirred under her skin. Nonetheless, she stepped round Hugh and into the firelight at his gesture, dropping onto her knees before the king.

"Your Majesty," she murmured, head bent.

"A pretty piece, as I have always said," the king commented, slurring his words, and she guessed he must be addressing the man next to him. "And yet you tell me she does not please you as she should, Lord Wolf."

With a shock that left her pale and breathless, Eloise realized that the other man in the room was Wolf.

What was he doing here with the king…and these disreputable women?

There was a roaring in her ears, and for a terrible moment she thought she would faint. Her hands began to tremble, and she clasped them tightly before her, not daring to look up for fear of what she might see.

"What are these disobedient women about, eh?" the king continued, blithely unaware of her struggle. "God's blood, a man of your standing should be allowed to divorce his wife for disappointing him in bed. But I daresay the priests would disagree once again, damn them, and I cannot tear all the churches down." He laughed richly. "So what do you intend to do about her, my lord?"

"I have not yet decided, Your Majesty." To her horror, Wolf sounded calm, almost amused. "What is your opinion on this matter of disappointing wives?"

King Henry laughed again, and glancing up from under her

lashes, she saw him clap Wolf on the back. "You have come to the right man for counsel, my friend. Divorce the wench, I say, and take yourself a new wife. Her father is a sound man, he will understand. If she has not been meddled with…"

"Oh, I have meddled with her," Wolf admitted lightly. "I must have an heir, Your Majesty, whether the begetting of him proves a trial or not."

"You do not have to say any more on that score." The king shifted angrily on the couch, and his tone became biting, even savage. "I understand your dilemma perfectly. Though you surprise me. I always had my eye on little Eloise when she was among Anne's maids of honor, for she has something about her…"

"Pray do not waste your time, Your Majesty," Wolf interrupted. "My wife is an icicle in bed."

His voice too was slurred, but more heavily, as though he had been drinking some hours. He lowered his voice as though to spare her feelings, though he must have known that she could hear every word of his drunken complaint. As could every other person in the room, she thought painfully.

"Eloise is one of these women who lie rigid as stone and wait for you to mount them, so that you feel like a rapist by the end of it. On our wedding night, Your Majesty, I would have had more joy with a marble statue. But Holy Church has seen us wed. So I must cleave to this sorry wife for an heir and take my pleasures in another's bed."

Her cheeks burned with humiliation, and her hands clenched into fists.

I hate you for this, Wolf.

King Henry had risen from the couch. He came toward her, stumbling in his drunkenness, and stood with his legs slightly apart, as though about to force her into some lewd act.

His hand came under her chin, dragging her face up into the

firelight. "Yes, you are right, you are right. Her mouth is over-large. She has not much beauty, and her hair is too fair."

She waited, unsure why she had been summoned, unless it was merely to be scourged with the shame of her husband's loathing and contempt.

"Speak truthfully now, for I am your king… Did you never see my wife with another man? I know you were often privily in Anne's chambers, you and your little friends from the Maidens' Hall."

King Henry's voice grew rough, and she suddenly realized that he was tortured by the same cruel stabs of jealousy which afflicted her.

"Do not look at me with such fear, Eloise. I shall not punish you for Anne's fault, you may speak freely here. Perhaps you overheard her speak too sweetly to one of her musicians? A Flemishman called Smeaton?"

"I did not, Your Majesty."

"Never?" he demanded, pressing her violently. "Never?"

"No, Your Majesty."

"For if you are lying to me, I swear before God that I will have your head for it, pretty or not." His voice thundered at her, his words beating about her ears. "Now tell the truth and shame the devil, did you ever see Queen Anne play me false?"

She shook her head, her throat tight with unshed tears. This at least she could do for the unfortunate queen. "I swear it on my honor, Your Majesty."

"On your honor, Lady Wolf?" His leering gaze dropped to her tight bodice, where her breasts swelled fashionably upward, as though inviting a man's touch. "I never knew a woman yet who held her honor dear enough to swear on it. Well, well." He licked his lips and his eyes glinted in the firelight, as though he had been suddenly distracted from his interrogation. "Your hair is truly lustrous…"

"Your Majesty," Hugh interjected, clearing his throat. "Forgive me, sire, but Sir Thomas Cromwell is at the door here, begging an urgent audience with Your Majesty."

As the king moved away, reluctantly turning his attention to the waiting men in the antechamber, Eloise took the opportunity to glance in Wolf's direction. At once, she wished she had not done so, or that she had looked with a more guarded heart.

Through the tears in her eyes she saw that he was not alone on the couch. A beautiful woman lay beside him, her arms draped about his neck, watching Eloise with a knowing smile. Her curly red hair hung loose to her waist, and her breasts were not even confined to her courtly gown but bulged freely over her bodice, displaying large, dusky nipples that had sharpened to points. She was some five years older than Eloise, her blue eyes full of cruel laughter, and her reddened mouth bore the signs of recent, vigorous kissing.

But that was not what Eloise was looking at.

Her gaze was fixed on Wolf's arm, wound so intimately about the woman's waist. He was looking down into her heart-shaped face, as though deeply in love, and Eloise could not prevent a tiny choking cry of rage and despair.

How dare Wolf come to her bed last night, demanding his rights to her body, when he had this shameless woman to pleasure him at court?

God's blood, if he had thought she was frigid before, she would soon teach him the meaning of ice.

"I am no marble statue, my lord Wolf," the woman whispered seductively, then stretched up to kiss him on the mouth.

Wolf kissed her deeply, then slid his mouth down her throat to the swell of her breasts. "That you are not, my sweet Kate," he said thickly, and Eloise heard the unmistakable slur of lust in his voice. "A creature of pure fire."

Behind her, King Henry had returned with Hugh Beaufort and

Cromwell, hovering dark-robed in his wake. His voice grown cold, he was saying to his chief advisor, "No, I have not yet decided the manner of her dispatch, given a verdict of guilt. I know the law prescribes death by burning in such a case. But whatever her sins toward me and God, I cannot... We must find another way."

"The block, Your Majesty?"

"Aye, perhaps." The king stared down into the fire. He wiped a hand across his brow, as though uncomfortably hot. "But not with a common ax. She is still a queen anointed."

"With a sword, then?" Cromwell mused. "It will be hard to find an executioner skilled enough."

"Then you must send to France for one. It is their custom there to behead with a sword, is it not?"

"As you say, Your Majesty."

The king turned and gave a sudden hoarse shout of laughter to see Wolf in the arms of another woman, and Eloise still kneeling red-faced before her husband.

"Sweet Jesu, my lord." He took up a cup of wine and drained it. "Your wife is still here, Wolf. Is this seemly?"

Wolf's face was flushed a hard red, his eyes glittering.

"Forgive me, sire. I forgot myself."

"I must speak privately with Cromwell," King Henry told him. He dismissed him with a wave of his hand. "You had best leave Mistress Langley to her husband and take your own pretty wife to bed. If you want my advice, you'll warm her up with your hand a little if you wish to have an heir."

"Yes, Your Majesty."

"Master Beaufort, I will speak with you more on the subject of the northern monasteries tomorrow."

Hugh bowed, and silently withdrew. From the doorway, his eyes sought hers, a pitying look in them, as though ready to offer her his help. Eloise felt herself color with shame, but looked away, keeping her chin high. She would not accept help from any man, even one as charming and friendly as Hugh.

However much her husband had humiliated her in the king's presence tonight, however badly he might hurt her in the future, this argument was between her and Wolf alone. She would not draw Master Beaufort into her private hell, however much she suffered there.

With some difficulty, Wolf disentangled himself from his mistress, staggering to his feet. On his way to the door he stumbled over a lost shoe, catching himself in time against the table where they had dined. Eloise rose and followed him, despising him for his vile licentiousness. Why had she been so foolish, blindly admiring her husband's determination and resolve, not seeing what lay behind that facade, the libertine who thought so little of his wedding vows that he would all but bed another woman before her?

"To bed," Wolf muttered, gripping her by the elbow as she tried to stalk ahead of him. "We will go together, madam wife, if you please, and at my pace."

The two women had been dismissed from the king's presence too, wrapping themselves in cloaks before being escorted away by one of the guards. Mistress Langley shot her a furious glare as she passed, then blew a kiss to Wolf, which he received with a hard look. No doubt even he found it uncomfortable to parade his mistress before his new bride.

"Until tomorrow eve, my lord," Kate promised him softly as she turned away.

Watching this exchange, the torment in her heart that Eloise had struggled to hold at bay during the king's questioning returned tenfold. It threatened to overwhelm her spirit, cast her down to a place where she would crawl like the abject fool that she was, all the pride whipped out of her.

Like a sick animal she allowed herself to be dragged along beside him through the torchlit corridors, not able to meet his eyes, though more than once she felt his gaze on her profile. She had feared he still loved Margerie after seeing him with that paper, marked with the name of his former betrothed, in his secret tower room. Instead she found there were other women in line for his attentions.

Turning her face away, Eloise sunk her teeth into her wrist rather than let him hear her moan of distress. Why could she not stop torturing herself like this? Wolf was a wealthy and influential nobleman, and a man with a strong sexual appetite.

Of course he had more than one mistress at court. What had she expected?

Wolf released her arm long before they reached their apartments, his face shuttered, unreadable. He passed the man-at-arms on the door with a nod, holding onto the wall as though he was finding it hard to stand. The man's look was amused when Wolf began dragging at his jacket before they were even inside, yawning and not quite managing to walk in a straight line.

"I need to sleep," he said roughly, limping inside the room and kicking the door shut once Eloise and Hugh were inside.

Mary had been asleep on the daybed by the fire, her mouth open as she snored gently. At the sound of the door slamming, she jumped up with a start, straightening her cap when she saw who it was.

"My lord, my lady," she managed, staring wide-eyed from one to the other.

"Take yourself to bed, Mary," he said curtly without looking at her, and began to struggle out of his tight jacket, his eyes on Eloise instead.

"But I must tend to my lady…"

"My lady can sleep in her gown for all I care," Wolf bit out, finally ridding himself of his jacket, and shot the maid a dangerous look. "Bed. Now."

"Aye, my lord."

Mary sketched a hurried curtsy and disappeared through the door into the narrow space that served as her bedchamber.

Now it was only the three of them, Hugh lingering by the closed door as though uncomfortable at remaining but clearly unwilling to leave her alone with Wolf.

She looked back at her drunken husband, meeting his gaze with a cold shuddering shock that felt like the end. The end of their marriage, the dying of that tiny light that had begun to kindle in her heart whenever he looked at her.

"I hate you," Eloise breathed, her heart breaking apart as what she had seen in the king's chamber flashed through her mind like scenes from a tragic play, how Wolf had held that woman, Kate Langley, in his arms, had kissed her begging mouth, all the while telling the king in that scathing tone how cold Eloise was in bed, how little she could please him as a woman…

"Is that so, my dearest love?" he drawled, his brows raised at her vehemence, clearly mocking her.

"Yes, and I'll never share your bed again," she hissed, just about hanging on to her self-control.

The urge to launch herself at him was so strong. To flay his handsome face with her nails, let him see what he had done to her tonight. Yet what would that achieve? Better to rein in her agony and keep some shred of pride with which to clothe herself in the morning.

He was drunk anyway; he would not remember any insults she might fling at him tonight, though if she scratched his face that might give him an inkling of her anger tomorrow.

"We'll see," Wolf remarked, tossing his jacket carelessly across the back of the daybed.

He limped to the table and poured himself a cup of wine, as if he had not already taken enough drink that night, then stood drinking with his back to her.

His shirt was already loose, his slashed-sleeve doublet open, his muscular thighs and buttocks outlined in the tight black hose. The sight of his hard soldierly body, given so freely to other women, tore her apart. She was his wife; his body should belong to her alone. When he turned back, she had to avert her eyes from the aggressively masculine thrust of his codpiece, knowing what lay beneath it—and that it was not for her.

Wolf had barely registered her threat not to sleep with him again, as though he did not believe her. Which was perhaps not surprising, given how she was staring at him, not bothering to hide how desire simmered below her contempt.

He put down the cup, wiped his mouth with the back of his hand, and glanced across at Hugh. His lip curled at his friend's wary expression.

"Still here, Beaufort?" The question was laconic, but there was steel beneath it.

Hugh hesitated, clearly reluctant either to argue with his friend or to abandon her when she might be in trouble.

He glanced at Eloise, as though seeking permission to leave. "My lady?"

"Pray do not alarm yourself on my account, sir," she managed, though her heart was beating wildly at the thought of being left alone with her husband in this dangerous mood. She went to bid the young man good night, anxious not to see him get hurt by interfering between her and Wolf. Their marriage was fast becoming a battleground, but she would fight this war without outside help. "You have been more than good to me tonight, Master Beaufort. But you need not stay."

"You are sure, my lady?"

"Perfectly."

Hugh bent gallantly over her hand, kissing it. Eloise looked at him with gratitude as he straightened.

"I am tired and will go to bed now," she murmured, and he released her hand. "Thank you for everything, sir. I shall see you tomorrow."

Narrow-eyed, watching the two of them talk softly together, Wolf gave a furious exhalation of breath. He folded his arms across his powerful chest, tension in every line of his body.

"I think not," Wolf said tightly. His hard gaze moved from Hugh's face to her own, the warning in that stare unmistakable.

Her gaze flickered across to him with disdain; she wondered how her husband could still stand, the amount of wine he must have drunk that night. Yet his stare did not falter.

It was almost as though he were jealous, she thought angrily. Which was a mockery of everything she knew to be true, of course. If he wanted her at all, Wolf saw her as a dog sees a bone: his to bite, and his to bury. She was his possession, and he was not willing to part with her, regardless of however many other women he might also possess.

The agony of seeing him in the arms of the beautiful Mistress Langley wrenched at her again, instinct telling her Wolf must have known her carnally before tonight. Just as there was no doubt in her heart that he would "know" that woman again, repeatedly, while they were in residence at court. She had grown to appreciate his powerful desire for sex and was not foolish enough to assume that she alone could satisfy a man like that.

With an expression of deep chagrin, Hugh Beaufort bowed to them both, cap in hand.

"Forgive me," he muttered. "I can see that I am in the way here, and will trespass on your time no longer."

He was about to take his leave when someone came thudding heavily along the corridor and hammered at the door with what sounded like a dagger hilt.

"Ho there within, open up!" a deep voice cried, full of urgency.

The hammering came again, even louder. "Open this door; I must speak with Lord Wolf at once!"

She did not see Wolf move. Yet suddenly he was right there at her side, his hands about her waist, whirling her behind him as though she weighed as little as a rag doll.

He sounded crisp and decisive, forestalling her protests with a raised hand. "Stay behind me, Eloise, or I shall not be answerable for my actions."

The air of drunken stupor had fallen away as her husband spoke, standing straight-backed before the door with a threatening hand on his dagger hilt.

She was amazed by this change of demeanor, feeling like a fool as she realized he had dissembled in the king's rooms. Wolf had never been drunk at all, merely playacting. But to what purpose?

"Hugh, open the door."

Sixteen

THE CLOAKED AND MUD-SPLATTERED man who entered their rooms threw back his hood at once, and Eloise gasped.

"Renford!"

It was one of her father's serving men, a sturdy fellow she had known since childhood.

She stared at him in sudden terrible apprehension and took a faltering step forward. "My father... He is not unwell? Not...?"

"Forgive me, my lady," Renford interrupted, and knelt wearily before her husband. He wrested a letter from his pouch. "My lord, I bear an urgent message from Sir John in Yorkshire."

Wolf took it without a word and unrolled the letter. His brows knitted together as he read. "God's blood."

"What is it?" she demanded at last, unable to bear the agony of waiting. "Is my father sick? Tell me, for pity's sake."

He glanced at her oddly, from under his lashes. "It is not Sir John who is in trouble, but your sister. Susannah has run away from home, and your father asks me... Nay, he begs me to send out a party of men to search for her."

She frowned. "But if she is in Yorkshire..."

"Sir John believes she was coming here, to court. She left a note to that effect and took one of his fastest horses. Money too."

"But a young woman, riding south unaccompanied..." Eloise shook her head, looking horrified from one man to the other. "Susannah will not get far, surely? She would be noticed in every village and hamlet on the road to London." A thought struck her with the force of a sword thrust, and she wrapped her arms about her stomach. "God forbid she should be set upon before she is found. That road is so dangerous…"

Wolf looked over her head at Hugh, whose face was suddenly gray with fear for the young Susannah. "Your father says she took precautions against such a fate. Her old nurse believes she left dressed as a man."

"D…dressed as a man?" she repeated, stammering, unable to imagine her fair-haired sister in a man's garb. It was shocking, and yet perhaps it might save her life. If Wolf could only reach her in time. "You must ride north and hope to intercept her, my lord. Then bring her on to court yourself."

"I admit, that is my own thought," Wolf mused, but his frown was dark as he met Hugh's gaze. "Yet I cannot leave court. Not now."

What on earth did he mean by that? She could find no significance in it, and guessed with a sudden painful insight that he would not stir for her sister when he had an assignation with his mistress that he would rather honor. Until tomorrow eve, my lord. That was what Kate Langley had murmured as she bid him farewell, her eyes promising more than just soft kisses on the king's couch.

Eloise felt her gut twist as she realized how little she and her family must mean to him.

Hugh nodded, as though his friend had spoken. "I will find your sister and bring her safely to court," he told her grimly, and put his hand on the hilt of his dagger. "Whatever it takes."

"You cannot ride that road alone," Wolf said swiftly, and handed the letter to Eloise, who was still waiting silently to read it. "As my wife has said, the way is dangerous, and her sister may not have traveled far. Sir John's messenger may have overtaken her on the road, had he but known it." He fetched his jacket from the daybed, frowning hard. "I shall seek out some half dozen of my men below; they can journey with you. You ride at first light, yes?"

Hugh nodded, though he seemed impatient enough to set off at once, even in the darkness.

"Come then, there is no time to waste. Let us bustle." Wolf clapped the messenger on the shoulder on his way out. "I give you thanks for your speed, man. Take some victuals now, and then a few days' rest."

"Aye, my lord."

Eloise drew an angry breath as Wolf limped back through the door, accompanied by Hugh, both men having forgotten her presence.

"My lord!" When Wolf turned to stare at her, his handsome face suddenly tense and wary, she could not help herself, much as she despised her own weakness. "When will you be back, my lord?"

"Later," was his curt reply.

She took a step forward, meaning to interrogate him further, and his eyes met hers with a look of such violent authority that it both shocked and silenced her.

"Go to bed, Eloise. You can do nothing here."

It was a command, not a suggestion, and they both knew it. Like her impotent fury over his mistress, this business was for him, not her, and her interference was unwelcome. He was her master, and it was clear he intended her to understand it, whether she liked it or not.

Wolf tore his gaze from hers and closed the door quietly behind him, leaving her alone. She stood in a whirl of exhausted confusion, no longer sure what was true in her life and what false, wishing she could rush after him and demand an explanation.

But she could not. She did not have that power. She was Wolf's bride, not his keeper.

―⁂―

It was dark when she was woken by a noise, lying facedown on the bed where she had thrown herself hours before, still in her gown but without her shoes and stockings. The candle had long since burned out, and the only light was from the glowing embers in the hearth. She sighed, turning her head drowsily, and noticed a thin yellow light through the open bed curtains, coming from under the bed-chamber door.

Eloise lay for a moment, still half-asleep, looking at that soft, flickering light and trying to work out what it was. Then she heard again the noise which had woken her, and sat up abruptly.

Someone was in the other room. And that crash had sounded like a weary man throwing his boots across the room, one after the other.

She slipped out of bed and padded barefoot to the door. It opened with a slight creaking sound, but nobody challenged her. Indeed, the chamber seemed empty at first glance. Then she saw him. Wandering across the rushes, her crumpled skirts gathered up in her hands, Eloise came to the side of the daybed and stopped, staring down in disbelief.

Her husband was lying on his back by the fire, one arm flung across his eyes as though to shut out the flickering glow. His jacket and boots were gone, his shirt was unlaced, and his short dark hair was disheveled.

She thought he looked thoroughly exhausted, as though he had just climbed out of another woman's bed. Jealousy pricked at her as she looked down at him, noting the dark stubble on his chin, the sensual line of his mouth—and his weary pallor.

Wolf was a player and a libertine, she had no doubt on that score. But was there anything left over for her, and if there was, could she ever be satisfied with that? To be the one he returned home to, not the one he went to for his pleasure?

She must have made a noise because he stirred. His arm fell back, then his eyes opened and met hers. That deep, intense blue gaze that always left her fighting for breath.

"Eloise." There was a wealth of heavy, ironic meaning in the way he said her name, as though he were saying "Trouble" or "Danger" instead.

"It's gone the middle of the night. Master Beaufort must have retired to bed long since. Where have you been?" she asked coldly, and dropped her skirts when she saw his gaze slide down her body to her bare legs and feet.

His mouth twisted at the question, as though she had amused him. "Elsewhere."

Her heart winced in pain and her breath hissed out, already knowing the answer before she asked the question.

"With Mistress Langley?"

Wolf opened his mouth to reply, then closed it again. His eyes held some shadow which she interpreted as guilt, though he sounded more angry than guilty.

"Why don't you go back to bed, Eloise? I shall not disturb you but sleep out here tonight." Wolf sat up and swung his legs to the floor, then reached for his wine cup, which she saw was still dark with red wine. "Forgive me if I woke you."

"Drinking again?"

Her voice was stormy, accusing.

Wolf looked up sharply, then shrugged and put the cup to his lips. She saw his throat swallow, then he lowered the cup, still looking directly at her. "As you see."

It was a challenge, she realized. He would drink whenever and whatever he wished. What was she going to do about it? Nothing, she thought wildly. Nothing.

"Why did you play drunk with the king tonight?" she demanded.

His eyes narrowed. "What?"

Her guard wavered and then abruptly dropped before his penetrating gaze, for she was too tired to fight him anymore. Instead she looked at him without dissimulation and let his physical spell work its mastery over her. There was no point pretending anymore that she did not want whatever crumbs Wolf might offer her when he had finished with his other women.

But she was still angry with him, and her pride would not allow her to fall to his feet in abject surrender.

Her body ached for his, yes. But he would have to take it. She tried to tell him what she wanted with her eyes, and guessed from the way he looked back at her that he had understood. Or understood that she was offering herself to him, at least.

"Wolf, please…" she managed thinly, barely holding onto her strength and self-control. At that instant nothing else mattered but that he wanted her back. "I need you."

Something flickered in the hot blue depths of his stare. Then he stood and took her arm, firmly steering her back toward her bedchamber.

"What you need is sleep," he muttered. "We both need to sleep tonight. It will be dawn soon."

She could feel the heat from his body, her senses tingling at his proximity. She had been dreaming of him in her sleep, she remembered now. He had been inside her in her dream, so male, so demanding, and she had not pushed him away but urged him on, whispering in his ear, even riding atop like a wanton.

She flushed, glad he could not read her thoughts. Though in truth she would not mind if Wolf crawled into bed with her, then rolled her over until she was lying on top. The thought of controlling him in bed was heady, intoxicating, like the rich red wine he had been drinking and that she could smell on his breath.

"Wolf," she whispered seductively as he pushed her before him into the darkened bedchamber.

"No," he said tightly.

"Yes," she insisted, not easily distracted from her goal. "You are my husband, are you not?"

He did not answer, but watched her in silence.

Eloise turned swiftly before he could leave her again, her mind made up, her hands dragging at his loosened shirt, tugging it over his head.

To her surprise, Wolf did not stop her, though his chest heaved as he stood before her, naked to the waist.

She had forgotten to close the shutters properly last night when she had fallen alone into bed, exhausted and still dressed, and now the milky light of dawn was creeping through the window slit.

By that light she admired his powerful chest and shoulders, running her fingers down his belly toward the leather bulge of his codpiece. His breathing increased, his eyes on her face, then he made a hoarse noise as her hand found and caught his cock, squeezing lightly through the codpiece.

"Eloise…"

"Hush," she told him, then pulled on his hose, releasing his cock. It sprang into her hands, thick and veined, already stiffening as her fingers closed about him, inciting the flames of desire she had tried to dampen down. "Oh, Wolf."

"You would take me into your bed, madam," he said harshly, "believing me a drunk and an adulterer?"

She sank to her knees before him, her hunger for his body so all-consuming that she could think of nothing else.

"I do not want to hear what you have done," she whispered, meaning every word at that moment, and laid her cheek against his body. "Only what you will do with me."

His shaft jerked, and she turned her head slightly, sighing as she took the mushroom-shaped crown into her mouth. His skin tasted salty, so masculine and enticing. He grew in her mouth, slowly stretching her lips, and with a strangled moan she shifted position, accepting more of his thick root into her throat.

He suddenly grabbed at her hair, pulling her closer. "All of it, then," he ordered her, and the silken authority in his voice made her shiver as she obeyed.

She sucked him in deep and let him withdraw slowly, his root hardening until it was rock in her mouth, the skin startlingly velvet against her lips. His breathing grew more rapid, and he began to thrust lightly in and out of her mouth, not hurting her but expertly showing her how much more she could take.

Daringly, she cupped his balls, taken aback by how large and powerful they felt, and rolled them gently in her hand. He exhaled sharply.

"God's blood," he muttered.

She looked up at him in the early morning light, and his blue gaze hooked onto hers. The flame in her heart burned more intensely at that look, making her his slave, his chattel, his lover. Yet even as she thought that, she knew Wolf was as much her slave in bed as she was his, for the same flame burned behind his eyes.

He stroked her hair, watching in apparent fascination as his thick root slipped in and out of her mouth. Her throat was held open to his shaft, her fingers stroking his balls, and with every inward thrust she made a tiny wet moaning noise that would not be silenced.

Suddenly he withdrew from her mouth, leaving her lips parted; she could still taste him on her tongue.

"Here," Wolf insisted, and turned her rapidly in his hands, positioning her so that she was kneeling on the bed. His hand tangled in her hair, dragging her head back so he could kiss her from behind. Their mouths met with a violence that shook her. Then she felt his cock pressing between her thighs, and moaned against his mouth, lost in a maelstrom of desire she had never known before.

He released her hair, then began to fuck her from behind with long, determined strokes. Grasping her hips, Wolf stamped himself on her flesh again and again. In that position, she could feel his cock rubbing back and forth against some sweet place deep inside, the constant pressure driving her out of her mind, her hips snapping back against his, her lips mouthing his name.

"Wolf," she managed, gasping as though she were dying.

"Yes, yes."

Eloise closed her eyes tight, jerking with passion, her entire body shattering in pieces as she came, surging powerfully against him. There was a dark well of joy in front of her, and she fell straight into it, head over heels, tumbling breathless through space.

It was like dying, she thought in a state of wonder. Like dying and being instantaneously reborn, with new skin and new eyes, born afresh into a world of pleasure.

When Eloise managed to open her eyes again, he was still fucking her, driving even harder inside. His hand gripped her neck, holding her still as he thrust and gasped, his breath tortured, taking her with all the desperation of a condemned man. It felt like their last time together, he was riding her so hard, so intensely. And his intensity seemed to burn into her too, scorching her flesh, devouring it until she was nothing but bones and blood beneath him, barely clinging to life.

Suddenly Wolf groaned and thrust deep, rolling and jarring his hips against hers, his heavy cock beginning to swell inside her. She hissed as his seed pulsed out in long, frantic bursts, flooding her cunt, wetly seeking her womb.

Everything blurred to a milky haze as she came for the second time, arching backward onto his cock with a high-pitched cry.

Sometime later she stirred, feeling him leaving the bed, and sleepily put out her hand to stop him.

"No," Wolf ordered her when she would have followed him, not letting her rise. His hand cupped her breast softly, rolling her nipple back and forth. "I have business to attend to this morning. Stay in bed, get some rest. I will instruct Mary not to rouse you before noon."

Then he was gone.

It was late morning by the time she rose from her bed, a bright spring sunshine lying warm across the floor. Mary helped her into one of her richer court gowns, a soft yellow silk with velvet trim and a high, jeweled bodice, then Eloise made the possibly rash decision to leave their apartment chambers unaccompanied. She knew Wolf would be angry, but she would be damned if she would wait in forever for her husband to return.

Mary stared when she asked for her best outdoor shoes. "My lady?"

"I am going to walk in the gardens. It is a fine day."

"But the master…"

"My shoes, Mary," she insisted. "And if news comes of my sister's whereabouts, be sure to run and find me. I will be walking near the river."

Feeling braver dressed in her court finery, long hair coiled up under a gold net, and with a book of Italian poems in her hand, Eloise descended to the palace gardens. The day was warm, with only a slight breeze from the river, and she was soon breathing in the sweet fragrance of young herbs and flowers growing along the pathways.

Eloise drew off her glove and stooped to rub a tall spike of rosemary against bare fingertips, letting its pungent aroma fill her senses.

She took the riverside path, trying to concentrate on her book of Italian poems as she wandered alongside the palace walls, but in truth deep in thought.

Wolf's lovemaking had such a powerful effect on her body she found it impossible to throw his offenses in his face when he took her to bed. Her own weakness unsettled her, made her wonder if she deserved to be married to a cheat and a liar. But perhaps that weakness was part of life at King Henry's court, a tacit acceptance of "doubleness" that kept courtiers' heads on their shoulders.

On such a glorious spring day it was even harder to remind herself of the darker side of the king. To look out across sunlight dancing on the river and remember that, in the Tower of London, the slender-necked queen of England might be looking out of her prison window at the same river, wondering when her last day on this earth would come.

"Eloise!"

She turned clumsily on her heel, taken off guard by the shout. It was Simon. He came striding toward her along the riverside path, thinner and more pale than she remembered, but otherwise as handsome as ever.

"Simon," she responded, and curtsied, unsure how to greet him after the manner of their parting. Then she had been on her way to marry Lord Wolf, to all intents a forced bride, her heart still smarting from Simon's lack of interest in her fate. Now she was a married woman, and to speak too freely with him might occasion gossip of a kind she could not afford at court.

Yet his was the first friendly face she had seen since her arrival, and he must have been badly frightened by the accusations he had faced. What harm would it do to speak with him for a few moments?

"Dearest Eloise." Simon bent his head to kiss her gloved fingertips, shooting her a wry look as he straightened. "Though I suppose I should address you as Lady Wolf now. How are you, Eloise? I have often thought of you up in Yorkshire with your brutish soldier husband." He admired her jeweled gown and the exposed swell of her breasts with undisguised lust. "And now you are returned to court."

"As you see," she agreed cautiously.

Simon seemed cheerful enough, but his pallor told her he had not fared well at the hands of the king's inquisitioners. She wondered if he had been confined to the Tower, knowing they suspected Simon of adulterous liaisons with the queen. If so, he had surely been released without charge, for she had no knowledge of any intimacy between Simon and Queen Anne.

Unless all the charges were false, as Wolf seemed to suspect, and the queen's trial merely an excuse for Henry to rid himself of another wife who was unlikely ever to bear him a son.

Eloise shuddered at the thought of such cruel treachery.

"Shall we walk?" Simon murmured.

She hesitated, then fell into step beside him with some small misgiving, closing her book of Italian poems.

Now that she considered it, it had been Simon who had given her the leather-bound poems. A love gift, he had called it, kissing her on the lips. Knowing now what love was, she found it hard to believe that Simon had ever loved anyone but himself.

"You gave testimony before Sir Thomas Cromwell last night," he remarked. It was not a question.

She glanced at him in some surprise. "How did you know?"

"Nothing is secret here," he said drily, then shrugged, his mouth twisting. "Or everything is secret, I cannot decide which. What did you tell him?"

"You do not know that too?"

"Perhaps I do," Simon admitted with a grin. He stooped to pick a long-stemmed daisy, twirling the small white flower between his fingers. "I know you spoke in my defense, and although I cannot be sure how helpful that was, I was released without charge this morning." He paused, a sudden grim expression on his face. "Not all those who were arrested have been so lucky."

"This is a terrible business."

Her former suitor opened his mouth as though to agree, then closed it again. Fear had made him wary of speaking his mind even before her. "You would have done better to stay in the north," he commented, trailing the white-petalled daisy down her silken yellow sleeve until it brushed her wrist.

She stood very still. "The king himself summoned us. We had no choice."

"Ah." A wealth of understanding went into that sound. His eyes flicked to hers, then away again. He crumpled the daisy in his fist, then tossed it away, studying the broad River Thames with apparent fascination. "My father believes I was arrested because I am a libertine, and any such men near the queen are now suspect. He tells me I should curtail my romantic adventures, as he so discreetly put it, until…"

He stopped abruptly.

"I would say your father is right," she said lightly, though both of them knew that he had intended to say, "until the queen is dead."

"He is a killjoy."

"Better alone in bed than alone in a prison cell," she pointed out, and he laughed, but she could see that she had annoyed him. Too near the truth, she thought.

"And how is your husband?" he asked silkily. "I remember you as a sweet virgin, how reluctant you were to indulge me. Does married life suit you, or are you ready for something a little…different?"

At first she thought he meant the king, and felt her cheeks flare with heat. Was what had passed between them in that intimate chamber last night common knowledge? Then she understood with a belated shock that he was propositioning her himself.

"I am not…" She stopped, unwilling to discuss her marriage with this young man who was already a stranger to her, though the river was empty on that stretch and there was no one there to see them.

"Hush, no matter," Simon murmured, smiling down into her eyes as he laid a finger on her lips. "I understand you perfectly. Come, let me show you my gratitude."

It was out of the sun there, close against the high palace wall, and the place was shady. Before she quite realized the danger she was in, Simon had taken her by the shoulders and bent his head to hers.

"Are your lips still as sweet, Eloise?" he whispered against her mouth, then kissed her.

She pushed at his chest, irritated that he should have taken advantage of her like that, and jerked her head away from his kiss.

"Simon!" she hissed, exasperated.

At the back of her mind though, she was already registering the startling realization that Simon's touch, the persuasive pressure of his mouth on hers, had meant nothing to her.

Nothing whatsoever.

There was a sharp rasp of metal, then her heart almost stopped at the sound of a coldly furious voice at his back.

"Get your insolent hands off my wife, sirrah, and draw your weapon."

Seventeen

SIMON DROPPED HIS HANDS from her shoulders as though she had stung him, and spun around.

Wolf was standing there, a long and brutal-looking dagger in his hand.

Eloise met his gaze and felt sick. Wolf's face was a mask of chilly contempt, his eyes hard. "No," she whispered, shaking her head.

But neither man was listening to her. Simon took one look at the glittering blade in Wolf's hand and drew his own dagger, though Eloise noticed that his hand shook.

"It's not what it seems," he began, but Wolf interrupted him, his voice a whiplash.

"I said, step away from my wife."

"My lord…"

"Now!"

Wolf lunged out at him, growling.

Simon skittered backward, nearly overbalancing in his haste to escape that long blade. He swore under his breath, back on his feet in a second, and for the first time she thought he understood that Wolf was not merely making a point for the sake of his honor but intended to end him.

The path ran close to the river bank at this point. Too close, she thought anxiously, watching their feet slip on the loose soil at the river's edge. The Thames was high that afternoon, the tidal river at its peak, deep gray-blue water swelling at the bank.

One slip, and a man could easily drown in its depths, weighed down with leather and stout boots.

"Be careful!" she exclaimed, and earned a grim look over his shoulder from her husband.

"What's the matter, Eloise?" He shifted the dagger from one hand to the other, then back again, watching Simon for the slightest movement, his whole body poised to do violence. "You enjoy a man's kisses, but not their consequence? Perhaps you should have thought of that before arranging this intimate little rendezvous. Now you will have to stand there and watch your lover spitted on my blade."

The icy flick of disdain in his voice did not fool her. His eyes were turbulent as they raked over her, letting her see precisely what he thought of her, then returned to the man he intended to kill.

Again he lunged, and again Simon danced just out of reach of his weapon. They had moved another few steps along the river into sunshine. Eloise looked at Simon and felt her heart wince. He was reckless and a libertine, but he did not deserve to die in this way. He was breathing hard, and perspiration had broken out on his forehead.

Like all men, Simon had been taught how to handle a blade, that was clear. But he was a courtier, not a born fighter. He would not last long in a hand-to-hand fight with a soldier of Wolf's experience.

"Wolf!"

She was suddenly angry herself, and bitterly so. It was not as though Wolf felt any emotion for her; this was merely his male possessiveness again, his insistence that she must belong to him and never look at another man. Meanwhile he could sleep with any woman he chose.

"Put up your dagger," she raged at him, sick with fear for them both. "What are you about? Stop this nonsense before one of you is killed."

"That is the idea," he pointed out coldly.

Simon feinted suddenly, taking advantage of this distraction, and Wolf ducked sideways at once. He turned on his heel, crouching low, a deadly smile on his face.

"Fool," he breathed.

Wolf thrust hard, catching Simon off guard, and their blades met with a sickening, steely impact. Simon staggered backward, a mere inch from the water's edge, fear in his face. Eloise gathered her skirts and ran forward, determined to stop them before it was too late.

Wolf whirled, perhaps mistaking her for a second enemy coming from behind, and struck out by blind instinct, the full force of his body behind the blow.

"Jesu!"

Somehow he managed to turn the blade sideways at the last second, just missing her chest. His body slammed abruptly into hers, unable to halt the momentum, and would have knocked her down but for his hand, which grabbed at her arm as she fell and jerked her upright again. He swore under his breath. His hot blue gaze met hers, wild as a summer storm.

"Are you out of your wits, woman? I could have killed you."

She stared at him and could not seem to breathe, slowly realizing how close she had come to death.

A shout behind them made her turn, and she almost sagged in relief when she saw a group of palace guards running along the river path toward them.

"Hurry, put up your daggers!" she hissed at them again. "Or you will both be arrested for public brawling."

Simon hesitated, then looked at Wolf and very slowly and deliberately slid his dagger back into his belt. He too seemed relieved by the appearance of the guards, for the fight had not been going his way.

"Another time perhaps," he managed breathlessly, then bowed. "My lord."

But Wolf leaned in close as he sheathed his weapon. His eyes narrowed to slits, his voice a snarl. "I catch you near my wife again, Thetford, I'll slit you open and toss your innards to the dogs. Do I make myself clear?"

Simon nodded, but she saw the heightened flush of anger in his cheeks, and feared he would try to take his revenge on Wolf if he could.

The palace guards closed in on them, flushed and breathless in the sunshine, their pikes lowered.

"What's this? Brawling within the jurisdiction of the king's palace?" one of them demanded harshly, perhaps not having seen who was involved in the disturbance. "It is forbidden to fight here. Speak or lose your liberty!"

Wolf turned at once, his back very straight, a cold authority in his voice. "A misunderstanding, Captain Tanner. Nothing more. We are finished."

The man considered him in silence, his gaze moving slowly from Simon's flushed face to Wolf's calm demeanor. Then he nodded. "Very well… I see." He gestured his men to turn back, and bowed before departing. "Lord Wolf."

"Captain Tanner."

Eloise was surprised by this exchange, but said nothing. Did her husband know every guard and soldier in the king's employ?

As the palace guards raised their pikes and marched swiftly back to the side gate, she looked about for Simon. But of course he had vanished. Slipped away while no one was watching, she thought drily, and could find nothing in her heart but contempt for him. Why had she ever thought herself in love with such a creature? But then, he was skilled at dissimulation. It was a lesson to be more careful with whom she trusted in future, for even those who seemed most like friends could be her enemies.

And now she was alone with Wolf. He looked at her and she

knew she was unforgiven. His face was hard, set in impassive lines, but his eyes gave him away.

He took her by the wrist, dragging her after him.

"Where are we going?" she demanded, suddenly afraid.

"Somewhere private."

—⁓—

Wolf did not know where he was taking her. All he knew was that he was incandescent with rage and hurt, and could not bear the thought of his shame being overheard by anyone at court. He had to get away from the palace before the tension inside him exploded like gunpowder at the merest touch of a spark.

"You're hurting me," she exclaimed, trying to wriggle free of his grasp.

The sound of her anger cut him to the quick. What right did Eloise have to be angry? What had she been whispering in her lover's ear when he came upon them just now, walking the river path in search of his wife only to find her in the arms of another man?

"Good," he told her bitingly.

"For pity's sake, it meant nothing. It was nothing."

He flicked her a lethal look, barely able to trust himself to reply without giving rein to his fury.

"Letting another man kiss you is not 'nothing,' Eloise. It is the first step on the path to adultery. Some husbands would reckon even a kiss adultery, and have you soundly whipped and put in the stocks for it."

"I did not let him kiss me. Simon took that kiss. I was unwilling."

That was not what he had seen, Wolf thought, unable to stop replaying the encounter in his mind, sick to his soul as he saw again her hands on Thetford's chest, her head tilted back eagerly, her mouth entwined with his.

Damn her, he thought. Damn them both to hell.

"Where is our queen now, and for what reason?" he growled, jerking her closer. "Answer me that."

She looked at him aghast. "Her Majesty is innocent."

"Not according to her accusers."

"You do not believe in the queen's guilt any more than I do," she muttered angrily, but Wolf noted that she could not meet his gaze.

"Perhaps not, but that does not mean I will allow my wife to play the same dangerous game unchallenged." He ground his teeth, wishing now that he had killed Thetford while he had the chance. The young courtier would be laughing at him, no doubt awaiting another opportunity to take his wife to bed. "I have not been a stern enough husband. I have given you too much liberty. It is time we laid this headstrong tendency of yours to rest."

She dug in her heels, looking toward the high palace walls as though for assistance, but Wolf merely tightened his grip and refused to let go. He would never let go of her again, he thought, his fingers curling tight about her gloved wrist. For whenever he did, her loose behavior demonstrated how little Eloise respected him as a man and her husband.

"I swear on my life, I am innocent too." Her tone was softer now, more placatory. No doubt she had seen the dangerous look in his face, his struggle to hold on to his self-control. "Simon kissed me. I did not kiss him back. I was pushing him away when you appeared."

They reached the end of the river path. Hesitating a moment, Wolf glanced toward the pennants flapping on the palace turrets, intending to take her back to their bedchamber.

A small group of ladies was wandering along the palace walls in the sunlight. Margerie was among them, her graceful figure only too familiar to him.

Impatiently, he turned and limped along the narrower path toward the nearby woodlands, dragging Eloise after him. He could not risk an encounter between his wife and the woman he had once intended to marry. Besides, his instincts were driving him to be alone with her, to find a place where no one could see them, and then…

What? Strangle his wife in a jealous rage and leave her lifeless body in the undergrowth?

Wolf dragged a hand across his forehead. He was not that man. Before God, he would never become that man.

He felt murderous, yes. But that side of his fury was directed entirely toward Thetford. The rage he reserved for Eloise was of a more passionate kind, a rage that could only be assuaged by her total surrender.

He glanced back at his wife, seeing her pale face, and knew he did not have it in him to cause Eloise harm. But he must have the truth, whatever it cost him. He only prayed his bride would not confess that she loved young Thetford, and had loved him throughout. The agony of such an admission would surely finish him.

God's blood, could he be falling in love with this woman? Was such a thing even possible?

He had put love aside the day Margerie cut him to the heart, and never thought it could blossom in him again.

He could not love Eloise. He must not love her.

"I did not see you push Thetford away." His words spilled out in a savage rush before he could control his jealousy. "I came along the river path and saw you in his arms, the man who would brazenly have taken your maidenhead before we married, who suggested you should visit him privately once you returned to court so he could fuck you behind my back."

She clearly did not know what to say, staring back at him, her cheeks flushed with shame.

They were inside the woodland shade now, the noisy bustle of the palace left behind, the only sound birdsong and the slow rustle of sunlit branches high above them. Wolf dragged her off the path and through the leafy undergrowth, paying no attention to the little noises of distress when she stumbled and nearly fell once, her gown snagged by a tangle of brambles.

"Stop!" she insisted, panting, but still he ignored her, leading her deeper and deeper into the woods.

"Here," he muttered at last, releasing her wrist and stepping back to look her up and down.

"So you have brought me alone and unprotected into these woods. What now?" She straightened her torn skirts and faced him angrily, as though refusing to be cowed by the murderous look in his eyes. "Is this where I am to meet my end?"

"Don't be a fool," he told her scathingly.

"I have been a fool ever since I agreed to marry you, my lord Wolf. Why change now?"

"This is mere distraction from your guilt. I saw his mouth on yours, madam." His voice deepened in accusation. "You invited his kiss, stood still for it."

"No!"

"Tell me the truth, is this the first time you have met privately with Thetford since coming to court? Or have there been other secret assignations?" He stopped, and swallowed convulsively. "Has he had you?"

She stood staring at him, her green-flecked eyes wide, rubbing her wrist above her kid glove as though he had bruised her there. Jealousy coiled within him like a serpent, whispering the deadly truth before she could confirm or deny it. Eloise was not replying because she was guilty; she had lain with Thetford behind his back since returning to court.

The thought ate him alive, making it hard to breathe, his chest hurting with every heave of his lungs.

"And would it matter to you if he had," she demanded in return, her voice suddenly hoarse, "except as a blow to your damned family pride? You did not bother to hide your lust with Mistress Langley last night. I saw you clearly, my lord. You kissed her even in the king's presence. It seems you can drink and whore as much you wish while I am forbidden such freedoms."

"You are my wife," he bit out.

His hands had clenched into fists by his sides. His skin felt drawn tight over his cheekbones, his lips barely moving as he spoke, the violence he was suppressing very near the surface.

"Yet you do not find me desirable."

Speechless, Wolf stared at her in disbelief. Did not find her desirable? "Have you lost your wits along with your honor?" he demanded with heavy irony.

A bird flew away out of the branches above their heads, startled by the sound of raised voices in the quiet woodland. As the clatter of its wings had died away, Wolf realized how alone they were. The wood was deserted, and though he could see flashes of the palace walls through the close-set trunks, he had dragged her far enough from the path that no one would hear or interrupt if he were to take her here and now.

"You think I do not desire you?"

Eloise seemed unable to decipher his words, her eyes filled with an emotion he recognized as close to agony. Her hands shook as she picked up her skirts and began to back away across the shady ground, staring at him.

"No," she whispered, and he heard tears behind her voice. "You only desire an heir for the Wolf dynasty."

Wolf swore under his breath, only then realizing how little she knew or understood him. On impulse, he made a grab for her, meaning to show her what he was feeling.

Eloise turned with a tiny cry of fear, and stumbled clumsily through the trees, beginning to run.

—∿—

Eloise did not know why she had to get away from Wolf. All she knew was that his stillness, the look in his eyes, and the rough note in his voice had frightened her. Not because she thought he meant to harm her, but because there was something about this man that hurt her soul more keenly than anyone else on earth, and if he so much as touched her again, even brushed a single finger across her skin, she would simply burn up before him, like a love letter put to the flame…

He caught her after only a hundred yards, his arms closing tightly about her waist. "Eloise!"

She sobbed, shaking her head, struggling to push him away. Not like this, she kept thinking wildly. "Stop, Wolf, please. I cannot bear to have you touch me."

His voice was hoarse in her ear, tinged with anger. "Strange, I do not recall you turning me out of your bed last night. Quite the reverse, indeed."

She could not answer that, but moaned in shame and anguish as he laid her weakness bare.

"Eloise." His hands were rough as he pushed her against the broad gnarled trunk of a beech tree, turning her to face him. His mouth came down on hers, hungry and almost violent at first, then abruptly slanting hotly, teasing her with his tongue, inciting her to kiss him back.

How could Wolf kiss her like this and not desire her? How could he turn her to flame every night, and then bed other women at court as though she meant nothing to him?

His hands cupped her breasts, tugging down her bodice, thumbs rubbing across her nipples, and the tide of desire rose in her so sharply she was drowning in seconds.

"Look at me," he ordered her harshly.

She had closed her eyes at his first kiss, losing herself in the urgent drive for pleasure. Now she opened them, reluctantly obeying his command.

Wolf's face was consumed with lust. His eyes glittered with it, a hard color in his cheeks, his breathing ragged. He seized her hand and pushed it between his legs, impatiently unfastening his codpiece so she could reach his erection beneath.

"That is how much I desire you. Never tell me I do not desire you, Eloise. This is my need for you right here." His eyes met hers. "Strip off your gloves and feel it if you do not believe me."

Greedily, she did as he bade her. Her bare fingers wrapped about the powerful girth of his cock, reveling in his length, the hot rigidity that told her precisely what she wanted to know.

She groaned and began to tremble. "Wolf…"

"Yes," he gasped, as though in response to some unspoken question, and dragged up her skirts, nudging her back against the tree trunk. His fierce blue gaze scorched her. "Open your legs to me, Eloise."

She obeyed, eager for the conflagration that was to come, and his fingers found her wet and ready, nothing to impede his progress.

He stroked between her legs, and her breath hissed in between her teeth, her hips straining toward his. "Sweet Lord," she cried.

For the first time, she felt free to show him the desire his body inspired in her. It was not as though she could hide it, she thought, and kissed him back hotly.

Wolf entered her with one urgent thrust, groaning against her mouth. She almost sobbed, clutching at his shoulders, no longer capable of thought. He seemed lost in their congress too, his face darkening with red, his chest and head tilted back for better balance as he possessed her.

"Here." The veins stood out on his neck as he raised her, banging her back into the trunk. His arms supported her, his muscular thighs too, holding her body aloft as he waited, deep inside her. "You want this? Eloise, you want this?"

"Yes." Her heart stuttered, needing him to declare himself, yet not daring to ask for more, to hope for anything greater than this violent, all-encompassing need. "Yes."

Wolf withdrew slowly, watching her with an intent expression, then stroked back into her. This time he pushed his large cock deep inside, so deep it stretched Eloise beyond her limits, so deep that she shook and gasped in his arms. Her whole body felt stuffed with his cock, unable to take another inch. Yet somehow it was still good. So good she thought she might die from it, in fact.

She felt faint from the acute pleasure of being filled to the hilt, her head ready to burst, her heart drumming with blood.

"This," he told her, his teeth gritted as he thrust in and out, "is what I think about when we are not in bed. This is what gets me hard."

"But your other women…"

His voice was like steel. "What other women?"

"Mistress Langley."

His eyes mocked her. "You mean Kate?"

Eloise was infused with helpless anger as he withdrew, toying with her, watching her through narrowed eyes as though threatening to stop what he was doing. She struggled with it, her body caught in the grip of delicious, almost painful pleasure as he slotted his cock back inside her.

"You…"

"Say it," he invited her silkily.

"Very well. You've made love to Kate Langley." Her breath hissed out, jealousy twisting inside her like a cold blade, killing her slowly. "You have done this to her. Then come back to our bed."

He shook his head.

She dug her fingers into his shoulders through the lavish black jacket, his sleeves fashionably slashed to reveal white silk beneath.

She hated how strong he was, the power of his body that allured and bewitched her, left her too weak to push him away.

"Why lie to me?" she demanded, furious again. "I saw you with her in the company of the king. You have lain with that woman; do not bother to deny it."

Wolf shrugged. There was sweat on his forehead as he moved in and out of her, slowly, deliberately, his eyes on hers. "Before we were wed, yes."

He closed his eyes as though remembering, then reopened them, focusing on her again. She felt sick, wishing he would just kill her and have done with it. Not torture her by making love to her and thinking of another woman at the same time.

"And why not? Kate is a handsome and passionate woman, and her husband rarely beds her. She must find satisfaction somewhere."

She fought to slap his face in the tiny confined space between their heaving bodies. "Bastard!"

"Stop hitting me," he exclaimed, and thrust more forcefully inside her, making her cry out. "I told you, you little termagant, I have not lain with Mistress Langley since we married. Even then it was only the one time. I was lonely. Hurt."

He seized her hand and pressed it down, forcing her to feel the heat between their moving hips. His voice was urgent. "Don't you understand? I was young then, a green fool. This is what I want now. You as my wife. This pleasure."

"Then why kiss Kate Langley in front of me and the king last night? Why say those things to me, touch her so intimately, make love to her?"

She forced the tears away, steeling herself for yet more pain. Even if the truth killed her, she must have it. She could not live a lie with this man. "If you truly want only me, Wolf, why would you wish to humiliate me like that?"

"*Rex uxorem meam cupiat,*" he whispered, looking into her face.

She stared back at him, slowly groping after each word, glad that her father had insisted she learn some rudimentary Latin as a girl. "The king…the king desires a wife?"

"The king, my beautiful fool, desires *my* wife."

Her heart almost stopped.

She pushed against him urgently now. "Wolf, you are not serious? The king?"

"You did not know?"

"I know the king always favored me as one of Queen Anne's maids. But he would never take me for his mistress. I was accused of being complicit with Her Majesty in her affairs. And I am married now. Married to you. And you—"

"Have just enough skill as a soldier to be worth keeping alive." He buried his mouth in her throat, and she could feel him shaking, still inside her. His voice was ragged. "I could not risk it though. It was imperative that I made you less attractive to His Majesty. The queen is in the Tower, Jane Seymour will soon be in his bed, but what the king most desires is to bed a new lady. Someone to take the edge off his appetite, but not a whore. For where would be the challenge in that? No, what he desires to bed before he remarries is a lady not too experienced, nor yet too innocent."

Eloise shivered. "A new bride."

"Last night, with the help of Mistress Langley, I sought to put a little doubt in his mind. To make my bride less appealing to his sensual tastes. But without arousing his suspicions. That is why I maligned your skills in bed, and made my preference for another woman painfully clear." He drew a sharp breath. "I knew you would hate me for it. Yet what else could I do?"

She was horrified by this confession, suddenly realizing that Wolf had put himself in terrible danger by trying to fool the king.

"If His Majesty discovers your deceit, you could pay for it with your life."

"You think my life is worth more to me than your honor?"

"My honor?" Eloise linked her legs about his waist, her body fired by his closeness, the way he was still moving gently inside her, driving her slowly insane. "Was it my honor you were thinking of when you drew your dagger on Simon by the river?"

He turned his head and gazed at her, the most honest look he had ever given her. "No," he admitted, and the word seemed to hurt him.

"Then what?"

There was a hard color in his face. "I wanted to kill him," he muttered. "For daring to put his hands on your body, his mouth… God's blood, I have never wanted so badly to kill a man, even in battle."

"Yet you did not," she reminded him softly.

Wolf kissed her hotly. "His death was not worth losing you over. I may be high in the king's favor, but even I cannot stab a courtier through the heart just for kissing my wife. I would have risked being condemned for his murder, leaving you a widow and defenseless. In time, the king would have made you his mistress. No, Thetford's death was not worth the risk."

His kiss had lit a hunger within her that would not be ignored. She wound her fingers in his hair, pulling him closer while she kissed him back.

"So you find me desirable," she whispered.

His cock jerked inside her, thickening. "As you see," he murmured, his words slightly slurred.

"And yet we seem to do nothing but scratch and bite at each other. Out of bed, we are enemies."

"You are a fiery bride," he conceded drily. He withdrew, teasing her, then pushed forward to fill her again, his mouth twisting in a smile as she gasped. "But you will not hear me complain. Your fieriness makes for some exciting nights."

"And days."

She thought of Margerie, whose name had been on that loose sheet he had dropped in the tower room.

The thought that Wolf might still be in love with his former betrothed, and writing letters to her, left her grieving inside. He had convinced her that he was not sleeping with the beautiful Mistress Langley, and that he had merely behaved like that before the king to make Eloise seem less appealing as a mistress. But there was still so much she did not know about her husband.

Now was not the time to demand answers though, Eloise told herself. Later, perhaps, when her sudden intense hunger for his body had been assuaged.

"Wolf," she said against his throat, kissing his warm, rough skin. "Stop teasing and take me."

"It will be my pleasure, my lady," he agreed hoarsely. "You had only to ask."

She thought he sounded as violently in need of release as her. Wolf carried her a few unsteady steps from the beech tree, laying her down upon a grassy spot where two trees parted in the green shade, bright shafts of sunlight dappling their high leaves. There he knelt and pressed his mouth between her legs, parting her moist flesh with his fingers and tonguing her greedily.

Eloise moaned in wild ecstasy, clawing at the loose earth on either side of her head, her fingers sinking deep into the soil, not caring if she dirtied herself or her yellow silk gown. This was what she had needed from the moment he came along the river path and found her with Simon, she realized. For Wolf to show her to whom she belonged, and why.

She climaxed easily, and thought her back would break as she arched with pleasure, crying out his name.

Wolf covered her at once, not waiting for her to come down from that sweet peak but thrusting urgently inside. He supported himself on his hands as he ploughed her body, grunting out his pleasure and working fiercely above her, showing her with every deep stroke how much he desired her. Both of them were still partially clothed, yet that lent an intense excitement to their lust, and the knowledge that at any moment someone might come walking through the woods and discover them.

When he came, it was with a violent shuddering cry, his cock pumping rush after rush of hot seed inside her. "Jesu," he groaned, and buried his face in her breasts.

She lay beneath him for a long while afterward, staring up at the flickering green canopy of leaves above their heads. She felt so drowsy and fulfilled, yet her heart was churning with barely veiled excitement. Something had changed between them, she was sure of it, a strange and sudden shifting of emotion in the air. Had Wolf felt it too?

But when he stood later, and held out his hand to help her up, Eloise saw once again that cool distance in his face, the cautious sidelong glance that told her Wolf was not yet ready to love her as he loved his elusive Margerie.

Perhaps he never would be ready.

Eighteen

ALMOST A WEEK HAD passed since the fight on the river bank when Wolf told her that Simon had left court. "It seems he has returned to Norfolk and will likely remain there some months," he commented, delicately boning a baked trout with his dagger before passing her the dish. They were taking a late luncheon together in the privacy of their apartment, away from the gloomy terrors of the court. "By order of the king, I heard."

She looked at him. "Poor Simon," she murmured, thinking aloud. "He so loves life at court. To be exiled…"

"Better exile than a shameful death on the scaffold, which the others under accusation may not so easily escape." Wolf hesitated, helping himself to a dish of pickled walnuts. He met her gaze steadily. "You will miss him, I expect."

She did not reply to that. His tone had not fooled her. She had seen the bitter flash of jealousy in his eyes, and knew herself how it felt to be in its grip.

"I only wish we had news of my sister," she remarked, pushing aside her trencher. "It has been days since Master Beaufort rode north in search of her. I fear something terrible must have happened."

Eloise kept remembering the day when their cavalcade had been attacked. They had been journeying north on the same road her sister had most likely taken on her way toward London, and in the company of stout soldiers. If Susannah had been attacked by men like those, a pack of northern ruffians with rape and murder on their minds, there would be little hope of her survival. A woman alone was an easy target, even one who had apparently taken the precaution of garbing herself like a man.

"Beaufort is no fool," he assured her, meticulously cleaning his fingers in the water bowl, then drying them on a damask napkin. She watched him, amused by the thought that her husband had better table manners than the king, despite his pretense that he was just a rough soldier. "Nor does he ride alone, remember. If your sister is still on that road, he will find her."

"I pray you are in the right, my lord."

"I am always in the right, my dear Eloise," he murmured, his sharp blue eyes mocking her across the table. "Have you never re-marked it before?"

"Forgive me, no. It must have escaped my attention."

"Ah, cruel."

She could not help smiling. Wolf was hard to dislike in this mood, so charming and at his ease. Events at court in recent months had turned everyone sour, and put that grim look in her husband's eyes. But perhaps when they were home again in Yorkshire, away from the dark clouds of Henry's court, his mood would lighten again and she would be able to fall in love with him.

To own the truth, she was halfway in love with him already. His hard, powerful body had long since captured her soul; but could his soul capture her body?

"Did you hear that young Wyatt is not to be executed?" he asked abruptly, watching her as though hoping to gauge her reaction to the news. "They are still holding him in the Tower, but his father has spoken for him and it seems the king has listened."

Her lips were bone dry. She licked them nervously, and saw his intense blue gaze narrow on the movement.

"I did not, no," she murmured. "But I am glad to hear it. Sir Thomas Wyatt is a fine poet and the most charming courtier. He is one of the few gentlemen at court whom I have always admired. Furthermore he is innocent and does not deserve to…"

Eloise stopped, and pushed her trembling hands into her lap. She could not bring herself to say the word.

Wolf's eyes brooded on her face. "I don't know Sir Thomas well enough to comment on his innocence, though I have fought beside him on a few campaigns. He is a fair soldier." He hesitated. "So he holds a special place in your heart, does he, this Wyatt?"

She glared at him, immediately angry at the unspoken inference. Why did Wolf always have to assume that if she expressed some liking for a man, he must have been her lover once?

"No more than any other innocent man whom I would not wish to see on the scaffold!"

His brows snapped together. "Oh, you will see nobody on the scaffold, I promise you that. You are not permitted to attend any of their executions, is that clear?"

How dare he? She had no intention of watching any of those unfortunate men die, nonetheless a wave of fury swept over her at his overbearing manner. It was like being married to her father, another man who had never seen her in any other light than as a possession, to be ordered about or locked away at will.

For such men, women were dim, carnally minded creatures, who were to be kept under harness and not allowed opinions or independent thought. Oh, but females must also be watched very carefully, lest they produce an heir by another man while their husband's back is turned.

"Yes, my lord. No, my lord. Whatever you say, my lord."

"Eloise…"

"Your doubleness makes my head spin. You accuse me of having a special place in my heart for Sir Thomas Wyatt. Yet you, my lord, will not give up your own lover."

"And who is that, pray?"

"Margerie."

"Be quiet," he growled.

Part of her knew that she was probably being unfair to Wolf. But he should not have baited her with what he had heard during Cromwell's interrogation. And now he was trying to impose his will on her again, regardless of the injustice.

Her temper got the better of her. She jumped up. "I will not be quiet."

"Sit down and do as you are as told."

"You do not believe those men to be guilty any more than I do," she threw at him. "It is all a sham."

"For pity's sake, will you not be silenced?" he ground out, something akin to panic suddenly flaring in his expression.

"Why should I obey you, Wolf?" she demanded, flushed and too angry to properly interpret his orders. "So you can gloat over my wifely subservience?"

Almost as though he could not help himself, Wolf's gaze shifted warily toward a decorative wooden screen set into the west wall, where a doorway into another chamber had once stood, now long since sealed off and no longer part of these apartments.

She glanced that way too, frowning, and saw a sudden, tiny movement behind the intricate friezework of the screen. As she stared it was hurriedly stilled.

The blood froze in her veins.

Somebody was watching them from behind that false panel. Listening to every word they said.

"Sit down," Wolf repeated gruffly, and this time she obeyed him without comment, grateful to be seated now that her legs were shaking.

"The evidence gathered against these men cannot be refuted," he said warningly, but she could see the message in his eyes was one of caution. He did not believe them to be guilty either. But to say so when they were being spied upon would be tantamount to slitting their own throats. The king would accept no talk of an unjust trial, and she knew it. She could hardly believe how close she had just come to condemning them both to death. "Their sentence is lawful, and must be carried out as given."

She took a deep breath, then nodded. "Yes, my lord."

"You have not drunk your wine," he commented, and leaned across to pour more into her cup. "Though these are difficult times, they will soon be over. Your generosity toward these criminals does you credit, Eloise, but you must be careful. Simply because you yourself are innocent, it does not follow that others are equally unblemished."

She managed a stiff smile. "Of course, you are right." She picked up her cup and drank a little wine, eyeing him over the rim as he stretched out his legs to the low fire burning in the hearth.

How long had he known that they were being watched? Was it only in this room or also in their bedchamber that they had to be careful? Her skin crawled at the thought of some sweaty-palmed spy watching them in bed together, then writing up a detailed report of their lovemaking for the king.

She could only hope their bedchamber at least was safe from those who watched. Wolf had lied to the king to keep her out of his arms, declaring her cold and unyielding to bed. Any act or conversation which might suggest the opposite would be highly dangerous, and put his life in jeopardy. So he would hardly have made love to her with such passion and abandon if he knew the king would hear of it.

Whenever they were alone here, she had longed to ask him about Margerie. Her jealousy was an itch in her blood. Yet she had fought it, afraid of disturbing the fragile equilibrium which had settled about them since his fight with Simon and the intense lovemaking that had followed that horror.

Now she was glad she had not asked. For everything they said or did in this place must be weighed very carefully, in case it was reported back to the king.

Besides, even if she could ask him such a question privately, what if Wolf confessed that he was indeed still in love with Margerie? The two had been betrothed once, long ago, and she knew how powerful his feelings must have been. And Margerie had spurned him, not the other way around. She had run off with her secret lover and married him.

Having seen how even the suggestion of betrayal could shatter Wolf's famous self-control, the discipline that made him such a great soldier and commander, it was hard not to wonder how he had dealt with Margerie's loss.

Not well, she thought drily, then lowered her gaze when Wolf looked up and caught her staring.

"Should I ask what you're thinking, my lady?" he drawled, his voice very cool, though she heard a sliver of doubt behind the easy arrogance. "Or would it be better not to know?"

Thankfully Eloise did not need to fumble for an answer to that, as a commotion at the door made them both turn their heads.

Wolf stood at once, his body tensed for action, reaching for the dagger he had used to bone the trout. He wiped the blade clean on the napkin, his face tense. "Who's there?"

The door opened and Hugh Beaufort stood in the doorway, swaying a little, his chin dark with stubble, his doublet and hose dusty from the road. Behind him stood a slender boy, booted, cloaked and hooded, his young face concealed in shadow—but with a tell-tale lock of fair hair tumbling down one shoulder.

"Susannah!" Eloise exclaimed, relief surging through her at the sight of these two weary figures, and jumped up to embrace her sister. "I never thought to see you again."

Her sister threw back her hood, a chastened look on her face. Her cheeks had more color than she remembered, but Eloise put that down to having ridden so far in the warm spring sunshine. She clasped Eloise's hands, not quite meeting her gaze.

"Forgive me," was all she seemed able to say, stumbling over even those few words. "Forgive me, Eloise."

"So you found her in the end," Wolf murmured, watching Eloise and Susannah with a curious expression on his face. He shook Hugh Beaufort's hand, then clapped the young man heartily on the back. "Well done, sir."

"I thank you, my lord."

"You look half-dead, man. Here, we had more food served than we needed." Wolf stepped aside, gesturing them both to sit down. "Will you not eat?"

Without any ceremony, still wearing her cloak, Susannah sat down and eagerly scooped up the last of the trout, eating as though she had not been fed for days.

Eloise helped her sister off with her cloak, bearing it away to have the dust beaten off. "Mary!" she called, and her maid appeared, looking astonished but deeply pleased to see Susannah safe and at the table. "Fetch more wine."

"And food," Susannah managed indistinctly, her mouth full. "More sauce. Manchet bread. Sweetmeats."

To Eloise's surprise, Hugh refused to sit at table, telling Wolf instead how he had come upon Susannah some fifty miles north of London, sleeping rough in a wood. He kept his face politely averted as Susannah ate, but something about his wary stance made Eloise suspect this was not merely good manners.

She wondered if the two young people had argued on the long road to London. Hardly surprising, Eloise thought, hurriedly concealing her smile. Susannah was a willful, headstrong girl, and she had been discovered in her crime as a runaway. Perhaps even scolded by Hugh for having caused so much trouble and heartache. Indeed, it would be a miracle if they had not argued.

"You took your time returning," Wolf said lightly, but it was a question.

"My lord, you must forgive my tardiness." Hugh looked awkwardly at Susannah, who said nothing but continued to eat. He hesitated, an odd tightness in his voice. "I had some difficulty persuading Mistress Tyrell to accompany me back to court."

Wolf frowned. "But was it not her intention to journey to court in the first place?"

"But not with him," Susannah said clearly, without looking at Hugh, then returned to her repast.

Mary bustled in with a full flagon of wine, a kitchen servant following close behind with a basket of warm bread, a jug of sauce, and a bowl of sweetmeats.

"Oh yes, please," Susannah murmured, and held out a cup. "I have not eaten for two days straight."

Eloise was surprised, and glanced across at Hugh Beaufort. "Surely you took your ease at roadside inns? Tell me you did not simply ride for court without stopping once you had found my sister?"

"We stopped every night." There was a hard color in Hugh's face now; he seemed almost angry, his voice sharper. "But your sister refused to eat in my company, and since I refused to leave her alone until we reached London, she took no sustenance at mealtimes."

Suppressing a burst of laughter, Eloise bit her lip. "I see," she managed unsteadily.

"And why should a lady eat at the same table as her abductor, pray?" Susannah stared at Hugh fiercely, and was rewarded by a stormy glare in return. A tiny spot of red burned in each cheek as she lifted her chin. "I shall certainly take care never to be alone in your company again."

"Nor I in yours, madam," Hugh Beaufort seethed at her, his face taut. His fists were clenched by his sides as though he longed to shake some sense into the girl, his knuckles white with strain. Eloise cleared her throat, and Hugh abruptly seemed to recollect where he was. He drew breath, turning to make his bow to Eloise. "Forgive my poor manners, Lady Wolf. It was not my intention to raise my voice in the company of ladies. I…I have not slept overmuch these past few days."

It seemed Susannah had met her match in Hugh Beaufort. They had been friendly enough in Yorkshire, spending time in each other's company, and Eloise suspected it was to see Hugh again that Susannah had run away from home in such a drastic manner. Yet clearly something had happened between them on the road to change Susannah's mind.

Perhaps her sister had not found it as easy to twist Hugh Beaufort around her finger as she had once innocently supposed. Whatever the truth of it, she was now aloof and he incensed. A happy pairing indeed.

She caught Wolf's eye, and he smiled drily.

"Come, Hugh," he said, thrusting his dagger back into his belt. "You are in dire need of a wash and fresh clothing. Let us walk to your chamber together, and you can tell me everything that has passed while you have been away."

"Aye, my lord," Hugh agreed, still very much on his dignity. On the threshold he paused, then turned back, bowing first to Eloise and then Susannah. "Lady Wolf," he murmured in farewell; then his eyes sought her sister's at last. "Mistress Tyrell."

Susannah said nothing, her head stubbornly bent.

Hugh straightened, still looking directly at her, then drew a sharp breath and swept after Wolf.

"Susannah, why on earth are you so upset with poor Master Beaufort?" Eloise asked as soon as the door had closed behind the men; she had dismissed Mary so they could talk without fear of being overheard. "He only rode north to see you safe to court. And at great risk to himself, for that road is one of the most dangerous in England."

When her sister did not reply but sat still, head down, staring fixedly at the table, Eloise added with a stab of spirit, "Forgive me, but I don't understand. I thought you liked Hugh, that the two of you were friends."

Susannah lifted her head, and Eloise saw that she had been crying. "Oh, Eloise," she burst out, pushing away her trencher as though her appetite had suddenly failed. "I did like Hugh Beaufort, very much. But now I hate him, I hate him. Everything's ruined. And it's all my fault!"

"Whatever do you mean by that?" she asked her sister, astonished. "Did something happen between you on the journey?"

But try as she might, Eloise could not bring Susannah to say any more. She very much feared some dreadful indiscretion must have occurred on the road back to court. But whatever had happened, it was probably for the best if they never spoke of it again, she thought warily, wrapping her arms about her sister's shoulders in a gesture of comfort. Her father still hoped Susannah would marry a man of his own choosing, and Hugh Beaufort did not strike her as a man in love.

Little said, soon amended, she told herself, and rummaged in her belt pouch for a handkerchief.

Days passed, with the atmosphere at court growing ever darker and gloomier as Anne's fate looked more certain, and one night in mid-May Wolf struggled out of sleep to find the bed curtains drawn back, and one of his men standing beside the bed, a candle flickering in his hand.

He sat up at once, immediately alert. He had not been asleep long, for his mind had been too occupied with dark matters, his psyche disturbed with a creeping horror that he could not shake off. Not that he was alone in that. Not tonight.

It was still dark, the early watches of the night judging by how low the fire had burned since he had retired. Beside him, Eloise was still sleeping, breathing softly, her back turned.

"What is it, Fletcher?"

"Forgive me for disturbing you, my lord. It would not wait until morning."

The man was holding out a letter. Wolf took it, frowning down at the distinctive royal seal.

"Hold the candle higher."

He broke the seal and read the contents, digesting the grim message with chill striking into his heart.

"Will there be any reply, my lord?"

"No." He looked down at his sleeping wife. "What hour is it, Fletcher?"

"A little after four of the clock, my lord."

"Come back in an hour and rouse me again. I must be on horseback by sunrise this morning."

"Aye, my lord."

"And leave the candle."

He glanced again at Eloise, seeing the slender column of her neck from behind, her golden hair fallen loosely to one side. Caught in the grip of some primeval terror, he could not prevent himself from imagining an ax being brought down upon that fragile neck, severing her throat, her life force…

He made a choking noise under his breath, his heart suddenly pounding, his palms damp with sweat.

Eloise stirred beside him in the candlelight, flushed from her warm pillow. Sleepily, she turned to look at him, her nightrail falling loosely off one shoulder to reveal pale skin, the curve of her breast below.

"What is it, my lord?"

He looked down at her grimly, considering what to say, how to word his admission. He could not conceal the agonizing truth from his wife, however much he knew it would distress her, but he could at least hide his own turmoil.

"Fletcher was just here," he told her sparingly. "He brought an urgent missive from King Henry. I have received a direct command from His Majesty and must obey it."

She sat up, staring. "Wolf?"

"I am ordered…"

He choked again mid-sentence and sat silent, staring at nothing, holding up his hand without looking at her when she tried to speak.

It was a struggle to regain his self-control. Yet regain it he must.

"I am ordered to the Tower of London this morning," he managed. "To witness the execution of our former queen, Anne Boleyn."

"Sweet Jesu." Her cheeks had lost their color, reflecting the same unspeakable horror he was feeling. Her hand went out to him, brushing his sleeve. "Do not go, you must not go."

"He is my king," he bit out, and meant every word, regardless of who might be listening. "I swore allegiance to His Majesty. I must obey his command; I cannot break my oath."

Her voice was hoarse. "A king who executes his queen…"

"Hush." He caught her wrist, but then released her at once, seeing the fear on her face. He would not have his wife afraid of him. It was too much to bear. "Be careful."

She hid her face in her hands for a long moment. "Poor, poor Anne."

"I had hoped when the marriage was dissolved that she would be spared this fate. That the king would change his mind at the last minute and simply put her away, as he did Queen Katherine, so he could marry Jane Seymour in her place. But there is to be no clemency…"

Wolf stopped, swallowing hard. He had said too much already. Even here in the dark privacy of his bedchamber he could not be certain they were not being spied upon.

"The law says she must die. So she will die."

"May God forgive them."

Unable to say what he truly felt, to admit the heaviness and agony of his heart, his eyes sought hers. "At least it is not the fire," he whispered. "Her Majesty does not go to the stake, though the law required it for treason. They have sent for an expert swordsman from France instead. The man is an executioner of great skill and judgment, I'm told. He will ensure that the queen…"

Again, his voice failed him, for he had remembered that Anne Boleyn was no longer the queen. "That her end will be swift," he finished hoarsely, then fell silent.

His wife knelt up beside him in bed, dragging her nightrail over her head. Her body was so pale and perfect in the flickering candle-light, he could not take his eyes off her. In his mind's eye, Wolf saw again what he must witness later that morning, the barbaric slaughter of a dark-eyed lady he had once danced with and knelt before, as entranced by her charm and wit as every other man at court. His heart stuttered at the cruelty of it.

Anne Boleyn. Sacrificed to the brutal whim of her husband and king so that Henry might beget an heir.

His hands trembled as he pulled Eloise toward him, his breathing quickening at the sight of her naked beauty.

"Make me forget," Wolf whispered in her ear. "Eloise…"

Nineteen

WOLF STOOD TO THE back of the crowd, arms folded, staring up into the clear blue sky rather than at the black-draped scaffold before him.

It was a fine mid-May morning: a day for hunting, or jousting, or lying with a lady-love on the greensward. Immaculate white blossom blown from the trees within the windy confines of the Tower enclosure signaled the advent of summer. Sunlight and budding flowers. Love and laughter. A newness and clean simplicity about the world. A time for fresh beginnings. The irony struck him again as he heard a stirring in the crowd and knew that Anne Boleyn was being led out from her lodgings.

He did not look round, not wishing to stare disrespectfully at Anne in extremis. He thought instead of young Sir Thomas Wyatt, the poet and courtier who had so enchanted his wife. He looked up at the miserable gray walls, the intimidating height of the White Tower looming above them.

Where was Wyatt held prisoner? Could the poet see this sorry spectacle from his cell window?

Anne Boleyn was climbing the scaffold steps with painful care, dressed demurely in dark gray damask, an ermine mantle draped about her shoulders. Her small band of ladies followed, pale-faced and watchful as they assembled behind her on the platform, only one of them weeping.

Not her own women, he realized, scanning their faces with a sinking heart. The king had not allowed his former queen the comfort of her own household about her in prison. Not even today, her last day on earth.

She had prepared her last words. Turning toward the crowd without looking down, she spoke them, her voice falling cool and clear in the sudden intent silence.

"Good Christian people," she began humbly, "according to the law and by the law I am judged to die, and therefore I will speak nothing against it."

Henry was far away, of course, preparing to marry Jane Seymour on receipt of the news that Anne was dead.

The king had been careful to stay away from his wife since early on in this process of false accusation and unfair trial. It was hardly surprising, for if the king could see her now, waiting so beautiful and resolute on the scaffold, he would surely dismiss the executioner and allow Anne to live out her days in some remote spot, as he had done with his first divorced wife, Katherine.

Wolf could not imagine how it would feel to watch his own wife die like this. Sweat broke out on his forehead. He swore silently that he would do everything in his power to protect Eloise and keep her from harm.

The last lines of one of Wyatt's poems came unbidden into his head; a poem some had whispered was about Anne Boleyn herself, though the poet had strenuously denied this. As well he might, given today's horror.

> *And graven with diamonds in letters plain*
> *There is written her fair neck round about:*
> *"Noli me tangere, for Caesar's I am,*
> *And wild for to hold, though I seem tame."*

Anne's pitifully short speech was over. She stepped back, still pale, but carefully showing no emotion.

She had not confessed her guilt, he realized slowly, thinking back through her words, nor yet condemned Henry for sending an innocent woman to her death. Anne Boleyn wished to safeguard her baby daughter's position with this politic speech, he guessed, and felt only admiration for her courage and resolve.

Prayers were being said on the scaffold, then a lengthy passage was read out from the Holy Bible, while the skirts of the women flapped uneasily in the wind coming off the river.

He watched the proceedings with a growing sense of desperation. This wait was unbearable. Why had he not told the king he was unwell, that he could not attend this appalling act of injustice? Because he was neither a liar nor a coward, he reminded himself grimly, and set his feet further apart, trying to gain strength from the earth itself. Henry was his sovereign, and Wolf one of his lords, sworn to obey him.

Even faced with this horror, he could not imagine a greater dishonor than to rebel against his king.

Anne had been standing slightly apart from the other women, head to one side, listening intently to the priest. When the man finished and closed the book, she started, looking about herself as though surprised that the time had arrived for her to die.

Slowly, the former queen removed her velvet gable hood and handed it to one of her ladies. She was still calm, no sign of tears or panic, though her dark eyes constantly searched the crowd as though hunting for a friendly face.

Wolf stared back at her, unable to help himself now, wishing he could call out some words of comfort to ease her last moments. But his throat was like dust, and he could not make a sound.

Anne's shining dark hair was hidden beneath a plain cap. She was blindfolded by one of her women, then guided gently to the spot where she was to die. There she knelt, achingly graceful to the last, her slim neck bared, her head held high at the muttered suggestion of the executioner.

She clasped her hands before her in prayer, calling out, "O Lord, have mercy on me. To God I commend my soul."

Wolf wanted to look away, as other noblemen there had already done, their heads hanging before this appalling sight. But he could not. Her chief accuser, Sir Thomas Cromwell, was staring too, his mouth slightly agape. But there was something compulsive about her slight figure on the scaffold. In the poignancy of her beauty, Anne seemed otherworldly, and so brilliantly, dramatically alive…

The French executioner was a younger man than Wolf had expected. He fumbled for his sword, hidden beneath a heap of straw so as not to frighten Anne when she ascended the scaffold. For a long moment he hesitated, looking down at his victim with what appeared to be pity. Then he called out in a heavily accented voice, "Where is my sword?"

Anne, blindfolded and still praying under her breath, gave a little jerk of her head. Perhaps she thought in that instant that she had been given a few moments' reprieve, that the Frenchman's sword really was missing.

Silently, the executioner lifted his sword and swung.

Wolf looked away.

He heard her body fall. A terrible groan went up amongst the watching crowd, then a hoarse shout of "God save the king!" from one of the nobles in the front. Less than a minute later, there came the roaring boom of cannon fire from the battlements, signaling London that the woman who had once been their queen was dead.

To his shock, Wolf found he was crying.

He turned away from the scaffold, walking head down with the rest of the crowd. Nobody spoke on the long return to the gate. Their feet shuffled at the same slow pace as though in shame. High above the broad river the gray-backed gulls were crying, specks wheeling overhead in a too-dazzling sky.

He rubbed the back of his hand across his face, and thought

longingly of Eloise, how his wife had watched from their bed as he dressed in the half-light that morning, her face flushed with desire but her eyes anxious, fearing for him.

I have been a fool, he thought simply. I love Eloise. So why can I not tell her? What is the matter with me?

"His Majesty, King Henry, and Her Majesty, Queen Jane!" the king's steward announced, solemnly thudding his staff on the floor three times.

The entire court sank to its knees, Eloise and Susannah with them. It was a few weeks since Anne Boleyn's execution. A fanfare sounded in the musician's gallery, and Eloise bowed her head as the king swept past, resplendent in gold and scarlet, his new bride on his arm, almost as magnificent in a full-skirted gown of silver and blue.

Behind them walked young Henry Fitzroy, the king's bastard and Duke of Richmond, whom some whispered might one day inherit the throne if his father failed to beget another son. After him came the king's advisors and Privy Councilors, the somber Sir Thomas Cromwell prominent amongst them, followed by the new queen's most favored ladies, giggling and smirking behind their hands at her fantastical elevation to the throne of England.

A pair of handsome shoes stopped in front of Eloise.

"Rise, my lady," a voice said mockingly, and she looked up, dazed by the length of those powerful thighs encased in hose, her attention caught immediately by the smooth bulge of his codpiece, the flat belly above and broad chest, his athletic build making her mouth water.

His eyes met hers, an intense blue, glinting with promise of pleasure to come, and Eloise smiled, taking his hand. That look always made her shiver with delicious anticipation, for it was how Wolf looked at his most aroused.

"I thank you, my lord Wolf."

The musicians had begun to play a jaunty galliard. The king was dancing with Jane Seymour, his hand clasped possessively about her waist. Around them the courtiers watched, applauding at every jump and turn, smiling on the new couple as though Anne Boleyn had never existed.

Indeed, no one had mentioned Anne since the day she died. They had not been told that it was forbidden, yet somehow it had seemed better to erase her from their memories, slowly unravelling the past to make Henry's second, imprudent marriage disappear into the cracks of history.

Wolf lifted her hand and led her forward, his limp barely discernible. Or was she merely so accustomed to his tigerish gait that she no longer noticed it?

He was still a man to be reckoned with, she thought, suddenly proud of who her husband was, of his courage and influence at court. The king seemed colder with him these days, more distant. Yet men still moved aside as he approached, their bows respectful; the bored noblewomen stared greedily at his hard body, no doubt trying to imagine what he would be like in bed.

Look away, he's all mine, she thought silently, glaring back at the women with her chin raised.

"Shall we dance?" Wolf asked, and she guessed from his arched brow that he knew what she was thinking.

He had barely danced with her before, and she had wrongly assumed he did not like to dance because of his leg. But he was strong and light on his feet, his dancing as rhythmic and compulsive to watch as the way he made love. He caught her by the waist as she jumped, aiding her to land gently, and she relished the way their mouths almost brushed in that slow descent.

"Jane looks radiant," she said softly. "Some are whispering that the new queen is already with child."

"For her sake, I pray it is a boy."

She turned away, weaving in and out of the other couples as the dance required, then returned to where he was waiting, his gaze fixed on her face.

"At least Susannah seems happier than when she first arrived," she commented. "She seems to have forgiven Hugh for whatever it was he did."

Wolf grunted. "They will make a match of it."

She stared, astonished by his certainty. "Hugh and Susannah?"

His smile was dry. "Wait and see."

As Eloise spun in his arms, she heard applause and turned to see that the king and Jane had stopped dancing. The royal couple were already on the dais instead, the king clearly out of breath, throwing himself back onto his throne with a sullen expression. Henry had injured himself in a fall from his horse earlier that year, she remembered, and was no longer so active as he had been. No doubt Jane Seymour would suit him then, for Anne had been an eager and skilled dancer, always light on her feet. Jane seemed to prefer to sit and watch the world go by.

She leaped again in the dance, suddenly uneasy. "Let us go home," she begged Wolf as he caught her, the words meant only for him. "Back to the north."

"Have a care, Eloise," he murmured warningly. His hands encircled her waist, drawing her close, and even that fleeting warmth lit a fire inside her. She could not stop staring at him these days, so hungry for his body she could happily have spent a week in bed with him. "You never know who is listening."

"All the more reason to go home. Besides, I miss Yorkshire." Aware of the other dancers moving around them, their sly sidelong glances, she made an excuse which sounded feeble even to her ears. "The court is grown so hot and close these past few weeks, the air itself stifles me."

"Soon," he promised her, but his face was aloof. "When His Majesty consents to release me."

She glanced round and saw the king watching from his throne on the dais, thick fingers tapping out the rhythm, heavy with jeweled rings. Beside him sat Jane, her figure neat but rounded, her eyes excited, seemingly unalarmed by the fate of his previous two wives.

Perhaps three is the charm, Eloise considered. And Queen Jane might be right. All it would take was one legitimate son, after all, and Henry would adore her forever.

"You are safe enough from that quarter," Wolf whispered in her ear, seeing in which direction she was looking. He meant the king, of course, she realized.

He took her hand to walk her through the next few steps, and a hot turmoil stirred inside her as their fingers met and linked together.

"How can you be so sure?"

"His Majesty has his hands full with a new bride. I remember that time only too well. A new wife takes time to bed in. She needs to be handled…" He paused, drawing her close as the music swelled to a close. His eyes were a very dark blue as he tweaked one of her nipples through the thin material of her bodice. "Delicately."

Over his shoulder, Eloise caught a glimpse of a woman staring at them from across the Great Hall. She had copper-red hair, curling out indiscreetly from below a French hood, and her wide eyes were fixed on Wolf as though she were drowning and he was the only man there who could save her.

"Who is that lady?" she asked, frowning, then fell silent when Wolf turned to look, suddenly realizing her mistake. She could not help but see his instinctive recoil, nor did she miss his sharp intake of breath.

"That's Margerie," he muttered, then looked sharply back at her as she tried to pull her hand away from his. "Don't."

"Don't what?"

"Eloise…"

"Forgive me, my lord," she bit out, flushed and breathing hard as though the dance had been too energetic for her. She dropped a hurried curtsy, just out of his reach. Jealousy boiled inside her, lending urgency to her clipped words. "I must find my sister. Susannah is still very new to court life. If I leave her alone too long, I fear some predator may attempt to seduce her."

Ignoring the angry hiss of her name as she turned her back, Eloise hurried through the crowd of courtiers toward the spot where she had left Susannah. Let him seek out his former lady. Yes, and dance with her too. She did not care.

She found her sister speaking to Hugh Beaufort, a distracted expression on her face.

"We are going," she muttered, grabbing her sister's arm. "Now, if you please."

"What?"

"I can't stay."

Eloise heard footsteps behind her and stiffened, turning on her heel, fully expecting to see Wolf there.

But it was Sir Thomas Cromwell.

She stared, her angry flush fading as she saw the look in his eyes. "Sir," she addressed him, sinking into a wary curtsy.

Her heart jerked in fear, warning her to be very careful with the king's most influential advisor. This man had almost single-handedly sent Anne Boleyn to the scaffold. If he could destroy a queen so effortlessly, he could crush her without a second thought.

"How may I help you, Sir Thomas?"

"Lady Wolf." Cromwell inclined his head, never taking his eyes off her face. "I trust you are well. Where, pray, is your husband?"

She hesitated, then stilled, seeing Wolf approaching, his face dark with confused anger. "He is behind you, sir."

Cromwell turned, bowing to Wolf. "The very man I need. My

lord, His Majesty has sent me to order you north. Word has reached the king tonight that an uprising has taken place along the north-east coast. His Majesty requires you to gather your men and put down this revolt before it spreads further south."

"At once?" Wolf demanded.

The king's advisor raised his brows at the sharp tone. "Naturally."

Wolf bowed. "I am at His Majesty's command."

"I am glad to hear it, my lord. His Majesty will speak with you in one hour." Cromwell turned away, drawing his fur-lined robes closer about him, his expression already dismissive. "In his privy chamber."

"I will be there."

In the silence that followed Cromwell's departure, Eloise met Wolf's angry blue eyes, and did not know what to say. She had not expected this. She had felt almost happy dancing with Wolf, and even the court had seemed to be settling again after the horror and upheaval of Anne Boleyn's execution. Now her husband was being ordered to ride north to put down a rebellion, and everything was topsy-turvy again.

"Madam," he said sharply, and she could see that Wolf had not forgiven her for walking away from him.

"My lord."

"She means nothing to me now," he muttered, staring down at her as he lifted her hand to his lips. "I swear it on my life."

Do not lie to me, her heart jeered.

Jealousy ate at her insides. She wanted to grab her hand away, scream at him, slap his face, demand that he admit his sins with Margerie so she could stop feverishly imagining them in bed together and hear the horrible truth from his own lips.

But what she said, calmly enough, was, "Pray do not disturb yourself on my account, my lord. You would do better preparing to leave."

His gaze searched her face, and she saw something in his

eyes that she could not explain. For a second, Wolf had looked almost vulnerable.

Then something shifted in his expression. His mouth tightened and his eyes hardened to sharp blue points of light, almost lupine under his short black hair. He straightened, looking at Hugh Beaufort. "My friend, yet again I must put you in danger by asking a favor of you."

"Name it."

"Would you escort my wife and her sister home to Yorkshire? I am to see the king tonight and take my orders from His Majesty. When I accept them, I also intend to ask his permission for Eloise to leave court. If the king grants it, she can leave immediately. But I cannot allow her to travel unprotected."

Hugh nodded, ignoring Susannah's angry intake of breath at this arrangement, and the two men shook hands. "I am happy to do this for you, Wolf."

"You have my thanks. And as many of the men under my command as you wish to accompany you."

"Half a dozen did the trick last time."

"Six it is then. I will speak with my men tonight, settle who is to ride north with you." Wolf seemed almost relieved now that their travel arrangements had been agreed, a smile lurking around the corners of his mouth. "So it seems I am going to fight, and you must take the long road north again. You will soon know that road more intimately than you know London, my friend."

"I don't wish to interrupt, but the king will never let me go," Eloise muttered, hurt and frustrated that he had shut her out of their conversation.

Did she have no say in any of this?

Wolf's head swung toward her. His blue gaze grew darker and more intense, dropping slowly from her hair to her eyes to her mouth as though memorizing every detail of her face.

"I am sure His Majesty will agree to your release if I tell him you are with child."

She stared, her color rising. "Tell him what?" she stammered. "But Wolf…"

"No more talk," he said abruptly, and laid a callused finger across her lips. A soldier's touch, rough and unmannerly, but determined and somehow desirable. The promise of that contact was enough to send her pulse wild, her eyes locked with his, her body straining toward his for one last kiss.

Only he did not kiss her.

Wolf did not love her, she reminded herself in desperation as he stared down into her face. He would never love her. She was his wife, his possession, his chattel. Not his beloved. Like many noblemen, he kept his other women closer than his wife; his attachment to Margerie was burningly apparent, whatever lies he might have told to protect his own heart.

If only she could hate him for it. That was surely what Wolf deserved. Yet all she had inside her was love.

"Come home safe," she said hoarsely as he turned away, and his grim look nearly broke her heart.

"Farewell, Eloise."

Twenty

WOLF COULD NOT FOCUS on the swaying torchlight for long. Whenever he tried, his vision blurred and he felt sick.

He closed his eyes instead and listened. He was lying down, and he could hear hooves on dry earth. Several horses, one in front, one to each side. Possibly more following. He needed to grasp where he was, what calamity had occurred. But it was too hard. His head throbbed and he kept losing consciousness; when he came round again, nothing seemed to have changed. The night was still dark beyond the flaming torches, and Wolf was being carried in a litter, his whole body rocking as though in a cradle.

The cart must have gone over a large stone in the road. The violent jolt shook him, and he groaned, feeling pain shoot through his groin.

"My lord?"

A man bent over him. It was Fletcher.

"God's blood, where am I?" He heard himself mumbling, and paused, frowning, aware that he must make himself understood. "What happened?"

"Try not to speak, my lord." Fletcher looked concerned. His voice seemed indistinct, though he was leaning close. "You are wounded. We are taking you home to Wolf Hall."

"The rebels…"

"They are all put down, my lord, or waiting to be hanged. Word has been sent to the king."

"I remember now, we were riding full tilt after the bastards," he said hoarsely, a dreamlike memory coming back to him of endless green flats and marshlands. "I...I fell from my horse and took some hurt."

One of the rebels must have hidden in a ditch behind a low hedge, crouched there, waiting for their approach. As their horses flew over the hedge, the cold glint of a pike had come thrusting up from beneath, slicing his horse's belly open and catching Wolf in the groin.

"My horse... Is he dead?"

"Aye, my lord. Like the cowardly ruffian who did this to you. We cut him down before he had run three paces, and stuck his head on his own pike as a warning to his fellows."

He sucked in an agonizing breath, fighting to stay awake as the darkness threatened to swallow him again.

"Is the wound bad? Will I live?"

He grabbed at the man but his fingers were useless, too weak even to open and close. The sickness returned abruptly, and he fell back, gasping up at the cool night air.

"Here, this will help you sleep." Fletcher tipped some flask to his mouth, and he swallowed reluctantly, then shuddered. The taste was loathsome. "My lord, you must rest. Calm yourself, and let the physick do its work. The surgeon who operated on you knew his trade, I made sure of that."

"How bad, Fletcher? The truth."

His servant's face was impassive. "Wolf Hall is another two days' ride. If you do not bleed further, or suffer an infection of the wound, you should reach there alive."

He lay still, his head burning. A fever?

"Have you sent word to Lady Wolf?"

Fletcher nodded, laying a hand on his forehead. "One of the boys rode ahead with a missive. You are expected, my lord."

Wolf tried to mumble another question, but his mouth would not work. He was simply too tired.

The question slid away, and when he opened his eyes again, the torches had burned low and it was almost dawn. The sky was flushed along the eastern horizon, the weather thankfully dry. He thought of Eloise, how she would be free if he died, free to marry a man who could love her as she ought to be loved, and berated himself for a fool and a coward.

"I should have told her," he muttered.

He looked about, meaning to write her a letter, but Fletcher was gone. He was alone on the litter, and so hot he had to kick off his blankets so he could breathe. He fumbled with his shirt, but his hands were too weak. Sweat was pumping off him. The cart jolted again over some crater in the road, and Wolf roared as a searing white agony pierced his groin.

He felt hands steadying him, and fought to escape them. The rebels had come back to finish the job, but they would not take him so easily. He thrashed wildly, hunting by his side for his dagger, his sword, any kind of weapon to stave them off.

"My lord!"

Something burned his throat. Poison, he thought, furious at their treachery.

He fell like a stone into darkness, and did not awake again until the litter had stopped moving and he could see a thousand pinpricks of stars above him in the black velvet sky. In a sudden moment of lucidity, he realized they had camped for the night, his men sleeping around the fire.

Then the sickness took hold of him again, and the nightmares returned.

Eloise was there, a welcoming smile on her face. He could hear water running sweetly behind her, and smelled moss, the tang of summer flowers. He was lying on his back in a sunlit meadow and Eloise was kneeling beside him, stroking his head. Her golden hair tumbled over him, brushing his cheek. She looked down at him, her eyes so warm and loving he felt he could tell her anything.

"I love you," he whispered. "Eloise."

But her face suddenly clouded over. She did not want his love. Her eyes grew cold. She told him his love was smothering her, like a hand across her mouth. Then they were arguing, and Eloise was saying she could not love him, that she had never felt anything for him, that she was in love with another man.

He reached for her. "Eloise, please…" He was begging, he realized. Begging like a fool for her love, as he had once begged Margerie.

Then it happened again, just as he had feared.

She rose and left him without a word. The meadow grew chill and silent, as though a dark cloud had covered the face of the sun and all the flowers had withered. Then the meadow itself vanished, and he was alone in a darkened chamber, only the glow of a fire to keep him company. He had driven his betrothed away with his obsessive love, and he knew she would never return.

Wolf lay hot and aching in the darkness, his heart in turmoil, his body on fire. What had he done amiss?

He slung an arm over his eyes, fighting back the tears that would betray his weakness. "I will never love again," he said hoarsely. "Never."

Eloise closed the door to their bedchamber and stood a moment in silence, her face hidden in her hands. It was so hard to watch him suffer. But at least his fever was subsiding. He would live. She had stripped and bathed Wolf in cool water as the physician had suggested, and given him poppy juice to help him sleep, and now he seemed over the worst.

He was still having nightmares, though. She feared his rambling, tormented dreams, wondering who was with him in that shadowy half-world into which he had retreated since his injury.

She had still not recovered from the horror of receiving that first missive, the news that her husband was gravely wounded and close to death. When their cavalcade arrived at the hall, Wolf tossing and sweating in his litter, half-crazed with fever, she had thought his death imminent. That first night had been spent on her knees beside his bed, praying relentlessly for his safe recovery and following the physician's instructions as carefully as she could.

By the time day broke, she had been almost dead herself, barely able to rise and lie down beside him, needing to close her eyes for a space.

If she had not fully appreciated his physical strength before, she knew it now. At the height of his fever, it had taken three men to restrain Wolf as he fought and lashed out, cursing them for traitors in his feverish dreams.

Hugh Beaufort appeared in the doorway to the hall. "My lady," he said deeply, bowing.

She smiled at him thankfully. Hugh had stayed on after escorting her and Susannah back to Wolf Hall, gallantly insisting he could not leave two women alone and unprotected when there was an uprising in the north country. Even when Susannah had been ordered back home to face her father's wrath at her running away to court, Hugh had stayed at the hall rather than return to London. "Lord Wolf would never forgive me if I left you alone here. I shall await his return, and make my way south after that."

Eloise had secretly suspected Hugh of wishing to spend time with Susannah, for the two seemed to have grown dangerously close again in recent weeks, despite their frequent quarrels. It should not be encouraged, for she knew her stubborn father still intended Susannah to marry one of his old friends, a local landowner, and would not look favorably on this match with a stranger, however influential with the king. Yet who was she to force them apart?

For now, she was deeply grateful to have another gentleman about the house, for she could think of nothing but Wolf while he lay so dangerously ill, and there were daily tasks to be done about the hall which Hugh had willingly taken on.

Hugh straightened, frowning at her appearance. He shook his head. No doubt she looked quite wild and disheveled, she thought wryly. "You should rest, my lady. You have not slept these two days."

"My lord needs constant care and attendance."

"Then let a servant attend him. You will do your husband no good by working yourself into the grave."

"Maybe an hour or two, then. But I cannot leave him alone for long. When they first carried Wolf inside, I feared…" She closed her eyes. "I thought he would die, Hugh."

"He is stronger than he looks."

"Yes." She drew a long breath, trying to prepare herself for the worst. "But his wound irks him. I worry it may fester and poison his blood. He is in great pain, though the fever has masked it. The physician fears that Wolf…that my husband…"

She halted, suddenly unable to go on.

"Speak it," Hugh urged her.

Eloise looked at him, her agony out in the open. "Wolf may never be a whole man again."

His expression was grim. "His groin?"

She nodded.

"Sweet Jesu," Hugh muttered, shaking his head in pity. "And Wolf is such a man that any doubt or shame cast on his manhood would kill him."

"I fear so too."

Her husband's friend came nearer, laying a hand gently on her sleeve. "And you, my lady? How do you fare under that burden?"

"What I feel is not important," she told him proudly, shaking away the tears.

Eloise straightened, squaring her shoulders and raising her chin. Yes, her heart was burning with agony, knowing she might never more feel Wolf's hard body driving into hers. Yet even if he never lay with her again, never gave her that hot, intense pleasure she had come to crave, she would not love him any less. Not even knowing that he loved another woman.

"Whatever tomorrow brings, Wolf is still my husband."

———

Wolf limped to the window and stared down into the sunlit gardens. Eloise was directly below, giving directions to the servants as they clipped and garnered herbs for the kitchen. She looked so radiant these days, her breasts swelling out of her bodice, her hips sweetly curved under the coarse apron she had donned for household work.

He felt a stirring of arousal and smiled hungrily, wishing she would hurry back upstairs. Though even if she came to him now, he knew they would not end up in bed together.

It was some three weeks now since he had woken to find his fever gone and his body weak, but healing slowly. He was glad to be home at Wolf Hall, to have these familiar old rooms about him as he regained his strength. But he was not a fool, and he could not help remarking how aloof Eloise had been since his body cooled and he opened his eyes to find her face beside him.

To see her at his bedside when he woke, a lovely, golden-haired siren in a white gown, had given him a simple joy he had never known before. He had wanted her as before, yet now his lust had turned to purified desire, a love he had never felt, even for Margerie. For that had been a boy's love, a burning need to possess and have his manhood confirmed by their mutual pleasure. Now he looked at Eloise and felt friendship as well as desire, the need to embrace and comfort her as well as take her to bed.

What was that if not a man's love?

It had not felt wise to declare his love too soon though, still in this damnable weakened state, a healing scar on his groin that could yet make him less than a man.

So Wolf had tried to express his love to her in smaller ways, kissing her hand and asking her to play chess with him or read aloud from Chaucer's tales, loving the hours they spent together in such idle pursuits. Eloise had not responded though, drawing away whenever he began to kiss her, her face shuttered.

Why?

It had to be his old ghost, Margerie. When they had parted at court, he had known Eloise feared he was still in love with his former betrothed. But she could not be more mistaken.

He loved Eloise to distraction. And he knew she was not indifferent to him. Far from it. His body ached with arousal, remembering how they had lain together so passionately before the king had ordered him north. He could have sworn then that she loved him, that Simon was forgotten at last and her heart belonged to him alone. Yet now she was strangely distant, avoiding his touch as though she feared it.

She looked up at that moment, seeing him at the window. His gaze met hers. He felt the shock through his body as she stared back, smoothing her blue gown over her hips, almost nervous. What was she thinking?

Frustration seized him and he spun away from the window, limping heavily back to his bed.

Moments later, she came into the bedchamber, closing the door quietly behind her when she saw him lying clothed on his bed. Slowly she unlaced her work apron and laid it aside, each movement unconsciously sensual, making his blood rise.

God, he wanted her.

But had she lost her desire for him now he was all but bedridden? He saw concern in her expression, and silently cursed his injury for reducing him to the status of an invalid.

He must show Eloise he was still a man, still capable of siring the child he was sure she must want. Then perhaps she would look on him less indifferently when she came to his bedside.

"My lord? What is this? You should not be out of bed yet. The physician says…"

"Damn the physician," he growled, and held out his hand. "Come here, woman."

"Wolf, I…" She shook her head, not moving.

"Yes? What would you say, Eloise?" He stared at her, his jaw tense, his body aching with need, dangerously close to that madness he had denied feeling before. "Am I not your husband? Are you not my wife?"

"You are not strong enough," she began tentatively, but he saw the flush in her cheeks, heard the tremble in her voice, and he knew she wanted him too.

"You would deny me my rights, is that it?"

"Wolf, please."

He slid his legs to the floor and crossed the room toward her, carefully schooling himself to hide the jarring pain in his leg. He stopped before her, and searched her face for signs that his touch might be unwelcome. He was her husband, but he was no rapist.

"Eloise, what is this foolish hesitation?" He brushed her cheek with his fingers, and frowned at how she recoiled from his touch. Pain flashed through him and he too winced, taking a step back. "God's blood, woman. Am I such an ogre?"

She shook her head, apparently struck dumb.

"Is this about Margerie?"

Her lips parted as though to agree, her face startled, her color rising, yet still she did not speak.

"I do not love Margerie," he told her bluntly. "She never loved me, but she was everything to me once, I admit it. That is all over. She came to see me at court. She knew the king desired you, and she offered us help. It was her idea for Kate Langley to accompany me to the king's privy chamber that night."

He turned away abruptly. Eloise did not care who he loved or did not love, she merely thought him an invalid. If he could no longer pleasure her, her thoughts would soon incline to Simon Thetford again. And why not? Thetford was younger than Wolf, and would no doubt fill her bed as readily as he had done.

The thought of her in bed with another man made him groan aloud, his fists clenched in helpless rage.

"My lord, what is it? Are you…are you in pain?"

"Yes," he bit out, and turned to face her. He took her by the shoulders, the scent of her skin driving him wild. "I am in agony over you, can you not see it?"

His voice broke, suddenly hoarse. "I lusted after you from the first, Eloise. Your smile makes a man want to come inside you. The king wanted you too. Hard to blame him, knowing how very beddable you are." He paused, then forced the words out. "But you were only ever a body to me, a female to bring me pleasure and bear me sons."

She made a rough sound under her breath. "Please…"

"No, you must listen. After Margerie, I told myself I would never be such a fool as to love another woman. Not even my wife. That was why I was happy to marry you, knowing you were in love with Thetford and would not demand a closer bond." He forced a smile to his lips, but it fell awry, twisting into a grimace. "Only I changed my mind once we were lovers. I could not help myself."

"And Margerie?"

"I told you, that's over."

"So easily?"

"Damn you, no, not so easily," he growled, his voice brittle with tension. "When I saw Margerie again at court, I realized what a fool I had been to hold on to her memory. If I loved anything, it was the dream of her. Not the woman she has become. There was nothing in my heart when I saw her again but pity."

"Pity?" she queried, frowning.

He nodded. "For the terrible life she has led since we parted, for she lost her reputation when she broke off our betrothal and ran away with another man. She has no hope of making a respectable marriage now."

"And what of that letter you wrote to her, my lord?"

"Letter?"

"When I came across you in the tower room, you had been writing a love letter to Margerie, had you not? I saw her name on the paper."

He stared, remembering. "That was no love letter. It was…"

She raised her brows, watching him coldly. Was that hatred in her eyes?

"A farewell," he finished awkwardly.

Eloise said nothing, but he saw incredulity on her face.

"Since she rejected my suit, I have been writing letters to her. Not sending them. Merely writing out my…my dark and twisted thoughts, then later throwing them on the fire."

He swallowed hard, a sudden heat in his face. How to persuade her that he was speaking the truth when she still thought him a liar and an adulterer?

"Do you not see?" he asked huskily. "If I had not found some way to write out my thoughts, I would have run mad. What you saw that day was my last secret letter to Margerie. A final farewell."

"Why?"

Pain twisted him in helpless desperation at that one icy word. Her body was frozen beneath his hands, as though it meant nothing to stand so close to him, when his whole soul was on fire for her.

Was there no way to rekindle the ravening heat that used to flare so intensely between them?

"Because it was time to let go of that boyish memory," he told her, not caring if he exposed his failings as a man with this confession. "I have since burned that letter. It is over and done with. Margerie was a dream, a shadow of love. Not love itself. Trust me when I say she is no longer in my soul." He stared down into her face, willing her to believe him. "There's only room for one woman there, and that's you, my Wolf bride, my Eloise."

He bent his head, driven by a frustration that was killing him, and took her mouth. Let her push him away if she must, tell him she did not want him, had never wanted him. He could not keep his hands off her a moment longer, his desire for her was such exquisite torture.

But Eloise did not reject him. Her lips parted beneath his and he slipped his tongue inside, tasting her sweetness, the delicious warmth he had been denied for so long.

She gave a little cry, her fingers slipping restlessly through his hair, stroking and gripping as he kissed her.

Encouraged, he pressed closer, his body suddenly alight with fever, his cock hardening inexorably against her belly. There was pain from the scar at his groin, but it was bearable. And the pleasure of their coupling would soon chase it away.

"No," she suddenly gasped, pulling away, panic and guilt in her face. "We must not. Your wound…"

"Is healed," he finished for her silkily. Their eyes met and he almost grinned, abruptly understanding her hesitation. God's blood, had she truly thought him incapable? If only she knew how he had woken that morning, gloriously erect, more than willing to perform his duties as a husband, but with no wife by his side.

He drawled, "You do not believe me, dear wife? Give me your hand."

She shook her head, starting to back away. "My lord, no, in truth I dare not… If you were not able to…"

He grabbed her hand and pressed it hard between his legs, his bulge only too apparent without a codpiece, and saw her eyes slowly widen…

Eloise could not believe it. After everything the physician had said, all his dire warnings about destroying Wolf's manhood by visiting his bed, one touch told her that her husband was far from rendered impotent.

Indeed, he was more rigid than she had ever known him, his cock hard as wood beneath her hand. It jerked as she stroked down its impressive length, then stiffened still further when she curled her fingers around its girth and squeezed.

"Did you fear I would never fuck you again, Eloise?" he mocked, though his smile warmed her heart even as he teased her. "That would be a privation of the most fearful kind indeed. But I assure you, my beautiful temptress, I am very much capable of mounting you. Yes, and of planting my seed in your belly. Which is precisely what I intend to do now. It is time I begot an heir."

"No need," she murmured, loving her husband with every bone in her body, and burning with pleasure that she could finally tell him what she had suspected for some days now. "The deed is done, my lord."

He stared, his eyes locked with hers. His whisper was hoarse. "What are you saying?"

"Give me your hand," she ordered him, deliberately echoing his own words.

Slowly he obeyed, his eyes questioning hers, and she pressed his hand against the gentle swell of her lower belly.

"I am with child, Wolf. Your child."

He seemed to be having trouble breathing, his blue eyes very dark. Then Wolf dropped to his knees before her and rubbed his rough cheek against her belly through her gown.

"A child? I am to be a father?"

"Yes."

"Is it…is it safe to…?"

She laughed, running her fingers through his black hair. Her whole body felt so free and alive, it was hard to remember the darkness she had carried in her heart for months now, thinking he would never love her.

Eloise looked down at him with love and joy as her husband knelt before her. She did believe that he no longer loved Margerie. There had been such a shaken look in his face as he spoke of his last letter to her, and their meeting at court. She knew this was Wolf stripped bare of his defenses, waiting for her either to destroy him forever or forgive his past sins.

Still, Wolf had not said the words she needed to hear. I love you. But that could wait for another day, if those words ever came at all. She would not spoil things by being impatient. Not this time, when all her dreams seemed to be coming true.

"I cannot think why it should not be."

"Thank God, for I must have you again, I cannot wait until the babe is born," he groaned, and pushed up her skirts, expertly finding her slick cleft with his fingers, stroking and pressing inside her until she gasped and writhed with hot ecstasy.

"Oh, my lord," she breathed, already so close to the edge that her legs were shaking with the need to come.

His mouth found her. He sucked hard, and Eloise sagged against him, climaxing with a wild cry.

Wolf dragged her down on top of him, their half-clothed bodies tumbling together in clumsy lust, his cock already exposed, its thick length leaving her mouth dry with sheer need.

His hands seized her hips, then he jerked her forward onto his cock, his head snapping back on a grunt of pleasure as he penetrated her slow and deep. He showed no sign of pain, his eyes closing, caught up in the spell of their lovemaking as deeply as she was.

She cried out too, and her heart filled with love for him, her mouth trembling with joy. She had come to him reluctantly, resigned to a marriage of cold couplings where his need for an heir would leave her unloved once the longed-for son was provided. Eloise knew the child inside her belly might be female, and indeed that she might never bear him a son, leaving him—like the king—without a male heir.

But she had grown to trust Wolf, and knew he would not put her aside for failing to provide him with an heir. Her husband had integrity, something she had failed to see in those early days before they were married. She was his wife now, and she trusted Wolf to keep his marriage oaths as solemnly as he had kept his oath of allegiance to the king, whatever hardship or sacrifices that might entail.

With sensual abandon, Eloise rose and fell on his hard body, aided by his hands on her hips, a heady pleasure spiraling in her body as she rode him. There was no more doubt in her heart, no more fear, no restraint. She was so sure of his steadfastness she was willing to put her happiness in his hands for the rest of her life. And her body too, for him to pleasure like this forever.

"Jesu Christ." He groaned, eyes still closed tight. His strong throat was corded with veins, his body tense. "Eloise, I love you."

She stilled above him, and Wolf looked up at her warily, his eyes guarded, suddenly defensive.

"What did you say?" she whispered, staring.

His mouth twisted on a pained smile, a bitter humor in his voice. "I said that I love you. Though I don't blame you for not believing me. I have not been a good husband to you, Eloise. All I can promise is that I will do better from now on."

She was crying, but they were tears of joy, salty in her mouth as she leaned forward and kissed him, sucking gently on his tongue and loving the way his cock swelled inside her.

"I do believe you, and I love you too," she told him softly, and met the blue intensity of his eyes without her usual quiver of trepidation, hands cupping and stroking his stubble-rough face. "My dear, sweet lord, my delectable Wolf."

"My love."

They kissed hotly and tenderly, their mouths meeting for the first time in love, revealing their true selves at last.

Wolf drew back a little to gaze at her, a smile lighting up his eyes with a warmth and tenderness she had never seen there before. The sight of such vulnerability on his hard, soldierly face tore at her heart, driving her even deeper in love with him than ever.

"You have made me a man, Eloise."

Wolf rolled her over on the floor and began to make love to her in earnest, his powerful arms supporting his weight as he thrust, his strokes fast and urgent.

She remembered the wolf he had drawn on the cave wall, and her heart ached for the boy he had been. She had no wish to replace the mother he had lost, nor the girl who had betrayed his trust. But she could be the woman he would love for the rest of his life, now that Wolf had left the darkness behind and was hunting in sunlight.

She ran her tongue delicately along his lips and heard him groan against her mouth, swelling and thickening inside her. Her thighs locked about his muscular back, dragging him closer, wanting to give him the same joy he had given her.

"And I will love you," he finished hoarsely, "as a man."

Eloise kissed his throat as he thrust deep and began to come. His cry of agonized pleasure was explosive, his cock wondrously hot and hard, leaping inside her, jolting and filling her with love.

Epilogue

Early autumn 1536, Yorkshire

"SUSANNAH? WHERE ARE YOU hiding, child?"

I am not a child.

The morning had been altogether too peaceful, Susannah thought, closing her eyes; and the hay loft above the threshing barn, a perfect hiding-place. Lying back in the shadowy warmth of the straw, she had been indulging a daydream which, even now, still held her hotly in its grip. But her peace was at an end, and she forced herself to kneel up, shaking off that dream with the straw caught in her hair.

There was no longer any point in pretending she had not heard the sound of a horseman approaching the house, then her voice being called from below.

A messenger must have arrived from her sister Eloise, come to invite her to stay at the great hall for a few days, or perhaps with some news about Eloise's growing pregnancy, for it had been a good month now since Lord Wolf had announced to the world that his wife was expecting an heir. It was lovely to see Eloise glowing with happiness, her rounded belly beginning to show beneath her gowns, and to watch her and Lord Wolf so in love. But her sister's joy was a reminder to Susannah that she too would be expected to marry soon and do her duty by her husband. And her father had no plans to find her a handsome suitor like Wolf, that was for certain.

Susannah unfolded her legs from beneath her and stood up.

"Coming, Morag!" she called down to the woman who had once been her wet-nurse, and now was… Well, she did not quite know how to describe Morag, except that since Eloise had settled into her new life at the great hall, her old nurse had been spending more time back here at the manor house, looking after her and Sir John.

Susannah hesitated, glancing down. While thinking and day-dreaming, she had been clutching a small but heavy gold ring, set with a modest ruby.

She weighed the ring in her palm, wondering if she should wear it—and what that might signify—then pushed it back into the leather pouch hanging from her belt. She pulled the drawstring tight, checking twice that it was secure. It must not fall out and be lost, she told herself.

Hugh had given her the ring, "Not as a promise, but as a gift," he had insisted, and it was precious to her.

Not that she was in love with the king's clerk. Not a whit.

Hugh meant nothing to her, just as she meant nothing to him. The ruby ring was valuable though, and she did not wish to lose it.

Hampered by her gown, Susannah hurried down the ladder, impatiently jumping the last few feet to the ground. Her heavy skirts billowed out, no doubt showing off her ankles, and her bodice was wrenched a little awry as she landed.

"Damn," she muttered, tidying herself, then looked up in sudden consternation, for Morag was not alone.

A man stood beside her old nurse, shielding his eyes against the bright sunshine. She knew him at once. Hugh Beaufort.

Once she had thought him a comely man, broad-shouldered, long-legged, and had shivered in maidenly anticipation of those incisive green eyes meeting hers. Now she knew him so much more intimately. More intimately, indeed, than any chaste unmarried girl should know a man. And now her breath caught in her throat as she stared at him, her cheeks grew warm, and her body ached deliciously, remembering his touch.

Comely?

She had not known the meaning of the word when she first applied it to Master Beaufort. He was the most sensual man of her acquaintance, his looks almost god-like in her eyes. Yet she could never admit such foolishness to him. She had betrayed herself enough already.

Hugh lowered his arm, looking back at her, and she could not help noting the dark stubby lashes through which he surveyed her, unsmiling; nor the abrupt gesture as he swept off his velvet cap, thrusting a hand through thick fair hair; and saw the jutting deter-mination of his chin...

He had come to offer her his hand in marriage.

Again.

"Hugh!" she exclaimed, a little shaken at the sight of him, and took an involuntary step forward. She saw Morag's eyes narrow on her face and hurriedly amended her speech. "I mean...M...Master Beaufort. What do you... Why are you here?"

Did she have to stutter and trip over her speech like a lovesick girl? Morag already suspected she had not returned to her father's house as innocent as she had left it. Susannah had noted her pursed lips whenever talk between her and Eloise turned to men and suitors. Though if Morag knew the truth, she would doubtless take a birch switch to Susannah for her loose and wanton conduct. And put her weight behind every stroke.

"Mistress Tyrell."

Hugh bowed, cap in hand, his face very stern. No one looking at him could think he had come here to court her; perhaps to offer for her hand this very day. Yet surely that was his intention in visiting? It must appear so to Morag. Unmarried gentlemen did not call upon unmarried women unless they intended to make a proposal.

She curtsied a little belatedly, wishing her hair was not loose to her shoulders and no doubt covered in straw, then shot Morag a fierce look. "Do you need me up at the house, Morag?"

Fists on hips, Morag looked shrewdly from Susannah's flushed face to Hugh's stern countenance. Slowly, she shook her head. "I cannot pretend to like this business, a young girl speaking with a man alone, without the company of your sister or one of the maids, but…if I leave Bess alone with the wash tub much longer, she'll mar the laundry, for she is a brainless flibbertigibbet." She glared at Hugh suddenly. "Do you wish to speak with the master before you leave, sir?"

Hugh met that hard look without flinching. "I shall pay my respects to Sir John if he is at home, yes."

Morag gave an abrupt nod, then turned on her heel, muttering under her breath as if she had already put them both from her mind. "I only hope Bess has not rubbed a hole in your father's best shirt!"

Left alone together, they stood a moment in the door of the threshing barn. Outside, the sunshine beckoned, but Susannah preferred to stay indoors, hiding the heat in her cheeks. Her heart began to beat faster. She had forgotten what an effect his proximity had on her body, and did not raise her eyes to his, determined not to speak first—nor even to speak at all.

"I know we did not part on pleasant terms," Hugh began stiffly, and unable to help herself, she abandoned her decision and interrupted at once.

"Pleasant? I should think not!"

"Susannah, for pity's sake, I have made my apologies for what happened. Hear me out, at least."

He reached for her.

"Don't touch me!" She turned back into the shadowy interior of the barn, her arms folded across her chest, instantly furious with him—and with herself, for allowing him to disturb her peace of mind again. Her voice sounded high and breathless, almost girlish. "You abducted me, k...kissed me, then dared to offer for my hand out of a sense of duty."

She whirled about to find him mere inches away. He had followed her closely, his green eyes as stormy as her own, his body hard with tension.

"That's not true," he said tightly. "That is, I do wish to marry you. But not out of duty."

"Then why?"

His eyes held hers. "You know why."

The air thickened between them. There was silence in the barn except for their breathing. She did know why. He still wanted her. It was in every line of his body. And she wanted him too.

They were standing on a soft, uneven floor of earth and straw, Susannah realized, and behind them were the shadowy stalls where the carthorses were kept in poor weather. It would be so simple for them to lie down together in the darkness there.

The naked desire must have shown on her face too, because something seemed to snap like a leash, and suddenly Hugh was dragging her forward, his mouth slanting down over hers, tasting her hungrily.

The weeks flew away and she was back in the dark forest with him, hiding from their pursuers, when their lips had met and passion had flared like a torch between them. Later he had insisted in a stilted voice that they must marry, not meeting her eyes, saying he had taken advantage of the lady he should have been protecting. She had rejected his offer, of course, for to her mind it would be no better than the marriage her father had arranged for her. She would not have married Hugh Beaufort if he had been the king of England himself, not merely to satisfy his honor because he had been too intimate with her.

Hugh's shock at her refusal had quickly given way to anger, and that curt tone which had become his habitual expression with her. He and his men had spent days searching for her, sent by Lord Wolf to bring her to court after she ran away from home, and she supposed it was understandable that he had found her rejection infuriating. But after all, there was no need for him to behave so nobly and marry where he did not love. She had wanted him to kiss her; he had not forced his kisses upon her.

Nobody knew what had happened on her journey to court that spring, and nobody needed to know if only Hugh Beaufort would stop so obstinately pursuing her when she had already said no.

And now he was kissing her again!

His hands cupped her breasts, and as they pressed together, she felt the swelling in his codpiece, and became almost delirious in her desire.

"Hugh," she moaned, and his tongue pushed between her parted lips, licking and teasing her, stabbing in and out, each thrust a promise and an invitation.

Her hands clutched at his shoulders, and suddenly she was in his arms, being carried into one of the dark stalls and laid upon a bed of musty straw. Their mouths met again fiercely, and then their bodies. Susannah wished she had the strength of mind to struggle against him, but to own the truth, she had thought of little else since they had parted. Still, she was no fool. The straw might be softer than the forest floor where they had once lain in each other's arms, but the place was far less private, and she whispered urgently, "Not here, not here!"

Hugh paid no attention to her objections, his chest heaving, his face possessed by desire.

"You want this as much as I do. God's blood, woman, I have been driven half out of my wits these past weeks." He yanked up her skirt, stroking along her inner thigh until he reached her hot moist core, unfettered by any undergarment. Her breath hissed in at his touch, and his answering groan told her how much he had been imagining this too. "Refuse my offer of marriage if you will, Susannah, but I cannot hold back any longer. I must touch you again."

Breathless, Hugh settled himself on top of her as though trying not to crush her with his large body. One finger already stroking in and out of her eager cunt, his tongue slipped into her mouth again, urging her to respond as she had done last time, willingly and with passion.

"You want this too," he muttered against her mouth, and it was not a question.

He pushed a second finger inside her, slowly. She moaned, unable to prevent herself, and her body arched toward his. Hugh withdrew both fingers, then pushed them back inside, this time more forcefully, stretching her tender flesh as though preparing the way for a deeper invasion. Her gasp was muffled by his kiss. Then a third finger was inside her, his thumb pressing against the moist nub above, playing her mercilessly.

Shifting above her, he kissed her throat, then tugged her bodice down with one brutal jerk, exposing her breasts.

"Beautiful," Hugh breathed, caressing one breast until her nipple stiffened to a peak under his fingers. His lips traveled down the valley between her breasts, then suddenly he turned his head and suckled first on one breast, then the other, licking and blowing on her wet nipples until her limbs turned to water and she had no memory of why she had been fighting him.

It was the most exquisite torture in the world.

"Yes," Susannah found herself whispering, lost to reason, lost to everything but the drumming of blood in her veins. "Take me."

Yet Hugh did not take her, as she had naively assumed he would. Dragging her gown to her waist, his head descended instead between her thighs, and Susannah cried out in wordless astonishment as his mouth found her most intimate place.

Surely he did not intend…?

His tongue snaked out, catching that sensitive nub of flesh he had played with before, and she caught her lip between her teeth, biting down hard so as not to scream with pleasure. His tongue lathed up and down her aching flesh, then pushed inside, his invasion shocking her again with its thrusts and stabs, its dark promise of ecstasy.

There was sweat on her forehead. She could no longer think, only feel. The center of her being was so hot and swollen, so desperately sensitive to every flick of his tongue, her body would surely burst into flames if he did not…

Writhing beneath him, shame left far behind, Susannah gripped his fair head and urged that tongue further inside, her thighs splayed wide.

"Please," she managed incoherently, her face on fire, her hands begging him, though she did not properly understand what it was she wanted. "I need to… Please don't stop."

But suddenly Hugh was gone, leaving her frustrated and confused. He was on his feet again, panting and hot-faced. He shoved a hand through his disheveled hair, then bent to help her up.

She was still staring up at him in shock, mystified, when she heard her father's voice, close by in the doorway to the threshing barn.

"Susannah? Come to me at once! Where are you?"

Her father sounded furious.

Swiftly, Hugh pulled her to her feet, smoothing down her crumpled gown and pulling straw from her hair. "Go out to him," he whispered. "I will remain here. No one need know…"

But it was too late. Her father was standing right inside the barn. No doubt he had heard some noise within, perhaps her cries of passion. He stared at them both, his lined face a mask of barely contained fury.

"Susannah, I want you to come here and stand behind me."

"Father, please," she began, stumbling over her words in rigid embarrassment, "it's not...what it seems."

"I told you to get behind me, girl!" His voice shook, and she was suddenly frightened that her father would burst his heart in this rage, so incontinent was it, so at odds with his age and infirmity. "For once in your life obey me and do as you are told."

Reluctantly she left Hugh's side, daring a swift glance at his face, which was resuming its usual control now their passion had been stemmed, and stood to one side behind her father.

"Now, Master Beaufort, what is the meaning of this? First I hear you have come on a visit, not to me but to my daughter, and now I find you alone with her, guilt written on both your faces."

He looked from Hugh's stony face to hers, but did not wait for an answer. Perhaps he feared what might be admitted, for if he was told that it had gone too far between them, he would be forced to insist that Hugh marry her. And Susannah knew her father had his mind set on her marrying one of his old friends.

"How dare you sully my daughter with your inky clerk's hands, you villain?" her father demanded. "If I were a younger man, I would run you through for this insult. No, do not move from that spot, you coward. I may yet send for my sword. What have you to say for yourself?"

Hugh looked at him directly. Although he held his large body still, it crackled with purpose and determination. "I intend to marry your daughter, sir," he told him calmly. "I wish to make Susannah my bride as soon as may be, if you will consent to the banns being read in church."

But her father shook his head, just as she had suspected he would. Sir John Tyrell was a Yorkshireman, and while he had respect for the king's authority, he was not impressed by smooth-talking southerners from court, nor by their learning. "You can wish all you like, boy. I will not give my consent. Not to such as you."

"Father," she remonstrated, not keen herself to be married to Hugh against his will, yet still embarrassed by the insult her father had thrown so carelessly in his direction, "you forget, Master Beaufort is the king's clerk, and much respected at court. He has the king's ear."

"I do not care if he has the king in his pocket. Silence, girl. This is none of your concern." Her father jerked his head at Hugh. "Be off with you. And do not come back or I shall have you whipped from my land like a beggar."

Hugh Beaufort stood a moment without responding, his hands by his sides, his expression under control, giving nothing away. She saw a dark storm in his eyes though, and felt the curbed restraint of violence behind his stillness, and she feared for her father, who was frailer than he seemed.

"Hugh, please…" she whispered, and shook her head. "My answer must be the same as my father's. It is over."

Stiffly, Hugh bowed, then took his leave of them. She could tell by his expression that he had no plans to return.

The barn seemed a smaller, colder place once he had gone, and even the sunshine pouring through the open doors could not warm her as it had done before.

Susannah shivered, wrapping her arms about herself. Was she a fool, turning down his proposal? Hugh Beaufort could make her happy in bed at least, even if her heart would mourn when she considered how he had been forced into their union, offering her his hand in marriage as an honorable gesture. Yet if Hugh truly cared for her, would he have allowed her father to turn him away so easily?

"I should have you whipped too," her father said bitterly. She spun on her heel, knowing she must face his wrath unprotected now. "I thought you more innocent than your sister. I kept you away from court as long as I could, so you would not lose the sweetness of your nature. But you behaved like a whore with that man."

"Yes, I did," she agreed angrily, not caring who else might hear. "So perhaps I should marry him."

His blow caught her across the face and Susannah fell to the ground, half-stunned, her cheek aflame.

"You will marry my good friend Sir William Hanney, who has been asking for your hand since you were fourteen years of age. And you will give him children, just as your sister is giving her lord an heir." He was shouting now, his face mottled red, although he must have known he could be heard from outside the door, where she could see a number of the manor servants loitering, no doubt hoping to hear what had fired their master into this temper. "I have held Sir William off long enough, out of sympathy for your innocence. But it is high time I gave you to him, for you are no longer the child I remember."

She turned over, staring up at her father. Her cheek throbbed, and she guessed there would be a bruise there by the evening. How dare he strike her? Rage at his brutality flamed through her too, swift as a forest fire, stripping away any sense of caution.

"Then he will be sorely disappointed in his bargain, sir," she gasped out. "For I am no longer a virgin."

Her father's eyes almost started from his head at this bold admission, and he made a choking noise, his face dark with fury. But to her amazement he did not relent from his decision, sweeping past her with a look of withering contempt, as though she were indeed a whore.

"Then I suggest you learn to feign the loss of your maidenhead," he threw back over his shoulder, "and swiftly. I have heard tell of unchaste brides strangled on their wedding night for failing to convince their husbands of their innocence."

When her father had gone, Susannah struggled to her feet and stood a while staring at nothing, her cheek still on fire from his blow. He had a heavy hand. There would be worse to come for shaming him, she thought. Far worse. And then an elderly husband who would…

But she could not continue that thought, closing her eyes instead. It did no good to dwell on her fate. Even if she had accepted Hugh, her father would never have released her to marry him, and she was not able to marry without his consent.

There was only one choice open to her. She would have to run away from home again. Only this time she must ensure she was never found. For under law she could be brought back to her father's home and either made to marry Sir William—if he would still have her—or forced into a nunnery. It was a cruel prospect. She would miss Eloise terribly, and it would mean a hard life ahead for her, a life of poverty and fear. Yet what else was there to do if she wanted to be free?

Reaching into her pocket, Susannah drew out the ring Hugh had given her, and turned the stone to the sunlight, admiring its fiery red glow. It was a small thing, but it belonged to her. Whatever happened, however desperate life became for her, she must never sell this ring, never lose it, never part with it until she died.

Hugh Beaufort had given her this jeweled ring after that long night in the forest. *Not as a promise, but as a gift.* That night had been the wildest, and most pleasurable, of her life. Susannah clenched her fist about the ruby ring, and remembered…

Acknowledgments

My grateful thanks as ever go to my fantastic agent Luigi Bonomi, not to mention the wondrous Alison and Ajda at LBA. You have made all this possible. Also to the team at Hodder & Stoughton, and in particular to editors Kate Howard and Lucy Foley for their insightful comments and marvelous enthusiasm from the very start.

Many thanks to all the Tudor fans on Twitter and Facebook who have kept me chatting as well as working, ahem. To my family for putting up with my distracted behavior when trying to meet deadlines, such as putting the car keys in the fridge. And to Wolf and Eloise for being such a brilliantly lusty Tudor couple, and for allowing me to tell their story.

And lastly my love and eternal thanks to my husband Steve, who has more than once provided the inspiration for this love story…

About the Author

Elizabeth Moss was born into a literary family in Essex, and currently lives in the southwest of England with her husband and young family. She also writes commercial fiction under another name. For more information about her, visit her blog at www.elizabethmossfiction.com.

Rebel Bride

Lust in the Tudor Court

by Elizabeth Moss

Don't miss the next book in the deliciously erotic
Lust in the Tudor Court Trilogy…

I cannot wait to continue with book two."
—*Victoria Loves Books*

He is under her spell

Hugh Beaufort, favored courtier of King Henry VIII, likes his women
quiet and biddable. Susannah Tyrell is neither of these things. She is
feisty, beautiful, opinionated, and brave. And Hugh is fascinated by her—
despite himself.

Their passion knows no bounds

When Susannah pulls her most outrageous stunt yet and finds herself lost
in the wilds of England, Hugh must go to her rescue. Neither of them
is prepared for the dangers that lie in wait. But most dangerous of all is
their desire for one another. Alone together, in the forest, far from the
restraints of court…

Praise for *Wolf Bride*:

"It's Fifty Shades of Tudor sex, by Harry!" —*The Sunday Times*

"[A] rollicking and rude romp through Tudor England… Well-
written and will sweep you breathlessly along." —*Star* magazine

For more Elizabeth Moss, visit:

www.sourcebooks.com

Rose Bride

Lust in the Tudor Court

by Elizabeth Moss

The deliciously erotic Lust in the Tudor Court Trilogy concludes...

She's a fallen woman, an object of men's lust...

Margerie Croft yielded up her virginity before her wedding, and then fled, knowing she couldn't marry a man she did not love. Now she is viewed as soiled goods, fit only for the role of a courtier's plaything.

He sees something in her others don't...

Virgil Elton is King Henry VIII's physician, working on a tonic to restore his sovereign's flagging libido. But first it must be tested. Virgil eyes the wanton Margerie Croft as an obvious subject. But as he gets to know her, Virgil discovers someone as intelligent and passionate as she is beautiful—someone who has been gravely misunderstood.

Praise for *Wolf Bride*:

It's not just the bodices that are being ripped off in
this rollicking and rude romp... Well-written and will
sweep you breathlessly along. —*Star* magazine

"It's Fifty Shades of Tudor sex, by Harry!" —*The Sunday Times*

"Wow... This truly exceeded all my expectations... This was a superb read, addictive, passionate, compelling, and hot." —*Victoria Loves Books*

For more Elizabeth Moss, visit:

www.sourcebooks.com

Control

by Charlotte Stein

Will she choose control or just let go?

When Madison Morris wanted to hire a shop assistant for her naughty little bookstore, she never dreamed she'd have two handsome men vying for the position—and a whole lot more. Does she choose dark and dangerous Andy with his sexy tattoos? Or quiet, serious Gabriel, whose lean physique and gentle touch tempt her more than she thought possible?

She loves the way Andy takes charge when it comes to sex. But the turmoil in Gabe's eyes hints at a deep well of complicated emotions locked inside. When the fun and games are over, only one man can have control of her heart.

What readers are saying:

"Forget *Fifty Shades of Grey*…take a look at this and see how long you can stay in control!"

"This is honest to god, hands down, the best erotic fiction I've ever read."

"Highly addictive!"

For more Xcite Books, visit:

www.sourcebooks.com

Telling Tales

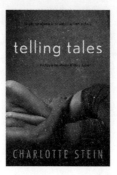

by Charlotte Stein

The only limit is their imagination.

Allie has held a torch for Wade since college. They were part of a writing group together, and everything about those days with him and their friends Kitty and Cameron fills her with longing. When their former professor leaves them his mansion in his will, it's a chance for them to reunite. But there's more than friendship bubbling beneath the surface.

As relationships are rekindled and secrets revealed, they indulge their most primal desires. With the stakes getting higher, Allie isn't quite sure who she wants…fun-loving Wade or quiet, restrained Cameron.

For more Xcite Books, visit:

www.sourcebooks.com

Awakening

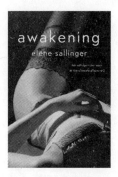

by Elene Sallinger

He will open her eyes to the ultimate pleasure...

The minute Claire walked into his shop, she aroused every protective instinct Evan ever had. She looked so fragile, so lost. He ached to be the one to show her a world she'd never dreamed of, to awaken within her the passion she was so ripe to share. It only takes one touch for him to see how open and responsive she is to his dominant side. But the true test will be whether he can let go at last and finally open his heart...

Festival of Romance Award Winner

What readers are saying:

"If *Fifty Shades of Grey* intrigued you, *Awakening* will take you to a whole new level of desire, submission, and unforgettable romance."
—Judge, Festival of Romance contest

"One of the absolute best BDSM novels I have read. (And I've read quite a few.) This one is absolutely amazing!" —Autumn Jean

"Finally! A well-told story that shows the characters' vulnerabilities and how they learned to trust and love again." —A. Hirsch

For more Xcite Books, visit:

www.sourcebooks.com

Reflection

Chrysalis

by Elene Sallinger

When two bodies collide...

The moment Bridget Ross and Connor Reynolds run into each other on the street—quite literally while out on a run—tempers flare. But when the two get together for an apology coffee date, it's clear that the coffee isn't the only thing steaming.

Connor is a charming artist without purpose. His tragic past prevents him from putting down roots or committing to anything. Bridget is feisty but guarded. She's aching to fill a void in her life but is wracked with guilt over her past and denies herself true pleasure. Can this gorgeous man tempt Bridget to finally succumb to her desires?

Praise for *Awakening*:

"Potent storytelling and characterization...with emotional depth and a sweeping romantic sensibility." —*Kirkus*

"Exquisitely beautiful, touchingly heart-wrenching, and hedonistic enough to keep your body on fire." —*Coffee Time Romance*, 5 stars

For more Xcite Books, visit:

www.sourcebooks.com